Bianca

DULCE VENGANZA GRIEGA
ANDIE BROCK

HARLEQUIN™

Editado por Harlequin Ibérica.
Una división de HarperCollins Ibérica, S.A.
Núñez de Balboa, 56
28001 Madrid

© 2017 Andrea Brock
© 2017 Harlequin Ibérica, una división de HarperCollins Ibérica, S.A.
Dulce venganza griega, n.º 2581 - 1.11.17
Título original: The Greek's Pleasurable Revenge
Publicada originalmente por Mills & Boon®, Ltd., Londres.

I.S.B.N.: 978-84-9170-116-3
Depósito legal: M-24980-2017
Impresión en CPI (Barcelona)
Fecha impresion para Argentina: 30.4.18
Distribuidor exclusivo para España: LOGISTA
Distribuidores para México: CODIPLYRSA y Despacho Flores
Distribuidores para Argentina: Interior, DGP, S.A. Alvarado 2118.
Cap. Fed./Buenos Aires y Gran Buenos Aires, VACCARO HNOS.

Capítulo 1

NO QUEREMOS problemas, Kalanos.

Lukas apartó la mano que el otro hombre había apoyado en la manga de su traje oscuro y lo miró con frialdad.

–¿Problemas? –repitió, clavando la vista en el rostro sudoroso de Yiannis, que intentaba sin éxito plantarle cara–. ¿Y qué te hace pensar que he venido a causaros problemas?

–Mira, Kalanos –le respondió el otro hombre, dando un paso atrás–, lo único que quiero decir es que es el entierro de mi padre. Solo te pido respeto.

–Ah, sí, respeto –susurró él–. Me alegro de que me lo recuerdes. Supongo que ese es el motivo por el que hay tantas personas presentes. Tantas personas deseosas de presentarle sus respetos a un gran hombre.

–No es más que un entierro íntimo, familiar –insistió Yiannis, evitando su mirada–. Y tu presencia no es bienvenida, Lukas.

–¿No? –inquirió él–. Pues qué pena.

En realidad, Lukas tampoco quería estar allí. No había deseado que aquel hombre muriese tan pronto, había querido vengarse del hombre por el que había fallecido su padre y que había hecho que él fuese a la cárcel por un delito que no había cometido.

Cuatro años y medio. Ese era el tiempo que Lukas había pasado en una de las cárceles más duras de Atenas, rodeado de lo peor de la sociedad. Había tenido mucho tiempo para pensar en la traición que lo había llevado allí y que, todavía peor, había terminado con la vida de su padre. Cuatro años y medio que lo habían convertido en un hombre duro y frío, lleno de odio.

Cuatro años y medio durante los cuales había planeado la venganza.

Y todo, para nada.

Porque el objeto de su odio, Aristotle Gianopoulous, había muerto el mismo día que él había salido de la cárcel.

Lukas observó cómo bajaban el ataúd a la tierra mientras el pope despedía el cuerpo y después pasó la vista por las personas presentes solo para hacer que se sintiesen incómodas.

A su lado, Yiannis Gianopoulous se movió nervioso. Era hijo del segundo matrimonio de Aristotle y Lukas no tenía ningún interés en él. También estaba allí su hermano, Christos, que lo miraba con el ceño fruncido desde el otro lado de la tumba. Un par de socios de Aristotle, su abogado, y una de sus amigas. A un lado, algo apartados, Petros y Dorcas, dos fieles empleados de Aristotle, que habían trabajado siempre para él.

Un grupo extraño de individuos rotos, desechos de la vida de Gianopoulous, reunidos bajo el justiciero sol de mediodía de aquella bella isla griega, para enterrar al hombre que, sin duda, les había arruinado la vida a todos, de un modo u otro. A Lukas no le importaba ninguno.

Bueno, sí.

Por fin posó la mirada en ella, en la joven con la cabeza ligeramente agachada, con un lirio blanco en la mano. Calista Gianopoulous. Callie. Hija de Aristotle y su tercera esposa, la más pequeña, la única hija. Lo único bueno que había hecho en su vida. O eso había pensado Lukas, hasta que ella lo había traicionado también.

Lukas saboreó su desazón. La había reconocido inmediatamente, nada más llegar.

El gesto de Calista al verlo había sido de pánico, sus ojos verdes lo habían mirado con temor.

En esos momentos los tenía clavados en el suelo e intentaba esconderse en el velo de encaje negro que también cubría su maravilloso pelo rojizo, como si así pudiese desaparecer. Pero eso era imposible.

«Mírame, Calista».

Deseó que lo mirase a los ojos. Quería ver culpabilidad en ellos, y vergüenza.

Aunque había una parte de él, muy pequeña, que todavía tenía la esperanza de haberse equivocado.

No obstante, la mirada de Calista estaba clavada en la tumba, como si quisiera meterse en ella también, pero no iba a escapar. Tal vez Aristotle hubiese fallecido antes de que Lukas hubiera podido vengarse de él, pero Calista estaba allí. La venganza sería muy distinta, pero igual de placentera.

Lukas la estudió con la mirada. Había creído conocerla bien, pero se había equivocado. Se habían hecho amigos con los años, o eso había pensado él, cuando pasaban los veranos en la isla de Thalassa, mientras sus padres, juntos, conseguían su primer millón con G&K Shipping, símbolo de su éxito y de su amistad.

Lukas, que tenía ocho años más que Calista, pensó en la niña cuyos padres se habían divorciado poco después de que ella dejase de usar pañales. Su madre, una neurótica, se había llevado a la niña a vivir a Inglaterra, pero la había enviado los veranos a Thalassa. Y la pequeña Calista se había dedicado a ir detrás de sus hermanastros por la enorme finca de los Gianopoulous.

Y también lo había buscado a él. Había ido a la parte de la isla que pertenecía a su familia, se había colado en su barco cuando salían a pescar, o se había encaramado a las rocas para verlo zambullirse en las cristalinas aguas del mar.

Más tarde se había convertido en una torpe adolescente. Ya sin madre, la habían mandado a un internado, pero había seguido pasando los veranos en Thalassa. Por aquel entonces, ya no había mostrado ningún interés en sus hermanastros, ni en Lukas.

Y, con dieciocho años, Callie, en esos momentos Calista, se había transformado en una joven muy bella, que lo había tentado para que se la llevase a la cama. Salvo que no habían llegado a la cama y lo habían hecho en el sofá del salón.

Lukas había sabido que aquello estaba mal, por supuesto, pero no había podido resistirse. El hecho de que Callie coquetease con él lo había sorprendido, se había sentido halagado de que quisiese entregarle su virginidad. Calista lo había embaucado.

Y se lo iba a hacer pagar.

Calista sintió que el suelo se movía bajo sus pies y la imagen del ataúd en el que estaba su padre se volvió borrosa.

«No, por favor, no».

Lukas, no. Allí, en ese momento, no. Pero no le cabía la menor duda de que estaba allí. Sus hombros parecían más anchos de lo que ella recordaba, su torso más fuerte, más imponente. Estaba de brazos cruzados, con los pies plantados con firmeza en el suelo, indicando claramente que no iba a marcharse a ninguna parte.

No era posible que aquello estuviese ocurriendo.

Lukas Kalanos estaba en la cárcel, todo el mundo lo sabía. Lo habían condenado por su papel en el negocio de contrabando de su padre, Stavros, que también había sido socio de su propio padre.

Calista sintió náuseas solo de pensar en lo ocurrido, en que el negocio de transporte marítimo de su padre se hubiese hundido por culpa de aquello, en cómo su familia se había arruinado. Con solo veintitrés años, había vivido en la opulencia y también había pasado por muchas dificultades. Y en esos momentos tenía claro qué era lo que prefería.

Aquel era el motivo por el que, cinco años antes, se había marchado y había decidido apartarse del negocio familiar, de los tejemanejes de sus hermanos. De los ataques de ira de su padre, de sus depresiones bañadas en alcohol.

Pensó en su hija y se puso a temblar. Se dijo que Effie estaba bien, sana y salva en casa, en Londres, probablemente jugando con la pobre Magda, amiga de Calista y compañera de sus estudios de enfermería, que iba a cuidar de la pequeña hasta que ella regresase. Solo iba a quedarse allí el tiempo estrictamente necesario, como mucho un par de días, para firmar los documentos que tuviese que firmar. Después, se marcharía de aquella isla para siempre.

Pero, de repente, le corría más prisa alejarse de Lukas Kalanos que de la isla.

La ceremonia casi había terminado. El pope los estaba invitando a unirse a él en una última oración antes de que cubriesen el ataúd de tierra. Calista se estremeció.

—¿No tendrás frío? —le preguntó él, agarrándola del codo—. ¿O ha sido una conmovedora muestra de dolor?

Hablaba inglés perfectamente, aunque Calista también lo habría entendido en griego. Lukas la hizo girarse hacia él y añadió:

—Si es así, estoy seguro de que no es necesario que te diga que no tiene ningún fundamento.

—Lukas, por favor... —respondió ella, preparándose para mirarlo a los ojos y notando que se le doblaban las rodillas.

Los rizos oscuros habían desaparecido, llevaba el pelo muy corto, lo que endurecía sus bonitas facciones y acentuaba la curva de su dura mandíbula y los ángulos de sus mejillas, pero su mirada seguía siendo la misma: marrón oscura, casi negra, y sobrecogedoramente intensa.

–He venido a enterrar a mi padre, no a escuchar tus insultos.

–Oh, créeme, *agapi mou*, con respecto a los insultos, no sabría por dónde empezar. Tardaría toda una vida, o más, en expresar la repugnancia que me causaba ese hombre.

Calista tragó saliva. Su padre había tenido defectos, sin duda. Había tratado muy mal a su madre y le había sido infiel muchas veces, lo que había ido haciendo mella en ella, que al final había terminado con una sobredosis. Y ella jamás se lo perdonaría.

Pero, no obstante, había sido su padre y por eso había ido a Thalassa por última vez. A despedirlo. Y, tal vez, a enterrar también los demonios del pasado.

Lo que no había sabido era que el mayor de aquellos demonios estaría también allí, agarrándola por la cintura en esos momentos.

–Te agradecería que no hablases de mi padre en esos términos.

Se apartó de Lukas y añadió:

–Es una falta de respeto, es insultante. Y, además, no creo que estés en una buena posición para juzgar a nadie.

–¿Yo, Calista? –le preguntó Lukas, arqueando las cejas–. ¿Y por qué no?

–Lo sabes muy bien.

–Ah, sí. El terrible crimen que cometí. De eso precisamente querría hablar contigo.

–No tenemos nada de qué hablar.

Si Lukas descubría que tenía una hija, solo Dios sabía cómo podría reaccionar. Y a Calista le aterraba la idea.

En realidad, ella nunca había pretendido mantener la existencia de Effie en secreto. Al menos, al principio. En realidad, no se había enterado de que estaba embarazada hasta el quinto mes. No había pensado que fuese posible quedarse embarazada la primera vez.

Había pensado que las náuseas y el cansancio, la falta de menstruación, se debían al estrés. Al estrés causado por la repentina muerte de Stavros, amigo y socio de su padre, por el escándalo que había hecho que se hundiese la empresa de ambos. Y, finalmente, por el repugnante descubrimiento de que Lukas estaba implicado en ello.

Para cuando había querido ir al médico, Lukas ya estaba esperando el juicio. Y el mismo día que ella se había puesto de parto, un mes antes de lo previsto, sola y asustada, a él lo habían declarado culpable y lo habían sentenciado a ocho años de cárcel.

Aquel mismo día, Calista había decidido que esperaría a que Lukas estuviese en libertad para contarle que tenía una hija. Ocho años le habían parecido una eternidad. Tiempo suficiente para que Effie y ella se construyesen una vida en el Reino Unido, se convirtiesen en un equipo fuerte y unido. Así que había mantenido el secreto.

No se lo había contado a nadie, ni a su propio padre, por miedo a que él se lo contase a toda la familia y la noticia llegase a oídos de Lukas. Aunque, en realidad, el motivo por el que no había querido que su padre lo supiese era otro. No había querido que Effie tuviese ninguna relación con él.

Sabía que su padre habría intentado tomar el control de la situación, de ella y de su nieta. Habría intentado manipularlas, doblegarlas, utilizarlas. Para evitarlo, la única solución había sido ocultarle la existencia de Effie.

Aristotle ya no sabría jamás que había tenido una nieta, pero Lukas... Tenía derecho a saber que era padre.

Pero todavía no era el momento. Ella necesitaba prepararse, y preparar a Effie.

—Calista, la gente se está marchando —dijo Yiannis, intentando llamar su atención sin acercarse demasiado—. Y quieren despedirse antes.

—¿Tan pronto? —preguntó Lukas en tono burlón—. ¿Nadie se va a quedar a brindar por la vida del gran hombre?

—Los barcos están esperando para llevarse a todo el mundo de la isla —continuó Yiannis, secándose el sudor de la frente—. Y tú deberías subirte a uno de ellos, si sabes lo que te conviene.

Lukas dejó escapar una carcajada.

—Qué gracioso, lo mismo estaba pensando yo de ti.

—Trajiste la ruina y la desgracia a nuestra familia, Kalanos, pero mi padre consiguió proteger sus propiedades en Thalassa. Media isla sigue siendo tuya, pero no por mucho tiempo.

—¿No?

—No. Vamos a pedir que nos la entregues como

compensación por haber arruinado a nuestra familia. Nuestros abogados confían en que vamos a ganar el caso.

–¿Vamos? ¿Quiénes?

–Mi hermano y yo. Y, por supuesto, Calista.

Al oír aquello, Lukas bajó la mano de su cintura y se giró a mirarla como si le causase repugnancia. Ella no sabía de qué estaba hablando Yiannis. No había dado su aprobación para nada. No quería saber nada de Thalassa, ni de nada que pudiese heredar de Aristotle tras su muerte. Y no tenía intención de denunciar a Lukas para conseguir su parte.

–Pues buena suerte –dijo él con el ceño fruncido, dándose la vuelta.

Pero entonces volvió a girarse y miró a Yiannis fijamente.

–O no. Porque quiero que sepáis, los dos, que la isla de Thalassa me pertenece. Entera.

–¿Nos tomas por tontos, Kalanos? –preguntó Christos, que se había acercado a ellos.

Lukas se limitó a apretar los labios.

–Es evidente que estás mintiendo.

–Me temo que no –respondió por fin–. Lo que me sorprende es que vuestros abogados no os lo hayan comunicado. Hace tiempo que adquirí la parte que vuestro padre tenía de la isla.

El gesto de Christos se descompuso, pero fue Yiannis quien habló.

–Eso no puede ser cierto. Aristotle jamás te la habría vendido a ti.

–No hizo falta. Cuando tanto él como mi padre compraron la isla, la pusieron a nombre de sus esposas. Un gesto enternecedor, ¿no? ¿O estoy siendo ingenuo? Tal vez lo hicieron solo para evitar impuestos. En cualquier caso, a mí me vino muy bien. Como es evidente, heredé mi mitad a la muerte de mi madre, que en paz descanse. Y para conseguir la mitad de Aristotle solo tuve que encontrar a su primera esposa y hacerle una oferta que no pudiese rechazar. No sabéis lo agradecida que se sintió, sobre todo, porque ni siquiera sabía que fuese la propietaria.

—Pero si has estado en la cárcel...

—Os sorprendería lo fácil que es hacer contactos ahí dentro. En estos momentos conozco a las personas adecuadas para hacer cualquier trabajo. Sea cual sea.

Yiannis palideció visiblemente. Desesperado, se giró hacia Calista, que se limitó a encogerse de hombros. Le daba igual de quién fuese la isla. Solo quería marcharse de allí lo antes posible.

Mientras tanto, Christos, que siempre había sido impulsivo, había levantado los puños.

—No te tengo miedo, Kalanos —dijo—. Y te lo demostraré si quieres.

—¿No habíais dicho que teníamos que tomar un barco? —replicó Lukas con indiferencia.

Christos dio un paso hacia él, pero Yiannis lo sujetó del brazo.

—¡Esto no va a quedar así, Kalanos! —lo amenazó Christos a gritos mientras su hermano tiraba de él—. Vas a pagar por esto.

Calista observó sorprendida cómo sus hermanastros desaparecían. Había pensado que sus hermanos iban a quedarse un par de noches en la isla a revisar los papeles de su padre y resolver sus asuntos pendientes, pero era evidente que eso no iba a ocurrir. Tampoco les había importado dejarla a solas con Lukas.

Se dio cuenta entonces de que seguía teniendo el lirio blanco en la mano y, acercándose a la tumba, lo dejó caer mientras se despedía en silencio de su padre. Se le hizo un nudo en la garganta. No solo se despedía de su padre, sino también de Thalassa, de su niñez, de su ascendencia griega. Aquel era el final de una era.

Se giró para marcharse inmediatamente y chocó contra el fuerte pecho de Lukas. Se agarró al bolso que llevaba colgado del hombro y dijo:

—Si me perdonas, tengo que marcharme.

—¿Marcharte? ¿Adónde exactamente?

—Marcharme de la isla con los demás. No tiene sentido que me quede aquí más tiempo.

—Por supuesto que sí, *agape*, no te vas a ir a ninguna parte —la contradijo Lukas, agarrándola por la muñeca y llevándosela al pecho.

Calista sintió pánico, pero, extrañamente, no fue una sensación completamente desagradable.

—¿Qué quieres decir?

—Lo que he dicho. Que tú y yo tenemos cosas de las que hablar. Y que no te vas a marchar de Thalassa hasta que no lo hayamos hecho.

—¿Me vas a retener por la fuerza?

—Si es necesario, sí.

—No seas ridículo.

Intentó mostrarse fuerte y dura. Clavó la vista en

la muñeca que Lukas le estaba agarrando y no la apartó hasta que él no la hubo soltado.

–¿Y de qué tenemos que hablar? Que yo sepa, no tenemos ningún tema pendiente –mintió.

–No me digas que se te ha olvidado, Calista. Porque yo todavía me acuerdo –le contestó él con la mirada brillante–. Digamos que la imagen de tu cuerpo medio desnudo en mi sofá, de tus piernas alrededor de mi cintura, me ha acompañado todos estos años. Tal vez demasiado. Supongo que es lo que ocurre cuando estás en la cárcel. Uno se tiene que conformar con lo que tiene.

Callie se ruborizó y dio gracias de llevar puesto el velo negro que ocultaba parcialmente su rostro. Al menos hasta que Lukas lo retiró suavemente. Por un instante, Calista pensó que iba a besarla como si fuese una novia.

–Así está mucho mejor.

La miró mientras ella contenía la respiración.

–Se me había olvidado lo bella que eres, Calista.

Ella respiró por fin con un gemido. Lo último que había esperado era un cumplido.

–No sabes cuánto deseo que retomemos nuestra relación. Llevo esperándolo casi cinco años.

Ella se puso tensa.

–Si piensas que voy a volver a acostarme contigo, Lukas, estás muy equivocado.

–No hace falta que nos metamos en una cama, podemos hacerlo en el sofá, contra la pared, o aquí mismo, frente a la tumba de tu padre. Me da igual. Te deseo, Calista. Y te advierto que siempre consigo lo que quiero.

Capítulo 2

LUKAS vio temor en el rostro de Calista. Pensó que todavía era más bella de lo que recordaba. Sus facciones habían cambiado ligeramente con el tiempo, pero todavía tenía la nariz respingona salpicada de pecas y la boca... la boca era tal y como la recordaba, generosa y deliciosamente rosa, incluso en esos momentos, en los que intentaba desafiarlo con una mueca.

No comprendía cómo era posible que Aristotle hubiese engendrado una criatura tan exquisita. Era evidente que Calista se parecía a su madre, Diana, que había sido actriz y modelo. Aunque no hubiese heredado la altura de su madre y tuviese muchas más curvas que ella. Lukas deseó aferrarse a sus caderas. Alargó la mano y tomó la suya.

–Ven.

Y tiró de ella para sacarla de allí, consciente de que se estaba comportando como un cavernícola.

–Lukas, para.

Él se sintió todavía más decidido a llevarla con él, a su casa y a su cama. Había esperado demasiado tiempo aquel momento.

–Lukas, ¡suéltame!

«De eso nada». Las protestas de Calista solo sir-

vieron para aumentar su determinación de llevársela a casa, a la cama. Había esperado demasiado
tiempo aquel momento y no iba a permitir que nada
se interpusiese en su camino.

–Lukas, ¡para, déjame!

Habían llegado a la pequeña arboleda que había
detrás de la vieja capilla, donde había dejado apar-
cada la moto. Colocó a Calista entre esta y su cuerpo
y entonces le soltó la mano.

Ella lo fulminó con la mirada.

–¿Se puede saber a qué estás jugando?

–No estoy jugando, Calista. No es un juego.

–Entonces, ¿qué es? ¿Qué intentas demostrar?
¿Por qué te estás comportando de un modo tan horrible, como un matón?

–Tal vez me haya convertido en eso –respondió
él–. Quizás sea lo que le ocurre a un hombre después de cuatro años y medio en la cárcel.

Calista apretó los labios.

–No entiendo por qué has salido ya. Te senten-
ciaron a ocho años.

–Por buen comportamiento –admitió Lukas en
tono frío–. Ya ves, he sido un buen chico. Espero
que no te moleste que me hayan soltado antes de
tiempo.

–No. De hecho, me da exactamente igual dónde
estés... o lo que hagas.

–Bien. En ese caso, sube a la moto. Vamos a
Villa Helene.

–Yo no voy a ir a ninguna parte contigo.

–Vaya, y yo que tenía la esperanza de no tener
que hacer esto por las malas.

La agarró por la cintura y la levantó en volandas para sentarla en la moto. Se le subió la falda, dejando al descubierto sus muslos, y su pecho subió y bajó con fuerza a causa de la indignación.

Lukas intentó contener el deseo.

—Si no me bajas de aquí ahora mismo, voy a gritar.

—Hazlo si quieres. Eso no cambiará nada. Tus queridos hermanos y el resto de almas en pena están ya en el barco. Nadie te oirá.

Calista lo fulminó con la mirada, pero no se movió. Su orgullo le impidió darle esa satisfacción. Y eso aumentó la admiración que Lukas sentía por ella. Allí sentada, Calista parecía una diosa, con la espalda recta y el pelo cayéndole sobre los hombros. El velo negro, por su parte, había ido a parar al suelo.

—Petros... y Dorcas todavía están en la isla. Siguen viviendo en Villa Melina.

Lukas respondió con la mirada.

—Mira... —añadió ella, cambiando de táctica—. No entiendo por qué haces esto.

—Te encantaba montar en moto, Callie. ¿Ya no te acuerdas? —comentó él—. Siempre me perseguías para que te diese una vuelta.

—Me parece que ambos hemos crecido desde entonces —replicó ella—. O, al menos, yo lo he hecho.

—En eso no te voy a contradecir —dijo Lukas riéndose—. Creo recordar que la última vez que nos vimos realizamos juntos una actividad de adultos.

Ella volvió a ruborizarse, como si el recuerdo de aquello le diese vergüenza.

—Pero es algo que no se va a repetir —le advirtió—. Te lo aseguro. Por mucho que me amenaces.

–No es una amenaza, Calista, sino más bien una promesa.

–Eres un arrogante, Lukas. Mi promesa es esta: lo que ocurrió entre ambos no se volverá a repetir.

–¿Estás segura?

–Sí.

–En ese caso, no te pasará nada por venir a casa conmigo un par de horas, ¿no? Salvo que no confíes en ti misma.

–En quien no confío es en ti, Lukas.

–Ah, claro, se me había vuelto a olvidar que aquí el malo de la película soy yo.

–¡Por supuesto que sí! –exclamó ella.

Y él tuvo que admitir que sus dotes de actriz habían mejorado con los años.

–En ese caso, permite que te tranquilice. No ocurrirá nada que tú no quieras que ocurra.

No estaba seguro de poder controlarse, pero tuvo que admitir que su plan inicial había sido embaucarla y hacer que se enamorase de él, como había hecho Calista tiempo atrás.

La miró y supo que caería rendida a sus pies.

Pasó una pierna por encima del asiento de la moto, la arrancó y notó cómo vibraba bajo su cuerpo.

–Si fuese tú, me agarraría –le dijo a Calista por encima del hombro.

Y, dicho aquello, salió hacia la carretera.

Calista tuvo que agarrar a Lukas por la cintura mientras se alejaban a toda velocidad del cementerio y tomaban la carretera que bordeaba la costa.

Supo que Lukas estaba conduciendo deprisa a propósito, para asustarla, para hacerla gritar, pero ya no era una niña de nueve años y no iba a darle la satisfacción de comportarse como tal. De hecho, en cuanto llegasen a la casa iba a dejarle claro que no iba a permitir que la amedrentase.

Clavó la vista en el brillante mar y supo que, de todos modos, no era miedo lo que sentía, sino emoción. Se sentía viva y le encantaba estar de vuelta en Thalassa. Se dio cuenta en ese momento de lo mucho que lo había echado de menos.

Cambió ligeramente de postura y notó cómo el cuerpo de Lukas respondía. Sintió el calor de su espalda en el pecho, los músculos de su abdomen contrayéndose. Y le gustó. La isla no era lo único que había echado de menos. Debía tener mucho cuidado.

La serpenteante carretera se alejó de Villa Melina, la casa de su familia, y continuó hacia el este, en dirección a Villa Helene, la casa de Lukas y su padre, el fallecido Stavros.

Era una carretera que conocía bien porque la había recorrido de niña muchas veces en bicicleta, para ir a ver a Lukas y a su padre, que siempre había sido muy amable con ella, mucho más agradable que su propio padre y sus aburridos hermanastros, con los que no había tenido absolutamente nada en común. Hasta entonces, no había prestado atención a los nombres de las casas. Melina era el nombre de la primera esposa de Aristotle y Helene, el de la madre de Lukas. Ella no había conocido a ninguna de las dos.

Tampoco había sabido que la isla les pertenecía. Esa información solo la había tenido Lukas, quien, evidentemente, la había utilizado para quedarse con la isla entera y vengarse así de los Gianopoulous. No tenía ni idea de lo que le había ocurrido al Lukas que ella había conocido...

Lukas salió de la carretera y tomó el camino de tierra que llevaba a Villa Helene para detenerse poco después delante de la puerta.

Desmontó y le tendió la mano a Calista, pero no lo hizo de modo caballeroso, sino más bien brusco. Después la empujó hacia la entrada, sacó una llave y abrió la puerta. Y a Calista le sorprendió el gesto, porque en la isla nadie se molestaba en cerrar las puertas con llave.

El interior de la casa seguía siendo tal y como ella recordaba. Incluso el olor le resultó familiar, cosa que la reconfortó y la inquietó a partes iguales. Siguió a Lukas hasta el gran salón, que estaba a oscuras, en silencio. Lukas se acercó a abrir las persianas, dejando entrar la luz del sol.

Calista parpadeó. Ante ellos aparecieron las increíbles vistas del mar Egeo, pero ella solo podía pensar en el sofá. El sofá en el que Effie había sido engendrada.

–¿Quieres beber algo? –preguntó Lukas, tomando un par de copas de un mueble y una botella de whisky.

–No, gracias.

–¿Te importa que lo haga yo?

Se sirvió una generosa cantidad, se la bebió de un trago, y repitió la operación.

Calista apartó la vista de él y recorrió la habitación, que tenía las paredes decoradas con coloridos cuadros y muebles rústicos, de madera. Siempre le había encantado aquella casa, mucho más que la de su propia familia, que estaba amueblada de manera mucho más lujosa, ya que Aristotle siempre había querido impresionar con ella a sus sucesivas conquistas.

Villa Helene era más modesta, más tradicionalmente griega, con las paredes altas y la carpintería exterior pintada de color azul mediterráneo. Al mismo tiempo, contaba con todas las comodidades necesarias, tenía una enorme cocina bien equipada, una preciosa piscina, cinco dormitorios, gimnasio y biblioteca. E incluso un helipuerto donde Calista había visto que esperaba el helicóptero en el que, al parecer, debía de haber llegado Lukas.

–Bueno, ¿de qué querías hablarme? –preguntó, girándose hacia él.

–Eso puede esperar. Ahora mismo lo que quiero es que me beses como me besaste la última vez que estuviste aquí, *agapi mou*. ¿Te acuerdas?

Calista sintió que se mareaba. Lukas le había puesto la mano en la nuca... su cálido aliento, con olor a whisky, la acarició. Por supuesto que se acordaba, perfectamente. Llevaba cinco años reviviéndolo.

Había sido el día de su decimoctavo cumpleaños, una bonita noche de junio, después de que hubiese terminado los exámenes y se hubiese marchado por fin del internado que tanto había detestado. Había ido a pasar unas semanas bajo el sol de Grecia antes de volver al Reino Unido, donde empezaría la universidad.

Le había gustado la idea de la fiesta, aunque su padre hubiese invitado a sus propios amigos. Él la había animado a invitar a sus amigos ingleses y se había ofrecido a pagarles el billete de avión. Aunque lo cierto era que Calista no había tenido muchos amigos, y no había querido espantar a esos pocos presentándoles a su padre.

Porque siempre se había avergonzado de él, de sus excesos con el alcohol, de las copiosas comidas que pedía todas las noches, de su carácter.

No obstante, Calista había querido ver a una persona: a Lukas. Y por eso había intentado domar su melena pelirroja, se había puesto pintalabios y máscara de pestañas, y un vestido verde esmeralda que le sentaba muy bien. Y, para terminar el conjunto, unas sandalias doradas de tacón.

Pero él no se había presentado.

Había sido su padre, Stavros, el que había llegado a la casa con la fiesta ya empezada, aparentemente enfadado, pidiéndole a Aristotle que entrasen al interior a hablar en privado. Calista no había podido ni preguntarle qué había sido de Lukas.

Al final, había decidido tomar las riendas de la situación.

Había tomado prestado el coche de Stavros, que había dejado las llaves puestas, y se había presentado en Villa Helene con una sonrisa, y una botella de champán en la mano.

Allí se había encontrado con Lukas, que parecía nervioso, agitado.

—¡Callie! ¿Qué haces aquí?

—He venido a verte. Es mi cumpleaños, por si se te había olvidado.

—No, no se me ha olvidado. Muchas felicidades —le había respondido él, de modo menos cariñoso de lo habitual—. ¿Has visto a mi padre?

—Sí, está en mi fiesta. Donde también deberías estar tú. Me lo habías prometido, Lukas.

—¿Y lo has visto bien?

—Sí, ¿por qué?

—Porque se ha marchado de aquí con muchas prisas y no ha querido decirme qué pasaba.

—Pues a mí me ha parecido que estaba bien. Se ha quedado hablando con mi padre. Y me ha dicho que viniese a buscarte.

—¿Te ha dado las llaves de su coche? —le había preguntado Lukas, claramente sorprendido.

Pero ella había pensado que no estaba allí para hablar de Stavros. Y se había dado cuenta del verdadero motivo por el que estaba allí. Porque quería que Lukas le hiciese el amor.

Todavía recordaba el gesto de sorpresa de él cuando se había acercado y le había echado los brazos al cuello, sin soltar la botella de champán, y se había pegado contra su espalda. Él se había reído y le había dicho que no hiciese tonterías, que había bebido demasiado, pero, al girarse y mirarla a los ojos, había entendido lo que ocurría.

Se había dado cuenta de que ya no era una niña. De que sabía lo que estaba haciendo. Y que lo deseaba.

Aun así, se había resistido, pero Calista había apretado su cuerpo contra el de él. Había dejado la botella de champán y había hundido las manos en su pelo para acercarlo más. Y, cuando lo había besado, él había reaccionado con pasión y la había llevado hasta el sofá, donde ya no había habido marcha atrás.

Volvían a estar allí otra vez. Y Calista se dio cuenta, horrorizada, de que la atracción seguía siendo igual de fuerte, que seguía deseándolo tanto como aquella noche de junio, a pesar de saber lo que había hecho, de saber en qué clase de hombre se había convertido.

Lukas ya no era el chico cariñoso y divertido del que se había enamorado. Su mirada era cruel y seria.

Y, no obstante, lo seguía deseando.

–Por supuesto que me acuerdo –respondió, intentando recuperar el control de la situación–, pero no voy a volver a cometer el mismo error.

–Entonces, ¿fue un error? Interesante...

–Sí, lo fue –dijo ella, sintiendo calor en las mejillas.

–Pues a mí no me lo pareció. A mí me pareció que lo tenías todo muy bien planeado.

–¿A qué te refieres? –susurró Calista.

–A que ahora me toca a mí seducirte –le contestó él, acercándose e inclinando la cabeza hacia sus labios.

–No, Lukas, ¡no seas ridículo! –exclamó ella, intentando apartarse.

–Y tengo que admitir que lo estoy deseando.

Entonces la besó, hundió los dedos en su pelo y Calista no pudo escapar.

Fue un beso intenso, urgente, despiadado. E imposible de resistir.

Porque, a pesar de todo, Calista sintió que se derretía entre sus brazos. Sintió que la hacía retroceder y notó la pared en la espalda y se dio cuenta de que no podía escapar.

Sus miradas se encontraron un instante, pero entonces Lukas la volvió a besar y ella se dejó llevar por el deseo que se había adueñado de todo su cuerpo.

Lukas le agarró la pierna y se la puso alrededor de la cintura, le acarició el muslo y apartó la ropa interior con impaciencia para sentir su calor. La hizo estremecerse de placer.

Él se apartó, dejó caer su pierna y buscó en el bolsillo de la chaqueta un preservativo, cuyo envoltorio rasgó con los dientes al mismo tiempo que se quitaba la chaqueta, se desabrochaba los pantalones y los dejaba caer al suelo. Hizo lo mismo con los calzoncillos y se puso el preservativo.

Entonces volvió a ella, la levantó del suelo porque supo que lo abrazaría con las piernas por la cintura, y volvió a apartarle las braguitas, pero no para acariciarla con los dedos, sino con la punta de la erección.

Y entonces, la penetró.

Calista no pudo pensar en nada más, el momento de placer se transformó en ansias de más, y se lo pidió sin palabras. Le pidió que la llevase a ese lugar al que se había temido no volver jamás.

Y Lukas obedeció. Sus cuerpos golpearon la pared hasta que Calista sintió que no podía más, y entonces gritó su nombre y se estremeció contra él. Notó que Lukas se ponía tenso y gemía contra la maraña de su pelo.

Capítulo 3

APOYÓ las manos contra la pared y atrapó a Calista entre sus brazos mientras intentaba recuperar la respiración. La miró y se dio cuenta de que temblaba mientras intentaba bajarse el vestido para fingir que no había ocurrido nada.

Pero sí que había ocurrido, Lukas había puesto en marcha su venganza.

Y todo había salido como él había planeado.

Pero lo cierto era que no se sentía satisfecho. No sabía por qué, pero aquello no era suficiente.

El sexo había sido tan estupendo como la primera vez, seguramente por la química y la conexión que había entre ambos. Y pensó que podía volver a hacerla suya una y otra vez. De hecho, podía retenerla allí y utilizarla hasta saciarse. Al fin y al cabo, Calista se lo merecía.

Casi estaba convencido de que era buena idea cuando se miró y pensó que era un hombre de treinta y un años, con los pantalones a la altura de los tobillos, y que deseaba tanto a una mujer que estaba a punto de perder el control.

Pensó que tal vez debiese dar un paso atrás y reexaminar sus motivos. Cuanto antes.

Bajó los brazos, se quitó el preservativo, se vistió y se dio la vuelta.

–¿Ahora quieres beber algo? –preguntó sin mirarla, por miedo a lo que podría ver en sus ojos.

Antes, necesitaba otra copa.

–Lukas... –susurró ella.

Él se giró con dos copas de whisky en las manos y vio confusión en los ojos verdes de Calista, confusión y dolor, y algo que no quería reconocer, y mucho menos analizar.

Había hecho que Calista se sintiese mal, pero ¿acaso no había sido esa su intención? Se negó a sentirse culpable.

Le dio la copa y vio que la tomaba con mano temblorosa y le daba un sorbo. El whisky pareció sentarle bien.

–Dime, Calista.

–¿Qué te ha pasado?

–Veamos... –empezó él–. Mentiras, traición, engaños, la muerte de mi padre y, ah, sí, cuatro años y medio pudriéndome en la cárcel en Atenas.

–Ya no te conozco, Lukas –dijo ella, sacudiendo la cabeza.

–¿No? Pues ya somos dos. ¿Y aun así me dejas que te haga mía contra una pared? ¿Por qué?

–No... no lo sé.

–Y, no obstante, te has puesto a temblar en cuanto te he tocado y has gritado mi nombre –continuó él, sintiéndose mejor–. Y eso que todavía estás vestida de negro y acabas de enterrar a tu padre. No creo que sea un comportamiento adecuado.

–No lo es. No tenía que haber ocurrido. Y créeme que lo lamento.

–Seguro que sí, pero eso no significa que no vaya

a volver a ocurrir –respondió Lukas, acercándose de nuevo–. Porque los dos sabemos, Calista, que puedo tenerte cuando quiera, y donde quiera.

Vio su gesto de dolor y le gustó.

–¿Así que de eso se trata? –inquirió ella, enfadada de repente–. ¿Solo querías demostrarme que puedes tener sexo conmigo cuando quieras?

–Más o menos.

Ella separó los labios, pero tardó en responder.

–Eres un ser despreciable y vil –dijo por fin.

–Sí, sí. Eso y mucho más. Insúltame todo lo que quieras si eso te hace sentir mejor, pero no va a cambiar nada. ¿Y sabes qué es lo peor?

La miró de arriba abajo.

–Que ni siquiera te has resistido. Ha sido tan fácil que casi resulta patético.

Ella se dobló por la mitad, como si la hubiese golpeado en el estómago, y tuvo que apoyarse en el respaldo de una silla. Tomó aire y entonces se incorporó. Lo miró con desprecio y se dio la vuelta para marcharse.

–No tan deprisa –dijo él, interponiéndose en su camino.

–Apártate, por favor.

–No te marcharás hasta que yo no lo diga.

–¿Forma esto parte de tu plan? ¿Vas a retenerme en contra de mi voluntad? ¿Todo para demostrarme que te has convertido en un canalla?

–¿Y si lo hiciera? –le preguntó él–. Ambos sabemos lo que pasaría. Que no querrías separarte de mí, Calista. Puedes fingir sentirte indignada e incluso resistirte por dignidad, pero en realidad bastaría con que chasquease los dedos para que fueses mía. Para que me suplicases que te hiciese el amor. Mira cómo acabas de comportarte. Es lamentable. Deberías darme pena.

Zas.

La mano de Calista aterrizó con fuerza en su mandíbula.

Lo había visto venir y podía haberlo evitado. Después de tanto tiempo rodeado de criminales, su instinto se había aguzado y había aprendido a anticipar situaciones antes de que ocurrieran. Siempre había sido rápido, pero en esos momentos lo era como el rayo. Y, no obstante, había permitido que ocurriera, había querido que aquella reacción tan primaria le demostrase que estaba vivo. Y la bofetada había hecho que se le acelerase el corazón.

Calista Gianopoulous, la joven a la que no había podido olvidar, cuya traición lo había consumido durante los últimos años. En esos momentos la tenía donde quería tenerla.

La estudió con la mirada y pensó que debía sentirse triunfante, vengado, pero no fue así. Lo único que sentía era la abrumadora necesidad de poseer su cuerpo otra vez. Solo podía pensar en lo bella que era.

Se quedó en silencio, a la espera del siguiente movimiento de Calista. La vio bajar la mano y la mirada, y que el labio inferior empezaba a temblarle.

–¿Recurres a la violencia, Calista? –se burló él–. Jamás lo habría imaginado de ti.

—No te mereces otra cosa.

—Tal vez no, pero, si vamos a ser sinceros, quizás deberías mirarte a ti misma.

—¿Qué quieres decir?

—Deja de fingir, Calista. Lo sé.

—¿El qué?

Si Lukas había tenido alguna duda de su traición, la expresión de culpabilidad del rostro de Calista se la confirmó.

—¿Quieres que te lo explique? Porque si es lo que quieres...

Se alejó un par de pasos de ella y después se giró para volver a mirarla.

—Volvamos a la noche de tu decimoctavo cumpleaños. La noche en que mi padre descubrió que la policía había registrado uno de los barcos y lo había encontrado lleno de armas. Mientras Stavros iba a Villa Melina, a intentar averiguar qué estaba pasando, tu padre te mandó aquí para que me entretuvieses. E hiciste un trabajo magnífico, lo tengo que admitir.

Hizo una pausa, su actitud era condescendiente.

—Aristotle debió de sentirse muy orgulloso de ti. Mientras a mi padre le daba un infarto, tú me seducías... Mientras a mi padre se lo llevaban en helicóptero, nosotros nos entregábamos a la pasión. Y, cuando él llegó al hospital, ya era demasiado tarde.

—No, Lukas. No fue así.

—Por supuesto que sí, Calista. Antes de que a mi padre le diese tiempo a enfrentarse al tuyo, a defenderse, le dio un infarto y se murió. Apuesto a que

Aristotle no pudo ni creerse la suerte que había tenido.

—Eso... eso que has dicho es terrible.

—Fue terrible, tienes razón —replicó él—. No solo traficaba con armas, sino que traicionó a su viejo amigo. No podría haber sido mucho más terrible, no.

—¡No es verdad! ¡No te creo! —gritó Calista, angustiada—. Mi padre no tenía nada que ver con el contrabando de armas. Él jamás habría traicionado a Stavros.

—Y supongo que tampoco fue el responsable de que me detuvieran a mí y me encerraran en la cárcel cuatro años y medio, ¿no?

—¡No! Eso tampoco es verdad. ¿Cómo iba a ser posible?

—Muy fácilmente. Tu padre tenía amigos corruptos en las altas esferas. O en las más bajas, dependiendo de cómo se mire.

—¡No! Te lo estás inventando.

—No insultes a mi inteligencia fingiendo que no lo sabías —continuó él, pasándose una mano por el pelo—. Me traicionaste igual que tu padre traicionó al mío. Solo espero que te mereciese la pena.

Calista se dio la vuelta y se tambaleó hacia las puertas abiertas de la terraza. No podía ni mirarlo y a Lukas no le extrañó.

Pero todavía no había terminado con ella.

—Así que, ya ves, *agape mou*, esta es mi venganza. Ahora me toca a mí hacerte ver cómo se siente uno cuando lo utilizan, cuando se aprovechan de él.

Se acercó a ella, apoyó una mano en su hombro y la hizo girarse para mirarla a los ojos.

–Dime, Calista, ¿cómo te sientes?

Calista intentó tragar saliva. Estaba tan bloqueada que casi no podía ni respirar. Tenía el corazón acelerado y todavía le ardía la palma de la mano con la que había golpeado a Lukas. Su cerebro funcionaba a cámara lenta, incapaz de procesar toda la información que él le había dado.

¿Su padre había sido el responsable del tráfico de armas y había culpado a Stavros y, más tarde, a Lukas? Y Lukas pensaba que ella formaba parte de aquella conspiración.

De repente, se sintió aturdida. Se dijo que, al menos, Lukas no sabía de la existencia de Effie...

Respiró hondo e intentó centrarse en aquello último.

Por un momento había pensado que Lukas lo sabía. Y había estado a punto de confesárselo.

Pero no, Lukas no sabía que tenía una hija y lo único que quería era hacerle daño a ella.

Pensó en cómo se había derretido entre sus brazos y sintió náuseas. Se pasó una mano temblorosa por la frente y pensó que tenía que salir de allí. Tenía que volver a Villa Melina, donde tenía su bolsa de viaje, y después marcharse de la isla y tomar un vuelo de vuelta a Londres.

Salió a la terraza y entrecerró los ojos contra la luz del sol.

–¿No tienes nada que decir, Calista? –le preguntó Lukas en tono burlón.

–Solo que tengo que marcharme –respondió ella.

–¿No te vas a disculpar? ¿No me vas a prometer que me compensarás por lo que hiciste?

–No tengo de qué disculparme –le contestó, girándose hacia él–. Tú eres quien debe responsabilizarse de lo que hizo.

–¿No has entendido lo que te he dicho? Yo no tuve nada que ver con el contrabando de armas, ni mi padre tampoco. La única persona responsable de aquella desgracia fue tu padre: Aristotle Gianopoulous.

–¡No! –exclamó ella, girándose para darle la espalda.

Lo cierto era que no lo tenía del todo claro.

–Sí, Calista.

–Pero en el juicio... se declaró culpable a Stavros... Y se demostró que tú habías estado implicado.

–Ya te he dicho que todo fue una trampa. Te sorprendería lo que el dinero puede llegar a comprar. Si tu padre siguiese vivo, tendría que pagar por lo que hizo, ahora que yo conozco a las personas adecuadas, porque por aquel entonces era tan ingenuo que pensaba que se iba a hacer justicia.

Calista se tapó la cara con las manos. No quería que aquello fuese verdad, quería poder defender a su padre, pero algo en la mirada de Lukas, en su tono de voz, hacía que le resultase imposible no creerlo.

De repente, sintió que no podía respirar.

–Bonita actuación –le dijo él–. ¿No pretenderás decirme que no sabías nada?

–No, Lukas, no sabía nada –admitió ella con un hilo de voz sin apartarse las manos de la cara.

–En ese caso, ¿qué te trajo a Villa Helene aquella noche, si no fue la orden de tu padre de mantenerme entretenido?

–Quería verte, nada más –le respondió, bajando las manos y clavando la vista en el suelo para evitar enfrentarse a la castigadora mirada de Lukas.

–Pues... me temo que vas a tener que inventarte una excusa mejor. Mucho mejor. Porque aquella noche venías con una misión, vestida para matar a tu presa, que era yo. Hiciste el papel de seductora muy bien, por orden de tu padre.

–Mi padre no sabía nada, te lo aseguro. Era mi cumpleaños y quería pasarlo contigo.

–¿Por qué, Calista?

Ella guardó silencio unos segundos. Luego tomó aire. Dadas las circunstancias, le daba igual contárselo.

–Porque estaba enamorada de ti –le confesó–. Había estado enamorada de ti desde los trece años, o incluso desde antes.

Lukas le puso un dedo en la barbilla para levantarle el rostro y que lo mirase.

–Si eras solo una niña.

–Eso era precisamente lo que quería, demostrarte que ya no era una niña.

Él apretó la mandíbula mientras asimilaba la información. Frunció el ceño.

—¿Y esperas que te crea? —replicó por fin—. ¿Esperas que crea que decidiste ofrecerte a mí en el mismo momento en que mi padre iba a plantarle cara al tuyo?

—Me da igual lo que quieras creer, Lukas —le dijo ella.

Se dio la vuelta porque tenía que marcharse de allí y atravesó la terraza para darle la vuelta a la casa y volver a Villa Melina. Con un poco de suerte, se encontraría con el viejo coche de Petros, si no, iría andando. Cualquier cosa era mejor que seguir aguantando las duras palabras de Lukas.

Pero solo había dado un par de pasos cuando él se interpuso en su camino.

—No tan deprisa —le dijo—. Todavía no he terminado contigo.

—Pues yo contigo sí. Apártate.

—¿No pensarías que iba a creerme eso de que estabas enamorada de mí?

—«Estaba», Lukas, en el pasado. Ahora mismo, te odio.

—Eso sí que me lo puedo creer. Y sé por qué tienes tanta prisa por huir. Porque te sientes culpable, Calista. Digas lo que digas, tienes la culpa escrita en el rostro.

Era cierto, se sentía culpable, pero no por el motivo que Lukas pensaba, sino por Effie. Sabía que tenía que contarle que tenía una hija, pero no era el momento ni el lugar. Y no tenía las fuerzas necesarias.

—Tal vez estés confundiendo mi expresión —le contestó—. No es de culpabilidad, sino de vergüenza.

–Llámalo como quieras –respondió él, acercándose más–. En cualquier caso, me alegra ver que aceptas la responsabilidad de tus actos.

–Por supuesto. Por mucho que quiera olvidar lo que acaba de ocurrir entre nosotros, no puedo. Y me da vergüenza haber permitido que me tocases, que me violases.

–¡Ja! –él se rio con crueldad–. ¿Te he violado? ¿Ha sido antes o después de que te abrazaras a mí y gritases mi nombre?

–¡Te odio!

–Sí, sí, ya me lo has dicho. ¿A quién intentas convencer? ¿A mí o a ti? Porque deberías saber que me da igual.

Entrecerró los ojos, pensativo, y después añadió:

–¿O acaso hay otro motivo por el que estás tan desesperada por salir de aquí? –inquirió–. ¿Sales con alguien? ¿Tienes novio, o un amante?

–Eso no es asunto tuyo –le dijo Calista.

–¿Es ese el motivo por el que no eres capaz de mirarme a los ojos? –insistió Lukas–. ¿Es por eso por lo que quieres, a toda costa, ponerme el cartel de malo de la historia?

–No. No tiene nada que ver con eso.

–Entonces, dime que no es verdad.

La agarró con fuerza por la muñeca.

–Muy bien –respondió ella con indignación–. No tengo ningún amante.

–¿Y novio? ¿Tienes pareja?

–No, nada de eso. Ahora, déjame marchar.

–Entonces, ¿qué es? Dímelo. Puedo ver en tus ojos que hay algo, Calista.

Ella dudó.

–No tengo ningún amante –insistió–, pero tengo una hija.

–¿Una hija? –repitió él, soltándole el brazo como si le quemase–. ¿Tienes una hija?

–Sí. Tengo una hija de cuatro años y medio.

Hizo una pausa. Tomó aire.

–Y tú, Lukas, también.

Capítulo 4

LUKAS miró a Calista, inmóvil, horrorizado. No podía ser verdad. No era posible que tuviese un hijo.

Aunque en el fondo sabía que sí. Habían tenido sexo... sin protección. Lo recordaba perfectamente.

Intentó controlar sus emociones y pensar. Calista era una manipuladora, eso ya lo sabía. ¿Cómo podía estar seguro de que no se estaba inventando aquello? Tal vez ni siquiera tuviese una hija, o que la tuviese, pero que no fuese suya.

Pero la creyese o no, el gesto del rostro de Calista lo decía todo. Parecía sentirse mal, estaba muy pálida.

–Siéntate –le dijo él, acercándole una silla de metal antes de que se cayese–. A ver si lo he entendido bien. ¿Has dicho que tengo una hija?

–Sí.

–¿Y me lo dices ahora?

–Estabas en la cárcel, Lukas.

–Eso ya lo sé –rugió él, furioso–, pero ese no es motivo para no contarme que era padre.

–Pensé que era mejor esperar... hasta que estuvieses en libertad.

–¿Ah, sí? –replicó él en tono sarcástico–. ¿Mejor para quién exactamente?

Calista agachó la cabeza.

–¿Y quién más lo sabe? ¿Tu familia? ¿Aristotle...?

–No, no se lo conté. No se lo he contado a nadie.

Él esperó que fuese verdad, por el bien de Calista.

–¿Y cómo se llama, esa hija mía?

–Effie.

–¿Effie?

–De Euphemia.

–¿Y ahora mismo dónde está?

–En casa, en Inglaterra.

–¿Y sabe de mi existencia?

Lukas fue haciendo las preguntas que se le iban ocurriendo, sin pensar en la reacción de Calista.

–Le he contado que vives en otro país. Muy lejos.

–Pues eso habrá que solucionarlo, ¿no?

Lukas se pasó una mano por el pelo y clavó la vista en el agua turquesa de la piscina antes de volver a mirar a Calista, que seguía con la cabeza agachada.

Acababa de tomar una decisión.

–Quiero verla. Lo antes posible. Quiero traer aquí a mi hija, inmediatamente.

–¿Qué?

–Puedo hacerla venir en mi avión privado –dijo él, mirándose el reloj–. Podría llegar esta misma noche.

–¿Esta noche? No esperarás que vaya a Inglaterra, recoja a Effie y la traiga de vuelta, ¿no?

–No. Tú no vas a ir a ninguna parte, te vas a quedar aquí hasta que me traigan a la niña sana y salva.

–¡No seas ridículo! –gritó ella, alarmada–. Effie tiene cuatro años. No puede viajar sola.

–Mi personal se encargará de ella.

–¡No! ¡No lo permitiré!

–No te estoy pidiendo permiso, Calista –le informó él–. Me he perdido cuatro años y medio de mi hija y no voy a perderme más.

–En ese caso, piensa en Effie –le respondió ella–. No ha viajado nunca en avión. Si la primera vez lo hace rodeada de desconocidos, se va a traumatizar. No sabes cómo es... lo sensible que es.

–Tienes razón.

Lukas vio alivio en el rostro de Calista y añadió:

–No sé cómo es.

El gesto de alivio desapareció.

–¿Y de quién es la culpa?

Calista bajó la mirada y, de repente, se sentó recta, como si se le acabase de ocurrir una idea.

–De todos modos, Effie no puede viajar al extranjero porque no tiene pasaporte.

–¿No será otra de tus mentiras? Porque si lo es...

–No, es la verdad.

–Muy bien –dijo él, buscando rápidamente otra solución–. En ese caso, tú y yo vamos a viajar a Inglaterra juntos. Así podrás presentarme a mi hija.

La mirada de Calista era de horror.

–Le pediré a mi piloto que tenga el avión preparado cuanto antes.

Muy a su pesar, cuando llegaron por fin a casa de Calista, en Londres, ya estaba empezando un nuevo día. El viaje había sido muy lento.

Bajaron del coche que había alquilado en el aeropuerto y Lukas estudió el edificio. No estaba mal. Era una casa de estilo victoriano de tres plantas, en una calle tranquila y estrecha.

A su lado, Calista buscó las llaves en el bolso. Casi no se había dirigido a él en todo el viaje, pero a Lukas le daba igual. Le había venido bien para poder ordenarse las ideas e intentar decidir cómo iba a actuar.

Calista había accedido a utilizar el dormitorio que había en el avión, pero, a juzgar por su cara, no debía de haber dormido mucho. Tenía ojeras.

—Hay que entrar con cuidado. Effie estará dormida. Y Magda también.

Él se imaginó que Magda debía de ser una especie de amiga que se había quedado al cuidado de la casa y de la niña. La tendría que investigar también, para asegurarse de que era la persona adecuada para estar cerca de su hija. Aunque probablemente ya fuese demasiado tarde para aquello. Cerró los puños al pensarlo.

Calista lo condujo por un pasillo en el que había bicicletas, una motocicleta de plástico y un montón de cartas.

—Sígueme, vivimos en el último piso.

—¿No es tuya toda la casa?

—Nada es mío, Lukas —respondió ella por encima del hombro—. Tengo un piso alquilado. Y si me lo puedo permitir es solo porque lo comparto con Magda.

Lukas guardó silencio. Si Calista pensaba que le iba a dar pena, estaba muy equivocada. Además, lo distrajo el balanceo de su trasero enfundado en unos ajustados vaqueros mientras subía las escaleras delante de él.

—Ya estamos.

Calista abrió la puerta y encendió la luz del estrecho pasillo. Lo condujo hasta la cocina. Por un instante, se quedaron mirándose el uno al otro. Lukas se sintió demasiado grande, fuera de lugar en aquel espacio tan pequeño.

—¿Cal? —llamó una voz desde el otro lado del pasillo—. ¿Eres tú?

—Sí, soy yo —respondió Calista en un susurro, antes de girarse hacia Lukas—. Voy a hablar con Magda. ¿Quieres prepararte un café?

Abrió un armario y sacó un paquete de café, se lo dio y señaló la cafetera.

—No hagas ruido.

Lukas llenó la cafetera y miró a las palomas que poblaban los tejados de Londres mientras esperaba a que el agua echase a hervir. Veinticuatro horas antes no se habría podido imaginar que estaría allí.

—Hola —lo saludó una voz de niña.

Él se giró y vio a una pequeña con la cabeza cubierta de rizos oscuros despeinados y ojos verdes soñolientos que lo miraban desde la puerta.

«Su hija».

—¿Quién eres?

Lo miró con curiosidad.

—Lukas. Lukas Kalanos —respondió él, alargando la mano para bajarla enseguida.

—Yo soy Effie.

—Umm, sí, ya lo sé.

—Es el diminutivo de Euphemia. Y tengo cuatro años y medio. ¿Cuántos años tienes tú?

—Esto... treinta y uno.

Effie lo estudió con la mirada.

—Mamá tiene veintitrés y Magda, veintitrés también, pero Magda es mayor porque cumple los años antes.

—De acuerdo. ¿Por qué no vas a buscar a tu mamá?

—Porque no puedo, tonto. Mamá se ha ido a Grecia a despedirse de mi abuelo. Yo no lo conocía. Se ha muerto. ¿Quieres un zumo?

Effie arrastró una silla y se subió a ella para abrir la puerta de la nevera. Estaba mirando dentro cuando volvió Calista.

—¿Effie?

—¡Mamá!

La pequeña cerró la puerta de un golpe y se lanzó hacia su madre, abrazándola con las piernas por la cintura, con mucha fuerza.

—¡Has vuelto! ¡Te he echado de menos!

—Y yo a ti, cariño.

—He sido muy valiente. Se lo puedes preguntar a Magda.

—Estoy segura de que es cierto.

Calista le dio un beso en la cabeza y la dejó en el suelo, pero no le soltó la mano.

—Veo que ya has conocido a Lukas.

—Sí. Tiene treinta y un años.

—Sí. Supongo que te preguntas qué hace aquí.

—A lo mejor se ha perdido —respondió la niña.

—No, Effie, no se ha perdido. Ha venido a conocerte.

–¡Ah! –dijo la niña, mirándolo con interés.

–El caso es... Effie, que tenemos algo que contarte. ¿Por qué no vienes aquí y te sientas en mi regazo?

Calista apartó una silla, se sentó y tomó a Effie
en brazos. A Lukas le sorprendió su cercanía, no
solo física, a pesar de que Effie abrazaba a su madre por el cuello y estaba pegada contra su cuerpo,
sino emocional. Parecían muy unidas, parecían una
sola persona.

En otras circunstancias, aquello le habría encantado, pero, en esos momentos, Lukas se sintió como
un extraño, como si no pintase nada allí.

–El motivo por el que Lukas está aquí es que
queremos contarte...

Effie los miró a ambos con sus grandes ojos verdes.

–El caso es que... Bueno, resulta que...

–Soy tu padre, Euphemia.

La voz de Lukas inundó la pequeña habitación,
sonó más alta y agresiva de lo que él había pretendido. Los ojos de la niña se dilataron con sorpresa
y Calista la abrazó, en los de ella había enfado.

–¡Lukas!

–¿Qué? –preguntó él–. La niña tiene que saberlo.

Lo que él había querido había sido retomar el
control de la situación, que no se le presentase
como al malo de la historia, pero, al parecer, esto
último era lo que había conseguido. La niña se había aferrado todavía más a su madre, que la mecía
suavemente, como queriendo consolarla, pero entonces Effie se zafó de ella, lo miró fijamente y se

metió un mechón de pelo detrás de la oreja. El gesto
era tan parecido al que hacía Calista que Lukas se
quedó sin respiración.

–¿Es verdad, mamá? –preguntó la pequeña, que,
al parecer, desconfiaba de él tanto como su madre.

–Sí, cariño. Yo quería habértelo dicho con más
suavidad, pero Lukas es tu papá.

Effie metió los dedos en el pelo de Calista.

–¿Y va a venir a vivir aquí, con nosotras y con
Magda?

–¡No! –respondieron al unísono Calista y Lukas.

–Lukas vive en Grecia, de donde yo vengo.

–¿Con mi abuelo?

–Bueno, más o menos...

–¿Y también está muy triste por la muerte del
abuelo?

–Umm... te voy a decir una cosa. ¿Por qué no
vas a vestirte? Después desayunaremos los tres juntos y hablaremos de todo. ¿Qué te parece?

Effie acababa de salir de la habitación cuando
Calista se giró hacia Lukas.

–¿Por qué has hecho eso? –le espetó–. Había-
mos acordado contárselo poco a poco, no así.

–Estabas tardando demasiado.

–¡Demasiado! ¡Si no hace ni dos minutos que
hemos llegado a casa!

–Bueno, pues ya está hecho. Y parece que la
niña está bien.

–¿Y tú qué sabes?

–Sé que necesita que le digan la verdad. La has
engañado durante demasiado tiempo.

–No la he engañado, la he protegido.

–A mí no me vengas con esos cuentos. Solo te estabas protegiendo a ti misma. Ha llegado el momento de que la niña aprenda valores, no mentiras.

–¿Cómo te atreves a criticar el modo en que educo a mi hija?

–También es mi hija, Calista, que no se te olvide.

–¡Ya estoy aquí!

Effie volvió a aparecer en la puerta. Se había puesto una camiseta, una especie de falda rosa y unas botas rojas.

–Bien hecho, cariño –respondió Calista, girándose a sonreírle–. ¿Qué te apetece desayunar?

–Tengo una idea mejor.

De repente, Lukas se sintió desesperado por salir de allí.

–¿Por qué no os invito a desayunar fuera?

–¡Sí! –gritó la niña–. ¿Podré tomarme un donut?

–Por supuesto que sí. Todos los que quieras.

Effie dejó de mirarlo a él para mirar a su madre con incredulidad. Y sonrió al ver que Calista guardaba silencio.

Lukas respiró aliviado. Había ganado el primer asalto gracias al donut. Tal vez fuese solo una pequeña victoria, pero le hizo sentirse bien.

–¡Más rápido! ¡Más rápido!

Calista miró hacia el columpio en el que Effie estaba sentada y que empujaba Lukas. Su hija tenía la cabeza echada hacia atrás y los ojos cerrados. Cualquiera que no los conociese pensaría que eran un padre y una hija, divirtiéndose juntos bajo la luz del sol, pero Calista se dio cuenta de que los hombros de Lukas estaban tensos, tenía la mandíbula apretada y una mano metida en el bolsillo del pantalón.

Habían desayunado en la terraza de una cafetería de Hyde Park. Lo había decidido Effie. Estaba cerca de un parque y del lago, dos de sus lugares favoritos. Effie se había comido dos donuts y medio y Lukas la había observado en silencio, probablemente esperando a que Calista reaccionase enfadada, cosa que ella se había negado a hacer.

No iba a meterse en aquel juego sucio. Había cosas mucho más importantes en juego. Además, como Lukas continuase columpiando a Effie con aquella fuerza, era posible que la naturaleza le devolviese el tanto a ella, de preferencia, encima de su inmaculado traje de diseño.

Dio otro sorbo a su café. Aquello era muy extraño, no parecía real. Los tres juntos, en aquel parque de Londres.

Siempre había sabido que, en algún momento, tendría que contarles la verdad a los dos. Era una de las muchas cosas que le había quitado el sueño por las noches.

Ya estaba hecho, pero, al mirarlos a ambos, Calista no sentía alivio, sino miedo.

Lukas había cambiado mucho, ya no era el chico divertido, abierto y generoso del que ella se había enamorado. Se había convertido en un hombre frío, calculador, despiadado. Un hombre dispuesto a cualquier cosa para conseguir su objetivo.

Un niño se acercó al columpio y Calista vio cómo miraba la madre a Lukas.

—Agárrate bien —le advirtió Effie al pequeño—. Mi papá empuja muy fuerte.

«Mi papá». ¿Era posible que lo hubiese aceptado tan pronto? ¿Y por qué hacía eso que Calista se sintiese todavía más incómoda?

Unos minutos después, Effie iba corriendo hacia ella, con los ojos brillantes y el otro niño a su lado.

—¿Puedo ir al tobogán con Noah, por favor?

—Sí, yo os miraré desde aquí.

Los dos salieron corriendo y Calista se dio cuenta de que la madre de Noah la miraba con decepción. Se sonrieron educadamente y la otra mujer siguió a los niños.

—¿Otro café? —preguntó Lukas, llamando al camarero.

—No, gracias. De hecho, tendríamos que irnos.

—¿Tenías otros planes para hoy? —le preguntó él en tono socarrón.

—¿Y qué si los tuviera? —replicó Calista—. Effie y yo tenemos una vida, ¿sabes? Una buena vida. He hecho todo lo que he podido para que crezca segura y feliz, y no le falta de nada.

—Salvo un padre, por supuesto —respondió él mientras se ponía azúcar en el café y se llevaba la taza a los labios.

Calista frunció el ceño.

—Por suerte, eso voy a poder cambiarlo.

—Tal vez —admitió ella—, pero no pienses que vas a poder irrumpir en nuestras vidas como si no pasase nada. Effie es feliz. Lo último que necesita es que le trastoquen la vida.

Lukas dejó lentamente la taza encima de su plato y la miró a los ojos.

–Cuanto antes te des cuenta de quién manda aquí, mejor para todos.

–¿Mandar? –replicó ella, ruborizándose, indignada–. En lo relativo a Effie soy yo la que toma las decisiones.

–Ya no, *thespinis mou*.

Con el corazón encogido, Calista vio cómo Effie los saludaba desde lo alto del tobogán. Ella le devolvió el saludo y la niña señaló a Lukas.

–Quiere que la saludes –le dijo Calista entre dientes.

Lukas levantó la mano y entonces Effie se lanzó tobogán abajo.

–¿Y cómo es esa vida que tanto deseas proteger? –preguntó Lukas, volviendo a mirarla a ella.

–Ya te lo he dicho, una vida normal.

–Háblame de ella. ¿Trabajas? ¿Va Effie al colegio?

–Effie acaba de terminar preescolar. Y yo estoy a punto de graduarme.

–¿De graduarte? ¿En qué?

–He estudiado enfermería.

–¿Enfermería? –preguntó él sorprendido.

–Sí –respondió ella, poniendo los hombros rectos–. Ha sido duro, estudiar y cuidar de Effie al mismo tiempo, pero Magda, que estaba en mi curso, me ha ayudado mucho. No lo habría conseguido sin ella.

–¿Y dónde trabajas? ¿En un hospital?

–Todavía no. Tengo que tener el diploma antes de poder solicitar un puesto de trabajo. Voy a intentar empezar en septiembre, cuando Effie vaya al colegio a tiempo completo.

Lukas frunció el ceño mientras absorbía la información.

—¿Y dices que nunca has llevado a Effie a Grecia?

—No.

—¿Por qué?

—Porque no ha sido necesario. Grecia ya no forma parte de mi vida. Ni siquiera habría vuelto yo si no hubiese sido por el entierro de mi padre.

—¿Y, no obstante, le has puesto a tu hija un nombre griego?

—Sí —respondió ella, consciente de que no sabía por qué lo había hecho—. Solo porque me parecía un nombre bonito.

—Tonterías. Tú eres medio griega. Y Effie, tres cuartos griega. Ambas tenéis sangre griega corriendo por vuestras venas. Eso no lo puedes evitar.

—No, pero...

—Grecia siempre será parte de tu vida, lo quieras o no. Y yo seré parte de la vida de Effie.

—¿Qué quieres decir con eso? —preguntó Calista, asustada.

—Quiero decir que no quiero seguir perdiéndome la vida de mi hija. Que voy a llevarme a Effie a Thalassa conmigo.

—¡No! No, Lukas, no puedes...

—Sí que puedo, Calista. Puede venir sola o la puedes acompañar. Tú decides. En cualquiera de los dos casos, mi hija volverá a Thalassa conmigo.

Capítulo 5

CUANDO las hélices del helicóptero dejaron de girar, Calista vio cómo Lukas apagaba el control y se quitaba el cinturón de seguridad. Habían pasado menos de veinticuatro horas y ya estaban de vuelta en Villa Helene, tal y como él había decidido.

Había ganado.

Calista no había querido que Effie viajase sola con él, así que había intentado convencerlo de que irían las dos unos días más tarde, o de que Lukas se quedase en Londres un tiempo, pero él no había cedido. Ni siquiera la excusa de que la niña no tenía pasaporte había funcionado. Lukas se había encargado de todo.

En esos momentos, Calista miró a Effie, que dormía profundamente entre sus brazos. El viaje hasta Thalassa había sido largo y cansado, sobre todo con cuatro años.

Lukas se giró hacia ellas con expresión indescifrable.

–He dado órdenes a Petros y a Dorcas para que preparen la casa. Me imagino que Effie querrá irse directamente a la cama.

Ella se preguntó si Petros y Dorcas trabajaban

para él, y cómo habrían reaccionado a la noticia de que Lukas y ella tenían una hija juntos.

Calista conocía a la agradable pareja desde siempre. Dorcas había hecho el papel de madre durante los largos veranos que ella había pasado en la isla.

Habían sido los únicos en trabajar de manera permanente en Villa Melina. La naturaleza irascible de Aristotle había hecho que nadie durase mucho tiempo trabajando para él.

Se quitó el cinturón de seguridad con cuidado, para no despertar a Effie, mientras Lukas les abría la puerta.

—Dámela.

Alargó los fuertes brazos hacia la niña y Calista obedeció a regañadientes. Vio cómo Effie se abrazaba a él mientras Lukas la llevaba hacia la casa.

La puerta principal se abrió y apareció Dorcas, que se llevó las manos al pecho al ver a Lukas con la niña.

—Entrad, entrad. Estaréis muy cansados después de un viaje tan largo.

—*Kalispera*, Dorcas —dijo ella, sintiéndose incómoda por no haberle contado a nadie, ni siquiera a su padre, que tenía una hija.

Pero Dorcas la tranquilizó con un fuerte abrazo.

—Mira que no haberme dicho que tienes una niña preciosa —la reprendió Dorcas—. ¡Y con Lukas!

Entraron en la casa y Dorcas dio instrucciones a su marido, que estaba saludando a Lukas. Cuando Petros se giró hacia Calista, lo hizo con una enorme sonrisa.

—Hemos arreglado una habitación para Effie. Petros ha pintado la pared de rosa claro, ¿verdad, Petros? Esperamos que le guste.

Petros asintió orgulloso y Calista se sintió incómoda.

—Gracias, Petros —le dijo, tomando a la niña de brazos de Lukas—. Si me decís cuál es, acostaré a Effie.

—Por supuesto. Sígueme.

Dorcas la guio hasta una habitación y abrió la puerta. Y Calista se quedó de piedra. La que había sido una habitación de invitados bastante espartana se había convertido en una preciosa habitación infantil, con muebles blancos, cortinas a rayas blancas y rosas, una pequeña cama y cuadros de hadas y de princesas en las paredes.

—¿Te gusta? —le preguntó Dorcas.

—Es preciosa, Dorcas, pero ¿cómo has conseguido todo esto en tan poco tiempo?

—Lukas dijo que no había tiempo que perder, así que Petros contrató a un pequeño equipo de decoradores. Lukas quería que todo fuese perfecto para su hija.

Aquello la alarmó.

Entre Dorcas y ella le quitaron la ropa a Effie y la metieron en la cama. Mientras lo hacían, Dorcas no dejó de susurrar que la niña era preciosa, tanto como su mamá, pero con los rizos oscuros de su padre. Calista cerró la persiana y casi tuvo que sacarla de la habitación a rastras. Dejó la puerta entreabierta.

—¿Ahora trabajáis aquí, Dorcas? —preguntó una vez en el pasillo.

–Sí. Lukas nos lo ha pedido.

–¿Y os parece bien? Quiero decir, después de todo lo ocurrido...

–Por supuesto que sí. Petros y yo conocemos a Lukas de toda la vida, desde que era un bebé, y jamás hemos creído que fuese culpable del delito del que se le acusaba.

–¿De verdad? Entonces... mi padre... ¿significa eso que sospechabais de él?

–Nosotros no somos quién para sospechar de nadie, cariño. Sobre todo, ahora que el Señor se lo ha llevado.

Calista tragó saliva.

–¿Y vivís aquí, en Villa Helene?

–No. Eso es lo mejor. A Lukas le parece bien que nos quedemos en Villa Melina. De hecho, dice que la casa es nuestra.

Cambió de gesto de repente.

–Lo siento, Calista. Sé que estoy hablando de tu casa. Yo le pregunté a Lukas si no quería mudarse allí, pero él me dijo que no, que vuestra casa sería esta.

–¿Nuestra casa?

–Sí, la de Lukas, Effie y tú. Y Petros y yo no podríamos estar más felices con la noticia. Nos encanta que los Gianopoulous y los Kalanos estén unidos. Es un sueño hecho realidad. Y pensar que Effie va a crecer...

Calista sintió que le temblaban las piernas.

Lukas pretendía que se quedasen allí, para siempre. O, mejor dicho, que Effie se quedase allí. Ella no le interesaba lo más mínimo.

Pero eso no podía ser.

Calista volvió al salón con los hombros rectos, dispuesta a pelear.

Pero Lukas parecía muy tranquilo.

—¿Va todo bien?

—No —replicó ella.

—¿No te gusta la habitación? —preguntó Petros, que estaba poniendo la mesa.

—No, Petros, no es eso. La habitación me encanta.

—Entonces, ¿no le gusta a la niña?

—Effie está dormida, pero estoy segura de que le encantará cuando se despierte.

—Me alegro —respondió Petros, sin dejar de poner la mesa.

—Creo que lo que Calista pretende decirte es que muchas gracias, Petros, a ti y a Dorcas, por haber hecho un trabajo tan fantástico en tan poco tiempo.

Todos se relajaron y Lukas miró a Calista con una ceja arqueada.

Ella sintió ganas de golpearlo y quitarle aquella sonrisa de la cara.

—Ha sido un placer, ¿verdad, Petros? —dijo Dorcas, llegando desde la cocina con una cacerola en las manos—. Ahora, sentaos a cenar, los dos. Estoy segura de que tenéis hambre.

Calista miró a Dorcas y a Lukas, y la idea de quedarse a solas con él le dio pánico.

—¿No os vais a sentar a cenar con nosotros?

—¿Petros y yo? Por supuesto que no —respondió Dorcas riéndose—. He preparado esto especialmente para Lukas y para ti. Es vuestra primera cena aquí juntos, como pareja, como familia...

–Gracias, Dorcas, estoy seguro de que estará delicioso –dijo Lukas–. Ahora, Petros y tú podéis marcharos, ya habéis hecho demasiado por nosotros. Calista y yo estaremos bien solos. ¿Verdad, Calista?

–Sí –respondió ella entre dientes.

Pero la puerta se acababa de cerrar cuando le preguntó, furiosa:

–¿Me puedes explicar qué está pasando aquí?

Él descorchó la botella de vino y la miró solo un instante antes de servir dos copas.

–¿Qué está pasando? –repitió mientras se disponía a servir la deliciosa comida, moussaka, en dos platos y le ponía uno delante–. Por favor, siéntate.

Calista se dejó caer en la silla.

–¿Por qué Dorcas y Petros piensan que nos vamos a quedar a vivir aquí, como una familia? ¿Se lo has dicho tú?

Él se metió un bocado de comida en la boca y lo masticó antes de contestar.

–Supongo que Dorcas se lo ha imaginado. Ya sabes que enseguida se emociona.

–Es cierto, pero le tienes que poner las cosas claras, Lukas. Tienes que decirle que Effie y yo solo vamos a pasar aquí unas breves vacaciones, que vamos a volver a Inglaterra.

–Yo me refería más bien a nuestra situación, a ti y a mí. Parece que Dorcas piensa que somos pareja. Supongo que es comprensible que cometa ese error,

teniendo en cuenta que siempre ha sido una román-
tica.

–Sí, por supuesto, en eso se equivoca también.

–¿No vas a comer nada? –le preguntó él–. Está
delicioso. Ahora entiendo que tu padre llegase tan
lejos, con Dorcas cocinando para él.

Calista se negó a responder a la provocación.

–¿Se lo vas a decir tú o se lo digo yo? Que no
vamos a quedarnos, quiero decir.

–Puedes decirle lo que quieras, Calista. Y puedes hacer lo que quieras. Me da igual. Pero Effie va
a quedarse aquí, conmigo. Todo el tiempo que yo
diga.

–¡No!

–Sí, Calista.

–No es eso lo que acordamos. Dijimos que iban
a ser unas vacaciones, como mucho quince días.

–¿Eso dijimos? Tal vez mentí un poco, pero no
pongas esa cara de sorpresa. Tú sabes bien lo que es
mentir.

–¡Eso no es justo!

–Nada de esto es justo, Calista. Que mi padre
falleciese de un infarto no fue justo, que a mí me
metieran en la cárcel cuatro años y medio no fue
justo, y que no supiese que tenía una hija, tampoco.
Pero ahora estoy intentando equilibrar la balanza.
Por el momento, se van a hacer las cosas a mi manera. Y vamos a empezar por que Effie se quede en
Thalassa conmigo.

–¡No! No puedes pagar con Effie la rabia que
sientes contra mi padre y contra mí.

–No tengo intención de pagar nada con ella.

Todo lo contrario, estoy deseando conocerla y formar parte de su vida.

—¡Pero no puedes mantenerla aquí!

—Yo pienso que sí. Podemos hacerlo por las buenas, o por las malas, con abogados, jueces, órdenes.
Yo no te lo recomiendo, porque ganaré. Te lo aseguro. No hace falta que te recuerde que estamos en
Grecia y que Effie es tres cuartas partes griega.

—Y no hace falta que yo te recuerde a ti que has
estado en la cárcel por tráfico de armas.

Calista se arrepintió nada más decir aquello.

—No, Calista —rugió Lukas, furioso—. No hace
falta que me lo recuerdes. Y te aseguro que pretendo limpiar mi nombre, pero, mientras tanto,
tengo dinero y contactos. Y estoy seguro de que las
autoridades griegas me concederían la custodia.

—¿Tienes pensado pedir la custodia de Effie?
—preguntó ella, pensando que se iba a desmayar.

—Tal vez... No estoy seguro. Depende.

—¿De qué?

—De ti. Si insistes en ponérmelo difícil, no tendré
otra alternativa.

—¿Y qué esperas que haga? ¿Que te entregue a mi
hija, sin más? ¿Que permita que hagas lo que quieras?

—Bueno... si me lo ofreces...

—No te estoy ofreciendo nada.

—¿No? —preguntó él con una sonrisa—. Qué pena.
Porque, si me permitieses hacer todo lo que quisiese, te aseguro que disfrutarías.

—Basta ya, Lukas.

—Tengo que admitir que, a pesar de todo lo que
has hecho, de quién eres, todavía te deseo.

–Pues yo no te deseo a ti –replicó ella, demasiado deprisa, con demasiada pasión.

–¿No? –le dijo Lukas en tono divertido–. Por supuesto que no.

Calista apartó la mirada.

–El caso es que todo depende de ti –continuó él–. Si permites a Effie quedarse aquí y aceptas que tengo tanto derecho como tú a que esté conmigo, podremos mantener una relación amistosa. No habrá juicios ni luchas por la custodia, al menos, por ahora. Sino un acuerdo civilizado entre los dos.

Ella se mordió el labio inferior, que le temblaba, no se sentía en absoluto civilizada, sino como una bestia salvaje, capaz de cualquier cosa por proteger a su cría. No obstante, sabía lo peligroso que podía llegar a ser enfrentarse a Lukas y estaba segura de que cumpliría su amenaza de luchar por la custodia de Effie. Y que lo más probable era que ganase él.

–Al parecer, no tengo elección –respondió.

Lukas se encogió de hombros.

–Pero no voy a dejar aquí a Effie sola. Si ella se queda, yo también.

–Como desees.

–Muy bien. Effie se quedará aquí, y yo también, al menos, por ahora, pero no de manera permanente, Lukas. Effie empieza el colegio en septiembre y es evidente que, para entonces, tendremos que estar de vuelta en Londres.

–Me alegro de que hayas decidido entrar en razón.

Lukas estudió su rostro colorado, bajó por la

garganta y hasta los pechos, donde se detuvo. Calista notó cómo se le endurecían los pezones y se cruzó de brazos para taparse. Lukas respondió arqueando una ceja.

–¿Y quién sabe? –comentó–. Tal vez no estemos tan mal. Quizás encontremos la manera de mantenernos entretenidos.

–Si estoy aquí es estrictamente por Effie. Nada más. ¿No te ha quedado claro?

–Como el agua, pero, por desgracia, tú también eres tan transparente como el agua y yo lo puedo ver todo –le respondió Lukas con una sonrisa–. ¿Y sabes lo que veo? A una mujer luchando contra sus deseos sexuales. A una mujer que sabe que es una batalla perdida porque me desea. Me desea mucho más de lo que es capaz de admitir.

–Te equivocas, Lukas Kalanos. Eres un iluso arrogante.

–Mira quién fue a hablar –respondió él con los ojos brillantes.

Lukas estudió a Calista con el ceño fruncido. Tal vez estuviese engañándose a sí misma, pero a él no lo engañaba. Su cuerpo la había delatado.

A Lukas nunca le había costado ningún esfuerzo atraer a las mujeres. Era moreno y guapo y, además, encantador, así que había sido un imán para el sexo contrario ya desde la pubertad. Incluso en la cárcel había conseguido engatusar a las pocas mujeres que habían trabajado en la cárcel: las trabajadoras sociales, la bibliotecaria, las cocineras. Todo el mundo había sabido que tenía privilegios especiales gracias a su encanto.

Pero el caso de Calista era especial. Quizás porque ella intentaba negarlo, o porque aquello le demostraba a Lukas que tenía un cierto poder sobre ella.

O, tal vez, solo porque era ella.

Lukas había sabido que Calista no dejaría a Effie sola con él. Por eso le había dicho sin pensarlo que le daba igual si se quedaba o se marchaba, había estado seguro de ganar. Porque, en realidad, sí que le importaba. Demasiado.

Darse cuenta de aquello no mejoró su humor.

Tomó la botella de vino y le hizo un gesto a Calista, pero ella negó con la cabeza, así que solo rellenó su copa. Clavó la vista en la pared del fondo, donde habían hecho el amor solo un par de días antes. No, no habían hecho el amor, habían tenido sexo. Un sexo rápido, furioso, frenético.

Tenía que admitir que, después de hacerlo, no se había sentido satisfecho, sino más bien disgustado.

No por Calista, ni por lo que habían hecho, sino porque se había dado cuenta de que quería más, mucho más. Y el disgusto provenía de cómo se había comportado con ella.

Dio un sorbo a la copa de vino e intentó encontrar alguna justificación a aquel repentino ataque de consideración. Tantos años sin estar con una mujer debían de haberlo trastornado.

Con veinte años, se había divertido mucho y había sacado el máximo partido a su belleza, dinero y poder. Había amado a muchas mujeres, y ellas a él, y pretendía volver a hacerlo, pero antes tenía que olvidarse de aquella.

Además, era padre. Tal vez ya no fuese apropiado que una sucesión de mujeres fuese pasando por su cama. Quizás hubiese llegado el momento de ser más responsable. No quería que su hija desayunase cada día con una amante diferente. Aunque aquel nunca hubiese sido su estilo. Siempre había preferido una habitación de hotel anónima, siempre había valorado la libertad de poder cerrar la puerta y marcharse. Siempre había valorado su intimidad.

Todo lo contrario que Aristotle.

Lukas miró a Calista, que estaba jugando con la comida, con las mejillas todavía coloradas. A Aristotle no le había importado pasear a sus conquistas delante de su hija, o de cualquiera.

Si es que podía llamarse «conquistas» a la sucesión de mujeres desesperadas y ambiciosas que habían pasado por su cama.

No había sido fiel a ninguna de sus tres esposas. Y los tres matrimonios habían terminado mal y, en el caso del de la madre de Calista, en tragedia. Y, no obstante, ella había ayudado a su padre y le había sido fiel hasta el final.

Lukas frunció el ceño y dejó el tenedor en el plato. Aquello no tenía ningún sentido. Salvo que Calista le hubiese dicho la verdad acerca de aquella fatídica noche.

No. Lukas se negaba a dejarse engañar. En cualquier caso, su comportamiento no se parecería en nada al de Aristotle Gianopoulous, solo de pensarlo se le revolvía el estómago.

Porque la pequeña Effie ya había conquistado su corazón.

Se dio cuenta, sorprendido, de que sería capaz de hacer cualquier cosa por ella. Y de que iba a formar parte de su vida para siempre.

La cuestión era qué iba a hacer con su madre.

Capítulo 6

DESPIERTA, dormilona.
Calista abrió los ojos y vio a su hija junto a la cama. En una mano llevaba un *koulouri* a medio comer y en la otra, un pan con forma de anillo, cubierto de semillas de sésamo que se estaban cayendo sobre la colcha.

–Tienes que levantarte.

Calista la abrazó y aspiró su olor a niña pequeña.

–Buenos días, cariño. ¿Has dormido bien?

–Sí –respondió Effie con impaciencia–, pero tienes que darte prisa. Tenemos mucho que hacer.

Calista se apoyó en un codo y se miró el reloj, sorprendida de lo tarde que era.

Había pasado la noche en la habitación más grande de la casa, que Dorcas había preparado para la feliz pareja llenándola de flores frescas y velas. Incluso había echado pétalos de rosa por la cama, detalle que había hecho que Lukas sonriese de medio lado al abrir la puerta.

En esos momentos, Calista se dio cuenta de la realidad a la que había accedido: a quedarse en Thalassa con Effie una temporada. En realidad, no había tenido elección. No tenía dinero ni contactos. Lukas, sí.

Pero se le aceleraba el pulso solo de pensar en él. Perdía el control, el raciocinio y la sensatez cuando lo tenía cerca. Por no hablar de lo que ocurría con su libido.

—Venga, mamá. Vamos a ir en el barco de mi papá.

Calista cerró los ojos, volvió a abrirlos y miró a Effie, que parecía feliz.

Lo único que le faltaba a ella era pasar el día en el barco de Lukas. Sabía que esa era su pasión, que era feliz subido a su barco, descalzo, con la brisa despeinando sus rizos oscuros.

—Date prisa, mamá. ¡Vístete!

Respiró hondo, apartó la sábana y se sentó al borde de la cama. Se detuvo. La imagen de Lukas, sonriendo y relajado, con los ojos brillantes porque iba a navegar, se había quedado anclada en su mente, no la podía borrar. Lukas había adorado la vida, había sido un chico alegre. Libre.

Y le habían arrebatado esa libertad.

Mientras se desperezaba, Calista pensó por primera vez en cómo debía de haber sido aquello para él. Que a Lukas le hubiesen privado del mundo exterior, del sol y del mar, que hubiese perdido su libertad durante cuatro años y medio...

Debía de haber sido toda una tortura. ¿Y si además no había sido culpable? ¿Y si era inocente?

Calista se llevó un puño a la boca y se mordió los nudillos. Al verse sola y embarazada, había sacado fuerzas de flaqueza para salir adelante, criar a su hija, estudiar. Y durante las horas más oscuras, durante las largas y solitarias noches, se había obligado a recordar lo que Lukas había hecho, el hombre que era en realidad.

Pero en esos momentos ya no estaba segura. O sí. Lukas era inocente. Estaba convencida. De hecho, siempre lo había estado.

Lo que significaba que su padre había sido el culpable.

–¡Mamá! –le gritó Effie, agarrándola de la mano para intentar ayudarla a ponerse en pie–. Papá nos está esperando.

Calista fue al baño. Tendría que hablar con Lukas y enfrentarse a la verdad, por dolorosa que fuese. Se lo debía.

Se protegió los ojos del sol y vio cómo Effie chapoteaba en el mar azul turquesa. Estaba con Lukas a cierta distancia del barco, pero Calista confiaba en él. Effie todavía no sabía nadar, pero le habían puesto unos flotadores y Lukas le estaba enseñando en esos momentos.

–Bien hecho, ya casi lo tienes –le estaba diciendo–. Ahora, a ver si puedes venir hasta donde estoy yo.

Se apartó un poco y esperó a que la niña chapotease hacia él.

–¡Muy bien, lo has conseguido! –la felicitó, tomándola en brazos mientras la pequeña gritaba contenta.

Entonces ambos se dirigieron hacia el barco. Y Calista volvió a clavar la vista en su libro.

–¿Has visto eso, mamá?

El barco se tambaleó mientras Effie y Lukas subían a bordo.

–He nadado sola.

–Eso es estupendo, cariño –le respondió ella, cerrando el libro y dejándolo a un lado para demostrar que en esos momentos era ella la que llevaba el mando–. Ahora, ven, tienes que secarte.

Effie la abrazó y el contraste de su cuerpo frío con el de Calista, caliente por el sol, hizo que a esta se le pusiese la piel de gallina. Consciente de que Lukas la miraba, ella se concentró en quitarle los flotadores a la niña. Luego le dio la mano y se la llevó hacia el camarote.

Pero Lukas estaba en medio.

–Perdona –dijo Calista, intentando pasar, pero él se negó a moverse y ella tuvo que levantar la vista hacia su magnífico cuerpo.

–La próxima vez voy a hacerlo sin flotadores –dijo Effie–. Papá dice que aprendo deprisa.

–Seguro que sí –respondió Calista, secándole el pelo, ya en el camarote–, pero, si no quieres, no hace falta que lo llames papá, puedes llamarlo Lukas.

–Me gusta llamarlo papá –respondió Effie–. Dice que los niños griegos llaman *bampas* a sus papás. Es gracioso, ¿verdad? ¿Tú llamabas así a tu papá?

«No», pensó ella en silencio. Siempre había utilizado con Aristotle la palabra formal: *pateras*.

–Y la palabra para decir sí es *nai* –continuó Effie mientras Calista la vestía–. Eso también es muy gracioso. Papá dice que tengo que aprender a hablar griego, así, podré hablar con todo el mundo.

–Bueno, ya veremos –respondió Calista–. En Londres no te va a hacer falta el griego.

–No, pero a mí me gusta estar aquí –respondió Effie, bostezando.

–Sí, las vacaciones son muy divertidas, ¿verdad? Pero en casa también se está bien. Apuesto a que Magda nos echa de menos.

–Umm –respondió Effie–. Podría venir también.

–No, cariño. Ahora, ¿quieres dormir la siesta?

Para su sorpresa, Effie asintió y permitió que Calista la tumbase en una cama. Cerró los ojos casi inmediatamente.

Calista miró a su alrededor. se sintió tentada a quedarse allí, en vez de volver a cubierta con Lukas, pero eso sería de cobardes. Y ella no era una cobarde.

Cuando subió, Lukas le estaba dando la espalda, haciendo algo con las amarras.

Al oír que se acercaba, le preguntó:

–¿Está bien Effie?

–Sí, está durmiendo. Debe de ser por el aire fresco –comentó riéndose.

–El aire fresco siempre es bueno para un niño.

Lukas abrió la nevera portátil.

–¿Quieres algo? ¿Más comida? ¿Una cerveza?

–No, gracias –respondió ella, que ya se arrepentía de la copa de vino blanco que se había tomado un rato antes. Entre eso y el sol, estaba empezando a sentirse aturdida–. Creo que me voy a sentar a la sombra, a leer un rato.

–Como desees.

Colocó unos cojines a la sombra y abrió su novela. Oyó que Lukas abría una cerveza y levantó la vista hacia él, que estaba ocupado con el barco. Las olas del mar golpeaban el casco, una gaviota pasó por encima. Ella cerró los ojos...

Lukas se puso cómodo al lado de Calista, que se había quedado dormida. Un mechón de pelo rojizo se había quedado entre sus labios y se movía con la respiración. Él la recorrió con la mirada y tragó saliva. La tentación de pasar las manos por su piel desnuda era demasiado fuerte. O de pasar la lengua, desatarle la parte de arriba del bikini y apartar la tela, para que su boca pudiese dedicar a aquellos pechos la atención que se merecían. Se excitó solo de pensarlo.

Apartó la vista y la clavó en el horizonte. Sabía que, si quería, podía tener a cualquier mujer. ¿Por qué torturarse con aquella?

¿Sería porque sabía que había sido su primer amante? No se le había olvidado el momento en el que ambos se habían dado cuenta de que no había marcha atrás.

Calista había sido tan apasionada, había estado tan excitada. En la cárcel, Lukas siempre había pensado que había sido toda una actuación, pero ya no estaba tan seguro. En esos momentos, cuando miraba aquellos ojos verdes veía en ellos muchas cosas: ira, dolor, miedo, pero no traición. Y cuando le había dicho que Aristotle era el culpable ella se había mostrado realmente destrozada. Rota.

Lukas se pasó la mano por el pelo mojado y

pensó que tenía que avanzar, tenía que dejar de sufrir por el pasado y concentrarse en el futuro. Un futuro en el que estaría su hija.

Porque Effie era lo más maravilloso que había salido de todo aquel embrollo. Todavía le costaba creer que tuviese una hija. Y, sobre todo, una hija tan especial como Effie. Se sentía feliz cada vez que la miraba... cuando pensaba en ella.

Pero había otra cosa que lo inquietaba. Él había sido el primer amante de Calista, pero ¿cuántos más había tenido desde entonces? Habían pasado cinco años, tiempo más que de sobra para que Calista hubiese tenido muchos compañeros.

Solo de imaginársela con otro hombre hizo que le ardiese la sangre en las venas, que le temblasen las manos de la impotencia y la ira.

Al menos no parecía que estuviese con nadie en esos momentos. Lukas lo había confirmado con Effie.

Lo que no significaba que fuese así. Aunque el modo en que Calista se había entregado a él el día del entierro, con tanta pasión, con tantas ansias, le sugería que no había nadie. Y que, si lo había habido, ya era parte del pasado. O iba a serlo pronto. Porque Calista iba a ser suya mientras él lo quisiese.

La decisión estaba tomada. Deseaba a Calista. Quería tenerla en su cama todas las noches. Y, además, iba a asegurarse de que ella también lo deseara.

Notó que se movía a su lado y se giró a mirarla. Vio cómo se humedecía los labios secos con la punta de la lengua y cambiaba de postura. Tomó el libro que había quedado pegado a su vientre, con las páginas ligeramente manchadas de crema solar. Lukas había visto cómo se la extendía por todo el cuerpo un rato antes y había deseado hacerlo él.

Calista abrió sus ojos verdes. Y Lukas estaba lo suficientemente cerca para darse cuenta de que, por un instante, lo miraba con deseo.

–¡Lukas! –le dijo entonces, indignada–. Me has asustado. ¿Qué haces aquí, mirándome?

–Solo estaba disfrutando de las vistas.

–Pues no lo hagas más.

Calista no sabía qué Lukas le resultaba más inti-midante, el vengativo y agresivo del entierro de su padre, o el sarcástico y arrogante que la recorría con la mirada en esos momentos.

Ninguno de ellos representaba al Lukas que ella había conocido. Del que se había enamorado. Y, no obstante, sabía que aquel hombre seguía es-tando en él. Lo había visto con Effie, cariñoso, pa-ciente. Lo había visto al subirse al yate, sonriendo, olvidándose por un instante de lo mucho que la odiaba.

Calista empezó a sentir calor bajo su mirada.

–¿Hay agua fría en la nevera? –le preguntó.

–Por supuesto.

Lukas se puso en pie rápidamente y volvió con una botella de agua mineral. Calista bebió y luego se dio cuenta de que estaba empezando a quemarse, algo que le ocurría con facilidad. Por suerte, Effie había heredado el color de piel de su padre, aunque un par de tonos más claro.

Calista hizo ademán de ponerse en pie.

—Voy a ver cómo está Effie.

—No hace falta. Acabo de hacerlo yo. Sigue dormida.

—Ah, de acuerdo —respondió ella, volviendo a sentarse.

Lukas había hablado en tono frío, como si hubiese esperado que ella le llevase la contraria, o como si estuviese esperando algo. La miró a los ojos un par de segundos y luego se tumbó en los cojines, con un brazo debajo de la cabeza.

Era un hombre impresionante, moreno y fuerte. Y a Calista le entraron ganas de tocarlo.

Así que dobló las rodillas y se abrazó a ellas.

Pasaron varios segundos en silencio, sin hacer nada. Calista tomó aire. Sabía que había una manera de romper la tensión sexual que Lukas estaba creando a propósito entre ellos.

Se aclaró la garganta.

—Lukas, he estado pensando —empezó, moviéndose con nerviosismo, obligándose a mirarlo a los ojos.

Él arqueó una ceja.

—Lo que me dijiste acerca de mi padre... es verdad, ¿no? El responsable del tráfico de armas era él.

—Sí, Calista. Es verdad —respondió él.

—Y Stavros... no tenía nada que ver, ¿no?

—Nada en absoluto.

—Ni tú tampoco.

Él se limitó a inclinar la cabeza. Le brillaron los ojos.

Pasaron varios segundos, Calista deseó poder meterse en el mar y huir de aquella horrible situación.

En vez de eso, se abrazó las rodillas con más fuerza.

—Lo siento mucho, Lukas —le dijo en un susurro.

—¿Que lo sientes? —preguntó él—. No creo que una disculpa sea suficiente, después de lo ocurrido.

—Bueno, no, pero...

—Me quedé sin libertad, mancharon mi nombre, me arruinaron la vida.

—Es evidente que no hay nada que pueda compensarte por todo eso.

—Por haber matado a mi padre.

Aquello hizo que Calista levantase la cabeza.

—Eso no es justo —le respondió—. El corazón de Stavros ya estaba débil, lo dijo la autopsia. Podría haber fallecido en cualquier momento.

—Y, no obstante, falleció mientras discutía con tu padre.

—No obstante...

—¿Todavía vas a defenderlo, Calista? ¿Al monstruo de tu padre?

—No.

—Porque, si es así, te sugiero que abras los ojos y veas que era un individuo abyecto.

—Sé que hizo algo terrible, Lukas.

A punto de echarse a llorar, Calista se tapó la cara con las manos temblorosas. Le resultaba muy doloroso enfrentarse a la culpabilidad de su padre, pero tenía que hacerlo. Y tenía que enfrentarse a Lukas también. Ella no era responsable de lo que Aristotle había hecho. Pensase lo que pensase Lukas, ella no había hecho nada malo. Y tenía que convencerlo de ello.

Tomó aire, apartó las manos y dijo:

—Te prometo que no tenía ni idea. Tienes que creerme.

—De acuerdo —dijo él—. Te creo.

—Bien. Entonces, ¿aceptas que no tuve nada que ver con ello?

—Si tú lo dices...

—Por supuesto que lo digo —replicó ella con firmeza—. Yo no soy culpable de los delitos que cometiera mi padre.

—No, pero sigues siendo culpable de haberme traicionado.

—No, ya te he dicho...

Él levantó la mano para interrumpirla.

—Aceptaste la versión de tu padre sin dudarlo. Creíste que yo era capaz de cometer los delitos de los que se me acusó y ni siquiera me preguntaste. Para mí eso es una traición.

—Me equivoqué... Ahora me doy cuenta —dijo Calista—. Y siento mucho no haber confiado en ti.

—¡No quiero tus disculpas! —exclamó él en tono duro, amargo—. Ya me da igual lo que pienses de mí.

La miró fijamente.

—Todavía no lo entiendes, ¿verdad?

Calista lo miró en silencio.

—Tal vez el responsable de que yo fuese a la cárcel fuera tu padre, pero tú, al creer sus mentiras, me negaste el derecho a saber que era padre. Me robaste los primeros cuatro años y medio de la vida de Effie –la acusó–. Y, si no nos hubiésemos visto en el entierro, si yo no te lo hubiese sacado, todavía no sabría de su existencia.

–No. Te lo habría contado. Iba a contártelo.

–¿De verdad? ¿Cuándo exactamente? ¿Cuando la niña tuviese dieciocho años? ¿O veintiuno?

–Tenía que pensar en Effie. Ella es lo primero... Tenía que hacer lo que era mejor para ella.

–¿Y lo mejor para ella era privarla de su padre? –inquirió Lukas–. Gracias por eso, Calista.

Ella no supo cómo responder.

–Para tu información, mi vida tampoco ha sido precisamente fácil estos años atrás.

–¿No me digas? ¿Has estado encerrada en una celda con un ladrón armado, capaz de rebanarte el cuello por un paquete de tabaco?

–Bueno, no, pero...

–¿Te has pasado una hora al día, la única hora al día en la que te dejaban ver la luz del sol, dando vueltas a un patio de prisión?

–No, por supuesto que no.

–Entonces, no te atrevas a decirme que tu vida ha sido dura.

–¡Yo no puedo arreglar el pasado, Lukas! –le gritó ella–. No sé qué más te puedo decir.

–Nada, no me puedes decir nada –le respondió él–, pero tal vez haya algo que puedas hacer.

Alargó un dedo, lo pasó por su mandíbula y después por los labios.

A Calista se le aceleró el corazón, se le dilataron las pupilas al ver que Lukas se acercaba más.

–Quizás haya una manera de poder empezar a compensarme –añadió, inclinando su magnífico cuerpo sobre ella.

Capítulo 7

EL CUERPO de Lukas se cernía sobre ella, con los brazos y los dedos de los pies apoyados con firmeza a su lado. Calista se quedó inmóvil, consciente de los músculos de sus bíceps, de su torso fuerte, que estaba a tan solo unos centímetros de su tembloroso cuerpo. Sentía el calor que irradiaba su cuerpo y penetraba en ella. Su aliento le acariciaba el rostro e hizo que cerrase los ojos, hasta que sus labios la tocaron y los volvió a abrir. Bastaba una caricia, el roce de sus labios, para que se pusiese a temblar de deseo. Para que se quebrase.

Lukas dobló los codos para bajar el cuerpo y profundizar el beso. Fue un beso persuasivo y sensual, con el que le dejó claro a Calista quién mandaba allí, quién tenía el poder.

Por un instante, ella intentó resistirse apretando los labios, pero no iba a servir de nada y ambos lo sabían. Al final se rindió y separó los labios e, inmediatamente, Lukas estaba allí, gimiendo mientras su lengua encontraba la de ella y se entrelazaban.

Calista hundió las manos en su pelo, se aferró a él. Por su parte, Lukas puso un brazo alrededor de su cintura para cambiar de posición y que ella estuviese encima, sin dejar de besarla. Sus cuerpos estaban prácticamente desnudos y Lukas la ayudó a

colocarse de tal manera que estuviese donde él quería: pegada contra su erección.

Calista se oyó gemir y el deseo de tenerlo dentro
fue tan intenso que tuvo que hacer un gran esfuerzo
para no rogárselo. En vez de eso, apretó las caderas
contra él.

Y Lukas lo entendió, gimió.

La tela de los bañadores era tan fina que corría el
peligro de deshacerse con el calor que ambos estaban generando. Calista metió una mano entre ambos y acarició los fuertes músculos del pecho de
Lukas, bajó por el vientre y metió la mano por debajo del bañador para acariciarlo. Lukas se estremeció y le fue desatando el bikini.

—Dios mío, Calista —gimió entre dientes—. Mira
cómo me pones.

Volvió a besarla mientras le acariciaba la piel
desnuda de las nalgas antes de hundir los dedos
donde ella más lo necesitaba.

—No puedo saciarme de ti —añadió entre dientes—. Jamás podré hacerlo.

¿Era una amenaza o una promesa? Calista no estaba segura, no le importaba. Solo podía pensar en
que lo deseaba tanto que tenía miedo de explotar.

Pero tenían que controlarse un poco. Effie estaba
dormida en el camarote, debajo de ellos. Tenían
que actuar con responsabilidad.

Ambos lo oyeron a la vez. Un ruido apagado
debajo de ellos y después una voz:

—Mamaaá.

Ella se apartó rápidamente de Lukas y se dio
cuenta de que la parte de arriba del bikini colgaba

de su cuerpo y, la de abajo, estaba arrugada entre sus piernas.

–Ya voy, cariño. Espera un momento.

Se ajustó los triángulos para cubrirse los pechos todavía duros y luego miró a Lukas, que la estaba observando con ojos oscuros y brillantes, pero con una cierta vulnerabilidad, y que entonces se movió para buscar unos pantalones cortos y ponérselos.

Acababan de vestirse los dos cuando una cabeza despeinada apareció por las escaleras, entrecerrando los ojos al ver la luz del sol.

–Aquí estáis –dijo Effie, mirándolos con curiosidad–. No sabía dónde estaba cuando me he despertado.

–¿No, cariño? –preguntó Calista sonriendo–. No pasa nada. Seguimos aquí, en el barco.

–¡Ya lo sé! –respondió Effie, poniendo los ojos en blanco–. ¿Puedo ir a nadar otra vez?

–Sí, por supuesto. Esta vez te acompañaré yo.

Calista pensó que le vendría bien un poco de agua fría.

–¡Sí! ¿Y papá también?

–Tal vez dentro de un rato –respondió él, apoyando una mano en el hombro de Calista e inclinándose para susurrarle al oído–: Continuará, señorita Gianopoulous.

Calista tragó saliva, pero Effie tiró de su mano y le impidió responder.

Estiró la espalda y se puso los brazos detrás de la cabeza. Lukas había estado trabajando en su despacho toda la tarde y necesitaba un descanso, pero después de tantos días sin hacer nada se le había acumulado el trabajo.

Su negocio de yates de lujo, Blue Sky Charters, había seguido funcionando bien en su ausencia. Sus empleados le habían sido leales y no tenía de qué preocuparse. Supuso que había tenido suerte, aunque la palabra «suerte» no era precisamente la que hubiese preferido utilizar, de que las autoridades no hubiesen embargado su negocio personal. No había ninguna relación entre este y G&K Shipping, que se había hundido con el escándalo.

Aunque Lukas pretendía volver a levantar la empresa, en honor a su padre. Ya habían conseguido volver a comprar siete cargueros. Aristotle Gianopoulous había tenido ochenta, pero era un comienzo. Lukas también había decidido limpiar su nombre y, lo que era mucho más importante, el de su padre. Quería que todo el mundo supiese quién había sido el responsable del tráfico de armas.

Se inclinó hacia delante y cerró el ordenador portátil. La casa estaba en silencio y todavía no se había puesto el sol. Pensó que, de hecho, había demasiado silencio. Hacía algo más de una semana que habían llegado los tres a Villa Helene y Lukas se había acostumbrado a tener por allí rondando a Calista y a Effie, a oír a la niña corriendo por los suelos de mármol de la casa, a oír su risa y sus gritos retumbando en las grandes habitaciones. En vez de disfrutar de su soledad, Lukas aguzó el oído para ver si habían vuelto ya de su excursión a la playa.

Después de la comida, Calista se había asomado

para anunciarle que iba a llevar a Effie a la pequeña cala que había cerca de la casa. Lukas había entendido por su tono de voz que no quería que las acompañase. Lo habría hecho de todos modos de no haber sido porque tenía trabajo. Además, Calista llevaba toda la semana jugando a guardar las distancias con él.

Y él había decidido seguirle la corriente. Aunque se estuviese volviendo loco, viéndola balancear las caderas por toda la casa, fingiendo indiferencia cuando en realidad la tensión sexual que había entre ambos fuese insoportable.

Se miró el reloj. Eran más de las seis. Tenían que haber vuelto ya, aunque sabía que siempre era difícil llevarse a Effie de la playa.

Le encantaba ver cómo disfrutaba la pequeña en Thalassa, y le encantaba que eso le fastidiase a su madre. Por un lado, a Calista le gustaba ver feliz a su hija, pero, por otro, no dejaba de recordarse, y de recordarle a él, que aquello no eran más que unas vacaciones, que pronto volverían a Londres.

Eso ya lo verían. Lukas todavía no tenía claro lo que iba a hacer, pero sí que no tenía la intención de dejar marchar a Effie.

Porque adoraba a su hija. Effie le había robado el corazón desde el primer momento y quería seguir teniéndola cerca. Si para ello tenía que domar a su madre, lo haría.

A pesar de que «domar» no era la palabra adecuada. Lukas no quería a una Calista dócil. Le encantaba que fuese salvaje.

Por su propio bien, Lukas había decidido concentrarse solo en la atracción sexual que había entre ambos. Solo habían hecho el amor dos veces, con un intervalo de más de cuatro años y medio, y ninguna de las dos había sido perfecta.

La siguiente vez que le hiciese el amor a Calista, porque estaba seguro de que iba a haber una siguiente vez, y pronto, se iba a asegurar de que las condiciones fuesen las correctas.

Por ese motivo, se había dedicado a elaborar cuidadosamente un plan.

Aquella mañana había llegado correo para Calista. Debía de habérselo enviado la mujer con la que compartía casa en Londres. Petros se lo había llevado junto con una muñeca para Effie, regalo de Dorcas y suyo. Effie había dado las gracias de manera educada, aunque Lukas se había dado cuenta de que miraba la muñeca con recelo. Cuando se había quedado sola, la había desnudado mientras su madre miraba las cartas y solo se molestaba en abrir una, leerla y volver a meterla en el sobre.

–¿Algo interesante? –había preguntado Lukas al ver que Calista apretaba los labios.

–No mucho –había respondido ella–. Es del abogado de mi padre. Van a leer el testamento el día veintiocho.

–¿Mañana?

Ella había mirado su teléfono para comprobar la fecha.

–Sí.

–¿Vas a ir?

–No. Tiene el despacho en Atenas. Además, no quiero saber nada de la herencia de mi padre... ahora que sé la verdad.

Lukas la había visto bajar la vista. El hecho de que por fin Calista hubiese aceptado la verdad no le había producido ninguna satisfacción. Más bien, su dolor había hecho que se le encogiese el corazón.

–Mis hermanastros pueden repartirse lo que haya quedado.

–Si tú no estás allí para firmar, no podrán –le había informado él–. Te sugiero que vayas a Atenas y que aproveches la oportunidad para dejar todos los cabos atados. Tal vez entonces puedas pasar página.

–Y yo te sugiero a ti que no te metas en los asuntos ajenos.

En vez de enfadarse al oír aquella respuesta, como habría sido de esperar, Lukas se había sentido casi aliviado al ver que Calista seguía luchando.

–¿He metido el dedo en la llaga?

–No. Es solo que no necesito que me digas lo que debo o no debo hacer, muchas gracias.

–Está bien. No obstante, permite que te informe de que yo tengo un negocio que atender en Atenas. Podríamos ir mañana... y, tal vez, hacer noche en mi apartamento.

–No –había contestado Calista con firmeza–. Va a ser un lío para Effie.

–¿Y por qué no la dejas aquí? –había sugerido él–. Estoy seguro de que Dorcas y Petros estarán encantados de cuidarla.

–Sí, por favor, mamá –había dicho Effie, a la que nunca se le escapaba nada–. ¿Puedo quedarme con Dorcas y Petros? Por favor.

–No sé... Quizás no quieran tener que estar pendientes de ti por la noche.

–No voy a molestar. Puedo ayudar a Dorcas a preparar galletas *kouloulou*.

–*Koulourakia* –la había corregido Calista.

–Sí, esas. ¿Puedo, mamá?

–Bueno, tal vez. Luego se lo preguntamos.

En ese punto, Lukas había esbozado una sonrisa. Gracias a su maravillosa hija había conseguido con éxito la primera fase de su plan.

En esos momentos, se dirigió a la terraza y se llevó la mano a la frente para hacerse sombra. Oyó a lo lejos la vocecita de Effie y poco después vio aparecer a madre e hija a su izquierda. Ambas coloradas y despeinadas por el viento. Calista llevaba un pareo atado a las caderas e iba cargada con un bolso de playa y una nevera portátil. Effie luchaba contra su cocodrilo hinchable que era casi el doble de grande que ella.

Lukas echó a andar y se dio cuenta, sorprendido, de la alegría que le daba verlas.

–¿Qué demonios está haciendo él aquí?

Los dos hermanastros de Calista se pusieron en pie de un salto al verla entrar con Lukas en el despacho del abogado. Ella notó cómo Lukas se ponía tenso a sus espaldas.

–Él no tiene nada que hacer aquí –le recriminó Christos–. Haz que se marche, Calista.

–Siéntate, Christos –le pidió ella con voz tranquila, aunque en el fondo estuviese muy nerviosa, mientras tomaba asiento–. Lukas solo ha venido a acompañarme.

–Ha venido a comprobar el daño que nos ha hecho –insistió Christos–. Ha diezmado nuestra herencia tanto como la suya propia.

–¿Por qué lo has traído? –intervino Yiannis.

En realidad, Calista no había querido que Lukas la acompañase, pero él había insistido en llevarla hasta allí, después, en acompañarla en el ascensor y, cuando había querido darse cuenta, había entrado con ella en el despacho.

–¿Por qué no nos sentamos todos? –propuso el señor Petrides desde el otro lado del escritorio.

Era el abogado de la familia Gianopoulous y debía de tener al menos ochenta años.

–La lectura del testamento no llevará mucho tiempo.

Christos volvió a sentarse y Yiannis lo imitó. Lukas tomó también una silla y la colocó al otro lado de Calista.

El señor Petrides se aclaró la garganta y empezó a leer despacio. Calista intentó concentrarse, pero le resultó difícil con Lukas a su lado, irradiando hostilidad contra los hermanos Gianopoulous. ¿Tenía planeado algún enfrentamiento? ¿Era aquel el motivo de su presencia allí? Por primera vez, Calista se preguntó si la habría engañado para tenerlos a todos juntos. Aunque, de ser así, no le importaba.

El tiempo fue pasando. El despacho era pequeño y hacía calor y, cuando se quiso dar cuenta, estaba con la cabeza en otra parte. Esperaba que Effie estuviese bien, aunque de aquello estaba segura, podía contar con Dorcas y Petros.

Ella, por su parte, había accedido a pasar la noche en el apartamento que Lukas tenía en Atenas. Todavía no lo conocía. De adolescente, había preferido no pensar en él, ya que se había imaginado que Lukas llevaría a muchas mujeres allí, aunque Lukas nunca le hubiese dado ningún motivo para pensarlo. Siempre había sido muy discreto en lo que a su vida privada se había referido. Lo que no significaba que no la hubiese tenido.

De lo que estaba segura era de que esa noche iba a tener que ser muy cauta si no quería terminar entre sus sábanas negras de satén. Durante toda la semana, desde el beso en el barco, había intentado luchar contra la atracción que había entre ambos. Solo de pensarlo temblaba por dentro.

Así que había hecho todo lo posible por guardar las distancias con él y había intentado estar siempre en compañía de Effie. Y, por las noches, después de acostar a la niña, se había puesto a leer o se había ido a la cama temprano.

Sorprendentemente, Lukas no había intentado presionarla. De hecho, se había comportado como todo un caballero.

Calista se había sentido muy aliviada. Era evidente que a Lukas se le había olvidado la promesa que, entre susurros, le había hecho en el barco. Al parecer, había decidido no intentar seducirla, darle espacio. Sin embargo, con el paso de los días ella había empezado a sentirse primero frustrada y después insegura. Había empezado a tener la sensación de que Lukas no se comportaba así por respeto, sino más bien por falta de interés, y eso tampoco le gustaba.

—Entonces, básicamente, nos está diciendo que no hay absolutamente nada.

La voz furiosa de Christos hizo que Calista volviese a la realidad.

El señor Petrides lo miró por encima de las gafas.

—Lo que estoy diciendo es que los pocos bienes que le quedaban a su padre tienen que dividirse entre los herederos.

—¿Y Thalassa? —inquirió Yiannis, echándose hacia delante—. ¿Tampoco queda nada de la isla?

—No se hace referencia a la isla de Thalassa —respondió el señor Petrides—. Tengo entendido que esa propiedad pertenecía a la primera esposa de su padre que, recientemente, la ha vendido al señor Kalanos.

—Eres un...

Christos había vuelto a ponerse en pie, pero Yiannis lo contuvo y lo obligó a volver a sentarse.

—Entonces, ¿es verdad? —le preguntó Yiannis a Lukas, con gesto de derrota.

—Por supuesto —respondió él en tono frío y tranquilo.

—En ese caso, ¿se puede saber a qué hemos venido? —le preguntó Christos al señor Petrides—. ¿Solo a que nos humillen? ¿A que este hombre pueda alardear de cómo nos ha engañado?

—No, Christos —respondió el anciano, que de repente parecía haber envejecido todavía más—. El motivo por el que os he reunido hoy aquí es que tengo algo que contaros. Creo que ha llegado el momento de que sepáis la verdad acerca de vuestro padre.

Apoyó la espalda en el sillón e hizo una pausa antes de continuar.

–He guardado silencio durante los últimos años. Al principio, pensé que lo hacía por lealtad, pero me he dado cuenta de que en realidad es cobardía. En cualquier caso, la situación ha cambiado. Me han diagnosticado una enfermedad terminal y necesito quitarme este peso de los hombros antes de morir.

–Lo siento mucho, señor Petrides –dijo Calista, inclinándose hacia delante para tocar su mano, pero el abogado la apartó.

–No me merezco tu compasión, Calista. Yo... he estado ocultando información, tanto a vosotros como a la policía. Y siento mucho tener que contaros esto... pero soy de la opinión de que vuestro padre fue el responsable del contrabando de armas, y no Stavros Kalanos.

–¡No! ¡Está mintiendo! –exclamó Christos, poniéndose en pie de nuevo–. Él le ha pagado para que nos diga eso, ¿verdad?

Señaló a Lukas y añadió:

–¡Es todo una sucia conspiración!

El anciano negó con la cabeza.

–No conozco los detalles de los negocios de vuestro padre, pero empecé a sospechar hace mucho tiempo. Sospechas que debí haber compartido con las autoridades. Y que ahora pretendo compartir con ellas. Lukas...

Con mucho esfuerzo, se puso en pie.

–Me alegro de que estés aquí hoy –le dijo–. No voy a pedirte que me perdones, porque sé que no me lo merezco, pero quiero expresarte mi más profundo arrepentimiento por no haber dicho la verdad antes, por la injusticia que sufriste y por haber arruinado el nombre de tu padre.

Lukas se puso en pie, rígido, pero tranquilo. Y tomó la mano temblorosa que el señor Petrides le ofrecía.

—Gracias, hijo —le dijo el abogado—. Es más de lo que me merezco. Puedes estar seguro de que a partir de ahora haré lo correcto.

—Un momento —lo interrumpió Yiannis—. Solo ha hablado de sospechas, Petrides. No se pueden hacer acusaciones tan fácilmente si no se tienen pruebas.

—De todos modos, nadie creerá a un viejo loco —añadió Christos.

—Es la verdad —intervino Calista—. Y es mejor que la sepáis, los dos. Nuestro padre fue el culpable, no Stavros, ni tampoco Lukas.

—¿Y tú qué sabes?

—Lo sé porque me lo ha contado todo Lukas, y lo creo.

—Pues peor para ti —le dijo Christos—. Todos sabemos que has andado detrás de Lukas desde siempre. Podría haberte dicho que lo negro era blanco y también lo habrías creído.

—Basta —dijo Lukas, poniéndose en pie justo detrás de la silla de Calista—. Deberías respetar a vuestra hermana. Los dos.

—¿Respetar? —repitió Christos—. ¿A esa? ¿Una criatura pelirroja que siempre ha sido un parásito?

Calista se quedó de piedra al oír aquello.

—¿Qué has dicho?

–Si no la quería ni su propia madre. La mandaba a Thalassa todos los veranos, hasta que al final decidió suicidarse. Y es probable que Calista haya heredado su locura, así que lo mejor es que tenga cuidado.

–¡Christos! –lo reprendió Yiannis, tirándole del brazo.

Pero Lukas ya lo estaba agarrando por el cuello, lo levantó en volandas.

–¡Suéltalo, Lukas! –le gritó Calista, temiendo por la vida de Christos–. No merece la pena.

Lukas dudó, respiró hondo y lo soltó por fin, a pesar de que era evidente que estaba furioso.

–No vuelvas a hablar así de Calista en la vida –lo amenazó.

Christos dejó escapar un gruñido.

–Ahora, discúlpate –le dijo Lukas, agarrándolo de los hombros para hacerlo girarse hacia Calista.

–No pasa nada, no me importa...

–Por supuesto que sí –insistió Lukas–. Este cretino va a disculparse, ahora mismo.

–Lo siento –dijo Christos, bajando la mirada a sus pies.

–No es suficiente. Mira a tu hermana a los ojos y discúlpate como es debido.

–No tenía que haber dicho todo eso –dijo entonces Christos–. Me disculpo.

–Siéntate –le dijo Lukas, y luego se giró hacia Yiannis–. Y tú también.

Yiannis obedeció.

–Ya va siendo hora de que os enteréis de un par de verdades. En primer lugar, vuestro padre era una mala persona, que mintió y traicionó a mi padre e hizo que me inculpasen a mí. En segundo lugar, si alguno de los dos vuelve a hablar mal de Calista, no seré responsable de mis actos. ¿Entendido?

Los dos hermanos asintieron.

–Y lo voy a dejar aquí por respeto a Calista –les advirtió Lukas–, no porque haya terminado con vosotros. No os merecéis una hermana como ella: valiente, fuerte, honrada y mucho más inteligente que vosotros dos, idiotas, juntos. Lo que me lleva a la tercera cosa que os quería decir: estoy muy orgulloso de anunciaros que es la madre de mi hija.

Yiannis y Christos dieron un grito ahogado al unísono.

–Sí, tenemos una hija. Y algún día heredará toda mi fortuna, y os aseguro que me voy a asegurar de que, en esta ocasión, nada ni nadie consiga perjudicarnos.

Capítulo 8

U NA COPA?
Lukas se acercó al bar y tomó una botella de brandy.

–Sí, ¿por qué no?

Calista aceptó la copa que él le ofrecía, le dio un sorbo y dejó que el líquido le calentase la garganta.

Acababan de llegar de cenar, habían estado en un pequeño restaurante familiar, escondido en uno de los muchos rincones de aquella bonita ciudad. Se habían sentado fuera, a una mesa tan pequeña que sus rodillas se habían chocado y Lukas se había visto obligado a estirar las piernas a un lado. Ella, por su parte, se había sentido mucho más relajada, después de todo lo ocurrido en el despacho del señor Petrides.

La comida había sido deliciosa, hacía una noche cálida y estrellada y el ambiente olía a jazmín y a flor de azahar, así que Calista se había olvidado de sus problemas por un rato y había disfrutado de la compañía de Lukas. Eso era sencillo cuando él estaba así: encantador, atento, divertido. El viejo Lukas. Ninguno de los dos había mencionado la desagradable escena del despacho del señor Petrides.

Pero, en esos momentos, Calista tuvo la sensación de que eso estaba a punto de cambiar. Hizo girar el brandy en la copa e intentó retrasar lo inevitable.

–Tu apartamento es precioso.

–Gracias –respondió Lukas, acercándose–, pero tengo la sensación de que te sorprende.

–¡Lo siento! –ella se rio–. Es que no me lo imaginaba así.

–¿Y cómo te lo imaginabas?

–Es mejor que no lo sepas.

–Deja que lo adivine: sofás de cuero negro y una enorme pantalla de televisión en el salón.

–Más o menos.

–¿Y tal vez una cama de agua y sábanas de satén? Y un cajón lleno de juguetes sexuales.

Calista se ruborizó. Se preguntó si Lukas podía leerle el pensamiento.

–¿En eso también me he equivocado? –preguntó, intentando disimular la vergüenza.

–Juega bien tus cartas y a lo mejor lo averiguas en un rato.

Calista tragó saliva.

Se apartó de él y paseó por el centro del salón.

–Me encantan todos tus cuadros. ¿Ese de ahí es un original?

–Lo es. Me interesa mucho el arte moderno. Además, es una buena inversión, pero no hay nada en mi colección que se pueda comparar a esto.

Apretó un botón y las cortinas se abrieron, dejando al descubierto un enorme ventanal.

–¿Qué te parece?

Calista dio un grito ahogado. Ante ella brillaban

las luces de la ciudad de Atenas, a lo lejos se veía la Acrópolis.

–¡Es increíble!

–Se ve mejor desde aquí.

Lukas atravesó la habitación, la agarró de la mano y, después de abrir las puertas de cristal, la hizo salir al balcón.

–Es bonito, ¿verdad?

Lo era. Era mágico. Echó la cabeza hacia atrás y disfrutó de la noche. Entonces, algo la hizo mirar a Lukas, que la estaba observando con fascinación. Cuando sus miradas se encontraron, la atracción que había entre ambos se avivó de golpe.

Él arqueó las cejas ligeramente, gesto que hizo que a Calista se le doblasen las rodillas.

Lo deseaba tanto... Y estaba segura de cómo terminarían si Lukas se acercaba más y la besaba.

Pero no lo hizo. Apartó la mirada y señaló hacia donde había dos sillas de metal.

–¿Nos sentamos?

–Ah, sí, ¿por qué no?

–Bueno... –añadió Lukas, volviendo a mirarla–. Parece que tus queridos hermanos por fin saben la verdad acerca de tu padre.

Calista hizo una mueca.

–No son mis queridos hermanos –respondió ella–. No quiero volver a verlos en toda mi vida.

–Ya somos dos.

Lukas hizo una breve pausa y añadió, muy serio:

–Si Christos vuelve a hablar de ti así, te prometo que no responderé de mis actos.

Calista vio cómo cerraba los puños.

–Todavía no sé por qué no lo he matado.

–Has conseguido controlarte muy bien –comentó ella, esbozando una sonrisa.

–No me importaría que me condenasen a cadena perpetua por haberlo matado.

–De eso nada –dijo ella, poniéndose seria de nuevo–. No merece la pena.

–Eso es cierto.

–En cualquier caso, gracias por haberme defendido –añadió Calista.

–No tiene importancia –respondió él–. Solo he dicho lo que pienso.

–Pues te lo agradezco mucho –repitió ella, apartando la mirada–. No obstante, lo que has dicho acerca de que Effie vaya a heredarlo todo... ¿No te parece un poco prematuro?

Lukas se encogió de hombros.

–No pasa nada por hacerles ver que la dinastía Kalanos va viento en popa.

–Umm...

Calista no se sentía cómoda con aquello, pero no quiso romper el alto el fuego llevándole la contraria.

–Tengo que admitir que siempre pensé que ese par de payasos sabían la verdad acerca de Aristotle –continuó Lukas–, pero, a juzgar por sus caras hoy, ya no estoy tan seguro.

–Yo pienso que también se habían creído las mentiras de nuestro padre –comentó Calista–. Lo siento mucho, Lukas.

Él sacudió la cabeza.

–Hagamos una tregua, al menos por esta noche.

Ella asintió. Le parecía bien. Si le diesen a elegir, no volvería a tocar el tema jamás, pero sabía que no era tan sencillo. Lukas había prometido limpiar su nombre y el de su padre. Al parecer, el señor Petrides iba a ayudarlo.

Todo el mundo sabría lo que había hecho Aristotle, cosa que a ella le parecía bien, pero también le daba un poco de miedo. Al fin y al cabo, Aristotle había sido su padre... y el abuelo de Effie.

–¿Puedo preguntarte qué pretendes hacer? –le dijo, dejando la copa en la mesita que había entre ambos–. ¿Cuándo tienes pensado hacerlo público?

–Cuando esté preparado. ¿Qué es lo que dicen...? La venganza es un plato que se sirve frío.

Calista se estremeció.

–Yo te agradecería que me previnieses antes...

–¿Para intentar cubrirte las espaldas, Calista?

–¡No! –replicó ella, indignada–. Solo estoy diciendo que, si me avisas, podré prepararme y asegurarme de que la prensa no molesta a Effie.

–Te aseguro que, haga lo que haga, pensaré siempre en lo que es mejor para Effie.

–Ah... gracias.

–Y, hablando de Effie, se me había olvidado comentarte algo.

A Calista se le subió el corazón a la garganta. Si Lukas iba a empezar a hablarle del tema de la custodia otra vez, lucharía con uñas y dientes por su hija.

–¿Sí? ¿El qué?

Lukas guardó silencio un instante. Divertido con su reacción.

–Solo, que me he dado cuenta de que no te he reconocido el mérito que tienes.

–¿A qué te refieres? –preguntó ella con el ceño fruncido.

–A lo maravillosamente bien que has criado a nuestra hija.

–Ah.

–Es evidente que Effie es feliz, una niña equilibrada y excepcional. Has hecho un trabajo estupendo.

–Gracias –respondió ella, ruborizándose.

–También me he dado cuenta de que es muy inteligente –continuó Lukas, sonriendo con franqueza–. Sospecho que eso lo ha heredado de mí.

–Por supuesto –le dijo Calista–. Junto con tu humildad y modestia.

Sus miradas se encontraron y la tensión desapareció, viéndose sustituida por algo mucho más peligroso.

–Brindemos por ello –añadió Lukas–. Por Effie, nuestra niña.

Chocaron sus copas y Calista notó que se le deshacía el nudo que tenía en la garganta con el sorbo de brandy. Notó que los ojos se le llenaban de lágrimas, pero no supo por qué.

–Y por el futuro, por supuesto –continuó él–. Nos depare lo que nos depare.

Calista se había quedado perdida en su mirada. Se dijo que tenía que decir algo, cuanto antes.

–Bueno... se está haciendo tarde –balbució–. Creo que me voy a ir a la cama.

Esperó a que Lukas dijese algo, hiciese algo. En

realidad, tenía la esperanza de que le impidiese marcharse, pero él se quedó inmóvil, sin dejar de mirarla.

–Buenas noches –añadió ella, poniéndose en pie con la intención de marcharse, pero sintió que tenía los pies anclados al suelo.

A sus espaldas, oyó reír a Lukas, fue una risa suave y arrogante. Ella se giró a mirarlo. A mirarlo mal.

Pero no pudo. Porque, de repente, tenía a Lukas muy cerca. Y la estaba tocando. Pasó las manos por sus hombros, por su espalda, trazó la curva de su cintura, la agarró del trasero y la apretó contra él. Y después volvió a subirlas para hundirlas en su pelo. Y besarla.

Y qué beso.

Hambriento, posesivo, dominante, que hizo que Calista se estremeciese y desease más. Respondió al instante y se apretó contra su cuerpo. Buscó su lengua con la de ella, notó que se le erguían los pechos. Se rindió al deseo.

–¿Habías mencionado la cama?

Lukas la tomó en brazos y la llevó al interior, atravesó el salón con Calista aferrada a su cuello y no la soltó hasta llegar al dormitorio, donde la dejó de manera casi reverencial encima de la enorme cama.

–Quédate así –le pidió Lukas en tono sensual.

Ella se estremeció y se dijo que no tenía pensado ir a ninguna parte. Contuvo la respiración mientras Lukas empezaba a quitarse la ropa, comenzando por los botones superiores de la camisa, que después se quitó con impaciencia por la cabeza, quedándose deliciosamente despeinado. Después fue el turno de los pantalones vaqueros y los calzoncillos, y entonces se quedó completamente desnudo ante ella. Su magnífico cuerpo brillaba bajo la luz tenue de la habitación... Calista recorrió su pecho con la mirada, siguió bajando hasta la V bien esculpida de su pelvis, llegó a la línea de vello oscuro y, por fin,... a la erección.

No tuvo mucho tiempo para disfrutar de las vistas, porque Lukas volvió a la cama enseguida, se colocó sobre ella y le bajó los tirantes del vestido antes de pasar a la cremallera de la espalda. Con su ayuda, Calista se quitó el vestido por la cabeza y después se desabrochó el sujetador. La mirada de deseo de Lukas hizo que se le endureciesen los pezones todavía más.

Luego se besaron apasionadamente y entonces Lukas bajó la mano para acariciarla entre los muslos.

Calista gimió contra sus labios y echó la cabeza hacia atrás. La sensación era maravillosa. Era ridículo que Lukas pudiese casi hacerla llegar al clímax con solo tocarla, pero tenía que admitir que era el único hombre al que había deseado, y amado, en toda su vida.

Estaba al borde del abismo cuando Lukas paró, se echó hacia atrás y le quitó las braguitas. Calista alargó los brazos hacia él, desesperada por volver a tenerlo cerca, pero Lukas tenía otra idea. Le separó las piernas y se colocó entre ellas, luego, bajó la cabeza.

–Lukas...

En cuanto su lengua la tocó, Calista no pudo decir nada más.

–¿Te gusta? –le preguntó él, sonriendo con picardía.

La respuesta de Calista consistió en agarrarle la cabeza para que continuase.

–Supongo que eso es un «sí».

Y volvió a acariciarla en el lugar adecuado una y otra vez hasta que Calista sintió que empezaba a caer. Caía por un precipicio que no estaba allí. Hacia un lugar que no existía.

Lukas cambió de posición y miró a Calista, que estaba tumbada boca arriba, saciada, recuperándose todavía. Se sintió orgulloso. Era él quien la había dejado así. Estaba preciosa, con los ojos cerrados, la piel cremosa, despeinada. No entendía cómo podía desearla tanto.

Se inclinó hacia delante y le dio un suave beso en los labios, vio cómo abría lentamente los ojos y se tumbó a su lado y la abrazó para acercarla a su pecho. El brillo de sus ojos le quitó el aliento.

La colocó donde quería tenerla, no, más bien donde necesitaba tenerla, para hacer lo que necesitaba hacer, penetrarla y oír su gemido de placer.

Poco después se rompían los dos por dentro y gritaban el uno el nombre del otro.

Capítulo 9

NADA más vislumbrar a lo lejos la isla de Thalassa, Calista se puso nerviosa. Estaba deseando ver a Effie. Solo habían estado separadas veinticuatro horas, pero la había echado mucho de menos. Además, Thalassa siempre había ocupado un lugar especial en su corazón.

Dos semanas antes, cuando había ido al entierro de su padre, se había prometido a sí misma que no regresaría jamás, pero las cosas habían cambiado. Todo había cambiado.

Había aparecido Lukas.

La noche anterior había sido increíble. Mucho más intensa y apasionada de lo que jamás se habría podido imaginar. Había sido como si no hubiesen estado separados nunca.

Y esa mañana, al despertar, Lukas había estado a su lado, mirándola, con sus ojos oscuros muy serios. Entonces le había dado un beso y le había dicho que tenían que levantarse.

Pero a Calista le había dado tiempo a ver aquella mirada cerrada, inescrutable, y se había dado cuenta de que se había entregado completamente a él, no solo le había entregado su cuerpo, sino también su corazón y su alma, sus emociones. Emociones que sabía que Lukas jamás compartiría con ella.

Habían desayunado en una pequeña cafetería y allí Lukas le había contado que tenía un negocio que atender en Atenas y que tendría que quedarse varios días más, le había propuesto que se quedase a hacerle compañía.

A ella le había costado un esfuerzo sobrehumano declinar la invitación. Tenía que volver con Effie. No quería estar sin ella otra noche más a pesar de saber que su hija estaría pasándoselo muy bien con Dorcas y Petros. Además, sabía que ya se había entregado demasiado a aquel hombre.

Así que Lukas le había organizado la vuelta a Thalassa en uno de sus barcos, manejado por dos dioses griegos, Nico y Tavi, que se paseaban por él exhibiéndose mucho más de lo que a Calista le parecía necesario. Aunque no le importó. Debían de tener la misma edad que ella, pero a Calista le parecieron dos niños. No podían compararse con Lukas. No obstante, disfrutó de sus atenciones, se sintió joven y sexy. Sintió que podía hacer cualquier cosa.

—¡Señorita Gianopoulous, mire! —la llamó Nico—. ¡Delfines! Y vienen hacia aquí.

Calista miró hacia donde Nico señalaba y vio un grupo de delfines que nadaba hacia ellos. De repente, estaban al lado del barco, saltando y haciendo piruetas a su lado. Ella sintió, emocionada, que la acompañaban a casa.

Contuvo las lágrimas y se dijo que era una tonta. Thalassa no era su casa. Jamás lo sería. No debía olvidar aquello. La noche anterior había sido maravillosa, pero, en lo relativo a su futuro, no había cambiado nada entre Lukas y ella.

¿Qué era lo que él había dicho? Que hicieran una tregua. Nada más.

Una vez de vuelta en Villa Helene, Calista comprobó que, tal y como había sospechado, Effie se lo había pasado estupendamente con Dorcas y Petros. Se alegró mucho de ver a su madre, por supuesto, pero lo primero que hizo fue preguntar por Lukas.

–¿Cuándo va a volver papá?

Estaban comiendo fuera, a la sombra de las viñas, compartiendo la deliciosa comida que había preparado Dorcas incluso con Nico y Tavi. Todo el mundo hablaba y se reía, pero era evidente que Effie echaba de menos a su padre.

–Ya te lo he dicho, cariño, volverá en un par de días.

–¿Cuántos días?

–No lo sé exactamente. Tal vez una semana.

Effie hizo un puchero.

–¿Echas de menos a tu *baba*? –le preguntó Nico–. Te voy a decir una cosa, Tavi y yo te vamos a llevar en barco para que veas los delfines. ¿Te apetece?

Effie asintió.

–Pues ya está decidido. Vamos a estar aquí un par de días más. Vamos a pasarlo bien.

Nico miró a Calista con complicidad, pero, una vez en tierra firme, a ella aquellos gestos le parecieron fuera de lugar. No quería que nadie se equivocase.

Ya en Inglaterra había rechazado siempre todos los avances de sus compañeros de estudios, dejándoles claro que no estaba interesada porque tenía responsabilidades. No obstante, en realidad tenía otro motivo. En el fondo, nunca le había interesado ningún otro hombre que no fuese Lukas Kalanos.

Lo que no significaba que no pudiese disfrutar de un par de días sin Lukas en Thalassa.

Después de la euforia de la noche anterior, Calista sabía que había llegado el momento de volver a poner los pies en la tierra. Así que, si Nico y Tavi querían entretenerlas durante un par de días, ¿por qué no lo iba a aprovechar?

–¿Cuántos días faltan?

Calista levantó la vista del teléfono. Había estado buscando ofertas de empleo para enfermeras por Internet, ya que sabía que necesitaría un trabajo a partir de septiembre.

–¿Cuántos días faltan para qué, cariño? –preguntó, a pesar de conocer la respuesta demasiado bien.

–Para que vuelva papá –añadió la niña con impaciencia.

–No estoy segura.

Calista volvió a mirar su teléfono. Llevaba nueve días sin tener noticias de Lukas. Tiró el teléfono al sofá que tenía al lado.

–De todos modos, lo estamos pasando muy bien sin él, ¿no? –comentó, sabiendo que no sonaba nada convincente.

–Supongo, pero sería mejor si estuviese papá.

Calista tomó aire. Aunque intentase disimular delante de Effie, lo cierto era que cada vez estaba más enfadada. Lukas le había dicho que estaría en Atenas dos o tres días porque tenía que trabajar. No era posible que las hubiese abandonado así, sin decirle cuándo iba a regresar. Al fin y al cabo, había sido él quien había insistido en que fuesen a Thalassa.

Ella pensaba que lo mejor sería hacer la maleta y marcharse con Effie a Londres, pero, por algún motivo, no era capaz. Le bastaba con mirar a su hija, que estaba deseando volver a encontrarse con su papá, para cambiar de opinión. No podía castigar a su hija solo porque ella tuviese el corazón roto.

Porque aquella era la realidad. Sentía que tenía el corazón roto. Y lo peor era que la culpa era solo suya. Había pensado que la noche que había pasado con Lukas podía convertirse en algo más, que podía ser el comienzo de una relación importante. Y se odiaba a sí misma, y a su estúpido corazón, por haber sido tan ingenua y tan tonta.

Porque había sabido desde el principio que el nuevo Lukas era frío, despiadado y calculador. Y ella había caído rendida a sus pies.

En esos momentos se daba cuenta de cómo la había manipulado para que cayese en sus redes y se entregase a él. Y Lukas, con su silencio, le estaba demostrando quién mandaba allí.

Calista se dijo que no podía remediar lo ya ocurrido, pero al menos podía cambiar de actitud en un futuro. Para empezar, no iba a contactar con él.

De hecho, se arrepentía del mensaje que le había enviado desde el barco, de camino a Thalassa, para darle las gracias por una noche maravillosa. Le había dado las gracias y le había mandado besos, y un emoticono con una carita sonriente. Se le encogió el estómago solo de pensarlo.

Pero tenía que dejar todo aquello atrás y mirar al frente. Necesitaba ser fuerte, olvidarse de finales felices y comportarse como la adulta sensata que siempre había sido, antes de reencontrar a Lukas. No iba a huir. Iba a enfrentarse a él cuando por fin volviese e iba a hacer todo lo posible por convencerlo de que lo que había ocurrido entre ambos no significaba nada para ella. Porque era evidente que no significaba nada para él.

—Es hora de irse a la cama, cariño —le dijo a Effie, dándole un abrazo.

—Todavía no... —protestó la pequeña al tiempo que bostezaba, cansada después de haber pasado otro día en la playa—. Espero que papá vuelva mañana. Quiero enseñarle mi colección de conchas.

—Sí, seguro que le va a encantar. Aunque ya sabes que papá está muy ocupado. Tiene mucho trabajo.

—Ya lo sé... me lo ha dicho —respondió Effie con otro bostezo—. Está comprando muchos barcos grandes. Barcos grandes que cruzan los océanos llenos de cosas de otras personas.

Aquella era la primera noticia que tenía Calista. Al parecer, Lukas quería volver a levantar el emporio familiar, y esa debía de ser su prioridad.

—¿Te ha contado algo más? —preguntó ella con toda naturalidad, presa de la curiosidad.

–Sí, pero es un secreto –admitió Effie, mirándola a los ojos.

–Ah, en ese caso, será mejor que no me lo cuentes –le dijo Calista a la niña, acariciándole el pelo.

No obstante, sabía que guardar secretos no era uno de los puntos fuertes de su hija de cuatro años.

–Te lo diré si me prometes que no se lo cuentas a nadie.

–Prometido.

–Bueno... –empezó Effie, sentándose recta, con los ojos brillantes de la emoción–. ¡Le va a poner mi nombre al próximo barco que compre!

–¿De verdad?

–Sí, le va a poner Euphemia, que es mi nombre de verdad, no Effie.

–Eso es estupendo.

–Lo sé. Supongo que es difícil comprar un barco grande, y que por eso está tardando tanto.

–Es posible. Ahora, vamos a la cama –respondió Calista, dándole otro abrazo.

Llevó a Effie a su habitación, le puso el pijama y la mandó a lavarse los dientes. Mientras esperaba, se sentó en la cama y vio una pequeña caja de cartón que había encima de la mesita de noche. Era la primera vez que la veía. Abrió la tapa y miró, sorprendida, en su interior.

–¿Qué es esto, Effie? –preguntó en voz alta, para que la niña la oyese desde el cuarto de baño.

Effie apareció en la puerta con el cepillo de dientes en la mano.

–Ah, eso. Es un mechón de pelo de papá.

–¿Y por qué tienes un mechón de pelo de papá?

–Hemos hecho un intercambio. Él se ha cortado un poco de pelo para dármelo a mí y yo le he dado otro poco del mío a él. Me ayudó papá con las tijeras.

Effie volvió al baño a dejar el cepillo.

–¡Ay! –exclamó desde allí–. Se me había olvidado que eso también era un secreto.

–No pasa nada, cariño –le dijo Calista, a pesar de que le temblaban las manos al entender lo que se proponía Lukas.

–No te preocupes, mamá –le dijo Effie, subiéndose a la cama y dándole un beso en la mejilla–. Fue solo un poco de pelo. Tengo mucho más.

–Por supuesto que sí.

Calista le devolvió el beso, la tapó, bajó la persiana y salió de la habitación.

Fue al salón, se sentó en el sofá y abrazó con fuerza un cojín.

Lukas ajustó el micrófono de sus cascos mientras esperaba a que le diesen el visto bueno para despegar. No estaba de humor para que le hiciesen esperar mucho, así que se alegró al ver, pocos segundos después, que tenía permiso para hacer que se elevase el helicóptero.

Habían sido un par de semanas agotadoras, pero por fin volvía a Thalassa, con planes de futuro claros. Planes que harían que Calista se plegase a sus deseos. Planes que iba a controlar él, con la cabeza y no con su traicionero cuerpo.

La noche que había pasado con ella había quedado muy atrás. Era como si aquel hombre no hubiese sido él, y no lo era.

Era evidente que tendría que tener la guardia bien alta con ella, porque sabía que Calista lo volvía loco y que, además, era adictiva.

Por eso le había pedido que se quedase con él en Atenas, para pasar otra noche con ella, y otra más, pero Calista le había dicho que no. Era probable que hubiese pensado que con una noche había sido suficiente para doblegarlo.

Al día siguiente, había estado reunido cuando lo habían asaltado las dudas. Había estado negociando la compra de un barco más para la flota de G&K Shipping, al que le pondría el nombre de su hija, *Euphemia*.

Entonces había recibido el mensaje de Calista, que le había hecho sonreír. Y se había dicho que la llamaría después, cuando pudiese darle la buena noticia de que Effie ya tenía su barco.

Había conseguido cerrar el trato y entonces, el presidente de la empresa rival, a la que le había comprado el barco, le había preguntado:

–Entonces, ¿es verdad? ¿Vas a intentar recuperar la vieja flota?

Lukas había asentido. No le había sorprendido que Georgios Papadakis lo supiese, ya no era un secreto.

–Sí.

–Admiro tu tenacidad, joven, pero una cosa será comprar los barcos y, otra muy distinta, que los clientes vuelvan a confiar en el apellido Kalanos, después del escándalo en el que os visteis envueltos tu padre y tú.

–Para su información –le había contestado él–, mi padre y yo éramos inocentes. El responsable del contrabando de armas fue Aristotle Gianopoulous, hecho que pronto podré demostrar al mundo entero.

–¿Y cómo pretendes hacer eso?

–Tengo mis métodos. Pronto saldrán a la luz nuevas pruebas.

Era la verdad. Además del testimonio del viejo abogado, aquella misma mañana se había abierto una nueva línea de investigación. Había habido detenciones relacionadas con un cártel de droga sudamericano y la policía había descubierto que este había recibido armas a través de G&K Shipping. Aquel debía de haber sido el último negocio que había hecho Aristotle antes de morir.

Lukas iba a volar a Bolivia aquella misma tarde para averiguar todo lo que pudiese y tener, por fin, las pruebas necesarias para demostrar la clase de hombre que había sido Aristotle.

–Interesante... –había comentado Papadakis–. ¿Y tu relación con la chica de Gianopoulous también forma parte del plan?

–¡Yo no tengo ninguna relación! –había respondido él.

–¿No? Bueno, eso es lo que había oído. Y admito que me había sorprendido. Aunque supongo que la idea es mantener cerca a tus enemigos. ¿O hay algo más? –le había preguntado el otro hombre–. ¿No habrás sido víctima de sus encantos femeninos?

–¡No!

–No serías el primero, eso es seguro. Y es una chica muy guapa, la verdad, pero yo te recomendaría que tuvieses cuidado y no confiases en nadie de la familia Gianopoulous. Si vas a sacar a la luz lo que hizo su padre, supongo que Calista intentará salvar su propio pellejo, sin importarle a quién se lleve por delante.

–No te preocupes, Papadakis, que ya te he dicho que no hay nada entre Calista y yo.

–Salvo una hija, por supuesto.

A Lukas le había sorprendido que también se supiese aquello.

–¿Euphemia? –había continuado Papadakis–. No hace falta ser un genio para atar cabos. ¿Así que la dinastía Gianopoulous-Kalanos está a punto de renacer de sus cenizas?

–No –había rugido Lukas–. La familia Gianopoulous no tiene nada que ver con esto. Va a ser una dinastía nueva, que llevará solo el apellido Kalanos.

–Pero la niña es nieta de Gianopoulous, ¿no?

–¡Pero es mi hija! –había replicado Lukas, poniéndose en pie–. Lo que significa que es una Kalanos. Y ya está.

–Si tú lo dices... –había respondido el otro hombre, dándole una palmadita en la espalda–. En cualquier caso, yo te recomendaría que lo tuvieses todo legalmente bien atado. Todo. En mi experiencia, mezclar los negocios con el placer puede ser una combinación letal.

Lukas sabía que tenía razón. Que tenía que hacer

las cosas bien con respecto a la empresa, y también en lo relativo a Effie.

De repente, no había podido dejar de analizar el reciente cambio de comportamiento de Calista. Sus comentarios acerca de que Effie era nieta de Aristotle, de que había que suavizar el impacto que la verdad tendría sobre la niña. Al parecer, a Calista se le había olvidado que Stavros Kalanos también había sido abuelo de Effie. ¿Había estado intentando manipularlo para que no hiciese públicas las atrocidades que había cometido su padre? ¿Para que siguiese cargando él con la culpa? ¿Era ese el motivo por el que había pasado aquella noche con él?

Si era así, Calista iba a llevarse una gran decepción. Porque para él, por mucho que la hubiese deseado, solo había sido sexo. Tal vez ella pensase que así podía meterse en su cabeza y apelar a su buena naturaleza, pero lo que no sabía Calista era que él no tenía buena naturaleza después de su paso por la cárcel.

Así que había borrado el mensaje del teléfono en ese mismo momento y había buscado en su bolsillo el pequeño mechón de pelo que Effie le había dado. Si había tenido alguna duda, si en algún momento se había sentido un poco culpable por lo que iba a hacer, ya lo tenía claro.

Después de diez duros días en Bolivia, Lukas había vuelto a Atenas aquella misma mañana, con la información que necesitaba. Antes de volver a Thalassa, había decidido pasar a dar una vuelta por Blue Sky Charters. Estaba a punto de entrar en las oficinas cuando oyó la conversación que estaba teniendo lugar en su interior.

–No tienes ninguna posibilidad con ella. Una chica como Calista Gianopoulous jamás se fijaría en ti.

–¿Eso piensas? Pues yo te digo que el día del barco sí que me miraba.

–¡En tus sueños!

–No subestimes al Tavi encantador, amigo mío. Siempre consigue lo que quiere.

–Yo diría que le gusté más yo, por eso me pidió que le enseñase a hacer nudos marineros.

–En ese caso, vamos a hacer una apuesta, Nico. El primero que consiga un beso de Calista, gana.

En ese momento, Lukas había abierto la puerta con brusquedad. Nico y Tavi se habían puesto en pie de un salto al verlo.

–¡Estáis despedidos! ¡Los dos! ¡Fuera de aquí! –había anunciado él.

En esos momentos, mientras sobrevolaba el azul mar Egeo en su helicóptero y veía a lo lejos la isla de Thalassa, Lukas seguía enfadado. Estaba furioso.

Calista Gianopoulous había demostrado cómo era en realidad y a él se le había caído la venda de los ojos, así que iba a demostrarle la clase de hombre que era él.

Capítulo 10

ACALISTA le dio un vuelco el corazón al oír aterrizar el helicóptero. Lukas había vuelto. Dejó su libro, se puso en pie y apoyó las manos en las caderas, pero según fueron pasando los segundos y no lo vio aparecer, empezó a ir y a venir por la habitación, alisándose la falda del vestido con manos temblorosas.

–*Kalispera* –la saludó Lukas, para después entrar a la cocina a por un vaso de agua–. ¿Dónde está Effie?

–No está aquí –le respondió ella.

–Eso ya lo veo –dijo él, dejando el vaso encima de una mesa–. ¿Dónde está?

–Eso da igual ahora, lo que yo quiero saber es dónde has estado tú.

–¿Me has echado de menos? –inquirió él en tono frío.

–No seas tan engreído. Habría sido todo un detalle decirnos cuándo pretendías volver.

–Yo nunca he sido precisamente detallista.

–No –admitió Calista, mirándolo a los ojos–. Es cierto, no sé cómo se me había olvidado.

Él sonrió, como si estuviese divirtiéndose, jugando con ella.

–Bueno, ya veo que estás encantada de verme. ¿Dónde has dicho que está Effie?

–No te lo he dicho, pero, ya que lo preguntas, está en Villa Melina. Dorcas va a darle la merienda y después Petros la traerá de vuelta.

–Interesante... –respondió él, acercándose más y mirándola fijamente–. Entonces, estamos solos.

–Sí. Mucho mejor así.

–Todavía más interesante. ¿En qué estás pensando, Calista? –le preguntó Lukas, tomando un mechón de pelo rojizo entre sus dedos.

–Te voy a contar en qué estoy pensando –replicó ella, alejándose para que no la pudiese tocar–. Vamos a empezar por hablar de lo que has estado haciendo estas dos últimas semanas.

–Eso no es asunto tuyo, *agape*.

–¿No? ¿Nada de lo que has estado haciendo es asunto mío?

–Eso he dicho.

–En ese caso, eres un mentiroso, Lukas Kalanos.

–¿Qué has dicho?

–Que eres un mentiroso –le repitió ella.

Tenía miedo, pero sabía que ya no había marcha atrás.

–Si yo fuese tú, retiraría eso, Calista. Te estás metiendo en aguas pantanosas.

–No, no voy a retirarlo.

–Entonces, voy a tener que dejarte varias cosas claras –contestó él–. No puedo creerme que tú, precisamente tú, me llames mentiroso. Tú, que no me contaste que había tenido una hija.

–Eso es diferente. No se puede comparar.

–Mentiste por omisión, Calista. Y eso es tan malo como mentirme a la cara. O peor. Es todavía más cobarde, así que no te molestes en intentar defenderte.

–No tengo ningún interés en defenderme.

–Hablando de mentirosos, ¿y tu padre?

–¡Esto no tiene nada que ver con mi padre ni conmigo! –le espetó ella, furiosa–. Estamos hablando de ti, que te has llevado un mechón de pelo de Effie para hacerle una prueba de ADN.

Lukas se quedó en silencio.

–Lo sé, así que no te molestes en negarlo –continuó Calista.

–Es cierto, he pedido una prueba de ADN para establecer la paternidad de mi hija –admitió Lukas, encogiéndose de hombros con indiferencia.

–Has mentido por omisión –replicó ella, utilizando su misma expresión.

–Que haya hecho lo necesario para establecer una base legal en la relación con mi propia hija no tiene comparación con las atrocidades que tu familia hizo conmigo.

–¿Una base legal? –inquirió Calista–. ¿Qué significa eso exactamente? No estabas seguro de que fuese tuya, ¿verdad?

–Todo lo contrario. Nunca he tenido la menor duda.

El pánico hizo que a Calista le temblasen las piernas.

–¿Entonces? ¿Para qué querías una prueba de ADN?

Lukas esbozó una sonrisa.

–Eres una chica lista, Calista. Estoy seguro de que ya sabes la respuesta. No obstante, si quieres que te la dé yo, te diré que para tener el control legal sobre mi hija, tengo que ser capaz de demostrar la paternidad. Para empezar, necesito que mi nombre aparezca en su partida de nacimiento.

Calista deseó decirle que no había podido pedirle que fuese con ella al registro, pero pensó que aquello solo podía empeorar las cosas, así que preguntó:

–¿Y para continuar?

–¿Para continuar? –repitió él, quedándose pensativo–. Bueno, te lo voy a contar. Después voy a pedir la custodia de mi hija.

–¡No! –gritó ella, horrorizada, lanzándose contra Lukas con los puños cerrados–. ¡Jamás!

Lukas no hizo nada para detenerla y eso la enfadó todavía más. Calista levantó una mano para golpearlo, pero él la agarró por la muñeca.

–No voy a permitir que me vuelvas a dar una bofetada.

–¡Suéltame! ¡Déjame! –gritó ella, intentando zafarse, pero Lukas siguió sujetándola.

Luego la acercó más a él y la soltó, pero para agarrarla por los brazos. Inclinó la cabeza y le susurró al oído:

–Te dejaré marchar cuando haya terminado.

Calista se quedó rígida, con el corazón a punto de salírsele del pecho. Y entonces volvió a sentirlo. «Deseo». Aunque aquella palabra no definía exactamente lo que había entre Lukas y ella. Era más bien ansia, hambre, anhelo, una obsesión que la desconcertaba y la debilitaba y que, al mismo tiempo, daba todo el poder a Lukas.

Lukas era mucho más alto que ella, la dominaba. La dominaba, pero en cuerpo y alma.

Estaba enamorada de él.

Y en aquellos momentos eso le parecía una terrible crueldad del destino.

Lukas aflojó las manos e inclinó la cabeza para mirarla, le apartó un mechón de pelo y, al hacerlo, le rozó la mejilla. Calista cerró los ojos. Sintió que él se acercaba más, que su aliento le acariciaba los labios y ella los separó ligeramente.

Tuvo que hacer un esfuerzo sobrehumano para controlarse y empujar a Lukas.

—Tal vez pienses que tienes todo el poder, Lukas, tienes dinero y contactos para hacerte con la custodia de Effie, pero estás equivocado. Jamás permitiré que me quites a mi hija. Jamás.

Se le quebró la voz del dolor, de la tristeza y de la ira.

—Antes prefiero estar muerta que sin mi hija.

Luego retrocedió varios pasos mientras lo fulminaba con la mirada a pesar de que, en realidad, nunca se había sentido tan asustada, tan vulnerable.

—¿No estamos siendo un poco melodramáticos?

Lukas se acercó y apoyó una mano en su hombro, pero ella se dio la vuelta y salió de la habitación. Oyó que Lukas la seguía por el pasillo, pero hizo caso omiso. Una vez en el dormitorio, empezó a vaciar cajones y armarios, y lo tiró todo encima de la cama mientras él la observaba desde la puerta.

Luego tomó una maleta, la abrió y empezó a llenarla.

—¿Puedo preguntarte qué estás haciendo?

—Eres un chico listo, Lukas, estoy segura de que ya sabes la respuesta –le contestó, repitiendo sus palabras, antes de meterse en el cuarto de baño a recoger sus cosas–. Es obvio. Me marcho.

—¿Te marchas? –le preguntó él, acercándose–. ¿O huyes?

—Llámalo como quieras.

Calista entró en la habitación de al lado, la habitación de Effie, y empezó a recoger también sus pertenencias. No podía detenerse a pensar, con Lukas tan cerca. Metió la ropa de la niña en su pequeña maleta y después miró a su alrededor, vio la colección de conchas, la muñeca que Dorcas y Petros le habían regalado, el barquito que Effie adoraba, regalo de su padre. Tomó la muñeca y dejó el barco.

—Y, por si te cupiese la menor duda, Effie viene conmigo.

No sabía lo que iba a hacer después, solo que tenía que salir de allí antes de que el dolor y la tristeza le impidiesen moverse.

—Huir no soluciona nada, Calista. Pensé que a estas alturas ya habrías aprendido eso.

—Todo lo contrario.

Pasó por su lado y salió de la habitación, con la maleta de Effie en una mano y la muñeca en la otra. De vuelta en el dormitorio, echó la muñeca en su maleta e intentó cerrar la cremallera, tarea difícil porque no había doblado la ropa.

–En estos momentos lo más importante es estar lejos de ti, tanto Effie como yo.

–¿Y por qué estás tan desesperada por alejarte de mí?

–Porque eres un matón mentiroso y malintencionado. Porque has estado planeando quitarme a mi hija. Porque...

Se calló cuando Lukas la agarró por la barbilla para que lo mirase a los ojos. Ella sintió calor, sintió que su cuerpo se ponía todavía más tenso.

–¿Por qué más, Calista, dímelo?

–Porque... ¡porque te odio! –respondió ella, presa de la emoción.

Entonces respiró hondo. Pensó que lo mejor que podía hacer era cruzar la delgada línea que separaba dos emociones tan extremas.

–Esas son palabras mayores, *agape*.

Lukas pasó un dedo por sus labios, como para acallarla, y después inclinó la cabeza para acercar sus labios peligrosamente a los de ella. Calista estaba a punto de caer en la tentación cuando...

–¡Hola!

La voz de su hija hizo que Calista despertase y saliese corriendo de la habitación. Lukas se quedó mirándola con exasperación, deseo, ira e impotencia, sentimientos que, al parecer, formaban parte de su relación con Calista. Si es que a aquello se le podía llamar relación.

–¡Hola, cariño! ¿Lo has pasado bien?

Oyó que Calista le preguntaba a la niña.

–¿Ha vuelto papá? –preguntó Effie–. El helicóptero está afuera.

–Sí, pero el caso es que...

–*Yassou*, Effie –dijo Lukas, entrando en el salón.

La niña corrió hacia él, que alargó los brazos para levantarla en volandas.

–¡Sí! ¡Has vuelto! –gritó la pequeña, abrazándolo por el cuello–. ¿Por qué has tardado tanto?

–Tenía mucho trabajo.

–¿Has comprado mi barco?

–Sí.

–Bien. ¿Cuándo puedo verlo?

–Bueno, la verdad es que... –empezó Calista de nuevo.

–Muy pronto.

–No va a poder ser tan pronto –añadió Calista, acercándose para tomar a Effie de brazos de Lukas–. Porque ha habido un cambio de planes, Effie. Vamos a volver a Inglaterra.

–Oh... –dijo la niña con decepción–. ¿Por qué?

–Porque tenemos que volver a casa.

–¿Por qué? A mí me gusta estar aquí.

–Lo sé, pero las vacaciones no duran eternamente.

Effie hizo un puchero.

–¿Y va a venir papá con nosotras?

–No.

Los grandes ojos verdes de Effie lo miraron y él sintió que se le encogía el corazón.

–¿Por qué no?

–Porque, como bien sabes, papá vive aquí –le respondió Calista a su hija en tono paciente–. Ya están las maletas hechas, así que si Petros nos lleva hasta el puerto...

–Yo creo que papá no quiere que nos marchemos, ¿verdad, papá?

Dos pares de ojos verdes lo miraron.

–Tienes que hacer lo que dice tu madre –respondió él.

Vio sorpresa en los ojos de Calista, y la oyó respirar aliviada.

Él tuvo que hacer un esfuerzo, pero supo que aquello era lo correcto. Lo más inteligente. No tenía intención de pelearse con Calista en ese momento, delante de Effie. Si Calista quería hacer las maletas y marcharse, no intentaría detenerla. Podría esperar... un poco más. Además, aquel era el tipo de comportamiento que le haría ganar la custodia de la niña. Porque la iba a ganar.

Sí, pronto tendría él todas las cartas y a Calista de rodillas rogándole. La mera idea le excitaba. Entonces, tendría a Calista donde quería, en su cama.

–Ven, pequeña –le dijo a Effie al ver que le temblaba el labio inferior–. No te pongas triste. Nos veremos muy pronto.

–¿Me lo prometes?

–Te lo prometo. Ahora tienes que marcharte con tu madre, pero enseguida volveremos a estar juntos.

La dejó en el suelo y le dio una palmadita en la espalda para que fuese hasta donde estaba Calista. Esta lo miró con miedo, como un animal acorralado que protegía a su cría.

–¿Quieres que os lleve con el helicóptero? –le preguntó él.

–No, gracias –respondió ella–. Podré arreglár-
melas sola.

–Como quieras –dijo él, girándose hacia Petros,
que estaba en la puerta, esperando instrucciones,
con gesto de preocupación–. Petros, por favor, ase-
gúrate de que hay barco disponible para llevarlas.

–Sí, señor.

–Vamos, Effie –dijo Calista, dirigiéndose hacia
la puerta–. Ah, las maletas...

–Yo lo haré –dijo Lukas, volviendo al dormitorio de Calista, donde tomó las dos maletas.

Luego las sacó a la calle y las metió en el male-
tero del coche. Esperó a que Calista le abrochase el
cinturón de seguridad a Effie y se inclinó a darle un
beso a la niña.

–Hasta muy pronto, *paidi mou*.

Effie asintió, estaba a punto de echarse a llorar.
Lukas se puso recto y miró a su madre.

–Calista –dijo a modo de despedida.

–Adiós, Lukas –respondió ella, orgullosa, desa-
fiante.

–Hasta pronto. Me pondré en contacto contigo
para que nos pongamos de acuerdo.

–Vas a perder el tiempo –replicó Calista–. Effie
es mi hija y va a quedarse conmigo.

Y luego fue hacia la puerta del copiloto.

–En ese caso, será mejor que te busques un buen
abogado, Calista, porque lo vas a necesitar.

Ella lo fulminó con la mirada y se subió al coche, se abrochó el cinturón de seguridad y alargó la
mano hacia atrás, para tomar la de Effie.

–Solo para que lo sepas, pronto haré pública la

información acerca de tu padre. Por si quieres mencionárselo a tu abogado también.

Dicho aquello, cerró la puerta y dio un golpe en el techo del coche, para que Petros supiese que podía arrancar.

Luego se quedó con los brazos en jarras hasta que el coche desapareció por el camino dejando tras de sí una nube de polvo.

Él volvió a la casa y cerró la puerta. Miró a su alrededor y pensó que nunca se había sentido más solo en toda su vida.

Capítulo 11

PÓNTELO, mamá –le dijo Effie, señalando el birrete que descansaba en el regazo de Calista.

Iban de camino a su ceremonia de graduación en la universidad, cosa que le apetecía mucho más a su hija que a ella. Calista dudó.

–Venga, mamá –insistió Effie–. Para que todo el mundo vea que hoy es tu día especial.

–De acuerdo –respondió ella, sonriendo y poniéndose el tonto sombrero en la cabeza–. Así. ¿Ya estás contenta?

Effie asintió y giró la cabeza para mirar por la ventanilla del taxi otra vez. Calista estudió su perfil. Lo más importante del mundo era que Effie estuviese feliz y se le rompía el corazón al pensar en lo callada que había estado en las últimas semanas. Se habría puesto un disfraz de payaso para la ceremonia de graduación si eso hubiese animado a su hija, pero sabía que solo había una cosa capaz de alegrarla: volver a estar con su padre.

Hacía tres semanas que habían vuelto a Londres, al principio Effie no había dejado de preguntar cuándo iba a volver a ver a su padre y, después, parecía haber aceptado con tristeza la realidad. Lo que solo había hecho que Calista se sintiese todavía peor.

No obstante, había intentado adoptar una actitud alegre y positiva, había decidido que iba a compensar la ausencia de Lukas. Habían ido al zoo y al parque, habían hecho picnics y habían comido helados. Había permitido que Effie se acostase un poco más tarde y que pasase más tiempo acurrucada con ella en el sofá, aunque lo cierto era que esto último se lo había permitido más bien porque le gustaba a ella. Porque cualquier cosa era mejor que la soledad... que quedarse sola y pensar en que su vida era un desastre.

Había estado esperando que saliese a la luz la noticia de que su padre había sido un ser horrible, o que le llegase una carta del abogado de Lukas pidiendo la custodia de Effie. O ambas cosas. Se levantaba con miedo todas las mañanas, pero después no pasaba nada. No había tenido noticias de Lukas, pero, en vez de sentirse aliviada, se sentía dolida. Era una tortura.

Un brusco frenazo hizo que volviese a la realidad, seguido por un golpe que las echó a ambas hacia delante a pesar de que llevaban puesto el cinturón de seguridad.

–¿Qué ha pasado, mamá?

–No estoy segura, cariño –respondió ella, mirando a su hija con nerviosismo–. ¿Estás bien?

–Sí, estoy bien –respondió Effie, mirando por la ventanilla–, pero creo que hay un hombre muerto.

Calista siguió su mirada y vio a un hombre joven que yacía en la calle. Se desabrochó el cinturón de seguridad rápidamente, pensando que, al fin y al cabo, era enfermera y podía ocuparse de aquello.

–Seguro que no está muerto. Tú quédate aquí. Voy a ver si puedo ayudarlo.

Effie asintió, obediente, y Calista salió del taxi y fue hasta el hombre, que estaba inconsciente. Todavía llevaba puesto el casco y tenía la cabeza girada hacia el otro lado. Tenía una herida en la pierna y estaba sangrando. A poca distancia de él estaba tirada su motocicleta. Calista se arrodilló a su lado y le buscó el pulso en el cuello. Estaba muy débil.

–¡No lo he visto! –gritó el taxista asustado–. Ha salido de repente, no sé de dónde.

–¡Llame a una ambulancia! –le ordenó Calista.

Un pequeño grupo de viandantes había empezado a arremolinarse a su alrededor.

–¿Alguien sabe hacer primeros auxilios? –preguntó ella.

Nadie respondió.

–Tú –dijo Calista, señalando a un joven que parecía inteligente–. Ven a ayudarme.

Él se acercó.

–¿Es usted médico, señorita?

Calista se puso muy recta, consciente de que su aspecto debía de ser un tanto extraño, vestida con la toga y el birrete.

–Soy enfermera –respondió, quitándose el birrete y la toga y dando esta al joven–. Rásgala, tenemos que hacer un torniquete para parar la hemorragia.

Volvió a inclinarse sobre el hombre y vio que se le iban los ojos hacia atrás. Pensó que no podía dejarlo morir. No podía.

Tomó el trozo de tela que el joven le tendía y lo ató con firmeza al muslo del herido. Después le desabrochó la cazadora de cuero y empezó a hacerle un masaje cardiaco.

Siguió así durante varios minutos, negándose a parar por mucho que le doliesen los brazos. Oyó a lo lejos la sirena de la ambulancia, que se acercaba, y se dijo que iba a mantener a aquel hombre con vida.

Lukas llamó de nuevo al timbre de casa de Calista, molesto. O ella no quería abrirle, o había salido. O, todavía peor, se había marchado de allí con Effie.

Tenía que haberla avisado de que iba a ir, aquello habría sido lo más sensato, pero cuando se trataba de Calista no era capaz de pensar con claridad. Además, había querido darle una sorpresa a Effie. Y a su madre también...

Había estado las semanas anteriores en Atenas, trabajando mucho, todo lo posible, para conseguir alcanzar su meta. Y lo había conseguido. Kalanos Shipping volvía a estar a flote. Y con respecto a Blue Sky Charters, después de haber despedido a Nico y a Tavi el resto de los empleados se había puesto a trabajar para impedir que les ocurriese lo mismo.

Por otro lado, Lukas había pedido a sus abogados que iniciasen los procedimientos necesarios para conseguir la custodia de su hija y había recabado más información acerca de Aristotle Gianopoulous.

Tenía que haberse sentido satisfecho con todo lo

que había conseguido, pero en realidad se sentía muy tenso, tenía la sensación de haberse portado muy mal con Calista desde el principio.

Y, por supuesto, echaba de menos a Effie. Villa Helene estaba muy vacía sin ella y su esperanza de sentirse mejor en el apartamento de Atenas tampoco había resultado. Más bien al contrario.

Se había sentido cada día peor, más irritable e irracional. Y la idea de salir por la noche a divertirse le había parecido tan repulsiva que se había preguntado si no estaría enfermo.

Pero no, no estaba enfermo. Sabía muy bien cuál era la fuente de su malestar. Calista Gianopoulous, que le había calado hondo, había hecho que se lo cuestionase todo: sus motivos, su moralidad. Tenía la certeza de que necesitaba tenerla en su vida. De manera permanente.

Y no solo en su cama por las noches. A pesar de que no podía dejar de pensar en su cuerpo desnudo, en su olor. No podía sacársela de la cabeza.

Por ese motivo, la noche anterior se había rendido y había tomado la decisión de ir a Londres y resolver aquel embrollo de una vez por todas. Aunque no tuviese ni idea de cómo iba a hacerlo.

Pero antes tenía que encontrarla.

La puerta se abrió y apareció Magda.

—Estoy buscando a Calista. ¿Está en casa? ¿Está aquí mi hija?

—No. Se han marchado.

—¿Se han marchado? —repitió él con el corazón acelerado, pensando que iba a buscarlas y a hacer lo que fuese necesario para recuperarlas.

–Sí, a nuestra ceremonia de graduación.

Magda levantó el brazo, en el que llevaba la toga, y señaló el taxi que estaba esperando en la calle.

–Ahí está mi taxi. Calista se ha marchado antes porque quería...

–Da igual el motivo –la interrumpió él.

Acompañó a Magda hasta el taxi y se subió con ella en la parte trasera.

–Vaya a donde ella le diga. Y rápido.

Pero cuando llevaban diez minutos circulando se vieron metidos en un atasco.

–Ha habido un accidente, amigo –comentó el taxista–. Es posible que lleguéis más rápidamente andando.

Lukas juró en silencio, pagó la carrera, agarró a Magda de la mano y tiró de ella.

–¿Conoces el camino? –le preguntó, ya en la acera.

–Debería –respondió ella–. He estudiado allí tres años.

–Pues vamos.

–¿Cómo está, doctor Lorton? –preguntó Calista al médico de urgencias.

–Fuera de peligro –respondió él, apoyando un brazo sobre sus hombros–. Ha hecho un trabajo excelente, enfermera Gianopoulous.

–¿Y la pierna?

–Vamos a operarlo, parece que podremos salvarla.

–Menos mal.

–En serio, Calista, le has salvado la vida a ese hombre. Tu mamá... –se inclinó para hablarle a Effie, que estaba entretenida coloreando– ¡es toda una heroína!

Effie le sonrió.

–Es una pena que te hayas perdido la ceremonia de graduación –le dijo el doctor Lorton a Calista.

–No pasa nada. Al menos la toga ha servido para algo.

–Y esto ha sido mucho más emocionante –añadió Effie–. He podido montar en ambulancia y todo.

–¡Eso me han dicho!

Calista levantó a su hija del suelo y la abrazó. Esperaba que la experiencia no hubiese sido demasiado traumática para ella.

La ambulancia que había acudido al lugar del accidente había ido directa al hospital en el que ella había realizado las prácticas y Calista conocía a sus ocupantes. Estos le habían sugerido que los acompañase hasta el hospital y ella había aceptado. De todos modos, no habría podido ir a la ceremonia de graduación con aquel aspecto, con la ropa toda arrugada y manchada de sangre. Además, con todo el lío se había dejado el bolso en el taxi, lo que significaba que no tenía ni monedero, ni teléfono ni llaves de casa.

Había llamado a la empresa de taxis, donde le habían prometido llevarle el bolso al hospital, pero mientras tanto se había dado una ducha y se había puesto la ropa que había dejado en su taquilla mientras varias compañeras cuidaban de Effie.

–Creo que, cuando crezca, voy a ser enfermera –dijo la niña, volviendo a ponerse a colorear–. O dueña de una naviera.

–¡Qué bien! –comentó el doctor Lorton.

Calista intentó sonreír también, pero no pudo.

–Como mi papá.

Lukas estaba empezando a perder la paciencia. Tuvo la sensación de que llevaba horas sentado en aquel salón de actos, viendo desfilar a estudiantes que recogían sus diplomas. Y todavía no había visto a Calista. En aquel momento vio que Magda subía al estrado y pensó que aquella debía de ser la clase de Calista, pero ¿dónde estaba ella?

–¡Calista Gianopoulous!

Oyó retumbar el nombre en el salón, pero solo hubo silencio, seguido de murmullos, y después pasaron al siguiente estudiante.

Lukas se puso en pie y miró a su alrededor, ni rastro de Calista. Fue hacia las escaleras del estrado y esperó a que bajase Magda.

–¿Dónde está? –le preguntó.

–¡No lo sé! –admitió ella preocupada–. Salió de casa con Effie antes que yo... Le he enviado varios mensajes... pero nada.

–Pues inténtalo otra vez –le pidió Lukas, sin contarle que él también le había dejado varios mensajes y no había obtenido respuesta.

Magda buscó su teléfono y miró la pantalla.

–Tengo un mensaje, pero no es de Calista.

Lukas frunció el ceño.

–Ah, sí que es ella, pero ha utilizado el teléfono de otra persona –añadió Magda entonces–. Ha habido un accidente... Effie y ella están en el hospital.

–¿Qué hospital? –inquirió Lukas, presa del pánico.

–A ver... St. George, pero dice que no me preocupe, que las dos están...

Antes de que a Magda le hubiese dado tiempo a terminar la frase, Lukas se había marchado corriendo hacia la calle.

–¿Cuánto tiempo vamos a tener que quedarnos aquí?

–No mucho. En cuanto me traigan mi bolso podremos marcharnos. Aléjate de las puertas.

Effie estaba cansada y se entretenía con las puertas automáticas que daban a la calle. Calista tiró la revista que tenía en las manos encima de una mesa y bostezó. Lo único que quería era irse a casa.

–¡Está aquí! –exclamó Effie, dando saltos.

–Está bien, cálmate.

Un taxi acababa de detenerse delante de la puerta.

–Mira, mira. ¡Es papá! ¡Está aquí!

Calista se sintió aturdida. ¿Lukas? No podía ser. Pero lo vio entrar en el hospital e ir en su dirección.

Como a cámara lenta, Calista vio cómo tomaba a Effie en brazos, la miraba de arriba abajo y sonreía antes de darle un beso en la frente. Luego se giró y puso toda su atención en ella.

Calista tragó saliva y se le aceleró el corazón.

Lukas lo era todo para ella y cuanto más intentaba olvidarlo, más lo necesitaba. Era como un pez atrapado en una red, intentando escapar, que, cuanto más se debatía, más se enredaba en ella.

–Calista. ¿Qué ha ocurrido? ¿Estás bien?

Ella se levantó y deseó gritarle que no, que no estaba bien. Que se sentía fatal por su culpa. Que estaba destrozada porque lo quería. Y que jamás se recuperaría.

Pero no podía decirle nada de aquello, así que se puso recta y tomó aire.

–Sí, estoy bien.

–¿Y Effie?

–También. Las dos estamos bien.

–Entonces, ¿qué estáis haciendo aquí?

–Lo mismo podría preguntarte yo a ti.

–Por favor, Calista. Dime qué ha pasado, según Magda, ha habido un accidente.

–De un señor en moto –intervino Effie–. Mamá le ha salvado la vida.

–¿Pero a vosotras no os ha pasado nada?

Calista negó con la cabeza.

–¡Gracias a Dios! –exclamó Lukas aliviado.

–Íbamos en el taxi que lo ha golpeado, nada más. ¿Dices que has visto a Magda? –preguntó Calista con el ceño fruncido, intentando comprender.

–Sí, en la ceremonia de graduación.

–¿Has estado en la ceremonia de graduación de Magda? –preguntó ella, sin entender nada.

–No... bueno, sí.

–¿Y qué hacías allí?

–Buscarte a ti, por supuesto.

–Ah... ¿Y puedo preguntarte el motivo? –añadió con cautela.

Se hizo un silencio. Las voces de las personas que los rodeaban se redujeron a un murmullo. Lukas la miró fijamente. Por primera vez, Calista vio vulnerabilidad en sus ojos oscuros. Se preguntó si tendría algún conflicto interno.

Sin dejar de mirarla, sacó la carpeta de cuero que llevaba debajo del brazo y la dejó en un asiento cercano.

–He venido a hacer esto.

La abrazó contra su cuerpo.

–Y esto.

Y la besó apasionadamente.

Calista se rindió, sintió que se derretía contra él.

Casi ni oyó los aplausos y silbidos. Y a Effie comentando:

–Ay, qué asco.

Capítulo 12

YA ESTÁ dormida –comentó Calista, saliendo del dormitorio de Effie y aceptando la copa de champán que Lukas le ofrecía antes de sentarse en el sofá–. Estaba agotada.

–No me sorprende –dijo Magda, sentándose a su lado–. ¡Vaya día!

Calista se echó a reír. Effie les había contado todo lo ocurrido a Magda y a Lukas, y después al chico que había ido a llevarles un ramo de flores de parte de la familia del muchacho herido.

–Qué rico –dijo Magda, dando un sorbo a su copa–. Muchas gracias, Lukas.

Y lo miró con una mezcla de curiosidad y admiración.

–Ha sido un placer.

Calista siguió la mirada de su amiga. Lukas estaba de espaldas a la ventana y su presencia dominaba toda la habitación a pesar de que se suponía que estaban en *su* territorio. Intentó mirarlo con desinterés, pero no pudo. Tenía el corazón acelerado, como siempre.

Lukas iba vestido con unos pantalones de traje grises oscuros y una camisa de rayas grises y blancas remangada. Era la personificación del hombre de negocios multimillonario relajado. Le había crecido el pelo desde el día en que se habían encontrado frente a la tumba de su padre. Ya no lo llevaba tan corto y los rizos oscuros le tapaban la base de la nuca y le caían sobre la frente.

Era lo único que había cambiado en él. Seguía teniendo un aire de austera autoridad.

—Me gustaría proponer un brindis —anunció.

—Buena idea —respondió Magda, levantando su copa.

—Por las dos nuevas enfermeras. Porque ambas tengáis una carrera larga y exitosa.

—Brindo por ello —dijo Magda sonriendo.

—Y, por supuesto, por Calista.

—¡Sí! ¡Callie! ¡Nuestra heroína!

Volvieron a brindar y Magda dio un abrazo a Calista, pero, al apartarse de ella, vio cómo su amiga y Lukas se miraban.

—Creo que me voy a ir a la cama —comentó Magda.

—No, no te vayas —dijo Calista con nerviosismo.

—La verdad, Magda —intervino Lukas—, es que quería pedirte un favor. ¿Podrías quedarte con Effie esta noche, para que pueda llevar a cenar a Calista?

—Por supuesto. Encantada.

—No, Magda —insistió Calista—. Seguro que tenías planes para esta noche.

—No, no tengo planes, salvo acabarme esa botella de champán. Salid vosotros. Y no tengáis prisa por volver.

Calista la fulminó con la mirada. ¿No se daba cuenta de que no quería estar a solas con Lukas?

—Perfecto —dijo Lukas, dejando su copa encima

de la mesa y tomando su chaqueta–. Tengo que hacer un par de cosas antes, así que te recogeré dentro de una hora.

Se dio la vuelta y después, volvió a girarse hacia ella.

–Ah... Será mejor que te pongas guapa. Al fin y al cabo, tenemos mucho que celebrar.

Lukas frunció el ceño mientras veía cómo Calista se comía un bocado de mousse de langosta y se limpiaba los labios con la punta de la lengua. Estaban en un exclusivo restaurante francés que había escogido con la esperanza de que el ambiente íntimo los ayudase a empezar a hablar. Y a empezar a resolver sus diferencias.

Calista había estado educada, pero muy centrada en la comida. Y su lenguaje corporal era tenso, casi hostil. Él, por su parte, estaba intentando controlar la lucha interna que había comenzado en cuanto había llegado a Londres, dispuesto a conseguir su objetivo.

No iba a pedir la custodia de Effie, no podía separar a la niña de su madre. Además, las quería a las dos, juntas, lo que no sabía era cómo iba a conseguirlas.

Bajó la vista e intentó ordenar sus pensamientos. Cosa hartamente complicada con Calista delante.

No había sido buena idea sugerirle que se pusiese guapa, porque el vestido de cóctel corto y dorado se pegaba a su cuerpo y era muy revelador, aunque más elegante que sexy y un poco extravagante, como la misma Calista. Se había recogido el pelo en un moño suelto en la nuca y varios mechones rizados caían suavemente alrededor de su rostro, dándole un aspecto renacentista, etéreo.

Estaba preciosa.

Calista era como una droga para él: peligrosa y adictiva. Le hacía actuar de maneras que no iban con él. Para empezar, en el entierro de su padre se había comportado como un bruto, y en esos momentos se sentía vulnerable. Ninguna otra mujer le había hecho sentirse así. Hambriento de algo más que deseo.

Lukas siempre había deseado a Calista, su cuerpo, pero se había dado cuenta de que también quería tener su alma. Y no era un capricho, sino algo mucho más profundo. Despertaba en él sentimientos que prefería no reconocer, emociones que cada vez le parecían más reales.

La palabra «amor» se le había pasado por la cabeza, pero no le parecía posible. La idea era ridícula. Así que se había dicho que lo que quería era que Calista lo amase a él. Eso lo podía entender.

Tomó su copa y dio un sorbo de vino tinto.

—Nuestra hija estaba muy orgullosa de ti.

—Sí —respondió Calista, esbozando una sonrisa—, pero espero que la situación no haya sido demasiado dura para ella, que no tenga pesadillas o algo así.

Se miró el reloj.

—No debería volver demasiado tarde.

—Effie estará bien —respondió él con firmeza—. Tenemos cosas de qué hablar.

Ella se sentó recta mientras el camarero se llevaba los platos. Se cruzó de brazos.

–Dime lo que me tengas que decir, pero te advierto, Lukas, que si se trata de quitarme a Effie...

–No.

Lukas vio esperanza en los ojos de Calista, la vio llevarse la mano a los labios, como aliviada.

–He decidido no pedir su custodia.

–¿De verdad? –le preguntó ella–. ¿Y qué te ha hecho cambiar de opinión?

–He encontrado una solución mejor –respondió él, intentando hablar con naturalidad, tranquilo–. Effie y tú vendréis a vivir conmigo a Grecia.

La mirada de Calista se nubló un instante.

–No, Lukas.

–A Atenas –continuó él.

Habló como si Calista no hubiese dicho nada.

–Aunque podría tener en cuenta otros lugares, mientras no estén demasiado lejos de Thalassa.

–No me estás escuchando. Effie y yo no vamos a marcharnos a ninguna parte. Vamos a quedarnos aquí, en Londres.

–Puedes elegir la propiedad, más de una, si quieres, todo lo grande que quieras. Encontraremos el mejor colegio para Effie.

Insistió a pesar de que tenía una especie de zumbido en los oídos y se estaba clavando las uñas en las palmas de las manos para intentar controlar la frustración que estaba creciendo en su interior, las ganas de agarrarla por los hombros y llevársela a su cueva en ese instante.

–He dicho que no.

–No os faltará nada –añadió Lukas.

–Nada, salvo mi libertad.

Por un instante, se miraron fijamente, la ira y la amargura les hizo guardar silencio. Y algo más, algo que ninguno de los dos podía controlar, por mucho que lo intentasen.

–No creo que estés en situación de hablar de pérdida de libertad –replicó él por fin.

–No, y tú no permitirás jamás que lo olvide, ¿verdad? –dijo ella, arrugando la servilleta–. De eso se trata, ¿no, Lukas? Todavía quieres hacerme pagar por los pecados cometidos por mi padre, amenazándome con quitarme a Effie.

–¡Maldita sea, Calista! –le espetó él, alzando la voz y haciendo que varias cabezas se girasen hacia ellos–. Esto no tiene nada que ver con tu maldito padre. Se trata de que Effie forme parte de mi vida. «Mi vida». No solo de la tuya. ¿No te das cuenta de que intento encontrar una solución?

–¿Insistiendo en que nos mudemos a Grecia? –inquirió ella–. ¿Metiendo a Effie en una jaula de oro y tirando la llave?

–¿He dicho yo eso?

–¿No? Entonces, cuéntame cómo sería.

Lukas tomó aire e intentó tener un poco más de paciencia.

–Tendrías tu propia vida, tus propios amigos. Si quisieses trabajar de enfermera, yo no tendría ningún inconveniente.

–Todo un detalle por tu parte.

Lukas apretó la mandíbula. Calista le estaba haciendo perder la paciencia.

Se inclinó hacia delante y le agarró las manos.

–Si yo fuese tú, *agapi mou*, cambiaría de actitud.

–¿Y si no?

«Te lo haré pagar», pensó él, pero no lo dijo. Se lo haría pagar debajo de su cuerpo, y encima. Haciendo que gritase su nombre y le rogase que le diese más. Podía hacerla suya allí mismo, encima del mantel, teniendo en cuenta el ímpetu de sus sentimientos.

Cerró los ojos un instante e intentó tranquilizarse.

–Si no, te arrepentirás.

La respuesta no era la que quería dar, ni lo que quería hacer, pero el camarero llegó con el siguiente plato y él bajó las manos y se echó hacia atrás.

Pasaron los minutos, Lukas empezó a comerse su filete. Calista jugó con el pescado que tenía en su plato.

–¿Y cómo piensas que sería? –preguntó Calista por fin, con un hilo de voz.

–¿A qué te refieres?

–Bueno... has dicho que yo podría tener mis propios amigos. ¿También hombres?

Lukas se puso tenso al instante, solo de pensarlo.

–Eso me parecía –añadió ella–. Mientras que tú sí que podrías ver a quien quisieras, ¿no? Y pasearte con una mujer tras otra, y llevarlas a tu cama.

–¿Y eso te molestaría?

–No, no me molestaría –le mintió–, pero no sería bueno para Effie.

–¿Y si te prometo que no habría mujeres?

–No hagas promesas que no puedas mantener, Lukas.

–Es la verdad. Si vivimos juntos, no habrá mujeres en mi cama.

–Ya, claro.

–Salvo tú, por supuesto.

–¿Yo? –preguntó Calista, ruborizándose.

–Sí, tú, Calista. Estoy seguro de que serás suficiente para satisfacer mis necesidades sexuales.

–Tu arrogancia no te permite pensar –le recriminó ella, furiosa–. ¿Qué te hace imaginar que voy a acceder a compartir tu cama?

–Lo pienso porque te he visto derretirte entre mis brazos, he sentido tus uñas clavadas en mi espalda, te he oído gritar mi nombre –respondió Lukas–. Puedes negarlo si quieres y hacerte la dura si eso te hace sentir mejor, pero ambos sabemos la verdad. Me deseas tanto como yo a ti. La atracción es mutua. Y, además, es algo que no podemos controlar.

–Habla por ti mismo. Yo soy completamente capaz de controlarme.

–¿Como hiciste después del entierro de tu padre? ¿O en mi apartamento de Atenas? ¿Es así como te vas a controlar?

–¿Sabes qué, Lukas? –dijo ella, poniéndose en pie–. Que me marcho.

–De eso nada.

La autoridad de su voz hizo que Calista se volviese a sentar. Él agarró su copa, dio un buen trago y se tomó un momento para tranquilizarse.

–Te marcharás cuando hayas oído lo que tengo que decirte.

–Ya he oído suficiente, gracias.

–No –respondió Lukas, bajando la vista a su copa y haciéndola girar entre los dedos–. Hace no tanto tiempo me dijiste que me habías querido.

–¿Y?

–Eso me ha llevado a una sorprendente conclusión –continuó él, levantando la vista.

Calista lo miró a los ojos con el ceño fruncido, pero con ternura al mismo tiempo.

–Te apuesto lo que quieras, Calista Gianopoulous... a que todavía me quieres.

Capítulo 13

CALISTA sintió que le ardía el rostro de la humillación. «Estúpida, estúpida, estúpida», pensó. Levantó las manos para intentar cubrirse el rostro, pero ya era demasiado tarde, Lukas la había visto.

Lo sabía.

Había pasado demasiado tiempo intentando ocultarlo, ocultárselo a él y a sí misma, a todo el mundo, y por un instante de patética esperanza había pensado que Lukas iba a decirle que era él el que la amaba.

Era evidente que se estaba volviendo loca. Estaba enferma.

Se agachó para tomar su bolso. Iba a marcharse y Lukas no podría hacer ni decir nada para detenerla. Echó la silla hacia atrás haciendo ruido y se puso en pie. Lukas la imitó. Calista notó su mirada clavada en ella, poniéndole la piel de gallina, como si la hubiese tocado para detenerla, pero no lo había hecho.

Empezó a moverse, avanzó entre las mesas y pasó por delante del maître, que estaba en la entrada, convencida de que, en algún momento, notaría los dedos de Lukas agarrándola con fuerza del brazo, pero no. Salió a la calle, bajó los escalones a toda prisa y llegó a la acera. Se detuvo allí un instante, sin saber qué hacer, con el corazón retumbándole en los oídos.

Llovía suavemente y las calles de Londres estaban mojadas. Calista giró a la derecha sin saber adónde iba, solo que quería alejarse de Lukas y estar sola para poder lamerse las heridas.

Caminó a paso ligero y se fue girando de vez en cuando para mirar por encima del hombro, a ver si Lukas la seguía. Se sintió aliviada y decepcionada a partes iguales al no verlo. Atravesó el parque de St. James, donde había gente paseando a sus perros, amantes que iban agarrados del brazo, hasta que llegó a la estación de Embankment y allí se apoyó en una pared y respiró hondo.

El río Támesis fluía lentamente ante sus ojos, las luces bailaban sobre la superficie negra, pequeños barcos se deslizaban por ella, todo ajeno a su dolor.

Lukas la observó desde donde estaba, apoyado en un árbol, a unos treinta metros. Había sido fácil seguir su cabello rojizo entre la multitud y el vestido dorado brillando bajo las luces de la ciudad.

Habría sido capaz de encontrarla incluso con los ojos cerrados, porque se sentía atraído por ella, lo hipnotizaba. Lo había embrujado...

Calista se estremeció, la fina lluvia se posó en su piel desnuda, bajó entre sus pechos. Pensó que debía tomar un taxi y volver a casa.

Entonces se le ocurrió que tal vez Lukas hubiese ido allí. ¿Para qué perseguirla por las calles de Londres cuando podía ir a instalarse en su viejo sofá y esperar a que regresase? O tal vez hubiese vuelto a su elegante habitación de hotel a celebrar la victoria.

–¿Calista?

Se giró sobresaltada y chocó contra el duro pecho de Lukas. Sus fuertes brazos la rodearon, la apretaron contra su cuerpo, y ella se sintió muy bien.

–Estás empapada –comentó él, apartándose para quitarse la chaqueta y ponérsela por encima de los hombros.

Luego la miró a los ojos.

–¿Por qué me estás siguiendo? –inquirió ella en tono débil.

Quería enfrentarse a él, pero estaba cansada de pelear. Estaba muy cansada.

Lukas dejó escapar una carcajada.

–¿No pensarías que te iba a dejar marchar?

Pasó una mano por sus rizos mojados y le metió un mechón de pelo detrás de la oreja.

–Jamás te dejaré marchar –añadió con voz muy tranquila.

Calista lo miró a los ojos.

–¿Y lo que yo opine no importa? –preguntó.

–No importa nada, en absoluto –respondió Lukas, inclinando la cabeza para rozar sus labios en un suave beso–. A partir de ahora, harás lo que yo diga.

–Eso piensas, ¿no?

–Sí, pero quiero que me respondas a la pregunta que te ha hecho salir corriendo del restaurante –le dijo él muy serio–. ¿Me quieres, Calista?

Ella esperó unos segundos y entonces se rindió.

—Sí.

—Entonces, dilo —insistió él, decidido a torturarla.

—Te quiero, Lukas.

No merecía la pena seguir negándolo.

—Preferiría no hacerlo, pero no puedo evitarlo.

—Umm... me gusta la primera parte de la confesión. La segunda, menos.

—No te burles de mí, por favor. No es gracioso.

—No me estoy riendo. Tenía miedo de que no me quisieras. Podía obligarte a compartir la custodia de Effie, a que vinieses a vivir conmigo a Grecia, o a donde fuese, pero todo eso no me importaba en realidad. A lo único que no podía obligarte era a que me amases.

—No te hacía falta obligarme.

—Ahora lo sé. Y me alegro de que ya no haya nada que se interponga en nuestro camino. Podemos ser pareja... una pareja de verdad. De hecho, me gustaría que fuésemos marido y mujer.

Ella dio un grito ahogado.

—¿Me estás pidiendo que me case contigo?

—¿Tanto te sorprende?

—Sí. No es posible.

—¿Por qué? Has admitido que me quieres. Ambos queremos a Effie...

—Para que una relación, un matrimonio, funcione, ambas partes deben amarse —lo interrumpió ella en voz baja—. Una sola no es suficiente.

Lukas la miró de arriba abajo. Calista tenía la cabeza agachada, el cuerpo perdido dentro de su chaqueta, el pelo mojado. La abrazó y le hizo levantar la cabeza, y vio que tenía lágrimas en los ojos.

Y los grilletes de su orgullo se vinieron abajo.

De repente, como por un milagro, fue capaz de decir lo que pensaba, de aceptar lo que siempre había sabido. Estaba enamorado de Calista. Nunca lo había dicho, ni siquiera a sí mismo, pero era la verdad.

Oyó las palabras en su cabeza. «Te quiero, Calista». Le resultaron sorprendentemente naturales, tuvo la sensación de que siempre habían estado allí, esperando a ser dichas, pero también tuvo una extraña sensación de pérdida. Porque entregar su corazón a Calista implicaba perder una parte de sí mismo. La parte amarga y resentida, la parte hostil y vengativa. Había estado con él tanto tiempo que Lukas había pensado que formaba parte del hombre que era.

Pero en esos momentos veía las cosas de otra manera. Sin ni siquiera intentarlo, sin saberlo, Calista lo había liberado de aquel horrible monstruo, dejándolo libre. Libre para amarla.

Lukas le tomó el rostro entre las manos y vio el dolor en su mirada. Quiso borrarlo de allí con un beso, pero supo que eso vendría después. En esos momentos, tenía que utilizar las palabras.

–Si el amor es lo que te preocupa, debes saber que no hay ningún impedimento para que nos casemos.

Calista lo miró como si no lo entendiese. Lo que no era de extrañar, porque hablando así Lukas parecía un abogado, un imbécil... o ambas cosas a la vez.

–Lo que te estoy intentando decir es que... –empezó, frotándose la mandíbula–. Lo que te quiero decir es...

–¿Sí?

Tomó aire.

–Calista, eres la mujer más obstinada, exasperante y maravillosa que he tenido la suerte de conocer. Y te quiero con todo mi corazón.

Se hizo el silencio.

–No, no es posible.

–Sí, sí que lo es.

–Solo lo dices para engañarme. O porque piensas que es lo que quiero oír. O porque estás mal de la cabeza.

–Bueno, eso último sí que es cierto –admitió él, sonriendo de oreja a oreja.

Ella hizo una mueca, pero Lukas pensó que aquello no era suficiente, que necesitaba más. Así que esperó con las cejas arqueadas, la cabeza ladeada y los ojos posados fijamente en los suyos. Y entonces la vio sonreír por fin, sonreír de verdad.

La abrazó, hundió el rostro en su pelo mojado y aspiró su delicioso olor.

–Te quiero, Calista. Lo creas o no, lo quieras o no. Y si eso me convierte en un loco... pues será que estoy loco.

–¡Oh, Lukas!

–Y quiero casarme contigo más que nada en este mundo.

Lukas apoyó una rodilla en el suelo y tomó sus manos.

—Calista Gianopoulous, ¿me harás el honor de convertirte en mi esposa?

Ella lo miró con los ojos llenos de lágrimas y amor. A lo lejos el Big Ben dio la hora. Lukas contó tres, cuatro, cinco agónicas campanadas antes de que Calista respondiese por fin.

—Sí, Lukas Kalanos, mi respuesta es sí. ¡Quiero casarme contigo!

Él sintió alivio, emoción y un amor infinito. Se puso en pie y la abrazó.

Dejaron de oír el Big Ben mientras cerraban los ojos y sus labios se unían en el beso más tierno y maravilloso que habían compartido.

—¿Te parece que estoy bien?

Calista se plantó delante de Lukas con una de sus camisas puestas encima del vestido, con un nudo en la cintura y las mangas subidas.

—No quiero volver con pinta de haber pasado la noche fuera de casa.

—Pero si eso es exactamente lo que has hecho —respondió él, abrazándola por la cintura—. Y estás muy sexy.

Al acercarse más, Calista notó su erección.

—¿Y si llamamos a Magda y le pedimos que cuide de Effie una hora más? —añadió Lukas.

—¡No! —ella se rio, empujándolo.

Había pasado la noche en el hotel de Lukas y a ambos les había costado mucho esfuerzo levantarse, ducharse y vestirse. Tras aquella noche de pasión, tan intensa emocionalmente, parecía mentira que todavía tuviesen ganas de más, pero las tenían. Las tendrían siempre.

–No podemos abusar más de Magda –le dijo Calista, dándole un beso rápido–. Además, Effie nos estará esperando. ¡Estoy deseando contarle que vamos a casarnos!

–¿Piensas que se alegrará?

–¡Se va a volver loca! Effie te adora, Lukas, lo mismo que su madre.

–¿Qué he hecho yo para mereceros? –preguntó él, poniéndose serio de repente–. He sido un idiota, Calista, por no permitirme amarte y por confundir mis sentimientos con ira y sed de venganza, cuando en realidad siempre he estado enamorado de ti.

–Tenías derecho a estar furioso después de lo que mi padre te hizo. Y de lo que hice yo.

–Tú no, Calista. Tú no tuviste ninguna culpa. Yo pensé que había sido así porque no me podía creer que hubieses venido a buscarme aquella noche solo porque me deseabas.

–No solo porque te deseaba, sino porque te quería ya por entonces, pero no podía decírtelo. El orgullo no me permitía contarte la verdad.

–Pues a mí me encanta tu orgullo. Y tu sonrisa, tu ceño fruncido, tu temperamento y tu enorme corazón. En especial, tu corazón –le dijo él, sonriendo de medio lado–. Aunque eso signifique tener que volver a contratar a empleados que había despedido.

Calista sonrió.

–Gracias por eso. Estoy segura de que Nico y Tavi han aprendido la lección, y tú mismo dijiste que eran buenos en su trabajo. Fue solo una tontería, y lo sabes.

–Es cierto.

Por un segundo, se miraron a los ojos en silencio. Entonces, Calista se mordió el labio inferior.

–Venga... suéltalo –la alentó Lukas–. ¿Qué es lo que te preocupa?

–Estaba pensando en mi padre... Supongo que todavía quieres sacar a la luz lo que hizo.

–No, ya no, sabiendo lo mucho que eso te afectaría. Vamos a dejar el pasado atrás. A mí ya no me importa. Lo único que me importa ahora mismo es el futuro, contigo y con Effie. El futuro más maravilloso que jamás me habría podido imaginar.

–Voy a ser yo misma la que vaya a la policía –decidió Calista–. Quiero liberarme del peso de todo lo que hizo mi padre.

Lukas le dio un beso.

–Eres extraordinariamente valiente, Calista. Lo sabes, ¿verdad?

–No soy valiente. Solo hago lo que tengo que hacer.

–En ese caso, estaré a tu lado para apoyarte. El mundo será nuestro. Nuestro... y de Effie. Es todo lo que podría desear y pedir. Salvo, tal vez...

–Sí, dime.

–Tal vez un hermanito o hermanita para Effie. O las dos cosas. O un par de cada... De hecho, podríamos empezar ahora mismo.

Ella se echó a reír.

—Te quiero, Lukas. Te quiero mucho.

—Y yo a ti, Calista, más de lo que soy capaz de expresar con palabras. Y estoy deseando pasar el resto de mi vida contigo.

—Y yo contigo, Lukas —susurró ella contra sus labios.

Bianca

Estaba dispuesto a traspasar los límitesde su acuerdo con tal de satisfacer su ardiente deseo

Violet Drummond no estaba dispuesta a asistir sin pareja a la fiesta de Navidad de su oficina, pero Cameron McKinnon, un amigo de la familia, parecía la pareja perfecta para el evento. Hasta que le contó a Violet que planeaba convertirla en su novia de conveniencia.

Cameron, un adinerado arquitecto, consideró esa farsa como la escapatoria perfecta ante la atención no deseada que le prestaba la esposa de un cliente. Sin embargo, los falsos sentimientos se convirtieron enseguida en atracción de verdad...

LA MENTIRA PERFECTA

MELANIE MILBURNE

Acepte 2 de nuestras mejores novelas de amor GRATIS

¡Y reciba un regalo sorpresa!

Oferta especial de tiempo limitado

Rellene el cupón y envíelo a

Harlequin Reader Service®
3010 Walden Ave.
P.O. Box 1867
Buffalo, N.Y. 14240-1867

¡Sí! Por favor, envíenme 2 novelas de amor de Harlequin (1 Bianca® y 1 Deseo®) gratis, más el regalo sorpresa. Luego remítanme 4 novelas nuevas todos los meses, las cuales recibiré mucho antes de que aparezcan en librerías, y factúrenme al bajo precio de $3,24 cada una, más $0,25 por envío e impuesto de ventas, si corresponde*. Este es el precio total, y es un ahorro de casi el 20% sobre el precio de portada. ¡Una oferta excelente! Entiendo que el hecho de aceptar estos libros y el regalo no me obliga en forma alguna a la compra de libros adicionales. Y también que puedo devolver cualquier envío y cancelar en cualquier momento. Aún si decido no comprar ningún otro libro de Harlequin, los 2 libros gratis y el regalo sorpresa son míos para siempre.

416 LBN DU7N

Nombre y apellido   (Por favor, letra de molde)

Dirección   Apartamento No.

Ciudad   Estado   Zona postal

Esta oferta se limita a un pedido por hogar y no está disponible para los subscriptores actuales de Deseo® y Bianca®.
*Los términos y precios quedan sujetos a cambios sin aviso previo.
Impuestos de ventas aplican en N.Y.

Deseo

Boda por contrato
Yvonne Lindsay

El rey Rocco, acostumbrado a conseguir lo que quería, se había encaprichado de Ottavia Romolo. Pero si quería sus servicios, ella le exigía firmar un contrato. Los términos eran tan abusivos que, si se hubiera tratado de otra mujer, Rocco se habría negado a sus disparatadas exigencias, pero la deseaba demasiado. Pronto comprendería que podría serle de gran utilidad, y no solo en la alcoba. La aparición de un supuesto hermanastro que reclamaba el trono lo tenía en la cuerda floja y, por una antigua ley, para no perder la Corona tenía que casarse y engendrar un heredero.

¿Sería una locura ampliar el contrato con Ottavia y convertirla en su reina?

Bianca

La deseaba como nunca
había deseado a una mujer

El banquero italiano Vito
Zaffari se había alejado de
Florencia durante las na-
vidades, esperando que la
prensa se olvidase de un
escándalo que podría hun-
dir su reputación. Para ello,
había ido a una casita en
medio del nevado campo inglés, decidido a alejarse del
mundo durante unos días.
Hasta que un bombón vestido de Santa Claus irrumpió
estrepitosamente allí.
La inocente Holly Cleaver
provocó una inmediata re-
acción en el serio banquero y Vito decidió seducirla.
Al día siguiente, cuando
ella se marchó sin decirle
adiós, pensó que sería fácil
olvidarla… hasta que des-
cubrió que una única noche
de pasión había tenido una
consecuencia inesperada.

HIJO DE LA NIEVE

LYNNE GRAHAM

The heat roared to life inside her

Laura caught a breath that made her chest rise and fall sharply. She could still see Dale's smile.

"You like that." He made it a statement, not a question, as his hands caressed her bare skin.

"I do."

There was an incredible unreality about the moment. Sensory overload from the feel of his mouth, the sight of his dark head poised over her, the promise in those smoky eyes.

This was Dale Emerson, the man who'd been haunting her subconscious for so long that watching him touch her was surreal in the extreme. It was a scene from one of her fantasies come to life while she stood barely dressed in front of a mirror, his tongue tasting her throat, a warm velvet stroke that left a gleam of dampness in its wake.

"I've wanted to be bad with you for a long time. And we're going to be bad together, Laura. *Very* bad."

Blaze™

Dear Reader,

Hot Sheets is the first book in my miniseries FALLING INN BED....
Since this series is all about how falling in bed leads to falling in love,
I promise lots of red-hot fun in this and the stories ahead.

In this story we have Dale Emerson. You may remember him from
About That Night, Blaze #53, where he laughed at the irony of his
best buddy succumbing to love. That attitude meant his time had
come. So what kind of woman would tempt this bad boy? Well,
there just happens to be a beautiful *bedding* consultant who works
at a sexy romance resort. Sounds like a perfect match, right?

Not exactly. Laura Granger likes romance with her sex. She won't
consider a fling no matter how hot her chemistry with Dale is. And
it's blazing! It doesn't take long before he's not only obsessing about
falling in bed, but falling in love.

I hope you enjoy Dale and Laura's love story. Let me know.
Drop me a line at www.JeanieLondon.com. And watch for the
next two books in the miniseries—#157, *Run for Covers* (Nov.),
and #161, *Pillow Chase* (Dec.).

Very truly yours,

Jeanie London

Books by Jeanie London

HOT SHEETS

Jeanie London

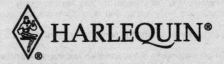

HARLEQUIN®

TORONTO • NEW YORK • LONDON
AMSTERDAM • PARIS • SYDNEY • HAMBURG
STOCKHOLM • ATHENS • TOKYO • MILAN • MADRID
PRAGUE • WARSAW • BUDAPEST • AUCKLAND

To Brenda Chin,
for your continuing encouragement
and all the *great* names!

ISBN 0-373-79157-7

HOT SHEETS

Copyright © 2004 by Jeanie LeGendre.

www.eHarlequin.com

Printed in U.S.A.

1

"LET THE SEX GAMES BEGIN!"

Truer words had never been spoken. Laura Granger had crammed the schedule with more erotic events during the next three weeks than this old hotel had ever seen. That said a lot since the property had been built well over a hundred years ago.

Falling Inn Bed, and Breakfast, or Falling Inn Bed as it was locally known, had started life during the 1880s boom that had earned Niagara Falls, New York, a place on the social calendar. Its evolution since that era had seen it alternately sparkle like a jewel and fade beneath the grime of the decades. But its most interesting development, as far as Laura was concerned, was its rebirth five years ago as a romance resort.

The term "romance resort" roughly translated into an upscale old hotel that specialized in sex, and as the inn's special events coordinator, or bedding consultant as she was commonly known, Laura knew firsthand just how much sex permeated the mood around here. She could call the newly updated promotional blurb into memory by heart.

Fun, active and romantic, Falling Inn Bed, and Breakfast is a unique resort, the perfect escape for energetic— and slightly wicked!—couples looking to ignite the spark.

Accommodations include suites exclusively designed for romance with lush settings such as the Roman Bagnio, Victorian Bordello, Sultan's Seraglio, Warlord's Tower, Wild West Brothel, Demimondaine's Boudoir, Roaring Twenties' Speakeasy, Sixties' Love Nest, Red-light District and the Space Odyssey.

A variety of exclusive shops offer erotic enhancements designed to drive couples wild, and with the grand opening of the new Wedding Wing, newlyweds will have a one-stop spot to accommodate all their naughty nuptial needs.

Unable to resist a smile, Laura gazed around the lobby of the inn's prized new addition. The Wedding Wing…this was her baby, an idea realized from conception through construction and now inauguration. She'd spent the past two years bringing her vision for this fantasy wedding operation to life and she couldn't possibly be prouder of the result.

Light from a crystal chandelier illuminated the New England antiques arranged in welcoming clusters around the lobby. A small-scale reservation desk ran along the west wall, directly opposite her pride and joy—a Mireille Marceaux oil painting, showcased behind museum-quality glass.

The glass display had depleted a chunk of her budget, but the expense had been necessary to meet the terms of arranging the painting's loan for the grand opening. And acquiring this art, even for a visit, had been quite a coup. Not only was the nude a regional beauty, but she set the whole tone for the new wing. And to Laura's mind brought good luck for the all-important grand opening events.

She needed all the good luck she could get right now.

Falling Woman would do the trick. Surrounded by lush

forest and mist from the falls, the woman in the painting held a sheer veil that spilled over her curves like a waterfall. Laura believed her sultry smile meant she approved of her new home, a place where newlyweds kicked off sensual happily-ever-afters.

As the name implied, the Wedding Wing's sole function was to accommodate weddings. Five floors of banquet halls, guest rooms, romance-themed honeymoon suites and even a brand-new full-service spa to pamper guests.

The grand opening had been officially dubbed the Naughty Nuptials, and the ensuing promotional campaign would span three weeks of highly publicized events. Week one was dedicated to Wild, Wild Weddings.

Laura had a typical slate of bridal functions scheduled, but with a Falling Inn Bed twist. A sex-toy shower, bad bachelor/ette parties and racy rehearsal dinner would culminate in a real wedding and kick off week two of the campaign—Risqué Receptions, which would be followed by Hottest Honeymoons in week three.

This grand opening promised to go down in history. It needed to. The management staff of Falling Inn Bed had wagered their personal and professional futures on the Wedding Wing's success. While they'd never expressed anything but total faith in Laura's ability to pull off this event, their trust underscored every decision she made, alternately empowering and weighing on her.

As if on cue, the radio affixed to her belt crackled and a Scottish burr rolled out on a wave of static. "Do you copy, bedding consultant?"

Unfastening the radio, Laura glanced down at her watch—almost check-in time. "Whisper sweet nothings, handyman."

"You've got a double date in the main lobby," the inn's maintenance supervisor, Dougray, said.

A double date. A *couple*.

Laura exhaled a breath she hadn't realized she'd held. The special guest she awaited hadn't arrived yet, but she knew he'd check in soon enough and end her suspense. She'd find out once and for all if he were bringing a date. Knowing what she knew about *him*, he'd not only bring a date, but a date who'd prove he'd completely forgotten how he'd once flirted with her.

But if luck rode with her and he arrived alone…

Until Laura knew either way, she distracted herself with the full house coming in for the inaugural events. She'd instructed the staff to let her know when her guests started to check in, so she could escort them to the Wedding Wing personally. Attentive service would start off the grand opening right.

"That's a copy, handyman," she said. "ETA a heartbeat."

"Show time," she said to the front desk clerk, who'd just reappeared from an office behind the desk.

The clerk, dressed smartly in Falling Inn Bed's gold-trimmed uniform, saluted, and Laura returned the salute before making her way from the lobby to the main portion of the inn.

Once again she couldn't help marveling at the smooth transition as the new building segued into the original. She could detect no discernible difference between the new architecture and that which dated one-hundred-plus years— a remarkable accomplishment by a brilliant architect, who'd worked for nearly two years to achieve the effect.

A *very attractive* architect, who would soon arrive for the grand opening events.

Hopefully *alone*.

Squelching the thought before she made herself crazy, Laura passed through the promenade of shops connecting the main lobby with the Wedding Wing and found herself face-to-face with her Hottest Honeymoon Couple.

Lieutenant Commander Troy Knight and his wife Miranda looked just as picture perfect as they had the last time she'd seen them, only now the Lieutenant Commander wore sportswear rather than an officer's uniform. Miranda looked…well, like Miranda always did—*perfect*. She was a vision in her sleeveless silk bouclé suit—with coordinating hat, purse and high-heeled slides, of course—perfectly attired for arrival at a romance resort on a beautiful summer day.

The butter color complemented the striking black hair that curled in an artful tumble down her back, and Laura suddenly felt the linen of her own tailored suit as if it had been hand-woven by someone with ten thumbs. Forcing steel into her smile, she made her way toward the couple.

"Miranda, lieutenant commander," she said in her most gracious voice. "I'm so pleased you could join us for the festivities."

She met Miranda's familiar gaze with a calm professionalism that made nine agonizing years of private school with this woman and *a lot* of water under the proverbial bridge evaporate.

"Laura." Miranda inclined her head in a gesture of greeting that was almost regal, but there was no missing the way her gaze flickered downward, taking in Laura with a glance that assessed the linen summer uniform as well.

Her husband extended his hand with a smile that actually reached his eyes. "Call me Troy, please. It's good to see you again. Thanks for the invitation. Miranda and I were pleased to be included in your grand opening."

Good thing someone was pleased, but all things considered, she found it much easier to smile at Troy Knight than at his wife. At least he seemed genuine.

Launching into the details of their itinerary, Laura focused on business and treated this couple the way she treated all her guests—as if they were welcome. These two would never know she hadn't been the one to add their names to the guest list.

"I'll take you to the Wedding Wing and give you an introductory packet." She wanted to get this show on the road. The sooner Miranda and Troy checked in, the sooner she'd be on her way to await one very handsome architect. They started walking across the lobby.

"We have a few things to discuss, but as our honeymoon couple, you've got the best job around here. You'll share the spotlight with our bridal couple at the events leading up to their wedding, and after they leave, you'll be on your own. Since two's company and three's a crowd on a honeymoon, all your events are scheduled for two. You'll have plenty of time to enjoy yourselves while you're here."

"We'll need it," Troy said. "Miranda hasn't been home in months. Everyone wants to see her."

What was new? Only the title as far as Laura could tell. Miss Popularity had married and become Mrs. Popularity.

"You'll have plenty of time for visiting family and friends. Just make sure you save some time to explore our facilities. We have a brand-new spa that has all the usual massage therapies and salon services, but we also have a few unusual ones like aromatherapy baths and couples massage. Everything for a honeymoon couple to pamper themselves."

"Speaking of, Laura." Miranda slowed to a halt in front of the lobby's fireplace, which had been draped with lush summer blossoms in keeping with the wedding theme. "I do hope you won't be working the entire time we're here. You're hosting so many events." She waved a perfectly manicured hand and gestured to their surroundings. "It would be a shame not to enjoy them."

Miranda may have sounded oh-so civil, but the woman was on a recon mission. She wanted to gauge the enemy to determine how much time she'd be forced to suffer Laura's company.

The moment could have been a time warp back to Westfalls Academy, the prestigious school Laura had attended until finances had forced her to go to a public high school. They might have been standing in study hall or in the dorm or on a sports team or at a dance. It never seemed to matter where, the attitude was always the same.

"You're defiling the air I breathe, Laura Granger."

What Laura couldn't understand was why Miranda hadn't simply declined the invitation to avoid breathing defiled air. Back at Westfalls they'd been forced to endure each other, but now Miranda had a choice. She hadn't needed to accept the invitation to participate in the Naughty Nuptials. She could have simply RSVPed with a "Thanks, but no thanks."

In fact nearly two years later, Laura still couldn't figure out why her long-time nemesis had chosen Falling Inn Bed for her wedding in the first place. There were plenty of other wedding hotels in Niagara Falls. A romance resort—especially one featuring Laura Granger—didn't seem in keeping with her stuffy social circles.

But Falling Inn Bed had been the rage ever since winning the "most romantic getaway" award, and Miranda could never resist a spotlight. As much as Laura hated to admit it, her nemesis was a perfect choice for a high-profile promotional campaign like the Naughty Nuptials.

Not only did Miranda present well, but she and her husband had been the last couple to get married at Falling Inn Bed before the inn had broken ground on the Wedding Wing. When her co-workers had suggested the Knights as the Hottest Honeymoon couple, Laura had opted to grin and bear Miranda's presence rather than argue a case where she'd had no professional grounds to launch a protest.

Only some very personal ones.

But she refused to let past history jinx her grand opening, especially where Miranda Knight was concerned.

"Our staff will participate in the grand opening events, Miranda. The Naughty Nuptials is a celebration after two long years of hard work pulling this Wedding Wing together."

"Correct me if I'm mistaken, but aren't these *events* intended for couples?"

She nodded. "We're all about two's-company-and-three's-a-crowd here at Falling Inn Bed. The Naughty Nuptials events are no different."

"So who's your escort? Anyone I know?"

There it was—the dig. Miranda never could resist reminding Laura that she didn't move in the same circles as her family. The woman had a gift for adding subtext to innocent remarks, and the subtext on this one was loud and clear—Laura dating anyone from her circle of acquaintances was a joke.

Once upon a time Laura had cared. Fortunately, she'd evolved into a woman who would never date anyone from such snobby circles. She'd had her fill of those types growing up in Miranda's shadow, thank you very much.

Even Miranda's husband watched them with a frown. More than polite interest was happening here, and while Laura wished she could commiserate with Troy, she couldn't. He might present himself as a normal, decent man, but he had to be flawed in some way to have married *this* woman.

"Well," Laura began, deliberating what to say. She'd lay down and die before letting Miranda know she didn't have a date yet. "Since my escort isn't from around here, I don't believe you know him, but I will introduce you. With all the events, we'll have plenty of opportunity."

She hoped. If her architect arrived with a date, she'd be stuck roping the assistant general manager into playing her escort. A dismal prospect even if the man knew the first thing about having fun, which he didn't.

A slight nod. A condescending smile. Then Miranda said, "I'll look forward to meeting him then."

Laura would just bet. But even if her plans for a date fell through, she wouldn't let that spoil her grand opening. Once upon a time she might have been easily shaken by unfavorable comparisons to this woman, but she'd grown to be a woman who'd learned from the experience.

Miranda Knight couldn't rattle her cage unless Laura let her.

And Laura wouldn't.

"Shall we, then?" She motioned them toward the promenade, pleased at how unfazed she sounded.

Miranda noticed. She arched one of those meticulously shaped eyebrows as she swept by on her husband's arm. Laura didn't care. She was closer to getting this couple checked in and out of her hair.

But as they moved across the main lobby, the man who'd been occupying a top slot in Laura's thoughts strolled through the inn's front doors.

He appeared as if conjured straight from her imagination, one of those stop-traffic gorgeous men who couldn't walk into a room without drawing attention. Not because he was loud or showy but simply because he was there.

He had that *something* about him, and it didn't matter whether he wore a business suit or workboots and a hard hat. A hint of bad boy lingered in his easy smile, in his smoky-gray eyes and the way he made everywhere seem like the perfect setting for his dark good looks.

Laura drank in the sight of him, her body instantly on red alert. The bottom dropped from her stomach, and the reaction was so intense, so automatic, that she might have laughed. But there was absolutely *nothing* funny about the sultry brunette dangling from this man's arm.

DALE EMERSON NOTICED the lovely Laura as soon as he walked through Falling Inn Bed's front door. She stood showcased in the open area that led to the promenade, breathtaking, her suit hinting at all the sleek curves hidden beneath its tailored lines. Not to mention showing off a great pair of legs.

Her gaze lingered over him as if she'd been waiting for his arrival, as though she somehow knew he hadn't been able to get her out of his head in the month since he'd left Niagara Falls.

Laura…what was it about her?

Dale couldn't answer the question, damn it. He only knew his own gaze lingered as if he'd been waiting every day of the last month to see her.

As always, she wore her long hair swept back in an elaborate French braid that hung heavily down her back. He'd had fantasies about unraveling her white-blond hair and draping it across his naked body. He'd had fantasies about how he'd enjoy her naked body, too, and about those long, long legs sweated up enough to glide sleekly through his.

Even the way she moved made him think of sex, all that graceful, breathless energy…just the thought made him aware, and too damned horny.

Oh, man, he *so* didn't want to see Laura again. If not for his obligation to attend this grand opening, he'd have spun the invitation back without opening it. But as project architect for the new addition, Dale was obligated.

This Wedding Wing marked his firm's first foray out of historic restoration and into construction, an expansion that had been solely his idea. He hadn't wanted to leave his firm for another job, but he had wanted to direct a team of his own, which meant finally breaking up the dynamic duo that he'd been with his buddy—the company's owner—Nick Fairfax.

He'd come up with the compromise of the expansion, a decision Dale hadn't made lightly. He'd been Nick's right hand for a long time, and the two of them had not only earned significant recognition with their restoration work, but had entertained themselves by chasing women on job sites all over the globe. But ever since Nick had married a fellow preservationist, things had been changing.

The beautiful Julienne had consumed Nick from the get-go, and Dale had laughed like hell while watching Nick do the bump and grind of making himself a serious contender for her affections.

He was still laughing when he stood beside Nick at the altar as his bride had walked down the aisle.

But Dale's humor eventually had started to fade when he discovered the thrill of chasing women wasn't nearly so much fun when he was pursuing them alone. He hadn't lost his best friend exactly…it was just damned hard to discuss the finer points of the opposite sex with a man who had everything he wanted in his bed every night.

This was a concept Dale flat-out didn't understand.

He'd never had a hard-on for a woman that the next beauty who walked by couldn't cure. Except for one…

The one who had zeroed in on him across an entire lobby of milling guests.

If it was any consolation—and it wasn't—Laura Granger had always been as aware of him as he was of her. When their gazes clashed across the distance, every muscle in his body galvanized at the appreciation he saw in her crystalline blue eyes.

They'd been wired with some sort of sex radar, and after all the time he'd spent working with her, he should be used to the effect. He wasn't. He'd been telling himself this acute awareness was nothing more than a side effect of this project. The Wedding Wing equaled sex, which had meant conversation after conversation about the topic with Laura.

He wouldn't be surprised if they'd talked more sex that he'd actually had in his lifetime—and he'd had his fair share. But sex had become an obsession with the Wedding Wing's *bedding* consultant, and while that might seem like a good thing given their chemistry, it wasn't.

Laura was an idealist. She believed in *romance* with her sex. Knights in shining armor, who rescued their damsels on white horses. She believed that fairy-tale weddings translated into happily-ever-afters.

She was exactly the kind of woman who usually shut

off his libido like a spigot. Except that every time she smiled one of those breath-stalling smiles, his temperature shot to full-blast and all he could think about was his body tangling around hers beneath that cool silk hair.

Almost as if she knew he was mentally undressing her again, Laura gave him one of *those* smiles. Then she took off, leading her guests along the promenade, her graceful steps putting more and more distance between them and giving him an incredible shot of the way she moved, all elegant swaying and subtle energy.

Running a hand through his hair, Dale stared after her, wondering what it was about her smile that made every nerve in his body tingle. *Tingle*, damn it.

"Remind me again why you bothered bringing me along." The demand in the accented voice jolted Dale from his thoughts enough to remember the woman beside him.

"Monique love, I brought you along to enjoy your company, of course," he said automatically.

"Then why are you staring after that blonde like some lovesick puppy?"

Lovesick puppy?

Glancing down at the beautiful French woman with cascades of rich brown hair and a pouting frown, Dale wondered how in hell to answer that question. He couldn't recall being lovesick in his thirty-three years, not even as a kid. He'd dived into dating headfirst and hadn't looked up since.

"How could I look at any woman with you on my arm?" He lifted her hand and brushed his mouth across her smooth skin.

"You promised to show me a good time."

"And I will." He directed her gaze to the lush main

lobby that surrounded them. "Look at this great old place. We've got three weeks together to enjoy ourselves in five-star luxury, far away from our lives. What could be better?"

From what he'd heard, Monique had needed a diversion after being dumped by some actor she'd been dating. When her scowl faded, he knew she'd forgiven his screwup and was looking forward to this vacation and putting her West Coast lover behind her.

"Let's check in and I'll give you a tour. Between these accommodations and the grand opening events, we'll have fun while we get acquainted." He only hoped Monique didn't let his mistake set the tone for the weeks ahead.

"Welcome back!" a familiar female voice called out.

"Great to be back, gorgeous." In his fantasies at least. "Monique, this is Annabelle Simmons, the inn's sales director."

With a regal expression, Monique held out her hand.

"Welcome, Monique," Annabelle said cordially but he didn't miss the assessing way she took in Monique. "You're in for an exciting visit. And, Dale, I'm so glad you could make it back for the grand opening. How's it been going?"

"Appreciated the time off." He appreciated a break from his Laura obsession, even if he hadn't gotten it under control.

"All that hard work—you deserve a chance to enjoy the fruits of your labors."

"I was on this property a long time, so I know all the hours you've put in, Annabelle. You make sure to pencil me in on your dance card because I expect you plan to follow that advice yourself."

Annabelle grinned. She was a hardworking, old-school businesswoman with a head full of gray curls who'd always struck Dale as out of place in a hotel that held weekly marketing strategy sessions to discuss new and improved ways to get their guests to do the nasty.

"All right, all right," she said. "No argument. There's always so much to do around here. You know that as well as anyone. But the staff intends to lighten up for Laura's grand opening and celebrate our achievement."

"Sounds like we're in for an interesting few weeks."

"Oh, we are." She rolled her eyes and motioned them to the front desk. "So come on. We've got to get our celebration underway. There's a whole new wing filled with sexy suites that need couples to play in them. Let's choose your poison."

Dale didn't know what to make of *that* statement, but when he caught sight of the new assistant general manager near the concierge desk, he steered the conversation back to business. "How's Adam making out? Have you worked your magic and gotten him into the spirit of things yet?"

Annabelle didn't slow her brisk steps. "Let's leave it with he's been trying to interject sanity into our grand opening."

"He's got his work cut out for him." Dale gave a low whistle before explaining to Monique, "There's nothing sane going on in this place on a good day."

She followed his gaze to the assistant general manager in question and he watched her take in the tall, athletic man with a penchant for custom-tailored suits and sanity in the workplace. She seemed to approve when she said, "He looks up to the job."

"We haven't given up hope for him yet," Annabelle told her. "Let me get behind this desk, and I'll check you in myself." Disappearing through a door, she reappeared behind the front desk a second later. "Now let's decide where to put you."

"The VIP treatment for the house architect, of course," Dale teased.

Annabelle nodded. "What else?"

Scanning the system, she kept them waiting for so long Dale began to wonder if there was a problem. Monique gave an impatient sigh, clearly disliking the delay. Dale patted her hand, silently imploring her patience, and she finally stepped away, flipped open her purse and withdrew a compact.

While reapplying her lipstick, she ran her dark gaze over a new arrival, checking the man out as thoroughly as he did her. Dale frowned, but apparently long hair and multiple piercings weren't to Monique's taste because she turned back to him and asked, "You did say five-star hotel, didn't you?"

One look at this grand lobby with sparkling crystal-cut chandeliers, mint-condition antiques and elaborate floral displays should have answered that question, but Dale nodded.

"Here we go," Annabelle finally said, and he pulled Monique closer to discourage her from checking out any more guests.

"I've got availability in the Bondage Boudoir with the chains on the walls and the Fetish Flat with the whips and spanking paddles. Or if you'd like, I could put you in the Waxworks Room. But you'd have to move next week. It's already booked for Risqué Receptions."

She delivered all this with such a straight face that Dale could only stare. She'd obviously lost her mind in the time he'd been gone, which surprised him since Annabelle was the most normal member of the Falling Inn Bed staff with the sole exception of the new sanity-loving assistant general manager.

"What are you talking about, gorgeous?" He forced a laugh. "Did you build some new suites while I was away? Or did you change some names?"

Falling Inn Bed was nothing if not upscale. There were romance-themed suites galore, but nothing so gauche as a Fetish Flat. If Annabelle wanted to prove she could lighten up for the grand opening, she'd hadn't gotten her mark. And he wasn't the only one who missed the punch line. Monique was scowling again.

"Just put us in a guest room on the third floor," he said.

"A guest room, Dale?" She shook her head. "You know better than that. You're practically one of the staff. You get nothing but VIP treatment around here."

"Excuse me, *ma'am*," Monique said, emphasis on the ma'am and the age difference that must indicate dementia. "This hotel has bondage and fetish suites and a...a waxing room?"

"The Bondage Boudoir and the Fetish Flat," Annabelle corrected. "And the Waxworks Room isn't a waxing room in the conventional sense, although we do offer that service in our new spa if you're interested."

Lifting a questioning gaze to Monique's exquisite—and momentarily stunned—face, Annabelle peered myopically as if checking to see if any waxing services were needed. "The Waxworks Room is a suite with protected furniture so couples can safely play with hot wax. Some people enjoy dripping it all over themselves. In fact, Dale, we just received a shipment of Busty Babe's Bodacious Beeswax. Your favorite. Did you want to go for the Waxworks Room and take a chance the reservation cancels?"

Busty Babe's Bodacious Beeswax? "Annabelle, what the hell are you—"

"Hot wax? Chains and *spanking* paddles?" Monique demanded on a rising crescendo that not only drowned him out, but drew the attention of the desk clerks, the long-haired guest and the assistant G.M. "Dale told me this bed-and-breakfast was called Falling Inn, not the pervert's palace."

"Annabelle's only joking, Monique. There's nothing perverted around here," he explained in his best attempt at damage control. He couldn't argue the existence of chains, spanking paddles and a multitude of other sex toys around here.

"You haven't quite got it right," Annabelle said. "Our name is Falling Inn Bed, and Breakfast." To prove her point, she handed Monique a promotional brochure from a display on the desk.

Monique darted her disbelieving gaze between the brochure and Dale. "You brought me to a bordello?"

"This isn't a bordello." He shot an equally disbelieving gaze at Annabelle. "Falling Inn Bed is a romance resort—"

"And we have Dale to thank for our newest addition." Annabelle swept her arms toward him in a motion reminiscent of a game show model pointing to the prize behind curtain number one. "He's the architect who designed the Bedding Wing, with five floors of sexy suites like the Coitus Chamber, the Mènage Motel and the Anal Atrium."

The Anal Atrium did it. Monique's eyes bulged, and she swung around to glare at him as if he'd sprouted a second head. "I thought you said the *Wedding* Wing, not the *Bedding* Wing!"

"I did—"

"Dale's one of our featured guests for the Naughty Nuptials. We've got weeks of erotic events planned and there'll be media to cover—"

"Monique, this isn't what it sounds like." He glared at Annabelle.

"Liar!" The word shot out as an enraged screech.

Annabelle's eyebrows disappeared into her hairline and every guest within earshot turned toward them. Adam Grant headed their way, clearly determined to bring sanity to the chaos.

"You men are all the same," Monique delivered in an explosion of sound. "'I need you to come for business,' you said. 'I'll take you across the country and pamper you until you forget Gerald ever existed.' You just wanted to get me into this bordello to have sex."

Dale caught her hand the split second before it connected with his cheek. "I came here to work."

"So I heard. You *built* this bordello."

"It's not a bordello," he ground out between clenched teeth. He was too busy dealing with Monique to handle Annabelle. But she was next in line. Guaranteed. "Let's get out of this lobby so we can talk. I'll explain. There's nothing disreputable about a romance resort."

"Get out is right." She tried to break his grip—to have another go at slapping him, no doubt—but Dale hung on.

"You're overreacting—"

"Me, overreacting? You're a *pervert*." She pulled away so forcefully, he had to let go or risk breaking her wrist.

She obviously intended to storm away, but found her way blocked by Adam, who said, "Excuse me. Is there a problem I can help with?"

Before Dale could open his mouth, Monique demanded a limo to take her to the airport.

Adam didn't miss a beat. "Of course, if you'll join me at the concierge desk, I'll make all the arrangements."

"Not necessary," Dale said. "I'll take you home, Monique. No problem. Let's go."

He'd think of something to tell his boss.

"Pervert," Monique snapped. "I'd walk back to California before I sat on a flight with you." In a swirl of red silk, she spun on her heel and headed toward the concierge desk.

"I'll take care of her," Adam said, his stoic gaze warning Dale to let him handle the arrangements before his date created even more of a scene.

Dale had never been abandoned like this before, so it took a moment to realize that he had no choice but to back down graciously. Monique obviously didn't want to be reasoned with, or to be here with him, either.

Fishing out the information for the return flight, he handed it to Adam and told him to bill her charges to his room.

Adam took off, and to his credit, he quickly calmed Monique down enough so the lobby couldn't overhear their conversation.

What the hell had Dale been thinking to bring a woman on the rebound to this event? Under normal circumstances, he would have been able to produce a more suitable date.

Unfortunately, these weren't normal circumstances.

Being the boss of his own job had meant enforced good behavior while building this *bordello*, so finding someone to attend an excursion had been a test of his social connections. After spending nearly two years in Niagara Falls constructing the Wedding Wing, his friends back at his West Coast home barely remembered what he looked like.

If he'd had any sense, he would have attended the grand opening alone. But the thought of three weeks spent lusting after Laura had driven him to action. Now he'd paid the price.

As Adam escorted Monique back to the entrance, Dale heard him reassure her that both she and her bags would be on their way to the airport immediately. She swept past, shooting Dale a dark look that should have shriveled him on the spot.

Turning to Annabelle, Dale thought about how this whole scene could have been worse. If Laura had been here to witness the carnage...

She'd hear about it, of course, but Dale didn't care. By then he'd have vented his anger on Annabelle, who had some serious explaining to do about why he was suddenly facing three weeks of erotic events *alone*.

2

"THE ANAL ATRIUM?" Dale sounded a lot calmer than he felt.

"It did the trick, didn't it?" Annabelle said.

"You chased her off on purpose."

"I did." No repentance whatsoever. "I saved you from a miserable three weeks. Monique wasn't your type, Dale. I'm surprised you even brought her."

"All I ever did was work around here, Annabelle, so what would you know about my type?"

She handed him a white envelope and a letter opener.

Scowling, Dale sliced through the heavy paper and withdrew what turned out to be an invitation. He flipped it open and found himself riveted by the familiar handwriting inside.

> Dale,
>
> I'd like you to be my guest for the Naughty Nuptials and to share the Castaway Honeymoon Isle suite. I haven't been able to stop thinking about you since you left. Your visit will give us the perfect chance to enjoy ourselves.
>
> Laura

"So what'll it be, Casanova?" Annabelle looked smug. "Do I check you into the Castaway Honeymoon Isle or have Adam hold the limo?"

Under normal circumstances Dale wasn't prone to mood swings. In fact, to hear his family and friends tell it, he was a downright good-natured guy. But, again, these weren't normal circumstances. He'd swung from mad as hell to happy camper so fast he felt dizzy.

I haven't been able to stop thinking about you.

Aside from the fact Annabelle was waiting for an answer about whether or not he wanted to make love to her co-worker, something coiled low in his gut…some wrenching feeling that was wholly unfamiliar.

He should feel guilty that Monique had flown clear across the country to turn around and make the trip back but he couldn't work up an ounce of regret. Not when Laura had decided to enjoy herself with him.

"Will I need the *Groom's Survival Guide* if I accept her invitation?"

"Check in and find out."

Dale searched Annabelle's expression. He thought she was joking, but given the events of the past twenty minutes, he wouldn't bet money. As much as he wanted to heat the sheets with Laura, a stubborn shred of reason insisted on knowing what had made Ms. In-Love-with-Love drag her head from the clouds long enough for a solid tumble on terra firma.

"You're not considering turning her down, are you?" Annabelle asked.

He'd spent too much time lusting after Laura to pass up this golden opportunity, but somehow when talking to Annabelle, he hated sounding easy.

"Around this place it's always a good idea to be clear on the details." An understatement, given the memory of Monique's departure. "The Anal Atrium, Annabelle?"

"I pulled that out on a dime, can you believe it?" Her laughter rang out loudly enough to draw another glance from the desk clerks, who were working hard to give their sales director some privacy in the limited space. "So what'll it be, Casanova?"

Tucking the letter carefully back into the envelope, he slipped it inside his jacket pocket. "The Castaway Honeymoon Isle, of course."

"An excellent choice." With a smile still on her face, she tapped out a mad burst on a computer keyboard, then handed him a card key. "Enjoy your stay at Falling Inn Bed."

"I will." He reached for her hand and brought it to his lips. "Thanks, gorgeous. I know the way."

"ALL RIGHT, ANNABELLE, who is she?" Pausing in the doorway of the sales office, Laura braced herself to hear about the curvy brunette who'd accompanied the man she'd waited too long to decide she'd wanted for herself.

"She's *gone*."

Laura must have braced herself too tightly because it took a second for that statement to register. "She's *gone*?"

Annabelle nodded. "Dale's date freaked when she found out we're a romance resort. She made quite a scene at the front desk and demanded a limo to take her back to the airport. Adam calmed her down and sent her on her way."

Laura had seen the brunette clinging to Dale and knew that two plus two did *not* equal four here. "All right, what did you do?"

"What makes you think I did anything?"

"Oh, please. I work here, remember? I know how we operate. Romance at all costs. If not you personally, then someone around here did something to chase her off. So fess up. What was it?"

Annabelle eyed her without remorse. "Do you really care when your date is in the Castaway Honeymoon Isle as we speak?"

Laura closed her eyes and exhaled slowly, letting the words filter through her and take hold in slow degrees.

No, she didn't care. She'd fantasized about Dale Emerson for so long that those fantasies had interfered with her life. While he'd been in town building the Wedding Wing, she'd spent way too much time hanging around after work, making excuses to run into him when she should have been dating.

She'd expected the problem to go away post-construction, but no such luck. If anything, she'd become more preoccupied with the man after he'd left, as if her subconscious worked overtime to make up for his absence. Only after she'd exhausted herself trying to banish Dale from her fantasies once and for all had she finally given in and decided to take action.

"Laura, are you all right?" Annabelle asked.

"You gave Dale my invitation?"

She nodded.

"What did he say?"

"He asked if he had to marry you."

Tension burst out as nervous laughter. "What did you say?"

"I told him to check in and find out." She winked. "I'd never tell him he couldn't marry you. You'd be good together."

"Oh, Annabelle, please. We've had this conversation before. I'm looking for a man with a compatible lifestyle and a career that doesn't make him a nomad."

Laura had learned the hard way to be very selective

about who she got involved with. After growing up with her head-over-heels parents, she had a healthy respect for the power of love. If she was going to fall for any man, she was going to make sure he was the *right* man.

But Dale had proven himself a special case. Even though he had heartbreak written all over him, she couldn't steer clear of him, not even after he'd left Niagara Falls for the West Coast. She'd been forced to resort to damage control—in this case a fling during Naughty Nuptials. Pure fantasy. Limited time frame. And work, work, work to distract her. She'd barely have time for sex, let alone a chance for her feelings to run away with her.

Unfortunately, Annabelle wasn't buying it, and she wasn't the only one who didn't. Laura's parents had been debating her views for *years*.

"You're looking for Mr. Perfect," Annabelle said. "And I hate to burst your bubble but he doesn't exist."

"I'm looking for Mr. Perfect-for-me and he *does* exist. I just haven't found him yet. But I've clarified exactly what I want from Dale in my invitation. I was clear, don't you think?"

"Very clear. You want to enjoy the celebration with him. You want to enjoy *him*."

"He really agreed?"

Annabelle nodded.

"I'm really going to do this?" It was a question. It shouldn't be. Laura could handle Dale Emerson. Of course she could. And there would never be a more perfect time.

"You issued the invitation, my girl. It would be poor form to change your mind now. Especially since I chased off his date."

"I knew it!"

Annabelle only steepled her hands before her and smiled.

While Laura appreciated the effort, she did feel a pang of guilt. Yet if the curvy brunette who had been hanging all over him was scared off by the concept of a romance resort, she was out of her league.

Laura hoped she was the only one.

"Well, I won't change my mind." She took a deep, fortifying breath. "As the bedding consultant around here, it's up to me to set a good example."

"Agreed. Which means you need to get upstairs and greet your guest. He seemed...*eager*."

"Did he?"

Annabelle smiled. "Very."

Well, most men would be eager with an invitation for sex in a room designed for lovers, wouldn't they? Especially a man with Dale's appetite. *Alleged* appetite.

Laura glanced down at her watch. "I can't go just yet. I'm waiting for Delia and Jackson. Oh, and don't forget, we're set for dinner with our featured couples and the press at seven."

"I'll be there with bells. But you need to make time to greet Dale. And don't worry. Your invitation was crystal clear."

"Okay."

"You're a beautiful young woman who has worked very hard to accomplish what you have, Laura. Celebrate. You like Dale and he likes you. Have a good time together and don't stress out about anything else. When will you ever get another chance to join in the fun and games around here? You're usually slaving away behind the scenes. This is a unique opportunity."

Wise advice. "What would I do without you?"

"You'd waste a lot more time angsting, no doubt," Annabelle said with a feigned scowl. She hated the mushy stuff. "You did the right thing by inviting the man to be your date. Now greet your guests and go have fun. You're wasting valuable time—yours and mine."

"I'm gone." Blowing her friend a kiss, Laura slipped back out the door.

The arrival of her featured bridal couple delayed thoughts of the man awaiting her upstairs, and she met her guests in the main lobby, genuinely pleased to see them.

Like the Knights, Delia Wallace and Jackson Marsh were the perfect couple to act as the honorees of her grand opening. Not only were they a very attractive pair—Delia was as blond as her fiancé was dark—but as interns on Dale's construction team, they had a history with the Wedding Wing.

"Delia, Jackson, welcome back. It's good to see you again."

"You, too." Delia extended her hands and gave Laura's a welcoming squeeze. "We've missed this place so much."

"Are you two ready for your big day?"

"Beyond ready," Jackson said. "This wedding has become a full-time job."

"How's that? You're supposed to be letting Falling Inn Bed do all the work."

He wrapped a protective arm around Delia. "That's what I thought. But my fiancée spends all her time explaining to my ultraconservative future in-laws that being the guests of honor at your Naughty Nuptials isn't the same thing as having our wedding featured in an X-rated movie."

Delia sighed. "I shouldn't have told them about the documentary."

The Worldwide Travel Association had sent a photojournalist to document the Wedding Wing's grand opening and as the featured bridal couple, Delia and Jackson would be front and center of the coverage. She could see where ultraconservative future in-laws might have trouble connecting the Naughty Nuptials with a legitimate hospitality industry documentary.

"What can I do to help?" she asked, needing more information to figure out how to address the problem. "I reserved your folks a regular room on the same guest floor where you'll be staying until the ceremony. They shouldn't run into anything too controversial there."

Unfortunately, that was about the only place they wouldn't run into anything *too* controversial.

"As long as we don't invite them to see our honeymoon suite," Jackson said.

"Oh, God, no," Delia agreed. "The Shangri-la Paradise would be enough to make my mother faint. And to be honest, I haven't figured out how to break the news about the sex-toy shower, either."

Laura understood. Falling Inn Bed dealt exclusively in sex and as sex was an intensely personal subject…by necessity, the staff had become skilled in assessing guests' reactions to put them at ease with the subject matter.

Fortunately, she had the advantage of knowing Delia. Beneath her fashion-model looks was actually a very shy woman who'd taken a while to warm up. And if Mom was anything like daughter…

Jackson wouldn't have mentioned the situation unless

he needed help. He knew Laura's specialty happened to be converting her guests into romance enthusiasts.

"What time do your parents arrive tomorrow?" she asked.

"Their flight's due early. A little after eight."

"Great, plenty of time before the festivities start." Looping her arm through Delia's, she steered her toward the promenade. "Come on. Let's get you checked in. We'll talk while we walk. I've got an idea."

Laura detailed her plan to have a limo pick up Delia's parents at the airport for a grand tour of Niagara Falls. "Let's give them a little VIP treatment and warm them up to the area before we bring them to the inn. You tell me what interests them, and I'll assign a concierge to be their guide."

She smiled, hoping to reassure an anxious Delia. "We've got a lot more than the falls around here and my staff is skilled at presenting our unique services. We'll break the news about the events in bits and pieces, and I'm sure we'll have them comfortable and ready to have fun before they even check in."

Jackson smiled appreciatively. "Sounds like a great place to start."

"And you're sure this won't be too much trouble?" Delia asked.

"Not at all, Delia," she said. "I'll have your folks back in plenty of time to get settled before the festivities. All you have to do is prepare them for the official Falling Inn Bed parents-of-the-bride VIP treatment. And now, are you ready for the unveiling?" Laura brought them to a stop beneath the entrance to survey the newly decorated lobby. "Ta-da! Here it is. What do you think?"

Delia and Jackson's obvious pleasure made Laura smile.

While they'd been involved with the construction of the new addition from the ground breaking, they'd left for their next project before the design crew had worked its magic. And the finished project—from the ornate ceilings and papered walls to the array of cranberry ware vases and the Mireille Marceaux displayed in prominence—was indeed magical.

"Laura, I can't tell you what it means that you chose us as special guests for your grand opening," Delia said.

"Special guests?" she repeated. "You're *the* honorary bridal couple for the Naughty Nuptials. And who better to inaugurate the Wedding Wing? Not only did you help build it, but you got engaged here. You'll be written into our history as the couple who started the matrimony ball rolling."

And establishing what Laura believed with her whole heart and soul—that a perfect man existed for every woman. What better place than the Wedding Wing to begin a marriage?

There wasn't one as far as she was concerned.

Motioning her bridal couple toward the wing's check-in desk, she said, "I've got a few things I need to cover and then you can go settle in. The events won't officially begin until the welcome reception tomorrow night, which is why I wanted you here early. You deserve to relax before your guests arrive."

Accepting a package from the desk clerk, a box gift-wrapped in white silk and wedding bells that contained the introductory packet, she passed it to Delia. "Inside is everything you need to prepare. Program. Itinerary. Maps. Checklist. I've also included copies of the *Bride's Guerrilla Handbook* and *Groom's Survival Guide*."

Jackson rolled his eyes. "The *Groom's Survival Guide*?"

"I wrote these handbooks myself," she explained. "And you need to know everything in them. Trust me."

"Of course we do," Delia said, coaching her fiancé.

"Good." Now if her staff could just win over the bride's reluctant parents, they'd be off to a good start. "Swear to me you'll look over everything and call if you have any questions. I'm 1-1 on the house phone."

After helping them to check-in, she saw Delia and Jackson settled before making her way up to her own honeymoon suite on the fifth floor. Beyond the door lay the suite she and Dale had designed together. A place for lovers.

And a man who might become her lover.

If he wasn't angry about his date.

Taking a deep breath, Laura slipped the card key from her pocket and unlocked the door.

The Castaway Honeymoon Isle was a penthouse suite with an open floor plan arranged around a central focal point—a tropical oasis complete with lush plants, a heated pool and rushing waterfall. It had been dubbed Lovers' Lagoon during construction and the name had stuck. Now it graced the promotional materials and the Web site.

The suite played to the fantasy of a couple being stranded on a deserted island alone, and every room in the place—including the bath—overlooked this oasis through a wall of glass.

There was a comfortable living area, a minikitchen and dining area, a master bath with a glass shower stall large enough for two and a bedroom with a bed large enough for plenty of sex play.

Laura had chosen the theme herself, a delightful Key West decor that was both airy and colorful and brought to mind translucent turquoise water and spun-sugar sand. Inhaling another calming breath, she closed the door and turned....

There he was, watching her from across the suite, where he'd sprawled in a chair with a vantage of the door. With his long legs outstretched and his elbows casually hooked on the chair arms, Dale looked equal parts expectant and predatory in a distinctly bad boy way.

She couldn't help but marvel at how her body went on red alert at the mere sight of him, a result of his overpowering good looks—black hair, cleanly chiseled features and a lethal grin. He had this hint-of-a-dark-shadow thing going on along his jaw that only added to the effect.

Even sitting, there was no missing that Dale was a tall man, athletic, a man who could move with fast, strong motion and energetic grace. Add that to the way he idly fingered her invitation while watching her with those smoky gray eyes, and her heart sped up its beat until she could barely breathe.

"Hello, Laura."

The minute he opened his mouth, Laura remembered exactly why she hadn't been able to get this man out of her head. His voice was pure sex—whiskey deep and silky smooth, a sound that conjured up images of bare bodies gliding against each other in a distinctly rhythmic way.

"Welcome back, Dale." She sounded breathless and that smile playing around the edges of his mouth suggested he'd noticed.

Not exactly the entrance she'd planned in her fantasies. She'd intended to breeze in and make herself comfortable and detail the game plan. But suddenly she needed him to react, to hear him say he'd accepted her invitation, that his arrival in this suite wasn't just morbid curiosity about why Annabelle had chased off his date.

Or, worse yet, a joke.

"Are you angry about your date?" She couldn't read a thing on his face.

"She'd still be here if she wanted to be."

Okay. He clearly wasn't too concerned about the runaway date. "Do you want to be my guest for the Naughty Nuptials?"

"I want to be your lover. I have since we met."

She didn't know whether it was his calmly issued declaration or the hungry look that sent a rush of awareness through her, but the pulse suddenly throbbing in her throat precluded any reply.

He held up the invitation. "This says you want to share this suite and have a good time. What's going on here, Laura?"

She took another deep breath. She'd known this would come out of left field for him. It had come out of left field for *her*. There was only one thing to do here—be honest.

"I changed my mind," she said simply.

"Now, after I've left town? How the hell did you reconcile our differences?"

"Do you mean declining to date you when you asked?"

He nodded.

"The limited time frame of the grand opening solves the problem, don't you think?"

He looked skeptical. "One of them, maybe. I'm leaving in three weeks, so there'll be no question about commitment."

"Problem solved then. As long as we're clear on what we want from each other."

"I know what I want from you, Laura. I've always known." His dark, silky tone promised enough bare skin and killer orgasms to send a shiver through her. "What exactly do you want from me?"

"I want to be your lover." She gave his words back to him, needing to give as good as she got, that familiar feeling rising up like it always did with him, that…*need* to do something to catch his attention, to make him notice her.

"Really?" He arched an inky brow. "You wouldn't go on a date with me because you don't do flings and I'm not the man of your dreams."

Now he shot her long-ago words back to her with that deep, sexy voice, his gaze holding hers so steadily that she could feel the effects low in her belly. "Can't a girl change her mind?"

"What made you change it?"

"You're the man of my fantasies." She watched his reaction flash across his handsome face. His nostrils flared. His jaw tightened. His whole body tensed. "It's this chemistry between us, Dale. It drove me crazy while you were here. I thought after you left I'd get over it." She shrugged. "Read my invitation. It's all there. I haven't been able to stop thinking about you."

His eyes bored into her as if demanding her truths, questioning, not quite daring to believe his sudden good fortune.

"Three weeks in this suite seemed like the perfect opportunity to get this chemistry out of the way…unless you don't want me."

"You know better."

The heat was pooling really low now, potent enough to make her take drastic action. Okay, so she'd have to convince him. Fair enough. She'd gone from red-hot to ice-cold when he'd asked her on a date so long ago.

Turning away, she opened the hall closet and slipped off her jacket. "I have to be back downstairs for dinner at seven."

Here was another perfect opportunity, this one designed to convince him that she was serious about wanting a fling. Swinging her braid over her shoulder, she unfastened the button at her nape.

"Did you tell Annabelle to chase off my date?" he asked.

Laura shook her head. While she might earn brownie points if he thought she'd masterminded the deal, she couldn't lie. Especially not when she still had pangs about the woman leaving.

"I only sent Annabelle to pick your brain. If you came in alone she was supposed to find out if you were expecting a date. If not, she could give you my invitation. If you arrived with someone, she was supposed to tear up my invitation and swallow the pieces so there wouldn't be any evidence."

He laughed. That husky-edged sound rippled through her but Laura still didn't look at him. It was easier to be calm, cool and courageous when she wasn't on the end of that gaze. Much, *much* easier.

Time to level the playing field.

Unfastening her skirt, Laura let it slip to the floor, leaving her standing in a shell, panty hose and practical pumps.

"What the hell are you doing, Laura?"

"I'm convincing you I'm serious about wanting a fling."

After their long business affiliation, undressing in front of this man was beyond outrageous. But as much as she wanted to see his reaction, she refused to let him see how important his reaction was to her. She hung her skirt on a hanger, instead.

"How can I be the man of your fantasies but not the man of your dreams?" He sounded unconvinced. "Please explain the difference to me."

His voice had lowered another sexy octave and Laura fought to keep her calm, as if stripping in front of an attractive man was a commonplace occurrence. "The man of my fantasies is a man I can enjoy myself with. When it's over, it's over. We both go our separate ways and take away some pleasant memories."

She tried not to wax too poetic when she said, "The man of my dreams is the man I want to share my life with. He'll be someone with similar values who wants similar things from life. He'll share some of my interests and be willing to explore new ones that we can share together. He'll bring out the best in me and I'll do the same for him."

Dale's snort sounded less than amused, so Laura placed the hanger in the closet and chanced a peek at him.

The frown darkening his expression warned her a storm was brewing so she wasn't entirely unprepared when he arched a brow and asked, "How do you know what I want from my life? I don't recall ever having that conversation with you. Or one about values, either."

She forced a laugh, unsure why she'd offended him. "You're a bad boy, Dale. The man of my dreams won't be."

"Define bad boy."

"The guys who drive fast cars and chase faster women."

"This is your opinion of me? Based on what? I behaved exemplarily while I was on this property."

He sounded so indignant that she had to swallow back a real laugh. "That may be the case, Dale, but let me point out that you can't help flirting no matter how young or old a woman might be. I don't think you'll deny that."

His frown morphed into a scowl. But on the up side, his heated gaze kept dipping from her face, and she thought he might have noticed that she didn't wear panties under her panty hose.

"Flirting doesn't make me a degenerate."

"I never said degenerate. I said *bad boy*. There's nothing wrong with bad boys but they don't stay forever. They like skirting the edges and pushing the limits. They like being challenged."

"This is bad?"

"Not at all. It can be perfectly exciting in a lover. But the man of *my* dreams won't work a job where he travels all over the world for extended periods of time—"

"Sounds like you have a problem with my job, not me."

"I don't have a problem with either," she clarified patiently. "I just didn't want to complicate our working relationship when you weren't what I was looking for in a man. It's not that I'm opposed to a fling per se, but a fling is meant to be short. We've been working on this project for two years and much of that time we were on this property together."

She wouldn't mention her own concerns about mixing sex and romance. They would undoubtedly send this man running.

"I find it interesting that the woman who single-handedly masterminded the Wedding Wing and the Naughty Nuptials, a woman who is the biggest romantic idealist I've ever met, and I've met my share of women, believe me—"

She certainly did!

"—can be so cold-bloodedly pragmatic about her own love life."

"What's cold-blooded? I know what I want and don't want to waste my time heading down roads that'll take me where I don't want to go."

"How do you know where a road will take you unless you go for a spin on it?"

He visibly struggled to keep his gaze on her face, so she propped a shoulder against the wall, folded her arms across her chest and hooking her ankles in a would-be casual pose that let him view her in all her full frontal glory.

His gaze dropped again.

"I've looked at the map, Dale. I know exactly where you'd take me—straight into bed. Then after the ride, you'd beep your horn, wave good-bye and not look in the rearview mirror. You would have shown up for work the next day as if nothing had happened between us. I just wasn't comfortable with that."

"You've looked at the map? What the hell does that mean?"

He didn't refute her charges, and that only reinforced what Laura already knew—Dale Emerson might be a dyed-in-the-wool bad boy, but there was honor beneath his fast grins and charming words. He wouldn't lie. Not even he could deny he was trouble on two very nice legs.

"It means I've looked at some of your past *rides* and they've confirmed my opinion." She hadn't meant to reveal that little tidbit but if he needed proof… "I did some home-work before I wrote my invitation."

"You checked out the women I dated while I was in town?"

"Yes."

He tossed the invitation onto an end table as if it sud-denly burned his fingers. "Enlighten me."

"My pleasure." But first…a distraction. Dragging the

hem of her silk shell upward, Laura stretched, another provocative move that was rewarded by a quick intake of breath. She schooled her smile before the blouse cleared her face.

"I heard that you had such a hot love life you could only date women who didn't live in Niagara Falls proper so you wouldn't damage your reputation."

"My former dates are talking about me?"

"No, Dale. They're *bragging*."

That stopped him. His expression went blank, and his mouth popped open enough to show a glint of teeth before he rallied, "Bragging? About what?"

"About what a studmuffin you are in bed," she informed him pleasantly. "From what I hear you can come four times a night and bring a woman to pleasure twice that number."

His scowl reappeared in force now, but he didn't dispute the claims, or agree, for that matter. Laura got the distinct impression he didn't know what to say, which came as another surprise. She'd meant to stroke his ego, had thought he'd be pleased to know his past lovers regarded him so highly.

Obviously not.

"How do you even know who I dated, Laura? I never visited the same town twice."

"You're in western New York, my friend. Mountains and valleys and miles do *not* equal anonymity."

"Apparently not."

He sounded so annoyed that she couldn't help but take pity on him. "I'm serious about wanting a fling, Dale. If it didn't work out during the grand opening, then I considered taking a much-deserved vacation to California to look you up. You sounded worth the trip."

He gave a grunt of disgust.

She smiled. "According to my research, you dated six women during the time you worked on the Wedding Wing. All six had rave reviews. That's something to be proud of."

"Except that I thought I was on good behavior because I was the senior project architect on this job."

"Oh." Pushing away from the wall, Laura headed toward the bedroom to retrieve her dinner dress and give him a performance along the way. "Case closed, Dale. You're a bad boy."

3

LAURA CONTINUED TO the bedroom closet, attempting to calm her pulse and reevaluate her strategy. She'd guessed that Dale would want an explanation about her change of heart, but she hadn't expected quite so much wariness about her offer. To be fair, she supposed that being a five-star Mr. Charming didn't necessarily mean he was careless about who he jumped into bed with.

She'd honestly never meant to imply that his actions were degenerate. She'd intended to compliment his prowess, reinforce her reasons for wanting a fling. But he'd seemed so surprised by her revelations about his past dates that she wondered if he'd expected her to crawl into bed with him without at least peeking at his history. That sort of negligence would have been reckless. Laura might be a lot of things—a romantic idealist among them—but she wasn't reckless.

She'd decided to switch gears and veer off the respectable relationship track, and while she knew Dale from work, she didn't know much about his personal life. She'd looked into it. Plain and simple.

Her choice of dates for the Naughty Nuptials would reflect on Falling Inn Bed during what was intended to be a media circus. Her choice in attire would reflect on the inn, too, so she selected a blue crochet dress and a pair of kid-skin slingbacks. Simple, tasteful and elegant. Heading back into the living room, she avoided Dale's gaze and hung the dress in the hall closet.

She'd answered his questions and given him a sneak preview of what she had to offer with the removal of her suit. He would make the next move. He'd either accept her offer or turn her down. If he turned her down, she'd simply dress for dinner as if changing in front of him had been nothing more than a necessity of time constraints. She'd pretend to have some dignity left.

Dale still hadn't said a word. Maybe he needed more time to decide. Maybe she'd just surprised him. Maybe he still didn't trust her. But whatever his reasoning, she began to feel naked and didn't like the feeling at all.

Just as she reached for her dress, she heard him get up. Glancing over her shoulder, she found him heading toward her, his expression nothing short of purposeful.

Now here was a look she'd never seen before. Gone was the professional who'd strategized and problem solved the design and construction of the Wedding Wing. Gone was the easy, smiling man she'd gotten to know while working together, a man who flirted as naturally as he breathed. And gone was the surprised, moody man she'd met only moments before.

This Dale Emerson had a fierce determination about him as he drew near, his long-legged strides powerful, his presence almost aggressive as he closed the distance between them.

Catching her in front of the closet, he moved behind her, and she braced herself, thinking he might whisper in her ear or kiss her cheek. Her whole body tensed expectantly, a boneless gathering of muscle as she stood poised and ready to react.

But he simply placed his hand above her head and slid the closet door shut, showcasing them in the full-length mirror. She lifted her gaze to the reflection of his face, a face that had lost much of its familiarity up close. Or perhaps all her bare skin was to blame.

Here was a man reputed to bring women pleasure. And from the way one look from him stoked the spark inside her to a flame, he'd earned his reputation with good reason.

He looked purposeful while she looked surprised. Laura thought she'd nailed this man for who he was, but soon realized that knowing Dale was a charmer and experiencing the effects of his charm were two distinctly different things.

Slipping his arms around her in a whipcord motion, he dragged her backward. She gasped as she came in full contact with his body. His broad chest surrounded her, his muscular thighs molded her backside. A rock-hard erection rode in the small of her back, and just as casually as he pleased, he rested his chin on the top of her head and met her gaze in the mirror.

"You feel good. I knew you would."

The breezy observation made her stomach swoop wildly. She could feel his every hard inch against her and relished how good *he* felt.

"But can Ms. Romantic Idealist really handle a fling?"

She understood why he might raise the question. Except for the bare skin, she really didn't look the part of a woman used to flings. Panty hose. Practical pumps. Nothing-special bra.

If she'd honestly believed Dale would arrive without a date, she might have dressed for a seduction. But her chances had been slim at best. Without Annabelle's help, she'd have been attending three weeks of events with Adam, who would much rather deal with erotic events from the outside looking in.

"I can handle you, Dale," she said, sounding very sure of herself. "Just because I declined a fling, doesn't mean I can't manage one. I'm a big girl."

"Yes, you are."

As if to prove the point, he dragged his hands up her ribs, a deliberate motion showcased in the mirror, visually erotic.

"So, Laura. What did you want to know about me? Were you interested in my stamina or did you ask my former dates for details?" The smoke in his gaze rode out on his voice so there was no missing that details meant *sexy* details.

"I wasn't so…*specific.*"

"No? You didn't want to know how I would touch you to make you come so many times in a night?" He arched a dark brow. "Or what I like to do to make me come?"

Damn if a blush didn't start creeping up from her breasts like the sunrise, the downside to her fair skin that she couldn't stop once it started. And she knew exactly what he was trying to do…well, not trying, *doing*, given the way her blush deepened.

He tested her, challenged her, because even though he touched her, he hadn't accepted her offer yet.

"Actually, Dale." He was about to find out that she was made of sterner stuff than he gave her credit for. "Your former dates were all so thrilled with your performances that they offered the information without much inducement."

"I'm glad I've left behind some happy women, but I much prefer to think about you asking for intimate details. Don't you want to know what I like to do in bed?"

"I'd like to find out for myself."

He chuckled, and his fingers began a slow glide down her neck. This was no tentative exploration. His hands pressed into her skin until she could feel a heat radiating downward, making her breasts grow heavy and her nipples stand at attention.

Yet Laura couldn't ignore that…*something* underlying his provocative manner. Something that hinted at how unexpected her revelations, and her opinion of him, had been.

"Does it bother you that I talked to those women?"

"Why should it?"

"I don't know," she replied silkily, even though the flush in her cheeks made a lie of her nonchalance. "I wouldn't want you to worry that a romantic idealist like me would set my sights too high and wind up disappointed."

That lethal grin kicked up the corners of his mouth, and he gave a laugh. "Never fear, lovely Laura. I'll live up to my press. Don't give that a second thought."

He nuzzled his face against hers, his smile still in place, and his faintly stubbled cheek abraded her skin, a simple touch that ignited her nerve endings everywhere.

"I don't doubt it, Dale, and I won't have any trouble handling you, either."

"Then I'll be your bad boy for the grand opening. If that's what you want from me."

"It is."

His gaze never left hers as he pressed an openmouthed kiss to the juncture between neck and shoulder. "I've wanted to be bad with you for a long time. We're going to be bad together, Laura. *Very* bad."

That heat roared inside, and Laura caught a breath that

made her chest rise and fall sharply. She could still see that smile where his mouth dragged against her skin.

"You like that."

"I do."

There was an incredible unreality about the moment. Sensory overload from the feel of his mouth, the sight of his dark head poised over her, the promise in those smoky eyes.

This was Dale Emerson, the man who'd been haunting her subconscious for so long that watching him touch her became surreal in the extreme. A scene from one of her fantasies come to life while she stood barely dressed in front of a mirror with him, his tongue darting out to taste her throat, a warm velvet stroke that left the gleam of dampness in its wake.

Suddenly he slipped his hands around her hips, dragged them along her stomach, up her ribs. His fingers looked so dark against her skin. They looked so sexy standing together, him fully dressed and her wearing only a bra and hose. The practical pumps—nothing much to look at normally, but professional and comfortable for long days running around the property—elevated her until her back arched and her breasts thrust forward.

"You're so beautiful," Dale whispered, and his gaze trailed down from hers, slowly taking in her reflection.

To her chagrin, that blush continued to deepen in a distinctly unbad-girl way. She resisted the urge to shut her eyes and block out the proof that Dale had been right. She was a romantic idealist looking to take a walk on the wild side.

She wanted to be a temptress, wanted to star in this man's fantasies the way he'd starred in hers. She wanted to wipe out the memories of the untold women who'd found pleasure in his arms before her turn had come around.

But even this aroused, Laura hadn't lost her senses completely. "We don't have time for this. Dinner, remember?"

His grip tightened, a possessive move that made her inhale sharply. "We have time. You're already undressed."

She couldn't refute his logic, especially when his head dropped out of sight behind her. She held her breath, waited. His mouth brushed her skin then his teeth…suddenly her bra sprang open and her breasts popped out.

She sucked in a hard breath as the climate-controlled air coaxed already hard nipples to tighter peaks, and he drew the straps over her shoulders, down her arms, and let the bra drop to the floor.

"I intend to find out what you like in bed," he said.

She heard the challenge in his voice, and her gaze zeroed in on the utterly decadent sight she presented as he cupped her in his palms, kneaded her skin with deep, erotic strokes that made her insides melt. She leaned into his touch without thinking, helpless to do anything but respond.

She couldn't have imagined feeling this way if she'd tried. She hadn't expected him to move so fast, hadn't in her heart of hearts believed this whole idea would work out. But Dale was back, and he'd agreed to be her date.

For three weeks of fantasy.

Resting his chin on her shoulder, he regarded her beneath heavy-lidded eyes, a look that drugged her with the promise of his next touch, a look that made it hard to draw a decent breath.

"You like how this feels." It wasn't a question, more a statement of fact that she couldn't deny. "What about this?"

He caught her nipples in a firm pinch and fire shot through her like a lightning bolt, one hot blast that singed every nerve ending from warm to blistering.

"Yes." The sound slipped out as a moan, an absurdly un-dignified sound that made his gaze twinkle.

"And this?"

He held on and tugged her nipples in a slow pull that splintered that bolt of heat until she could feel it every-where. Her nipples flushed pink. Her breasts swelled vis-ibly. She couldn't stop herself from rising up on tiptoes to arch her whole body into his touch.

"Oh!"

Not the most articulate of replies, but given his grin, Dale got the general idea. He thumbed the now-swollen peaks and each stroke made her tremble in reply, full-bodied quivers that mirrored their achy counterparts deep inside.

"You have such beautiful skin." His deep voice whis-pered against her ear, the caress of his warm breath mak-ing her sigh aloud. Trailing his fingers away from her nipples, he traced a vein that shone faintly along her breast. "You've got skin meant to be handled carefully and to be cherished."

He touched her with teasing swirls of his fingers, leav-ing her to savor the ache he'd started, an awareness that echoed down to her toes.

Dale understood pleasure. He understood how to make a woman respond to his touch, and he handled that knowl-edge with as much skill and experience as he'd ever dem-onstrated at work.

On the job he'd known how to interpret her architectural needs. He'd taken her vision to create the Wedding Wing. In this honeymoon suite, he understood her desires and how to fulfill them. He took her unspoken fantasies and made them reality.

She thought about making a few demands of her own.

She wanted to kiss his mouth, wanted to wrap herself around him and learn the feel of all his hard places. She wanted to taste him and tempt him the way he tasted and tempted her, *so* much.

She wanted to prove that even though she didn't normally indulge in flings, she would play by the rules. *Bad* was an attitude, after all, and she could wield attitude if it meant this man pleasuring her. And getting a chance to pleasure him.

But even through the haze of steamy sensation that made her melt against him, Laura recognized that she'd both offended and challenged Dale with her frankness about his personal life. She hadn't intended to, but explaining herself had brought his actions and her opinion up for discussion.

Dale Emerson might be a lot of things—a brilliant architect and construction manager, an oh-so charming man—but first and foremost he was *male*. He wanted to prove himself.

Right now she would let him. She'd told him she could handle a fling, and she would have plenty of time during the upcoming weeks to back up her statement with proof. At the moment, Dale wanted the upper hand so she gave up all thoughts of demands and let him do what he did best—be *bad*.

Raising her arms, she stretched until she could slip her hands around his neck and contented herself with fingering the silky hairs at his nape. He raked a hungry gaze over her reflection and dragged his strong hands over her, solid, persuasive strokes that skidded along her skin, made her imagine what it would feel like to press her body full against him.

Running his palms over her hose-clad backside, he massaged her cheeks, rounded her hips, then drove his fingers between her thighs with an intimacy that made her gasp. He anchored her close, riding that rock-hard erection against her, and his expression sharpened into a look of white-hot need.

"I want you," he said.

"You said we have time," she reminded him in a stranger's voice.

His eyes closed. He exhaled a sound that wasn't quite a groan, a sound so needy Laura knew instinctively that her effect on him rivaled his on her. And knowing she was the object of this man's desire blindsided her with its potency, a physical reaction that made her tingle with arousal.

"We do." He exhaled those words on a kiss. "If we move fast. But I've waited so long to make love to you that I won't be rushed." He brushed another kiss along her temple. "Do you know I've never seen your hair down? Will you take out your braid for me later? I want to see you wearing nothing but hair."

Even such a simple request meant he'd been thinking about her, perhaps even fantasizing, and she found the thought exciting. "It'll be my pleasure."

His eyes fluttered open again, and he speared her on a heated gaze. "Mine, too. And speaking of pleasure..." His voice trailed off as he slipped his fingers into the waistband of her hose and dragged them down.

She suddenly stood there with her arms wrapped around his neck, her breasts thrust outward and her sex exposed, looking decadently bare with the hose tangled around her thighs.

His low growl rumbled near her ear, and he ground that

hot erection against her for good measure. But before she had a chance to ride his length and share some of her excitement, he stepped away. The air suddenly caressed her bottom, punctuating the distance he put between them.

"I'm going to bring you pleasure, Laura." His husky-voiced declaration filtered through her, almost as potent as the hands he grazed along her bare skin.

Threading one hand between her thighs, he zeroed right in on the knot of nerve endings there. Coaxing the tiny bundle from its hiding place, he expertly rolled his fingers, sending a jolt through her.

Their gazes locked in the mirror. The intensity on his handsome face, those thick lashes hooding smoky eyes, promised her more pleasure than she'd ever imagined, promised that he would enjoy making her come apart at his command.

Forcing her to part her thighs, he explored her at his leisure. With sleek curls of his fingers, he spread moist arousal along her most intimate places, and Laura arched back against him, surrendering to the heat, letting him have all the control, payback for having resisted him for so long.

And he welcomed her payment, taking liberties that seemed astonishingly brazen for two people who'd only just decided to get intimate. But obviously Dale felt as if two years of unrequited attraction entitled him to privileges.

He thrust those fingers silkily in, and her body grew slick beneath his skilled touch. The mirror displayed every nuance of her expression, the way he worked her in long pleasured strokes, the way she swayed sinuously to feed this awakening need within.

"I want to watch you come," he whispered. "Let go."

Let go? She barely hung on. She rode his hand with an urgency she'd never known before, didn't want to control, a need that tossed her normally sound reason to the winds to keep up this steady rocking motion... A motion that created friction exactly where she needed it.

Dale promised to bring her pleasure and he did. Tension mounted, a coiling pressure that wound its way through her, and took over until she recognized the look of casual determination on his face. He hadn't been joking. He wouldn't stop until he made her come. Right here. Right now.

While he watched.

And when he hauled her back against him to find a deeper position, she did let go. She couldn't keep her eyes open anymore, wasn't sure she even wanted to as her body moved decadently in time with his strokes. Let him enjoy the show because once he used the heel of his palm to knead her orgasm into breaking, she couldn't worry about anything but the way her body had started to vibrate....

When Laura came, it was an expansive, glorious sensation that rolled through her body, as if two years of longing had crested and finally broke. Two years of fantasies that had grown into almost an obsession. A climax that shocked her with its intensity, left her panting as she leaned against him to support herself because her legs wouldn't do the job.

She wasn't sure how long it was until she could force her eyes open, but when she did, she almost wished she hadn't. Dale still watched her with that hungry expression, seemingly content to stand there forever with his hands wedged between her thighs.

She wasn't sure what to say, but Dale proved that bad

boys could still be gentlemen when he eased his hands away and slid her hose back into place with a few efficient moves.

Steadying her until she could stand on her own, he leaned over and kissed her cheek.

His smile was pure male satisfaction, his voice a dare when he whispered, "One down. Seven to go."

4

DALE ADJUSTED HIS tie in front of the dresser mirror, surprised and content with this turn of events.

A bad boy.

Leave it to Laura to dissect him. Yes, he'd enjoyed an active sex life before he'd starting building the Wedding Wing. And had he been enjoying himself during this job as he ordinarily would, he would never have had the kind of hard-on for this gorgeous blonde that wouldn't go away. The kind that had made him desperate enough to invite heartbroken Monique on this trip.

He shook his head, exasperated by his own obsession with a woman, and at Laura's idealistic notions about him and sex. If she wanted *bad*, he'd give her *bad* beyond her wildest dreams.

I haven't been able to stop thinking about you.

It went a long way to salvage his pride that he wasn't the only one suffering a serious case of unrequited lust. Just the memory of her smooth skin had his fingertips tingling. He had it so bad that he wanted tonight's dinner over with so he could get her back to this room and start exorcising his demons.

He hoped Laura understood what she was getting into, because Dale meant exactly what he'd said—he didn't intend to be rushed. He was going to make slow, careful love to her and explore this chemistry they shared. He would learn every inch of her tempting body and what touches made her melt the way she had in his arms.

"Heading out tonight?" Laura asked.

He glanced around to find her standing in the doorway dressed in a clingy blue dress that invited his gaze to linger over every shapely inch of her. "I'm escorting you to dinner."

"Oh."

Her beautiful face still looked soft-edged with pleasure, and with the dress accentuating the unusual blue of her eyes, she looked more edible than any feast Falling Inn Bed's chef could prepare. Covering the distance between them, he slid his arm around her waist and tucked her close so he could feel all those sleek curves neatly against him.

A soft gasp slipped from that kissable mouth and she slid into his arms with such gratifying ease that he couldn't resist a taste. Just one taste to test the reality against the fantasy.

He brushed his mouth across hers, sampled velvet moistness and his own lightning-hot response. Just a taste.

"We only have three weeks together, Laura, and I don't plan to miss a second." He traced her full lower lip with his tongue. "Not even for your business dinners."

"I'd like you to come."

"I plan to—four times, remember?"

Her gaze darted upward, her eyes so wide with surprise that he kissed her again to stop from laughing. What was it about this woman that pushed his buttons on such an instinctive level?

Deprivation, maybe. For a guy who usually dated a different woman each week he'd curtailed his dating for an obscene amount of time to behave like a boss on this project. Or perhaps deprivation had only intensified the effect. He recalled feeling as wildly attracted to her the day they'd met. A feeling that translated into a desire to distract her so he could keep stealing kisses.

Her mouth parted beneath his and he thrust his tongue inside, tasting her sweet warmth, savoring the easy way she responded. She tasted of inevitability. She wanted him as much as he wanted her and had finally accepted that this heat raging between them was a gift to be explored and enjoyed. Her kiss told him that she'd stopped resisting the truth and abandoned any thoughts of wasting more time.

They'd wasted too much already.

Back to deprivation again, which just might account for the urgency Dale felt right now, the need to thread his hands around her neck, tilt her head back just enough so he could plunge a little deeper, taste a little more. Her body rode his, all swells and hollows of sleek muscle, enticing him with the memory of the way her skin had felt beneath his hands, tempting him to shift his hips to ease the ache of another growing erection.

Her tongue tangled with his, met each thrust with a demand of her own, a willingness to savor this phenomenon. Lovely Laura had decided to play and she wouldn't hold back. He sensed her eagerness in her excited touches that proved she'd meant what she'd said in her invitation.

I haven't been able to stop thinking about you.

"What is it about you, Laura?" he whispered against her mouth.

She didn't open her eyes, just looked dreamy and beautiful when she said, "It's not really me, Dale. It's all that good behavior. You're horny."

"It is you, Laura." He rained light kisses along the curve of her cheek, caught her earlobe with a quick bite.

Laura finally met his gaze with that drugged-with-pleasure look. For all her fairness and white-blond hair, her brows and lashes were as black as his and the effect on her crystal eyes was startling. One glance ignited a need that tested his control, inspired him to absolute craziness, like forgetting everything in a quest to make her look at him with those eyes. To hear her breathe out on those excited little gasps. To feel her thighs part in a subtle signal that his body caught hers in all the right places.

Mmm-mm. His return trip to Falling Inn Bed had taken a glorious turn for the better, and he was grateful.

Twirling his tongue around her pearl earring, he dragged his mouth along the shell of her ear and breathed lightly. She shivered and that slight tremor brought her against him just enough to make him ache. She felt so damn good.

"Is it time for bed yet?" he asked, only half joking.

"Bed?" Her eyes widened, and she broke out of his arms. "Oh, no, Dale, dinner. We're going to be late."

He'd barely rallied his pleasure-numb thoughts enough to grasp what she'd said before he found himself sprinting after her.

And admiring the view from behind.

Streamlined and clingy, her dress shimmied around her with every hurried step as she sailed through the suite and out the door. He was on her heels, still admiring the view when she stopped suddenly and changed direction. He brought himself up short before he collided into her.

"The stairs," she said. "We can't wait for the elevator."

Catching her elbow, he kept pace by her side then grabbed the exit door. He braced himself to catch her when she wheeled into the stairwell at top speed on those strappy little heels that made her legs look so good.

But Laura just brushed past, skimming against him with all those trim curves. A hint of floral fragrance caught him as she moved by, hurrying down the stairs with her heels tapping out a measured beat.

He followed, asking, "So what's on the agenda tonight?"

"Introducing our featured guests to the press and laying down the ground rules."

"Who's coming from the inn staff?"

"Annabelle and Adam."

"How's Adam doing? Annabelle told me you haven't given up hope yet."

She shrugged. "We haven't, but he needs to lighten up and have fun. Dougray suggested locking him up in the Turkish steam room and not letting him out until he learns how to relax."

"Worth a shot, I guess."

"I thought so, too, but Annabelle's worried he'll shrivel away to nothing, and we'll be liable. After building the Wedding Wing, we can't afford our insurance premiums to go up." She shot a look over her shoulder that made him smile. "We're currently brainstorming if you have any suggestions."

"I'm surprised Ms. J. hasn't cut him loose," Dale commented, referring to the inn's general manager.

"Don't be. Adam's top-notch. He's implemented some really great ideas since he's been here. Not to mention he's awesome with the guests. It's only us he's making nuts. He just can't seem to make peace with selling romance."

That could definitely be a problem around here, and

Dale wasn't inclined to place all the blame on Adam Grant. Falling Inn Bed and its concentration on sex had an interesting effect on people. Monique had run screaming. Dale had learned firsthand that it was best not to analyze or fight the effect but to go with the flow. When in Rome…

His gaze swept over Laura, from her braid that bounced with her light steps to the sound of her clicking heels, and readily admitted that his time spent at the inn had given him an appreciation for all things Roman.

Sidestepping her as they rounded the last flight, he pulled open the door that led to the promenade. She glanced into the windows of the restaurant as they strode past, and groaned.

"Everyone's been seated. There's no graceful way to make this entrance."

"We're not that late."

She didn't reply, only took a deep breath as he looped his arm through hers and led her into the restaurant.

Bruno's Place paid tribute to the turn-of-the-last-century charm so unique to Falling Inn Bed and this was the exact atmosphere Dale had successfully emulated in the new Wedding Wing. Victorian-influenced romance permeated the place where soft light from crystal-cut chandeliers sparkled against walls papered with busy florals and pinstripes. Decorative shelves displayed china and ornamental glassware.

Couples whispered together and savored five-star dishes over dark wood tables draped with lace-trimmed linens. Bruno's Place promoted togetherness with a capital *T* and Dale cast a yearning glance at one of those tables for two where he could have enjoyed some of that togetherness with Laura.

"Your guests are waiting at A-4, Ms. Granger," the hostess greeted them and Laura smiled in acknowledgment.

Their party had been seated in a windowed nook affording a semblance of privacy in the busy restaurant. But the arrangement wasn't private enough for Dale's tastes. He'd been waiting too long for Laura. He wanted her all to himself tonight.

"Annabelle, my love." He leaned over to kiss her cheek then extended his hand to Adam, who stood. "Good to see you again."

He inclined his head in silent thanks for Adam's help in getting Monique safely on her way earlier.

Adam nodded. "Glad you could make it."

"Excuse our delay. I asked Laura to show me the atrium, so I can get a crew in to deal with the problem skylight before this grand opening gets underway. I don't want work to interfere with your events."

It was an outright lie. While there was a problem in the atrium construction, he and Laura hadn't even gotten close to that topic yet. They'd gotten close, and he intended to get a lot closer, but not to talk business. And he didn't mind lying one bit when it meant Laura gazing up at him with a grateful smile.

"Hello everyone," Laura said. "I'd like you to meet Dale Emerson, the senior project manager with Architectural Design Firm. He's the brilliant architect responsible for our Wedding Wing."

Dale smiled while sliding a chair out for her and taking his seat as she introduced the guests.

"You already know our bridal couple," she said as Dale shifted his chair so they could bump knees under the table.

"I do, indeed. Good to see you two again." During the

Wedding Wing project, Dale had been training Jackson and Delia to move into the final phase of their internship before taking their places on one of ADF's junior restoration teams as full architects.

Laura treated him to one of those hospitality-perfect smiles that managed to make him feel as if it was for him alone. "But you're not acquainted with our Hottest Honeymoon couple, Lieutenant Commander Troy Knight and his wife Miranda."

Dale dragged his gaze to the lieutenant commander and his wife, who went out of her way to lean around her husband to shake Dale's hand.

"A pleasure to meet you," she said in a cultured voice.

One glimpse at the dark-haired woman and her gracious smile told Dale that this woman knew her power over a man and exactly how to wield it to best effect. He usually steered as far away from these highbrow society types as he did from rebounding beauties and romantic idealists like Laura.

But this trip had him breaking all the rules. And he wasn't sorry. Shifting in his seat, he brushed his knee against Laura's silk-clad leg as a promise of what was to come.

She gazed up at him through the thick fringe of her lashes, a sassy look that told him she got his meaning loud and clear. "These gentlemen are covering the press for our grand opening." She continued, "Benjamin Harris is a local reporter from the *Niagara Falls Journal* and Tyler Tripp is the photojournalist commissioned by the Worldwide Travel Association to film a documentary of our Naughty Nuptials events."

With his sports coat and tape recorder, Benjamin fit right in with the group at the table, but Tyler looked as though he should be shooting runway models in Paris. Dale recognized him as the guest who'd been checking out Monique at the front desk earlier.

Tyler darted a knowing gaze at Laura, and gave a nod of approval. Dale got the man's message, and this stranger noticing he'd replaced Monique with Laura bugged him. He wasn't sure why. Maybe he was still raw after Laura's revelations about his gossiping former dates.

He forced himself to forget about any woman but the one at his side, who was both smiling and relaxed as she ordered lemon-laced mineral water from their waiter. He ordered wine, hoping alcohol would take the edge off of his impatience.

But the only thing that seemed to help was touching her.

Now that they'd started the ball rolling, he wanted some connection with her beautiful body. His need had been bordering on obsession *before* he'd gotten her undressed. Now that he'd seen her in the blush of passion and heard her pleasured sighs, he realized that a table filled with people wasn't curbing the effect she had on him.

He made a valiant attempt to distract himself by paying attention to the conversation, but even watching Laura interact with Annabelle and Adam wasn't doing the trick. The three of them took turns leading the conversation.

They made suggestions when the waitstaff returned to take orders, proving they all were on top of what took place in their kitchen, and were overall very gracious hosts, the epitome of luxury hoteliers. Their unity put their guests at ease long before Laura steered the conversation to the business at hand.

"Benjamin, Tyler, will you tell everyone your plans for the grand opening, so they'll know what to expect?" she asked.

"I'm your on-the-scenes reporter for the Naughty Nuptials," Benjamin explained. "I'll attend the functions and interview guests then report back to the paper."

Adam eyed them curiously. "I don't believe I heard how often you'd be reporting on the events."

"I'm running a daily article," Benjamin said. "We want our readership to be a part of the Naughty Nuptials from start to finish. An event of this magnitude can't help but make a big splash in our town."

"Sex can have that effect," Tyler of the piercings added.

"Speaking of," Annabelle said. "In case any of you are wondering how this coverage will work, Benjamin and Tyler won't have to attend the functions together. The general manager and I will be taking turns escorting these charming gentlemen to our various events."

"Two's company but three's a crowd." Dale raised his glass to Annabelle, deciding he'd never been happier with that particular philosophy in his life.

The Castaway Honeymoon Isle and a willing Laura.

Annabelle seemed in similarly high spirits. "That's our motto at Falling Inn Bed, as Dale knows after working with us for so long. I'm sure Jackson and Delia would agree."

"Without a doubt." Jackson idly wound an arm around his fiancée and addressed the group. "Delia and I were on this project with Dale through the entire construction, and let me tell you that we had more conversations about sex than you would believe."

"That's the truth," Dale agreed.

It was no damn wonder he'd gotten a hard-on for this gorgeous blonde by his side. Setting his glass back on the table, he rested his hand on her leg, brushing his fingers along her thigh. Her eyes widened, and he knew he'd surprised her.

"As we're a romance resort and all that," she said, "I'm sure you'll agree the conversations got the job done, Jackson. You were inspired to pop the big question."

Jackson nodded and Delia beamed one of those smiles that confirmed what Dale already guessed—Delia was as much of a romantic idealist as Laura.

"You got engaged here?" Benjamin asked. "What's the scoop?"

Delia explained how Jackson had popped the big question inside the new Wedding Wing, after the roof had enclosed the structure but before the first sheet of drywall had gone up.

Dale vividly remembered the day. It had been a wild gesture that had his crew cheering, and Laura popping open bottles of complimentary champagne in the middle of the workday. They'd gotten behind schedule because of the party.

"It's this place." Jackson laughed. "Romance is serious business around here. I don't think a day passed when Laura and Dale weren't going head-to-head about what constituted a decent size for a couples' bathtub—"

"Head-to-head?" Dale seized another opportunity to defend Laura's honor and hopefully earn a few more points to cash in later when they were alone. And naked. "Laura and I never argued. We *negotiated*. Construction involves compromises."

Delia eyed him pointedly. "You compromised very well, boss, because Laura generally won those negotiations."

Laura laughed, shooting Delia a conspiratorial look. "You noticed?"

"Hard not to." Delia exchanged a knowing glance with Annabelle, who agreed. "Laura's relentless in her pursuit of creating the perfect atmosphere for romance. She has a gift."

"As our special events coordinator and wedding consultant, Laura's function is to ensure our guests a perfect fantasy event," Adam explained to the guests. "Delia and Jackson will experience a perfect fantasy wedding this week. And from what I've heard the Knights did as well."

"Our wedding definitely qualified as a fantasy," Troy said.

His wife set her wineglass back on the table. "Special events coordinator and wedding consultant? I've heard Laura referred to as the *bedding* consultant."

Some women might have bristled at the emphasis this woman placed on her informal title, but not Laura. She faced Miranda with an easy smile and a lot of pride. "A resort like ours requires a few unique job titles to accommodate our guests. I'm fortunate enough to have claimed one."

"Is that how you managed to come out ahead in all those negotiations with your architect?" Miranda asked.

There wasn't anything in the woman's question to make Dale take notice, but on a good day he was tuned in to Laura. With his fingers brushing her thigh and the promise of sex in the weeks ahead, he was more closely in tune than usual. Her expression never changed, but he got the sense that her control came at a price.

"As the Wedding Wing director, I was fortunate enough to have the final say," she said neutrally.

Tyler laughed. "But I want to know how hard Dale could argue with one of the owners. What do you say, Dale? Did you ever stand a chance?"

He gazed down at Laura and her perfectly amiable expression, and shook his head. "Not really."

He hadn't stood a chance around this woman, not ever. He just hadn't realized it until he'd finally gotten to kiss her.

Miranda looked puzzled. "One of the owners? Laura's the owner of what exactly?"

"We have a rather unusual arrangement on our property," Annabelle explained. "The members of our management staff are the stockholders in our corporation, which makes us all personally invested in our guests' satisfaction."

Troy gave a low whistle. "I'll say."

"It's one of those unique features Laura mentioned," Tyler added. "When the management company that held the property went bankrupt a few years back, the inn's supervisors pooled their resources and leveraged a buyout. A very innovative move. This hotel is known for them."

"So we have the pleasure of dining with the owners," Miranda said, and something about her gaze suggested she was taking stock of Laura.

"Not all of them." Adam wasn't one to let details slide. "I'm new on board."

From his days on the property, Dale knew that Adam wouldn't be eligible to purchase company stock until his probationary period ended. Given the speculation about the guy's fit for the job, Dale couldn't help but wonder if the stockholders would vote him in. Or if Adam would still be as committed to bringing sanity to Falling Inn Bed when his probation period ended.

Dale also couldn't help but wonder what had gotten into Laura. She'd leaned forward onto the edge of her chair with a slight air of tension. He tightened his fingers on her thigh, a gesture of reassurance he wasn't sure why he felt the need to give.

"That certainly explains the level of service around here. Miranda and I were amazed during our wedding." Troy glanced at Jackson. "You and Delia will be well cared for."

"No complaints so far," Jackson replied. "Laura and her staff have taken care of details we'd never considered."

Delia nodded her agreement. "We're very pleased."

"And we love pleased guests." Annabelle shifted her gaze between her journalists. "Please take note, Tyler and Benjamin, and make sure all this customer satisfaction gets a mention in the press. We simply can't pass up this kind of golden opportunity to toot our horn."

"I'll find some inspired way to work it into my documentary," Tyler said.

"Speaking of..." Laura didn't miss a beat and zoomed right in on her chance to change the subject. "Tyler, why don't you tell us what you're planning? For those of you who might not be aware, the Worldwide Travel Association sponsors the annual Most Romantic Getaway contest."

"Tyler has sat on the judges' panel for the past three years. He'd been very instrumental in helping us win." Annabelle looked fondly at the man by her side and didn't seem to mind the piercings. "Winning that award factored into our decision to expand our services with the Wedding Wing. In a way, we all have him to thank for being together right now."

Applause rippled around the table, and Tyler stepped into the spotlight to detail why WTA had commissioned a documentary. "Laura's Wedding Wing and Naughty Nuptials campaign are groundbreakers in the hospitality industry. I'll record the trend and establish a standard for future generations of resorts looking to target the couples' market. WTA wants every hotel to live up to the upscale standards Falling Inn Bed has set."

"Here, here, Laura." Raising his glass, Dale toasted his date. "To being an innovator in your industry."

More applause followed. Laura smiled graciously, and Dale dragged his gaze away with a reluctance that almost made him laugh. His fixation with her had been bad when sex hadn't been a possibility. Anticipation made him downright dangerous now.

Dinner arrived, and Laura, Annabelle and Adam skillfully kept the conversation flowing while everyone ate. The meal progressed harmoniously, but too damn slowly for Dale's taste. Laura could only express a cursory interest in him, and as much as he would have enjoyed Bruno's apple cobbler at any other time, the dessert cart's appearance now only meant more of a delay in getting her back to their suite where he could claim her undivided attention.

This impatience wasn't something he'd dealt with before. Then again, Dale had never waited so long for *any* woman. He needed a distraction and this never-ending meal wasn't it.

He kicked off his shoe.

The exact moment he made contact was reflected in Laura's eyes, and he dragged his toes around her anklebone, lingered up the sweep of her calf.

"Tyler wants to capture how romance drives everything around here," Laura was saying. "Our atmosphere, our services, even our dining experience. Bruno runs an entire specialty menu seasoned with natural aphrodisiacs that has become very popular with our guests."

Aphrodisiacs, hmm? Dale didn't need any help enhancing his desire. If he could just get Laura alone, she wouldn't either.

Working his way slowly upward, he wondered just how far he could inch up her leg before he wound up kneeing the lieutenant commander. But he hadn't made it far when...

"Oh, excuse me," Laura said. "I dropped my napkin."

Leaning over before he got the chance, she scooped up the napkin and draped it over her lap. She performed the move one-handed because her other hand hadn't re-emerged above the table. Dale didn't get to wonder where it had gone before her fingers molded his groin and gave a solid squeeze.

Looked like two could play this game.

5

"ENJOY YOUR EVENING," Laura said as her guests departed the elevator on the Wedding Wing's third floor.

Delia waved before the doors hissed shut again.

Off duty. *Finally.*

With the preliminary meetings behind her, she savored a feeling of mingled relief and pleasure that they'd successfully established the tone for the upcoming events. While the future Mr. and Mrs. Jackson Marsh had been a guaranteed pleasure to deal with, Miranda and her husband had been a question mark.

They were off to a decent start. She'd handled the Knights professionally and laid the groundwork for the weeks ahead. Troy might not have understood the significance of this welcome dinner but Miranda had. No doubt.

Falling Inn Bed was *not* Westfalls Academy. Nor was Laura still the odd one out in a preparatory school filled with overprivileged girls who didn't bat an eyelash when tossing around comments meant to hurt.

"Laura Granger is a strange ranger."

Once upon a time that remark would have hit the bull's-eye. Not because the words were so horrible but because the sentiment behind them had cut to the quick.

Laura Granger isn't good enough.

Granted, as bedding consultant and stockholder of Falling Inn Properties, Incorporated, she still didn't live a run-of-the-mill life by anyone's standards, but she'd made the choices that suited her. Miranda's arrival could have reacquainted her with hurtful feelings from the past, but, instead, her appearance had steeled Laura's commitment not to let the past shadow her grand opening.

This strange ranger had grown up strong as a result of her upbringing and was content with the paths she'd taken. She wasn't worried about what people thought about her anymore. Except for one yummy person, who'd given her a chance to prove she did indeed possess a few bold genes.

That same person shook Laura from her thoughts when he brought the elevator to a sudden stop between the fourth and fifth floors. Glancing up, she found Dale purposely pressing the emergency stop button.

"What are you—"

"You look way too serious." Wielding his body like a weapon, he crowded her into the corner and braced a hand above her head. "Dinner's over and the night's finally ours, Laura. You're supposed to be excited."

"I am excited."

"You don't look excited."

The heat radiating off him blasted right through her dress, but it was the expression on his handsome face that ignited her nerve endings. All hard lines, dark shadows and lusty promise, his expression smoldered from the fire in his eyes to his inviting grin.

"That's because I wasn't thinking about you." She shot him a sassy smile, refusing to let thoughts of Miranda interfere with the night ahead. Not when Dale gazed at her as if he wanted to eat her. "Start the elevator—"

"Not until I have your undivided attention."

"You have it."

He arched a brow, questioned her with that intense gaze.

"I was just thinking about dinner tonight," she explained. "But I'm through. Promise."

"Good." He leaned in just enough to surround her, his broad shoulders crowding out everything but the sight of him. He filled her world with the promise of the night ahead, of finally indulging their attraction.

Slipping her arms around his waist, she tipped her face upward for a taste of his lightly stubbled jaw. "We should get back to our room."

Apparently her bold genes had only needed this man and her permission to fire up.

"Now that I've got you, Laura, I don't want to let you go. Dinner was torture. All I wanted to do was touch you."

"You *did* touch me," she said. "I was trying to work and you were playing footsie under the table."

"I've been waiting a long time to play footsie with you. *Too* damn long."

He'd always been honest about his feelings. Up front. No games. She liked that about him.

"No more waiting." Pressing full-length against him, she trailed those kisses toward his mouth as a sexy offering. "I'm all yours."

Her temperature upped a few more degrees at the sight of his face at close range, the planes and angles skewed by the distance, suddenly sharper, harder. A deep breath helped manage the feeling and treated her to another intoxicating breath of him, a hint of musky fragrance and all man.

"Excuse me if I need a little proof. All I've done is wait for you. While we worked together. Tonight. You were making me crazy with that hand job under the table. Adam knew what you were doing. He kept frowning at you."

"He kept frowning at me because the S-word kept coming out of my mouth. He doesn't care to discuss sex over dinner. But, Dale, you started the whole under-the-table thing. I had to counter. You don't think I can handle you and I'm determined to prove you wrong."

"I want you to prove me wrong. I want it *bad*."

Thrilled at his words, she rubbed her hips against him, riding the promising bulge she'd acquainted herself with under the table tonight, a move inspired by his earlier words.

One down, seven to go.

She sighed. He caught the sound on his lips, driving his tongue inside. Laura melted against him, drawn to his body, to the way he fitted against her. Running her hands along his face, she learned the angles of his cheeks, the feel of his stubbled jaw, the curl of his ears. This was her chance to explore, to live out the desire she'd felt for so long, a desire so dangerously out of control that she'd steered off her careful course for the future and asked this man to have a fling.

Thumbing the line of his jaw, she whispered against his mouth, "Let's get to our suite."

He growled low before stepping away and reaching for the panel, and her heart pounded so hard in reply, she could barely hear the piped-in elevator music.

They lurched into motion again, and when the doors finally opened, Laura brushed past him, her card key in hand. She didn't say a word while hurrying down the hall toward their suite but she felt him behind her every step of the way.

The Castaway Honeymoon Isle. Dale couldn't know how often she'd fantasized about him, a different fantasy

for each new suite they'd constructed. But this was her favorite. The idea of being stranded on a desert island with
Dale Emerson had caught hold of her imagination.

And now just the thought of her and him alone, with
nothing between them except the promise of pleasure… No
work, no romantic ideals. Gone were all the reasons why
she shouldn't be attracted to him and only the truth that she
was. *Very* attracted.

Dale closed and locked the door behind them, and she
swept through the suite toward the lagoon, knowing exactly
which fantasy she wanted to satisfy first.

"First one in gets the first orgasm," she called over her
shoulder.

Bad was just an attitude, and she could have one, too.

While reaching for her zipper, she pushed through the
glass doors that separated the living room from the lagoon.
Moisture lay thick in the air, a combination of mist from
the waterfall and temperature-controlled pool/spa combo.

Dragging in a tight breath, she stepped out of her shoes
and made her way to the edge, listening to the bubbling
quiet beneath the splash of the waterfall, experiencing a
boldness that had everything to do with the man who
pushed his way through the doors behind her.

From the corner of her eye, she caught him tugging his
shoes off and smiled. Didn't matter how much this bad boy
had honed his undressing skills, she could slither out of this
dress in a heartbeat, long before he could deal with that tie
and all those shirt buttons.

Shrugging out of his jacket as he drew near, he surprised
her by dropping the jacket over her head. She brushed a
lapel out of her face with an indignant, "Hey! What are
you—" then broke off when she heard a splash.

Sweeping the jacket away, Laura stared at the dark blur streaking through the water. He surfaced at the opposite end of the pool, still fully clothed, water exploding as he burst from the surface and turned to face her.

Shoving his hair out of his face, he looked supremely satisfied, and she let her gaze drift over him, sitting on the underwater ledge running the rim of the pool, elbows braced against the outer edge, wearing a lot of dripping fabric and a very bold smile.

"I don't believe you did that," she said.

"I'm ready for that orgasm."

She could hear the laughter in his voice and held up his jacket. "You ruined your suit."

"I've got others." He shrugged. "But I win, so now you'll have to undress me before you can give me my prize."

He let his legs drift out before him, buoyant, all that dark wet fabric taunting her with another challenge. This bad boy might have outmaneuvered her, but no matter who got the next orgasm, they were both winners in her book.

But Dale wasn't the only one who could issue challenges.

"You'll have to watch me undress before I'll get in that water, Dale. I happen to like this dress."

"I like it, too."

Laura could feel his eyes on her, a glance that seemed to see through the blue crochet and silk lining to the bare skin below. A glance that filled her head with the memory of how she'd looked in the closet mirror with his hands on her.

"Take good care of that dress, Laura. Did you know the lace catches the light when you walk?"

"No, I didn't."

"It shimmers over your curves like a waterfall. The lace hugs your bottom and makes a shadow where your thighs meet. I kept walking behind you so I could look. I wanted to touch that spot and feel if you were warm. Were you hot for me tonight?"

The simple act of inhaling suddenly required effort. "I'm definitely hot now."

His laughter resounded over the rushing water. "Will you wear that dress for me again so I can slide that lace up your thighs and feel for myself?"

Denying this man anything at the moment was beyond her and Laura thrilled to the husky sound of his voice, the potency of his intimate promises. "My pleasure."

"It will be."

No doubt.

But she wasn't above showing him that he wasn't the only one who could dish it out here with that sexy voice and his seductive remarks. She might not be as experienced at flings, but she'd devoted a lot of energy to fantasizing about him. And now that she had his undivided attention…

Turning, she gave him her back, so he could see that shadowy, shimmery place between her thighs to best advantage. Closing her eyes, she focused on the sound of the waterfall breaking the surface of the pool, refused to let nerves or shyness dull her excitement of the moment. She had the floor, and here was the perfect opportunity to prove beyond all doubt that even a romantic idealist could break free of ideals for a while to engage in hot, steamy sex for sex's sake.

She wasn't looking for candlelight and roses. She wanted a good time. This man had nothing to worry about except how to get those wet pants off with an erection that would be bigger than any he'd ever had before.

That thought made her smile and Laura hoped Mr. An-Orgasm-Is-Worth-a-Thousand-Suits was ready to find out just how far she could take him.

Flipping her braid over her shoulder, she let it dangle between her breasts while dragging that zipper lower and lower. The back of her dress parted, and she eased the sleeves from her shoulders with a few provocative rolls. Too far away to hear if his breathing quickened, she did sense his gaze on her, wondered if his smile widened as she eased the shimmery fabric down, down, down....

Stepping out of the dress, she draped it over the custom-designed condom dispenser on the wall. Every themed suite at Falling Inn Bed had similar dispensers strategically located for the guests' convenience. A resort that promoted romance also promoted safe sex and made the essentials easily available.

Then Laura bent over to treat Dale to a shot of that place between her thighs he seemed so enamored of.

"I'm definitely hot." The words came out sounding sultry and inviting, a stranger's voice.

"You are hot, Laura. So, *so* hot."

His appreciation transformed her nothing-special bra and hose into props fit for a striptease. She wanted this man more aroused than he'd ever been, to prove she'd been worth the wait and reassure her she'd made the right choice taking a side trip off the respectable road down this sexy alley.

She didn't have nifty tricks in her repertoire like Dale did—unfastening her bra with his teeth. But she could move to entice. Her mom hadn't forced her to attend Westfalls for no reason. Learning French and dance had only been two of them.

Starting up a provocative motion, she moved her hips to the rhythm of the waterfall, rolled her shoulders to the same beat. Peeling the bra straps down her arms became a ballet of simple motion, each move an erotic enticement meant to lure his gaze to the path they traveled along her skin, to invite him to imagine what he'd see if only she'd turn around.

But not yet....

The moisture-swollen air caressed her breasts as she released the cups. She sprang free with a heaviness that proved she didn't need Dale close to become aroused. Just imagining the hungry expression on his face, the hardness of that erection she'd handled so boldly through his pants during dinner, made her whole body want.

The hose went the same way as her bra, only with a stretching of muscles as she bent to strip away the clingy silk. Inch by inch she revealed her legs, her bottom high in the air, swaying steadily, revealing intimate places she didn't think he could see from this distance but hoped he was imagining. She hoped all that wet fabric wasn't restricting that special body part she so wanted to impress.

After pulling the hose away, she stood naked, silently thanking her mom for excellent muscle tone and her dad for his obsession with physical endurance. While she wasn't exactly shy, she'd never been so bold before. Then again, she'd never had so much incentive before.

And now for the pièce de résistance...

She never stopped swaying to the sound of the waterfall when she caught the tail of her braid and tugged the band off. With nimble movements, she unwound the strands with a practice honed by years of dealing with her straight hair. Her dad used to joke that she had enough to share with her friends. Back then she didn't have many friends to share with but now she was glad for each and every strand.

Shaking the braid out, she let her hair fall around her like a shield, covering her back almost to her waist. Some slithered around her shoulders to play peeka boo with her breasts and the feel of those heavy strands grazing her nipples sent waves of heat curling through her.

Was she hot for Dale? *Big-time.*

And she hoped the sight of her hair down was as good as he'd imagined. She couldn't see his expression or gauge if his chest rose and fell on hard breaths. She had only the sight of his face in her memory and the remembered sound of that hungry growl that warned he couldn't resist touching.

When the tension became too much, she circled around, letting him drink his fill of her body as she drank in the sight of his starved expression. His gaze cut the distance between them, flaring with an intensity that she could see not only in his face but gathering his body as if it was taking a supreme effort of will not to slice through the water toward her.

For a moment she thought he might launch into motion, but instead he simply said, "Come over here, Laura."

Strolling around the pool became an exercise in *bad* that Laura hadn't expected. While her hair covered a good bit, she could feel every inch of her swaying breasts and bare legs. She felt the lure of the water, the urge to conceal herself from the power of his gaze, to put herself on comfortable ground again.

But Laura didn't want comfortable. She'd lusted after this man for too long, and there'd been nothing comfortable about discovering her desire had controlled her rather than the other way around. There'd been nothing comfortable about being desperate enough to have a fling with a man who was too charming to trust with even the tiniest piece of her heart.

Sex with Dale meant a chance to satisfy a desire bigger than she was and each measured step brought her closer to fulfillment, to the excitement of what would happen next. They owned the night. Until the sun rose through these glass walls and painted their tropical paradise in dawn.

Anticipation made her forget to breathe. His hair a dark slash against his wet face, his soaked shirt and tie incongruous as he angled around to follow her progress.

She drew near and suddenly towered above him, feeling the power of her nudity with all that moist air clinging to her skin. He glanced up her legs, a look as potent as a caress.

She'd always felt too tall, too thin, too pale, a wispy presence people could see through unless they looked hard. But Dale's face filled with an appreciation that made a lie out of her self-image. He looked at her as if she was the most beautiful woman alive and he was the luckiest man to be with her.

Laura reminded herself that this was a sexy trick. What experienced man wouldn't know how to make the woman he was with feel like the most beautiful in the world? She couldn't let herself confuse romantic fancy with fact. They had three weeks together. No more, no less. But it was so easy to forget when she gazed into those smoky eyes....

"Come here," he said, motioning her down beside hi

She sank to her knees beside the pool in slow mo and he tipped his head back to peer straight betw thighs, a look so hot she grew dizzy. She felt nak posed in a way she'd never been exposed before, but she didn't blush. His chest rose and fell sharply, proving she wasn't the only one affected. And when he sat up, stretched his hand outward...

He threaded his fingers through her hair with a focus that seemed wildly out of sync with the moment. "You look like a goddess with all this hair."

His soft voice made her trembly and vulnerable. But she didn't want compliments. Or reassurances. *Bad* was an attitude that meant being comfortable with her sensuality, which meant feeling worthy of having a delicious man lust after her. The purely male smile on Dale's face was all the proof she needed.

"I'm glad you think so." She forced the words out, willed herself to sound casual, confident.

"Oh, I think so, all right." He slipped his hand between her thighs and the impact of his wet fingers against her most private places chased away all thoughts. "I knew you'd be hot."

He shot her a look of pure sex, and she braced back on her hands, arched her hips to press into his touch, another bold move that invited him to further exploration.

"Very hot," she agreed.

Caressing her with those wet fingers, he separated her skin enough to make her shiver. "Like that, hmm?"

She only nodded, her voice lost somewhere between her throat and her mouth. He replied with a gruff laugh then, in a move she never expected, he pushed her over.

She fell onto her backside and never got a chance to protest before he knelt on the ledge. He should have looked ridiculous with the water sluicing off him, the dripping tie ~ngling from his throat, but there was nothing ridiculous about this man, not his appearance or the purposeful way he wedged his shoulders between her knees and slid his hands underneath her.

Water splashed, trailing down her legs like ribbons of warm silk over her bare skin.

"I've got you where I want you." He pressed his fingers around her cheeks and lifted her off the pool deck toward him.

Just the sight of his dark face poised so purposefully stopped her heart in midbeat. She watched as he angled her bottom to his best advantage, then pressed his face toward her.

He lashed out with his tongue, an intimate stroke that began deep between her thighs and traveled out. Moist folds unfurled. Every nerve in her body gathered to savor the bursts of his warm breath, his stubbled jaw as it abraded her thighs.

Her heartbeat jump-started back into action as he delved deeper, hot curls of that silky tongue tasting and testing, tempting her to close her eyes and surrender.

Her lashes fluttered shut, and she blocked out one sense only to heighten the others. The lapping strokes of his tongue. The heat shooting through her, fierce, fast, urgent. Water dripped in silky runnels down her legs, and her thighs vibrated until Laura couldn't stop rocking her bottom against his face to increase the friction of his exquisite attention.

The intensity between them was startling and if she thought he'd fulfilled her fondest fantasies, she was wrong, wrong, wrong. Dale had so much more in store for her.

He cajoled that sensitive bundle of nerve endings out of its hiding place with sharp flicks of that devilish tongue, as though he had nothing better to do all night than kneel between her thighs and indulge her.

Her idea of proving herself vanished beneath his sexy assault. She could barely string two coherent thoughts together. How could she think with her thighs trembling and her sex clenching in slow, wet pulls? And when he sucked that oh-so sensitive bundle between his lips, swirled his tongue around it, Laura's whole body bucked on one rolling wave of pleasure.

A moan skittered out from between suddenly dry lips as her body arched on a wave of sensation. She had the wild thought that he'd claimed the right to first orgasm, but he couldn't possibly think she'd withstand this sort of assault. Not when he started suckling that sensitive bud, giving it an intermittent flick for good measure, sending pleasure bolting through her.

He knew exactly when to drag his mouth away and delve his tongue inside, to dig his fingers into her backside, to lift her to create the friction she needed. And when her orgasm broke, her moan carried out even over the splash of the waterfall.

And only when he trailed his mouth away to press tiny kisses along the inside of her thigh did she breathe again.

"I thought you wanted the first orgasm," she finally said, laying back on the floor, knees bent and spread, sex still clenching in fading bursts.

"Can't a guy change his mind?"

Her sex gave another spasm for good measure and she laughed. "Not a problem in my book."

After all, fair was fair.

6

LUST WAS AN APPETITE that shouldn't be deprived and given his hunger for Laura, Dale didn't think it was any damn surprise he'd gotten obsessed. This woman aroused him in ways he hadn't realized he could be aroused. When she'd started to strip, she'd had him sitting here with a hard-on as solid as a support beam, cursing his craziness for jumping in the pool.

He should have dragged her in with him. They could have had that first orgasm together.

Then again, he wouldn't have missed a second of exploring Laura's delicious body at his leisure. She responded to him as if she'd been created for that purpose, and he found himself content to sit between her thighs, watching her stomach contract whenever he pressed a kiss to her tempting skin. He was as turned on by her pleasure as the promise of his own.

He let his gaze roam the terrain of her beautiful body, all that sleek skin, the blush-colored nipples rising and falling on hard breaths. Her hair spread around her in a white-blond cloud and he smiled, his cheek pressed to her thigh, glad he'd asked her to release her hair from the braid, grateful she'd granted his request in such an inspired performance.

Laura had assured him she could handle a good time and was making a believer out of him. He didn't offer any romantic, idealistic vows of eternal love, just good old-fashioned sex, and she seemed to have embraced the idea. About time, too. He'd waited long enough.

But he wasn't complaining.

He nibbled his way under her knee, and she scrambled back trying to escape his mouth.

"Ticklish, hmm?"

"Yes." She breathed the word in a sound that made every muscle below his waist tighten painfully then rolled out of his reach and rose to her feet in a burst of liquid motion.

"I have a question," she said.

Dale dragged his gaze upward along her never-ending legs and by the time his gaze arrived at her face, he could barely get out the word, "Shoot."

"Define night. Your former dates claimed you could do amazing things. Were they talking about a real night or using night as a figure of speech?"

Dale usually didn't second-guess himself, but eight orgasms? Once he got past the fact that someone had been counting, he couldn't deny the figure sounded impressive.

"Nights with me aren't confined to the dark, Laura," he said in his best make-her-sigh-with-pleasure voice.

She exhaled a breathy little sound that was close enough to a sigh to satisfy him. "So if we're going to keep up with your press, you get one orgasm to every two of mine. That means I have to get busy."

"Be still my heart." The words popped out, leaving him wondering about his choice of words. He never mixed hearts and sex.

All the blood in his brain must have drained to his

crotch. Had to be. He almost couldn't believe it only had been this morning that he'd been on a flight from California, with a rebound beauty by his side while his thoughts had been stuck on this woman who'd wanted nothing to do with him.

Man, could life toss out the surprises, or what?

"Cold?" he asked when she poised one slim foot on the ledge beside him and he noticed the goose bumps spraying along her shapely calf. "I'll warm you up again."

She shook her head, sending that blanket of heavy hair shimmering around her. "My turn."

Dale laughed, spellbound at the sight of her as she stepped into the water. She didn't go under but dipped gracefully with her hair flowing around her.

They'd designed this pool together with sex in mind so while the actual square footage was impressive, the depth remained consistent at the perfect height for sexy water play. And testing the finished product gave Dale an appreciation of just how perfect.

Water lapped at Laura's breasts, broke below rosy nipples. She met his gaze, and her melting expression at such close range made him fight the urge to pull her into his arms.

"Time for those clothes to come off," she said.

Shifting off the ledge, he stood, intending to help, but Laura slipped her fingers around his tie and pulled him close.

"Allow me."

Dale wouldn't be rushing straight to that next orgasm. Oh, no. Not when Laura brushed her lips against his, an openmouthed effort that gave him a taste of what was coming. She began unwrapping him like a present, appearing to savor his body as thoroughly as he'd just savored hers.

One glancing kiss from those lush lips and she drew his

ruined tie away and tossed it onto the pool deck. Slim fingers worked each stubborn button patiently. Dale wasn't so patient. Bracing his legs wide, he captured her between his thighs.

This had been a fantasy of his for too long not to seize the moment. Ever since Halloween when Falling Inn Bed had hosted a masquerade for its guests and the staff members had costumed themselves as a cadre of superheroes, he'd been dreaming about what Laura kept hidden beneath her skirts. The micro shorts she'd worn that had hugged her bottom combined with her never-ending legs had captured his imagination.

At the time he'd thought she'd dressed purposely to torture him. Maybe that hadn't been her motive but the effect had been the same. Serious lust. Now he wasn't missing a chance to acquaint himself with those awesome legs in person.

Clearly great minds thought alike. Button by button she freed him from the clinging fabric, taking time to explore the skin she revealed along the way. Loosening his collar, she pressed soft kisses over his throat, the moist heat of her mouth making him struggle to stand still when the entire lower half wanted him to pull her close and tangle his legs around her.

The warm scent of woman assaulted his senses, an effect that he couldn't remember ever having been so potent before. Laura took her damn sweet time, torturing him with those feathery kisses, along his jaw, over his chin, down his neck.

"You taste so good." She dragged her tongue in the scoop between neck and shoulder, a stroke that made him ache.

Tightening his grip on the wall, he mentally cautioned himself to relax. He'd been waiting forever to get this woman in the buff and needed to kick back and enjoy every second of the experience.

Laura continued unbuttoning buttons, dropping those kisses onto his chest as she peeled his shirt away. If it was any consolation, she seemed as eager to make the most of the experience as he was. Her smile as she slid the sleeves down his arms was nothing short of wicked.

Dale wasn't consoled. He wanted to drag her underneath him, and she hadn't even gotten to his pants yet. Dropping his gaze, he distracted himself with the sight of her hair playing over her breasts and the water.

But looking only made him want to touch so, reaching out, he cupped the satin weight, thumbed her nipples. Touching only fueled his need even more.

Latching on to his belt, she unfastened his pants and began working them down his hips. Dale's muscles contracted with each glancing stroke of slim fingers against wet skin, and when she unleashed his aching erection, he had no choice but to let her go, to lean back on his hands to resist the urge to pull her against him.

She finally worked the soggy jumble down his legs and the waterlogged mess caught around his ankles. She didn't bother removing it, caught his erection with her wet fingers instead and gave a playful tug.

"Oh my, Dale. You do live up to your press."

He really didn't want to hear she'd been hearing *that* sort of information, so he forced out a casual, "Glad you're pleased." And hoped she dropped the subject.

"Very pleased." Easing her fingers down, she gave a stroke that made him buck hard, and he braced himself while those tempting fingers continued the exploration, slipped under his balls to cup him in her wet palm.

Gritting his teeth, he ordered himself to hang on. She shot him from zero to sixty in a touch, and he struggled…man, did he struggle. This pleasure neared torture. She rolled him in a teasing motion that sent shock waves to his toes. He'd waited so long that when he finally had Laura where he wanted her, he was too damn close to losing it.

Suddenly she went boneless and slid beneath the water. He gazed down at her, the woman he'd lusted after for so long with her hair floating out around her like a halo of silk.

And her face at crotch level.

Stopping that drive-me-crazy fondling, she went straight for the kill and sucked the head of his dick into her mouth with one hot swallow.

"Damn, Laura." He jerked so hard that his spine bounced off the pool's edge and hurt.

He didn't care. How could he care about anything when her wicked tongue twirled around him in teasing strokes, when she started up an easy sucking motion as if she wanted to swallow him whole?

Closing his eyes, he hung on as sensation blasted him. If she kept this up, she'd blow the top of his head off. Yet Dale knew that she couldn't go on forever and his reprieve finally came when she broke the surface to take a gasping breath.

He inhaled, too, willed himself back under control. But he didn't manage the job before she slid underwater and started up her sexy torture all over again.

He ground out a sound that echoed pathetically in the damp room, and threaded his hands into all that magnificent hair, unable to stop from riding the exquisite motion. He was losing it, and if this is what lusting after Laura did to him, he wasn't keen to experience the phenomenon ever again.

Awareness faded beneath the heat of need. He didn't know anything except those hot sucking pulls of her lush mouth and the warm-velvet strokes of her tongue. The desperately welcomed reprieves when she surfaced for a breath. His entire body ebbed and flowed with the motion, swelling, then receding, then crashing back again, even more intensely.

He was gone on the sensation, so gone that when the familiar onslaught of orgasm threatened to push him over the edge too early in the game, he speared his fingers into her hair and dragged her away.

Laura slithered upward in a shimmer of wet skin, soft curves and laughter. She didn't let go of his dick on her way up, and he groaned as she continued to fondle him.

Suddenly, she came up full against him, raising up on tiptoes so she could kiss the sound from his mouth. "Can you taste yourself on me?"

She dragged her tongue along his lower lip, and damn if he didn't taste himself mingled with the chlorinated water on her sweet lips.

Her hot words and another tug was all it took to send him into a climax that was totally beyond his control, and by the time he could think again, only one question mattered.

What the hell was going on here?

He *never* lost control. Not even when he'd been a kid maneuvering his way inside girls' pants in the back seat of his mint-condition Mustang. *Never*.

Gulping in another deep breath, he opened his eyes to find Laura watching him from beneath half-hooded eyes. Arousal blurred the edges of her expression. And judging by the smile playing at the corners of those pouty lips, she was proud of her performance. She had every right to be.

What was it about this woman?

"One down, three to go," she said, flashing him that killer smile. Then she turned, dived in and streaked away in a blur of pale skin that made his dick give an appreciative throb.

Live up to his press? Damn straight.

With a warning yell like a battle cry, he shot after her. And realized a second too late that his pants were still tangled around his ankles.

He smacked the water face-first and sank like a stone. After splashing his arms stupidly to regain his balance, he had no choice but to retreat to the side of the pool again, hike himself onto the ledge and free his feet from the sodden mess that had once been a decent suit.

It didn't help matters that Laura's silvery laughter bubbled out over the splash of water. One look and he found her poised on the submerged ledge beside the waterfall like a mermaid, knees drawn up beneath her chin and hair tumbling all around her body. Her laughter spurred him to greater speed. She'd made him lose control. She knew it, and she liked it.

He finally dragged the sodden vise away and tore after her at full-tilt, an unfamiliar urgency spurring him on, blocking out all thoughts except one—he wanted this woman beneath him.

He heard her laughter again and caught a glimpse of her slithering off the ledge into the water. He cut across the distance with clean strokes. There was only one place to hide in this pool, and he'd not only designed that place but built it.

He caught her beneath the waterfall. With the spray from the rock ledge pouring full into his face and nearly drowning him, he latched on to her arm and dragged her underwater. He heard her gasp for a breath before he had her in his arms, all her slithery curves tucked close.

The impact of their bodies fueled that urgency, a need to hang on tight and not let go. He wanted to savor the way her face fitted perfectly against his shoulder, the way her breasts molded his chest, the way her abdomen cradled his reawakening erection and her long, long legs twined smoothly through his.

She tried playfully to break free, but her best efforts failed because he stood half a foot taller and outweighed her by a hundred pounds. And Dale wasn't feeling playful right now. He had something to prove, and he was going to prove it all over her luscious body.

Gaining his feet, he brought her upright behind the falls. She broke from the surface laughing and he didn't give her a chance to stop before he captured her mouth, delving into the silken recesses, searching for a clue that her need burned as fiercely as his own.

He found his answer in how she melted against him, her tongue seeking his. Her thighs parted, her hips mirroring each thrust with an erotic motion that sent the blood throbbing through his veins. That urgency rose inside him, almost overwhelming. He threaded his hands around her neck, arched her head back to trail moist kisses down her throat. He couldn't stop touching her.

He glided his hands over her shoulders and down her back, over each silken inch that aroused some new reaction inside him, won another fiery response. She half sat on his thigh, riding him with languorous strokes, a motion that grazed hard-tipped nipples through his wet chest hair.

Their hips moved in time. His erection rode between them, their bodies creating a slick vise that caught him up in the feel of her, the taste of her. He couldn't look beyond the silk of her tangled hair, the sound of her breaths breaking against his lips, her heat riding his thigh with smooth strokes.

He tested her body's responses, needing to know what would spur her higher. Pressing his fingers into her sweet bottom, he anchored her higher along his thigh, tasted her low moan when he caught her pleasure point with the motion. He trailed his kisses from her lips, sampled the flavor of her wet skin, the texture of her cheek, her temple, her hairline. He traced her ear with his tongue, delving a little deeper until she shivered.

Caught up in the luxury of touching Laura, *finally*, his need to be inside her suddenly had him realigning her around his body. He slipped his hand between them, levered his erection along the folds of her sex. She never stopped that sinuous motion of her hips and each stroke dragged him a little deeper, tempted him with the feel of her heat until he arched his hips and pressed upward, helpless to do anything but thrust.

His breath constricted as her body stretched to accommodate him, molded around him tightly. He fought the urge to start up the rhythm that he craved, forced himself to stop, to wait, to relish each second of this sensation.

Then Laura grabbed at his back, her fingers digging into his skin almost painfully as she pushed herself down, a full-bodied motion that sank him in to the hilt. She locked her ankles around his waist and Dale cried out at the sheer power of her body working his, the need to make love to her as urgent as the need to breathe.

He braced his legs apart and gave a short driving thrust, then another, his whole body melting into hers with a pulsing completion he'd simply never felt before.

The intensity of the sensation proved too much. He took a few halting steps and levered back onto the ledge where Laura had sat like a mermaid. She scrambled to her knees above him, riding out a stroke as she did.

He groaned aloud, stunned by the sound coming from his mouth, stunned by their bodies together. He caught her breasts, molded his fingers around her firm softness, an anchor.

Laura's slim body bent back. Her wet hair streamed down her back. She presented a vision as lovely as he'd always imagined, and he thrust into her again, watched her sway erotically with the collision. He wanted to take her apart like he had at the edge of the pool. He wanted to prove he still had control, that this overwhelming sex was totally normal, natural.

But his body betrayed him.

He couldn't pace himself, couldn't focus on anything but the feel of her heat contracting around him, clenching, working him like she'd worked him with her sweet mouth.

He could do no more than slide his hands down her waist, around her hips and hang on. They found a pace that made her gasp on each upstroke, and she bent toward him, bracing her hands on his shoulders, riding him with a look of pure pleasure. Her moist heat spasmed around him and her body tightened on a crescendo, such an awesome sight that she stole away his control again, pushed him so far beyond his normal discipline that he barely recognized what was happening.

"Damn, Laura. *Damn.*"

The words registered on some level, but Dale couldn't comprehend that the broken plea had burst from his lips. Not when his body exploded in sensation, a rushing climax that

wrested reason so far from his grasp that all he could do was
go for the ride. He drove into her again and again, unable
to think beyond the need to keep pushing inside her, though
his strength depleted and the effort became monumental.

And still he couldn't stop.

Laura collapsed, draping him in warm skin and muscle,
and Dale could only inhale her scent, savor her pounding
heartbeats and be grateful that she'd been similarly affected. He held her close and kissed her mouth to reassure
her, and himself, that this chemistry made sense for how
long they'd denied it.

"Ohmigosh," she breathed the word out on lingering syl-
lables. "You designed this ledge to have sex on, didn't you?"

Some numbed part of his brain remembered the three-
day argument they'd had about continuing the ledge *beside*
the waterfall rather than *beneath* the waterfall where she'd
wanted it, but he couldn't seem to reply.

He was totally wasted. *Totally.*

But she wasn't moving on from this line of questioning.
"You told me you wanted this seat here so couples could
sit together and enjoy the spray from the falls. Were you
really thinking about making a place to have sex?"

He shook his head, too far gone for anything but honesty.

She searched his face with those baby blues. "Why
didn't you tell me? I'd have given in a lot sooner. I'm all
for anything that promotes togetherness."

"I didn't want you to know I was thinking about sex. I
was still raw from when you blew me off."

"I didn't think it would faze you."

"Yeah, well, I'm not used to being turned down." And
he wasn't used to feeling bugged that she'd thought it
wouldn't faze him, either.

"I'm sorry." She pressed an openmouthed kiss to his ear. "It wasn't that I didn't want you. I was just looking for something different in a relationship."

Yeah, he'd gotten that part loud and clear. She hadn't wanted a *bad boy*.

But if he really was the love 'em and leave 'em type would this one beautiful woman have the power to make him lose control?

7

WITH A FEELING of unusual serenity, a sense that everything in his world was perfectly right, Dale sat back on the bed with Laura sandwiched between his legs. They were naked and he could catch glimpses of all her fair skin whenever he dragged the brush through her hair.

Such a small task, yet one that brought him pleasure. He took pride in his work for ADF, had enjoyed a full sex life, but performing this small task, earning each pleasured sigh from Laura, contented him on a soul-deep level that humbled him.

He dragged the brush through her hair again and the heavy strands trailed along her shoulders, down her back, over his thighs. Each stroke separated the cool silk strands, sent them pouring through his fingers and over his erection, teasing him to life with wispy caresses. Each brush-stroke a unique assault on his senses.

"You've got guests coming in tomorrow and a full day of events scheduled," he said when she yawned. "We should probably get some sleep. It's late."

Laura tilted her head so she could stare into his face. "We can't go to sleep yet. You've only come three times."

"Orgasms with you are the concentrated kind." He liked that she was thinking about his pleasure. "Another one to-night and I won't be able to walk tomorrow."

She sank back against him, her warm body fitted neatly against his. He rested his chin on the top of her head, tucked himself around her like a spoon, so he could sandwich his erection against her bottom.

Only touching Laura seemed to calm the unsettling urgency that had hounded him since they'd met, and he'd be happy to sit here and hold her forever. Something about that should bother him, but he felt too content to figure out what.

"Y'know, Dale, I like the idea of you lounging around this suite waiting for me to pop in for a climax whenever I can get away from work."

"Sounds like you want a sex slave."

She smiled playfully. "I do. It would give me a lot to look forward to."

"Me, too." Dale meant it. Just the thought of hanging out in this island suite, waiting for the lock to click and the door to open made him press a kiss to Laura's head and smile.

He'd like nothing better than to spend the rest of his life as lovely Laura's sex slave.

Dale jolted awake to the image of his face plastered with a mindless grin. His heart thudded. His throat constricted. His breath burned as if his chest would explode.

I'll do anything to please Laura.

He blinked to break from the aftereffects of the too realistic dream and stared into the starlit bedroom. Only a silvery shimmer from the skylights over the lagoon penetrated the wall of glass, and the waterfall splashed, the bubbling muted by the closed doors.

Inhaling deeply, he wiped his brow and found himself bathed in sweat. He glanced down at Laura, who'd rolled away sometime during the night. Only her feet still tangled around his, a point of contact though the rest of her had gotten away. Her chest rose and fell deeply, and he knew he wasn't disturbing her dreams the way she'd disturbed his.

Had one night of sex cured her obsession?

The question unsettled him more, and he wasn't sure why. He'd gotten exactly what he'd wanted tonight—sex so hot his ears were still steaming. So why had he awakened with his throat clamped tight like he was suffocating?

The thought that Laura had done something to him flickered through his brain. She spread out before him, a fantasy vision in the starlit darkness, her hair gleaming like silver.

He'd been dreaming of that hair.

And then it hit him. She had done something to him tonight. She'd made him lose control. Not once, but twice, and only after he'd gotten her into this bed and between these sheets had he been able to put aside his own needs in favor of hers. He didn't know how many times he'd pleasured her.

But she would. She was keeping count.

He'd never cared about impressing a woman, or living up to his reputation. Of course he'd never realized he'd had this kind of press. Sure, women talked…when he'd needed a date for this grand opening a call to an ex-lover had served up Monique.

But Dale didn't remember ever caring about what any woman thought about his performance in bed. He'd always been casual about dating. He knew how to satisfy a woman and on the rare occasion a date didn't work out…well, that was life.

Things couldn't always go his way, and he'd be a fool to expect them to. Like with Monique today—it hadn't worked out so he did his best to make a graceful exit. It happened.

Gazing down at the exquisite woman beside him, Dale wasn't sorry, either. Unhappy he'd inconvenienced Monique, yes, but not sorry to be spending the next three weeks with Laura.

The need to curl back around her hit him hard and to his amazement, he didn't want to kiss her awake. Rather, he wanted the warm, solid feel of her to chase away this unsettled feeling that still lingered from a fading dream. He wanted comfort in her arms and instinctively knew he'd find it.

What the hell was wrong with him?

"STILL OPEN IN HERE, Clyde?" Dale asked from the doorway of the bar. "It's got to be past the end of your shift."

Despite the low lighting, the bartender's smile looked like a spotlight. Or maybe it was simply because a smile seemed welcoming right now.

That's why Dale had slipped out of bed at three o'clock in the morning and left Laura sleeping peacefully. He'd gotten to know Clyde during his stint at Falling Inn Bed and knew the retired businessman had become head bartender because "idleness was a shortcut to an early grave and he'd played enough golf during his working years to last a lifetime."

He knew Clyde would offer some simple male companionship that would help soothe his racing thoughts, help him make sense of what was going on in his head.

"You can sit here till the sun comes up, Dale," Clyde said. "You've earned the privilege around here."

"As long as I'm not keeping you from going home."

"Don't worry about me. Since my Alice passed, I keep my own time and don't worry anyone with my comings and goings."

"I owe you, then."

"Clyde likes taking care of the powers-that-be around here. As the house architect, you qualify."

Dale recognized the voice and glanced down the bar to find Tyler of the multipiercings proving he was another of the sleepless crowd.

"You all right, man?" he asked, frowning. "You look like you've seen a ghost."

"No ghosts. No sleep, either," Dale admitted.

"Then you've come to the right place."

"Sit down and have a beer, Dale," Clyde said.

He slid onto a bar stool and waited patiently while Clyde washed his hands. This gentleman bartender might be among the fellow sleepless and a welcome beacon for lost ships in the night, but at well over seventy, he was moving against the tide.

"Here you go." Clyde finally placed a frothy glass in front of him, and it only took one sip to realize that alcohol wasn't going to dull the edge of his mood.

What had Laura done to him?

He looked into the bottom of his glass for an answer, but Clyde had neglected to pour one along with the beer. He turned to Tyler and asked, "So what's happening? Is Clyde giving you a story?"

Tyler shook his head. "I already got his story when I came to judge the first most romantic getaway contest. He's been catching me up on all the news."

"And Tyler here has been telling me about the stories he's been covering lately," Clyde added. "He had to choose between visiting us or covering an Alaskan nudist colony. Last place in the world you'd expect to find one of those, eh, Dale?"

Dale gave a noncommittal shrug. "At least you won't freeze off any body parts at Falling Inn Bed. Unless someone's added a refrigerator suite I'm not aware of."

"So what about you?" Tyler asked. "Late-night building inspection?"

"That would be better than staring at the bedroom ceiling, waxing philosophic about love."

"I say again—you've come to the right place."

"No doubt," Clyde agreed. "And Dale knows it as he built a chunk of this place himself."

Dale had known, but Falling Inn Bed hadn't been the first time he'd worked on a project focused on sex. The Risqué Theatre in Savannah had fit that bill, too, and he hadn't ended up tied up in knots while he obsessed over a woman, *dreamed* about one.

Had it been all the conversations about sex with Laura that had worn him down?

"This place is contagious," he said. "You want to get in and out fast, otherwise you might catch it, too."

Tyler looked curious. "Catch what?"

"Romance on the brain. I've been here so long I caught it."

Clyde laughed, but Tyler grabbed his beer and moved to a bar stool within spitting distance. "Romance on the brain. That's a good way to phrase it. Mind if I steal it for my documentary?"

He shook his head.

"Romance on the brain. That's what I like about this place," Clyde said. "I'm reminded of my Alice."

Here was another perspective on romance Dale didn't have a bead on. Nothing in his own long and illustrious dating history had ever given him a frame of reference for

Clyde's loss. His nomad career precluded being in any one place long enough to conduct long-term relationships even if he'd wanted to, which he hadn't. Ever. While Clyde working as a bartender to get away from memories of his late wife made sense, holing up at this inn to be reminded of her didn't.

"Doesn't being at home remind you of Alice?" he asked.

"Sure it does, but home reminds me that she's not there anymore. While this place…" He swept a hand around in a gesture that encompassed the grand old hotel. "This place makes me remember the special things we shared. We celebrate love here at Falling Inn Bed."

Okay, Dale got this part.

"That's poetic. Tyler, maybe you should phrase it that way in your documentary," he suggested.

"That's the plan."

Clyde brought a tray of glassware to their side of the bar so he could polish glasses while he talked. "Tyler's an old hand at letting folks know that what we do around here is special."

"I am indeed, and I hope you don't mind me saying that you're in for a ride if you've already had your fill of romance, Dale. The events haven't even started yet and as the bedding consultant's escort, you'll have a backstage pass."

Dale swung a tired glance his way. "Yeah."

"Not to mention the accolades. You'll be hailed as an architectural genius. I've seen my share of properties up close and agree what you've done here is extraordinary."

"Thanks." Dale eyed Tyler curiously. "So what sort of stuff goes into an industry documentary about a romance resort?"

His conversations with Laura replayed in his head, and

he had no trouble imagining a service film about the pros and cons of placing theme-decorated condom dispensers in guest suites. He wondered how many documentaries wound up with a mature audiences' rating.

"The usual," Tyler said. "Service objective. Staff and guest perspectives. An in-depth look at how this inn manages to pull off sex and stay upscale about it."

"How Falling Inn Bed, and Breakfast celebrates love." Clyde shot them a white-toothed grin.

Tyler nodded. "That's basically it. Your prepackaged holidays and singles resorts are a dime a dozen. This place isn't about pickups, it's about *romance*. There's nothing comparable anywhere, which is why this inn keeps winning the Most Romantic Getaway award. They come at sex from the romance angle, and romance is a tough sell. My focus will be on how they've grown a niche into a market. I'll explain the secret of their success."

"I thought the secret of their success was Laura. How are you planning to feature her?" He wouldn't mind insight into the woman who was confusing the hell out of him right now.

"Laura Granger, bedding consultant extraordinare." Clyde raised a glass in salute. "That girl's a pioneer."

Dale recalled the striptease she'd done for him beside Lovers' Lagoon tonight. Laura was *something*, all right. The first woman who'd ever managed to turn his brain inside out.

Tyler clapped him on the back and said, "If you're worried about how you'll factor in, Dale, don't be. Got you covered. As the house architect, you don't really require much explanation. All I'm interested in is your read on what it was like to create a place geared toward romance. I want to hear about all those conversations about sex that Jackson mentioned tonight."

"There were a lot of them," he said dryly.

Clyde hooted with laughter, but Tyler smiled. "FYI, the G.M. made sure she has final approval over the finished product."

"You know Ms. J. will keep him on the up and up," Clyde assured him, and Dale agreed.

Mary Johnson, known among her staff as Ms. J., ran a tight ship—another woman who, like Annabelle, hadn't struck him as the type to be affiliated with a romance resort under normal circumstances. But nothing around this place was normal.

"What makes someone so obsessed with romance?" He tossed out the question, just desperate enough to want anyone's spin.

"You talking about Ms. J.?" Clyde asked.

Tyler didn't give Dale a chance to answer. He gazed knowingly over the rim of his glass. "I'm betting he's talking about our Laura."

Dale shrugged, didn't think that was much of a stretch. Not after watching Monique's scene in the lobby earlier.

Setting his glass on the bar, Tyler faced him with a knowing expression that for some reason bugged Dale. "Laura Granger is obsessed with romance. You've got special events coordinators and wedding consultants all over this industry. You've only got one *bedding* consultant. She always struck me as *Cinderella* meets *Sex and the City*."

Dale nodded. "A romantic idealist."

"Yeah, that sums her up to a *T*."

"How is any one man supposed to blast through all that idealistic crap? Why would one even want to?"

"Now there's the real question," Clyde said. "My Alice gave me a run for my money way back when. Thought I was crazy to chase after her, but I tell you, gents. You go with your gut on this. Love slaps you upside the head when you least expect it. Some folks analyze it. Some folks run in the other direction. Me, I had enough sense to know to stay put." He smiled fondly. "I did what it took to catch my woman, and I'm grateful for each and every day we had together."

Maybe it was the lateness of the night, or the dim quiet of the empty bar. Dale didn't know, but the obvious truth in Clyde's statement filtered through the air like a tangible thing. Tyler drank his beer in silence, while Dale stared at the reminiscent smile on the old man's face, witnessing an appreciation in his withered expression that was nothing short of humbling.

Love slaps you upside the head when you least expect it. No, it couldn't be…could it?

LAURA COULD BARELY force open her eyes when the wake-up call arrived via an annoying blare from the phone. Lunging for the receiver, she managed to knock it from the cradle and made even more of a racket to replace it. And just as she fell back onto the pillow, a morning-gruff grunt sent the where, what, when and with whom crashing through her semiconsciousness.

Castaway Honeymoon Isle. Scrumptious sex. All night long. Hunky Dale Emerson.

Mmm-mmm. Every achy muscle brought the feel of his mouth and hands exploring her body back to vivid life, the abandon she'd experienced with him. The *orgasms*.

Dale's former dates hadn't been kidding. This man knew his way around a bedroom, or a lagoon as it was. And even in this drowsy stupor, Laura couldn't deny that she had it much worse for Dale than she'd ever realized. One night had proven that beyond any doubt and thank goodness this whole fling thing had worked out. If it hadn't, she'd have probably made a cross-country trip to see the man, and that situation would have been loaded. She needed work to distract her from thinking about romance.

She had three weeks to satisfy her desire for Mr. Wrong. Three weeks to get over her obsession, starting…now.

Rolling over, Laura slipped her arm around Dale's waist and molded herself around him like a spoon, all his hard places to her soft ones. Her breasts melted into the curve of his back, her lap folded neatly around his bottom, her thighs outlined his to the knee. She could even hook her toes around his ankle, and she couldn't help but smile at the way they came together, two bodies sculpted to fit perfectly.

Resting her cheek against his warm shoulder, she pressed her lips to his skin. "Good morning."

A hint of chlorine still lingered, bringing back visions of their escapades in Lovers' Lagoon. A shimmer of delicate heat awoke inside with the memory. But overpowering the chlorine was the scent of his morning skin, more potent, more…*male*.

Inhaling deeply, she traced the curve of his shoulder with her mouth, tasted skin and the drowsy closeness that was all warm muscle and promise. Dale made another grunt that broke the stillness, not quite a coherent reply, but the only sound other than the muted splash of the falls.

Tonight she'd remember to open the doors so they could fall asleep to the sound of bubbling water, the fantasy that they were two people alone in the world with no purpose more pressing than to enjoy each other.

Tonight. Just the thought of another night with this man sent a wave of heat through her, only stronger this time, insistent. Her body awakened slowly and with it a need that had grown remarkably stronger for having been indulged.

And she had been indulged. Dale had gone wild after they'd made love beside the falls. He'd carried her out of the lagoon and attentively dried every inch of her with warm towels.

And given her yet another orgasm.

Once upon a time, he'd argued that the towel warmer was an extravagance that, like the themed condom dispensers, had challenged him to find ways to build modern devices into stylized designs. But after Laura had returned the favor on his wet body, she knew he'd been glad he'd made the effort.

And that he'd agreed to be her date, too.

Trailing her fingers down his tight stomach, she aimed for his still-sleepy morning erection and waited for life signs.

"You feel good," he said thickly, shifting his buns back to nestle closer.

"I can feel even better." She gave a leisurely stroke, felt him pulse beneath her fingers. Heat pooled low in her belly and an answering throb awakened deep inside her.

She stroked again.

Dale shivered this time, a full-bodied tremor that hinted at the impressive conditioning of a man who lived an active life. A man who could chase her across a lagoon without breathing hard. A man who could scoop her into his arms as if she weighed next-to-nothing and carry her wherever he wanted.

"Another tally for the score sheet?" he asked.

"Technically, we're ahead of schedule. You said a night with you doesn't necessarily mean the dark."

"You've really analyzed this."

She didn't answer, didn't feel like talking at all. She only wanted to savor the sleepy moment and pressed tiny kisses along his shoulder as a distraction. He surprised her by slipping his hand over hers, assisting in that slow, steady stroking that seemed a very nice way to start the day.

Laura enjoyed the intimacy of awakening together, a warm camaraderie as they worked together to bring him pleasure. She liked that about Dale. He was so easy about sex, as if it was just a perfectly natural part of life to be relished, as natural as eating or sleeping.

Some of the architects she'd interviewed in the planning stages of the Wedding Wing project had been thrown by all the talk about how sex would factor into the new addition. Some were men's men who thought talking sex with her meant preening their feathers to impress her. Others had gotten tongue-tied. One had even blushed so hard that he'd made her blush, too. All had been scratched off her list, and the situation hadn't looked good.

Her co-workers on the board of Falling Inn Properties had been wagering their futures on this expansion. They were counting on her to launch the Wedding Wing so new business brought in revenue that remained steady on-season and off. After all, couples didn't only get married during the gorgeous summer months in western New York, and the inn wanted that business, too. Whoever built the new addition had to understand the unique function this addition would serve.

Dale Emerson had been that man, even though his company had no track record with construction and their bid hadn't been low. But Laura had known by talking with him that he was the right man for the job. She hadn't doubted her decision once.

"I'm going to come," he warned gruffly.

"I was hoping you would." She continued stroking, riding his bottom and teasing herself into a frenzied awareness with a growing friction that was just shy of satisfying her ache.

"I've got some work to do catching up," he said. "How many times did you come last night?"

Laura forced her thoughts from that exasperating ache between her thighs to the events of the previous night. In front of the mirror. Beside the lagoon. In the lagoon. Beside the lagoon again. How many times in bed?

"I've lost count," she admitted.

But before the glow of warm satisfaction at having had enough orgasms to obliterate memory dimmed, Dale's hand caught hers. In a sudden move, he pulled her fingers away, and with a burst of fluid motion that startled the sleepy moment, he straddled her, rising in a breathtaking display of lean male.

"You lost count, Laura?" he demanded, trapping her against the mattress and staring down with a roguish look that managed to challenge her despite the wrinkled impressions of the pillow on his cheek and the black hair that stood on end.

"Are you saying that every orgasm wasn't a totally memorable experience?"

He looked so offended that Laura couldn't help but laugh. "I'm saying they were so memorable I'm brain-dead. Last night is just one big blur of pleasure."

With both hands propped on either side of her head, he braced himself above her, careful to support his weight while he filled her vision with broad shoulders, muscled chest and a very sardonic expression.

"Brain-dead, hmm? Do you want to make love to me now?"

She nodded.

"So you want me to touch you? Like this…" Listing slightly, he balanced on one hand while the other slithered down to cup her breast. "And like this." He tweaked her nipple and she shivered. "Do you like how that feels?"

Couldn't he see the flush suddenly searing her skin?

She nodded again.

He continued to lazily fondle her breast while kneeing his way between her legs. She thrilled at the feel of lightly furred muscle grazing her sensitive skin, at the touch of his hot, hard erection when he turned his attention away from her breast to take himself in hand.

"Do you want to be under me this time, Laura?" He repositioned himself until he could work the head of his newly awakened erection along her intimate places, easing himself in just enough to make her gasp. "Do you want me inside you?"

"I do."

"Your brain seems to be working fine to me." He smiled that devastating grin and drove in another forceful inch. "Which means I just have to be more memorable."

Laura's whole body melted, whether from his awesome smile or the feel of that thick erection pressing inside, she couldn't say. She only knew that she wanted more.

His deep voice excited her, a dark, arousing sound that placed her at his mercy in a purely erotic way. She had no idea what tempting tortures he'd use to bring her to pleasure again. She only knew she couldn't wait to see what happened next.

And it pleased her that Dale looked as caught up in the

moment, a small consolation for the way her needy sex clenched him tight and wouldn't let go.

"I want you under me, Laura. I want to sink deep and not stop moving until I'm brain-dead, too." There was such heat in his voice that she could only reach up, slip her arms around his neck and welcome him.

He sank inside her by breathtaking degrees, anchoring himself so deep that she groaned at the sheer power of his presence. He caught the sound with his mouth, a kiss that wasn't playful or demanding, but possessive in a way she recognized on some soul-deep level. She kissed him with that same need, driving out everything else except how they felt with their bodies close.

Rocking her hips, she lifted against him, needing to salve this ache, needing him to move. And he knew exactly what to do. Arching his powerful body, he slowly withdrew, the friction so intense she gasped.

He didn't stop. He made love to her mouth with his tongue, to her body with slow, big thrusts that dragged him nearly all the way out before he drove back with such force that she cried out this time. And again.

A trembling built inside, a mounting vibration that stole her breath as he carried her away with the strength of his desire. She met him thrust for thrust, rising toward a climax that worked its way through her with pulsing force.

And triggered his.

"Laura," he breathed against her mouth, a growl of pleasure as his body gathered tight.

He didn't bother acting as if this monumental explosion of the senses was in any way ordinary, and she wasn't sure if that pleased or scared her. She wasn't sure of anything right now, except that she'd never felt this way. Not with her heart pounding and her breathing hard and her body seizing in tiny climaxes that seemed to go on forever.

Pressing her face into the crook of his shoulder, she shot for levity. "I think we might break your record."

"Or die in the process."

He sounded just as wasted, and from somewhere in her orgasm-fried brain came the thought that this man shouldn't be as totally gone as she was. She couldn't dwell on why. Not now when she was trying so hard to act as if everything was normal, as if he hadn't thoroughly taken her apart. She'd have to trust that he knew what he was doing because her experience with record-setting orgasms was limited.

But Dale had been wrong about one thing. Her brain wasn't working all right, because when she'd finally rallied enough energy to open her eyes again, she caught a glimpse of the bedside clock.

"Oh, no!" she burst out loud enough to make Dale rear back and stare at her. "I've got a staff meeting in Ms. J.'s office in fifteen minutes."

He didn't have the advantage of adrenaline to get him moving, but she did, and almost broke off an important body part in her frenzy to get out from underneath him.

"Sorry," she said, without a backward glance, which was just as well because he either couldn't or didn't answer.

Laura didn't want to know which. She'd never make it downstairs in presentable condition in time for the meeting. Razor burn still stung her cheeks and her hair had dried in a tangle—a scary thought given its length. She'd never showered after playing mermaid last night and had just worked up another sweat with a man who hadn't showered either.

Just wielding a washcloth and painting on enough makeup to cover razor rash blew through her allotted fifteen minutes. She burst back into the bedroom, only nominally refreshed, to find Dale sitting on the edge of the bed, staring out at the lagoon looking as out of it as she felt.

"I'll take a look at that skylight in the atrium this morning," he said as she disappeared inside the closet to dig for an outfit.

She reemerged with a freshly dry-cleaned suit, which would be about the only thing fresh about her this morning.

"I'll get a crew together as soon as I diagnose the problem. Who knows, maybe I'll luck out and it'll be something Jackson and I can fix."

"Don't you dare. The man's here for his wedding. You can't ask him to work." She dragged a silk shell over her head and reappeared to find Dale suddenly close enough to kiss. She took a surprised step backward and he reached out to steady her.

Just the feel of his fingers on her arm sent a tingle through her, proving that all those orgasms hadn't satisfied her hunger for him, but heightened her awareness. Great. Three weeks of breaking records and Dale would be right—they'd wind up killing each other.

"Jackson won't mind, trust me," Dale said. "It'll be a break from the in-laws. From what I hear, they're a hoot. Career military."

"Did it ever occur to you that he might like his future in-laws?" When Dale only frowned, Laura added, "I'd forgotten they were military, though. I'm glad you mentioned it."

Not only did it suggest one possible explanation for Delia's mother's concerns about appearances, but it gave

Laura the perfect way to mingle her guests. Mentally filing the information for later, she decided she might work it to her advantage when warming up Delia's parents to Falling Inn Bed's unique features.

Dale ran his fingers through his hair, making the glossy waves stand up on end. Laura couldn't help but smile as she pulled the skirt into place around her waist, which earned her a full-fledged scowl.

"I'm taking a shower," he said.

"This isn't fair. I'm not going to have time to get back here until after lunch. I smell terrible."

Leaning close, he trailed his open mouth along her neck and made her shiver. "You *taste* like a beautiful woman who's happy she's finally spending time with the man of her fantasies." Another kiss. Another shiver. "Now go to work."

Then he headed toward the bathroom, leaving Laura staring after him, admiring the sculpted power of his broad shoulders and back, the nice tight flex of his butt. And realizing that Dale was exactly right.

She was *very* happy. Shower or no shower.

8

LAURA ARRIVED AT the staff meeting over fifteen minutes late and slipped into the conference room muttering an apology. Taking her seat, she dragged her gaze around the table to make eye contact with her co-workers.

Ms. J. peered at her from over the report she held, her dark gaze not missing a thing, leaving Laura desperately wishing that this morning wasn't day one of mixing business with pleasure. She'd been late to dinner last night, too, and while she couldn't be sure that tidbit had made it back to her general manager, several of her co-workers were very well aware of her lapse.

Being late again didn't look good. Making excuses would only draw attention to the fact, and excuses wouldn't work here. Ms. J. deemed actions far more valuable than words.

Laura had known that from their first meeting during her preliminary interview for the position of wedding concierge. She'd been twenty-two and fresh from college, enthusiastic about Falling Inn Bed's unique status as a romance resort.

The inn had been renovated during her senior year, and the moment she'd heard the plans for the place, she'd abandoned her own plan to hightail it from Niagara Falls to take on the world. She considered the opening of this unusual hotel an omen that she should stay in her hometown and make peace with her past. She'd shown up to that first interview a nervous wreck but determined to prove she was the only woman for the job.

An ultraprofessional woman, Ms. J. was tall, attractive and seriously formidable after surviving decades in hotel management in the then male-dominated hospitality industry.

Had Laura not wanted the job so badly, she might have let Ms. J.'s tough questions and serious demeanor intimidate her. But she had been determined to succeed, and after years working for this woman, Laura knew there was nothing to say to excuse her tardiness. Last night she'd been fashionably late. This morning she'd been just plain late. And she didn't have Dale along to gallantly take the blame.

"Join us, please," Ms. J. said.

Dougray couldn't leave well enough alone. "Och, lassie, I dinna think I've ever seen your hair unbound. Ye look like Rapunzel from the tower."

"Thank you," she said automatically, not sure whether to take his comment as a compliment or not. She wished he hadn't called attention to the fact that she wasn't presentable and sat down, silently willing Ms. J. to get the show rolling again.

To Laura's relief, her general manager did exactly that, and continued to review the night audit. Quietly propping her briefcase against the chair leg, she left her things inside, refusing to draw any more notice until her turn came to give a department report.

Of course she should have known she'd never get off that easy. They weren't halfway through the night audit when Annabelle slid a note her way. Glancing down at the familiar handwriting, she read:

New perfume? Smells like chlorine.

Laura scowled, but Annabelle just smiled, withdrew the note and slid it into her day planner.

Here was a reminder why Dale could never be the man of her dreams. Practical, reliable Laura was never late for a staff meeting. This man with his killer orgasms was trouble.

Fortunately the meeting continued smoothly—without further mention of her tardiness—and Ms. J. called a short recess not too far into the proceedings to let her menagerie of dogs out for a walk.

Laura had been watching the ladies, as she liked to call the little dogs, and knew a walk hadn't been on any of their minds. The motley crew, consisting of an English bulldog, a boxer and two teacup poodles, had been slumbering peacefully in their corner of the conference room, an impressive display of good doggy manners honed by lifetimes of hotel living.

But with Ms. J.'s direction, the ladies filed obediently out the door, leaving Laura free to hit the side bar for a desperately needed cup of coffee.

She sucked down a few grateful gulps, topped off her cup and brought a second to the table before Ms. J. resumed the meeting. Bless her. Laura never went long without a reminder of why she liked working here so well.

"If we're through with department reports, then," Ms. J said, rejoining them, "we'll move on to Naughty Nuptials. Laura, if you please."

The caffeine revived her, and Laura recapped yesterday's arrivals and the success of the evening's dinner with the press, before launching into a rundown of the day's scheduled events.

"The only problem I foresee is with the Bad Bachelorette Party," Laura said. "Annabelle said something at dinner last night about you two escorting our male reporters that got me thinking…. They can cover Jackson's Bad Bachelor Party but I can't very well invite them to join the ladies at the spa. Especially not with all I've heard about Delia's conservative parents."

"But why, lassie?" Dougray asked, shooting her a twinkling look from beneath grizzled gray brows. "I thought that man of yours built the place for lads and lassies to enjoy *together*."

Dale had been on this property since they'd broken ground on the Wedding Wing and no one had ever referred to him as *her* man. Laura narrowed her gaze at the maintenance supervisor, a warning to behave. He clearly found ribbing her publicly about Dale amusing—the very last thing she needed right now.

"I think the ladies might find having strange men around while they're being wrapped head-to-toe in seaweed intrusive."

Dougray laughed. "The laddies wouldnae mind, I'm sure."

"No doubt."

She caught sight of Adam eyeing them stoically across the table. "What if you invite Benjamin and Tyler to interview the guests afterward?"

"That's a good idea, Adam," she said. "Perhaps if I arrange the time right after the party, we'll still have that just-pampered glow so they can capture the feel of the event."

"Good thinking, team." Ms. J. inclined her head in approval. "This might also be a good opportunity to let the press tour the spa and interview the staff. They'll be fresh and fired up from the bachelorette party, too, which should only help convey their excitement over the Naughty Nuptials. And that's exactly what we need the press to see."

"Especially since we're counting on building local name recognition for our spa," Annabelle added.

Local name recognition translated into local business to keep the spa thriving off-season. Another important detail to the continued health and stability of Falling Inn Bed, as everyone at this table well knew.

"All right then," Ms. J. continued. "Anything else from the departments?"

"No," voices chorused from all around the table, and she gave a satisfied nod then moved on.

"I have an item of new business to discuss." She passed around a stack of photocopies. "Bruno asked me to run by his Naughty Nuptials specialty menu for comments."

As the house chef, Bruno refused to leave his kitchen during his on-season breakfast rush for what he called a managers' coffee klatch, and since Bruno's Place routinely earned five-star ratings from local reviewers that brought business into the inn from the surrounding locals, Ms. J. didn't insist otherwise.

Laura accepted a copy from Annabelle and quickly assessed the layout. Simple. Accessible. Elegant. But she hadn't glanced at the content before Adam said dryly, "*Inter Courses*. It's…*raw*, don't you think?"

"Raw is how we like our guests around here," Dougray said and Laura stifled a laugh behind a cough. "That's the point of the menu—eat Bruno's aphrodisiac-spiced food and crave sex."

Annabelle rolled her eyes. "I'm with Adam on this one, Mary. *Inter Courses* isn't in the same league as the Naughty Nuptials or Risqué Receptions."

Ms. J. peered at the menu. "I don't know that I agree. It's overt but not necessarily too raw, or tactless."

"You don't think so? *Inter Courses*." Annabelle sampled the words. "It does get the point across. Then again, so does the Anal Atrium."

Laura almost choked on a gulp of hot coffee, and there was no stifling the sound this time, not even over Dougray who burst into laughter. Even Ms. J. smiled. Clearly the story of Annabelle's antics yesterday had made the rounds of the staff and management.

Annabelle clapped Laura on her back while Adam closed his eyes and looked as if his blood had chosen that exact moment to turn into battery acid and start eating him from the inside out.

"For the record," Laura managed. "It's a little edgy but I don't think it's in the same league as Anal Atrium."

"All right, team, comments noted." Ms. J.'s eyes twinkled. "I'll consider your opinions, discuss the situation with Bruno and let you know what we decide. Which leads me to our last item of business before you all can get about your day." Her warm gaze riveted straight to Laura, who shifted uncomfortably in her chair. "A reminder to have fun. It has been a long haul since we first conceived of the Wedding Wing idea. We've placed a lot on the line and worked hard for this grand opening. We've earned the opportunity to enjoy ourselves, and I know none of you will have trouble mixing business with pleasure. We're also fortunate enough to have Adam, who'll staff the fort so we can relax."

Ms. J. slid the agenda inside her day planner and smiled. "All right, team, have a great day and good luck."

Heading to her office, Laura braced herself for the invariable crises that had arisen during the night and found herself pleasantly surprised that nothing catastrophic had cropped up. Checking in with her assistant, Frank, currently en route to Old Fort Niagara with Delia's parents, she received a thumbs-up and breathed a sigh of relief. The first day of Naughty Nuptials seemed to be off to a decent start.

Okay, she could have lived without showing up late to a staff meeting and becoming the butt of Annabelle and Dougray's jokes, but she really had no regrets about waking up to Dale, either.

The concierges she'd scheduled on duty this morning were easily accommodating the guests, attending their business needs, directing them to off-property attractions or educating them to the variety of features Falling Inn Bed offered.

On-season meant gorgeous June weather and many summertime activities. Not only were the waterfront bungalows opened for guests who wanted a more rustic experience, but guided adventure tours for all levels of hiking enthusiasts took place in the vast array of footpaths through the state park that separated the inn from the falls. Falling Inn Bed also boasted tennis courts and a marina for boat trips on the river.

Satisfied that her staff had the day under control, Laura headed to the front desk to check on the status of impending check-ins. When she bumped into Delia and Jackson in the lobby, she took the opportunity to ask them about their wedding party's arrival before popping into a specialty store on the promenade to check on the party favors for the sex-toy shower. While there, she picked up a surprise gift for Dale.

Work distracted her from any and all thoughts of how badly she wanted a shower and another cup of coffee straight through until lunch, when her radio vibrated with news that the bride's parents had arrived on property exactly on schedule. Laura headed back to the lobby to greet her newest guests.

She couldn't have missed Major General and Mrs. Wallace even if Frank hadn't been with them. The major general, casually dressed in slacks and Polo shirt, still had the commanding presence of a high-ranking military officer, and the woman by his side could only be Delia's mother. They were both smiling as Frank led them into the lobby.

So far so good.

"Welcome to Falling Inn Bed, and Breakfast." Accent on bed and breakfast as one phrase, Laura introduced herself. "I hope you enjoyed your tour of the town."

"Turns out Major General and Mrs. Wallace have a passion for historical sites," Frank said. "We managed to see two this morning."

"We have our share in the area. And a number of military sites, as well. Any chance you can make some time after the wedding to let Frank show you the Canadian side of the border?"

"We're counting on it," the major general said. "Don't want to leave the area until I see Fort Erie."

Laura knew the history of the British garrison, a strategic military site during the War of 1812. "Definitely worth the trip. They use authentically dressed guards and interpreters to recreate the operations base for the invasion of Canada."

The major general looked enthusiastic but, as expected, Mrs. Wallace proved a tougher sell. She only inclined her

The Harlequin Reader Service® — Here's how it works:

Accepting your 2 free books and gift places you under no obligation to buy anything. You may keep the books and gift and return the shipping statement marked "cancel." If you do not cancel, about a month later we'll send you 4 additional books and bill you just $3.99 each in the U.S., or $4.47 each in Canada, plus 25¢ shipping & handling per book and applicable taxes if any.* That's the complete price and — compared to cover prices of $4.75 each in the U.S. and $5.75 each in Canada — it's quite a bargain! You may cancel at any time, but if you choose to continue, every month we'll send you 4 more books, which you may either purchase at the discount price or return to us and cancel your subscription.

*Terms and prices subject to change without notice. Sales tax applicable in N.Y. Canadian residents will be charged applicable provincial taxes and GST. Credit or debit balances in a customer's account(s) may be offset by any other outstanding balance owed by or to the customer.

If offer card is missing write to: Harlequin Reader Service, 3010 Walden Ave., P.O. Box 1867, Buffalo NY 14240-1867

NO POSTAGE
NECESSARY
IF MAILED
IN THE
UNITED STATES

BUSINESS REPLY MAIL

FIRST-CLASS MAIL   PERMIT NO. 717-003   BUFFALO, NY

POSTAGE WILL BE PAID BY ADDRESSEE

HARLEQUIN READER SERVICE
3010 WALDEN AVE
PO BOX 1867
BUFFALO NY 14240-9952

Play the Lucky Hearts Game

and get...

2 FREE BOOKS

and a **FREE MYSTERY GIFT...**

yes! **YOURS to KEEP!**

I have scratched off the silver card.
Please send me my **2 FREE BOOKS** and
FREE mystery GIFT. I understand that I am
under no obligation to purchase any books as
explained on the back of this card.

Scratch Here!

then look below to see
what your cards get you...
2 Free Books & a Free
Mystery Gift!

350 HDL D346   150 HDL D35Q

FIRST NAME

LAST NAME

ADDRESS

APT.#

CITY

STATE/PROV.

ZIP/POSTAL CODE

(H-B-10/04)

Twenty-one gets you
2 FREE BOOKS
and a **FREE MYSTERY GIFT!**

Twenty gets you
2 FREE BOOKS!

Nineteen gets you
1 FREE BOOK!

TRY AGAIN!

head. "You were kind to have arranged our tour, Ms. Granger."

"My pleasure. As our honorary bride's parents, you get special treatment. And I have to tell you how very fond we are of Delia and Jackson. Not only do we owe them our new Wedding Wing, but they worked on the property long enough to become part of the family. Just wait until you see the result of all their hard work. It's amazing."

"They promised us a grand tour after lunch." Mrs. Wallace smiled, a real smile that suggested while the tour had been pleasant, the concern for her daughter and future son-in-law meant much more.

"Excellent," Laura said. "I'll let the staff know that you'll be coming. We've got a brand-new full-service spa and our beautiful atrium where Delia and Jackson's wedding will be." She'd keep them focused on the amenities and out of the romance-themed honeymoon suites.

Motioning them across the lobby, she said, "Bruno's cooking up something special and I happen to know that Delia and Jackson have been seated already and are looking forward to seeing you."

By the time Laura got her bridal couple and family settled at Bruno's Place, it was close to one o'clock and her stomach had started protesting a lack of food. She thought about sneaking into her office for a quick bite but decided even more pressing than hunger was her need for a shower. She'd wilted like a flower and still had a long afternoon and night ahead.

Changing direction in midstride, she headed back into the restaurant, reaching for her radio. "Got a copy, King Cuisine?"

"This better be good," Bruno replied over the crackling channel. "You're interfering with an artist at work."

"Must have food," she chanted. "Must have food."

"You know where to come, little lady."

"Bless you, Bruno."

Smiling at several of the waitstaff herding around the window as the steward called out prepared orders, she slipped through the doors to the kitchen and headed in the direction of the voice that boomed over the chaotic lunch rush.

Falling Inn Bed's head chef and restaurateur was a brawny man with a balding pate that disappeared neatly beneath his toque. He knew his kitchen as intimately as Laura knew her Wedding Wing and might have had eyes in the back of his head for the way he directed everything taking place around him. She'd barely made it through the door before he waved her back.

Striding through the food preparation tables where prep cooks competently worked under Bruno's watchful eyes, she smiled appreciatively as he plucked three steaming jumbo shrimp off a platter and dropped them into a garnish cup.

"Wonton shrimp. *Squisito!*"

"You darling man." She accepted her cup and kissed his cheek. "What would I do without you?"

"You'd waste away to nothing." Rocking back on his heels, he eyed her assessingly. "Now eat up or else you won't have the strength to enjoy that new man of yours."

"You're as bad as Dougray." Scooping up a shrimp, she took a bite. The taste of ginger and green onion burst in her mouth and she gave an ecstatic moan before swallowing. "And for the record, Dale's not *my* man."

Bruno waggled his brows. "Shellfish—the *sine qua non* of aphrodisiacs. If he's not your man yet, he soon will be."

The tender shrimp and the delicate taste were so welcome Laura couldn't even work up a decent reprimand. "*Inter Courses*, Bruno? Were you drinking decaf when you came up with that?"

Without taking his gaze from hers, he yelled, "Eh, eh, what are you doing, Ray Jay? B-2 doesn't want almonds on those chicken crêpes."

Laura watched as the cook arranging food on a plate shot a startled look their way, gave a quick nod and sprinkled the handful of nuts back into a container.

"Prepare the food with natural aphrodisiacs and call the dishes names that make guests think of sex." Bruno gave a laugh. "Next thing you know, they're naked in their rooms. Good for business, don't you think?"

"I think, definitely."

He replaced the shrimp she'd eaten and said, "Now get out of my kitchen. You're breaking my concentration."

As the recipient of his largess, she didn't argue, just thanked him and headed out a side door leading to the promenade.

She finished the last shrimp while climbing the stairs to the fifth floor and arrived back at the Castaway Honeymoon Isle to find it empty. A blessing, she decided, tossing the remains of her lunch into the trash and washing her hands in the kitchen.

Fortified and ready for a shower, she set the shopping bag on the table and withdrew the foil-wrapped package. This had been an impulse buy, a little something she'd seen and thought Dale might enjoy. Since he seemed so determined to live up to his press, she wouldn't miss a chance to live up to her promises, too.

Placing the package front and center on the dining room table where he couldn't miss it, she headed toward the bathroom. Time was short before she had to get back to oversee the final arrangements for the welcome reception.

The shower spray hit her in a hot burst, melting away the vestiges of the night and infusing her with new energy, and Laura was so absorbed in the shower spray pounding away at her senses that she never noticed Dale's arrival in the bathroom. After she'd lathered and rinsed her hair, she opened her eyes to find him standing there, wearing jeans, a flannel shirt and work boots. He looked exactly like the man she'd gotten used to seeing around the Wedding Wing construction site, only his knowing smile was new. A reminder of what they'd shared last night.

He didn't say a word, just lazily raked his gaze over her as she twisted her wet hair over her shoulder. She was suddenly aware of how each rivulet of water coursed over her and flowed off her breasts, how the gloss of steam caressed her bare skin in the wake of his appreciative gaze. It took a moment to realize he held her gift.

He gave the red ball a suggestive shake. "A magic ball?"

It was an erotic knockoff of those Laura remembered from her youth, the kind she'd ask questions of and receive answers like, "Yes, definitely," or "Try again later."

Except this one magically offered *sexy* suggestions....

Flipping it over, he peered myopically at the tiny window on the bottom. "Touch a body part of choice."

A wicked thrill sizzled through her when he reached for his belt and flipped it open. "I'll need to get undressed for this."

And she forgot all about running late.

9

DALE RETRIEVED TWO more flutes of champagne from a passing waiter and pressed one into Laura's hand. She wasn't doing more than taking an odd sip as she mingled with her guests and he watched glass after glass go flat. He, on the other hand, wasn't using his champagne as a prop. He seemed to be thirsty tonight, the blame for which he placed on Laura, who stood beside him looking even lovelier than usual.

The pale pink number she wore hugged her curves and left her shoulders bare, showcasing her breasts to such perfection that the sight made his mouth dry. Now that she'd braided her hair again, he could obsess over all that bare skin. Her heart-shaped face and delicate jaw angled down to the slim column of her throat, the curve of her shoulders.

And all that cleavage.

He kept going back to the cleavage. Dale just couldn't look at her without being blindsided by the memory of touching her, doing all those pleasurable things that inspired her to the breathy little moans that drove him wild.

When she smiled up at him, just an offhand look while explaining the differences between a romance resort and a singles resort, he felt the conversation slide out of his head.

He'd attended more social events working for ADF than he cared to recall, shmoozing with the members of historic preservation boards, city council members who voted on the proposed project budgets and various fund-raising arts and cultural groups. He knew how to play this game, but tonight he couldn't look at Laura and focus on much but the sight of her.

The major general had mentioned his wife was an avid reader, and Laura zeroed in on that as their topic. She compared Falling Inn Bed to a romance novel that dealt with the journey to happily-ever-after as opposed to erotica stories where characters had sex for the joys of sex alone.

Having never read a romance novel, Dale basically had no clue what she was talking about, and a glance at the major general suggested he didn't either. But Delia's mother seemed engrossed and the ensuing conversation left the men to enjoy a few moments' respite from the constant demands of party chatter.

This break was well earned, too, because Laura had been dragging him through this ballroom all night. He'd followed along at her heels, playing date to the reception hostess as if he'd been born to the job. He'd laughed with her guests, supplied her with champagne and stood close enough to admire the view of her cleavage.

Obsession? he asked himself again. *Or something more?*

Whatever his problem, he'd picked it up at this inn and hoped like hell that three weeks of sexual indulgence at the scene of the crime would cure him.

He wouldn't take that bet. After two years of Laura's rejection, a month-long separation and some seriously mind-blowing sex, he shouldn't be this distracted by her. Bottom line, the dating game he usually played had turned into a mating game with rules he didn't understand.

The closest he'd ever come was watching his boss and long-time buddy Nick in hot pursuit of the woman who'd wound up changing both their lives.

Dale remembered the night he and Nick had met Julienne as if it had been yesterday. They'd commissioned the restoration of the Risqué Theatre and had arrived in Savannah geared up to work like they had on a hundred jobs over the past decade. But on their first night in town, Nick had taken one look at Julienne and had been consumed, which had altered Dale's way of life forever.

He'd laughed like hell while watching Nick muddle through the bump and grind of becoming a contender for Julienne's affections. He'd laughed even harder as he stood beside Nick at the altar when his bride had walked down the aisle.

He hadn't exactly lost his best friend…but seeing Nick so obviously satisfied and apparently missing nothing about his bachelor days made Dale stop to consider.

Could he be content with the same woman in his bed every night?

When Laura laughed her silvery laugh, a sound that filtered through him with more potency than the champagne, Dale thought he could—if that woman was Laura. He'd have never guessed that Nick would ever meet a woman to satisfy him, yet *years* had passed and Nick still seemed as wrapped up in his beautiful wife as he'd been since they'd met.

Dale glanced at the woman who had his thoughts traveling down unfamiliar roads, and for the first time all night managed to keep his gaze above her neck. The light caught and held her eyes. Her mouth tipped up when she smiled, a full, sensuous look that brought to mind kissing.

Who knew he'd still be pining for this woman after two years? He wasn't generally one who liked banging his head against a wall, and Laura had made it clear he wasn't what she wanted in a man. Yet he'd kept right on lusting.

And he wasn't sorry. If every night was like last night…every morning like this morning…every afternoon like this afternoon…he was all for persistence.

Even losing control in the Lovers' Lagoon hadn't been bad—surprising, but not bad. His control had always been a given, predictable. But not with Laura. She challenged him, tested him and even managed to make a boring social event enjoyable when she laughed that chiming laugh, and told everyone in the room what a brilliant architect he was.

Maybe he shouldn't have laughed so hard at Nick. He'd obviously invited karma to laugh back at him. For the very first time he had *feelings* for a woman, and she was dead convinced he wasn't suitable.

You're the man of my fantasies, not the man of my dreams.

"Don't you think so, Dale?" Laura asked, obviously assuming he'd been following the conversation.

But Dale didn't have a clue what she was talking about, so he nodded, taking his fifty-fifty chance of nailing the right response. And when she flashed that high-beam smile, he decided that karma might be on his side, for tonight at least.

"Then let's migrate in that direction," Laura said, and he forced his attention on her words rather than the way that shimmery pink fabric clung to her breasts when she motioned toward the bar. "Delia and Jackson got cornered by our local reporter and, unless I miss my guess, he'll hang on to them for a bit. I see the Knights are free, though. Troy is with a different branch of the service, Major General, but I think you'll enjoy meeting him."

By now, Dale had the basic gist of the conversation so he located the couple in question and led Laura and the Wallaces across the ballroom. Tyler joined their party along the way, keeping pace at Laura's other side to discuss the video footage he'd been shooting of the event.

They finally reached the Knights and congregated around the couple while Laura performed the introductions.

"Major General and Mrs. Wallace are the parents of our bride, and I thought two military couples might enjoy meeting each other."

After a round of greetings, the major general and Troy Knight talked shop, or rank and barracks as it was, steering the conversation away from the current conflicts but making sure to include the group. Laura seemed pleased these two officers appeared to hit it off and there was no missing that Mrs. Wallace approved of her military wife counterpart.

Miranda Knight was a vision of impeccable high society dressed in a beaded blue gown that matched her sapphire eyes, a blue so unlike Laura's as to be night and day. She shifted that deep gaze between him and Laura, and though her expression never changed, Dale sensed she was checking them out.

Not so long ago, he'd have checked her out back, husband or not. But tonight, he just leaned closer to Laura, giving into an unfamiliar possessive feeling. He couldn't have cared less how long they stood here talking. He recalled Nick trying to explain this very phenomenon, and at the time it had only explained why Nick was no longer any fun at parties.

Now Dale scrambled to remember what his buddy had said, knowing that Nick would've laughed himself stupid if he could have seen Dale now.

When Delia and Jackson arrived with the local reporter in tow, they escorted the major general and Mrs. Wallace to a family photo shoot in the atrium, leaving him and Laura alone with the photojournalist and the Knights.

"Any chance we can sneak away for a few minutes?" he whispered to Laura. "Don't you need to check on some details in the kitchen or something?" He'd drag her into some sheltered alcove for a steamy kiss...

Laura managed to make the moment theirs with a glance, but Dale's hopes went bust when Tyler began to grill the Hottest Honeymoon couple.

"Troy, you mentioned you were the son of a career military officer," Tyler said. "How did you and Miranda meet?"

"She visited the naval base I was stationed at with one of her college courses, and I lucked into being assigned as her tour guide." Troy smiled at his wife, one of those I've-only-got-eyes-for-you looks that Dale was getting familiar with.

"He talked me into having our wedding here," Miranda added.

"So Laura coordinated your wedding?" Tyler asked.

Something in Laura's expression shuttered. Dale brought the champagne flute to his lips to occupy himself so he looked as though he was doing something more than just staring at this woman like some lovesick fool.

"No, I didn't, Tyler," she said. "I was so tied up with the design of the Wedding Wing that it would have been impossible to attend to the details properly, so I scheduled my assistant full-time on the project. To my understanding, Miranda and Troy were very pleased with the result."

"Everything went off without a hitch," Troy said. "Even Miranda's parents agreed. And that's saying a lot."

"Your parents tough to please, Miranda?" Tyler asked.

She eyed the photojournalist coolly over the rim of her flute. "Not really. But any event involving a Prescott tends to draw media attention around Niagara Falls. My parents prefer the attention to be positive."

Dale watched the silver stud in Tyler's brow travel halfway up his forehead.

"Prescott?" he asked. "As in Senator Let's-Free-America-from-Dependence-on-Foreign-Oil Prescott?"

Miranda nodded. "My grandfather."

"So before meeting the lieutenant commander here, you were Miranda Prescott?"

"Miranda Ford. My mother is the Prescott."

Dale gave a low whistle. "I'll say you needed your wedding to go smoothly."

"We considered having the wedding out of town to avoid the media but then decided leaving would only draw attention to why we'd left," Troy explained. "Once we decided to stay, Falling Inn Bed seemed like the perfect place to get married. Miranda took a little convincing but the staff proved top-notch."

Dale wasn't surprised. He'd watched the running of this operation up close for nearly two years now, and they were a class act from the word go.

"We were sorry the infamous bedding consultant couldn't take care of us," Miranda added.

Dale found that downright strange.

He knew from experience that Laura oversaw every aspect of whatever project she dipped her fingers into. She'd nearly driven him insane with her attention to detail, and he didn't think there could be too many people in the ballroom tonight who hadn't heard of powerful Senator Prescott. Hosting a wedding for the senator's granddaughter must have been a serious coup for the inn.

He also knew the real work on the Wedding Wing hadn't started until he'd brought his team onto the property. Sure, there'd been months of debates over the plans before then, but they'd been nothing compared to Laura dogging his heels to make sure every detail lived up to her expectations.

"I was sorry to pass along Miranda and Troy's wedding." Somehow Laura's regret didn't ring entirely true, and Dale glanced down to find her smile strained around the edges.

Tyler shifted his gaze between Troy and Miranda curiously. "Senator Prescott didn't have any trouble with this place being a romance resort?"

"My grandfather values a strong family unit. That's always been part of his platform," Miranda said smoothly.

"Given what I've read about the senator, if he'd had a problem with Falling Inn Bed in his town, he'd have rallied the troops against it and shut it down."

Dale would have guessed as much himself, but Troy just shrugged as if a high-profile life with a politician was all in a day's work.

"My grandfather also supports renewed interest in our town. We need industries that generate tourist dollars. If nothing else, Laura's hotel is a part of our local landscape."

Dale had never considered what it must have been like to have a politician in the family. He recalled when Nick had accepted a presidential appointment to the national board of historic preservation a number of years back and the annoying amount of media attention the appointment had drawn. The firm had been under such close scrutiny during Nick's fifteen minutes in the spotlight that even *he'd* had to curtail his activities to avoid finding his name plastered in some newspaper.

He could understand why Miranda's delivery would be so articulate. She'd obviously had practice performing for the press. He also didn't miss the reference to *Laura's* hotel. That wasn't an entirely accurate statement as Miranda had learned last night at dinner, so he had to wonder what she meant, and why Laura suddenly seemed so guarded.

He had the wild urge to slip his arm around her and pull her close, to press a kiss to her temple, her cheek, her jaw, until the tension he saw there faded. Dale knew such a public display of affection would be too personal for this situation. These people were guests, not friends, and while he was Laura's date for this event, that role had boundaries of professional behavior outside the Castaway Honeymoon Isle.

"We were delighted to host an event for the senator's family," Laura said with that fixed smile. "Doubly so to have the opportunity to invite Miranda and Troy back as our honeymoon couple. And she's right about Falling Inn Bed. The locals are very protective and supportive of our town history and legends."

Laura was as articulate as the senator's granddaughter, and Dale knew women well enough to sense there was more between these two than one event at Falling Inn Bed.

"Laura," he said, following up on his hunch. "Am I right to assume that you know Miranda from outside of the inn?"

"Assume, Dale?" Miranda didn't give Laura a chance to answer. "Does that mean Laura never mentioned me? Just how long have you two been together?"

"We met well over two years ago," Laura said, leaving everyone to guess if they'd been dating for the duration.

"And you've never told your beau about me?" Her tone implied she was hurt by the omission. "Well, Dale. I'll fill you in myself. Laura and I attended Westfalls Academy together. We were in the same house in the same year all through school, until we parted ways for high school. Isn't that right, Laura?"

Laura nodded, that smile etched in place.

"That's why I was so surprised last night to hear about Laura's partnership in this hotel," Miranda went on. "I knew she worked here but…well, I didn't think I'd been gone from Niagara Falls that long. Clearly I'm out of the loop."

"We've got three weeks home on this trip to do some catching up," Troy said.

Miranda nodded. "So you own a romance resort, Laura, you're dating the architect of your new addition and the press hails you as a visionary. I leave town and look at all these exciting things that happen."

Dale could sense the undercurrent between these two. He also knew Laura well enough to guess she must have a reason for letting everyone believe they'd been dating a lot longer than they had. He looked forward to finding out what it was. Until then, he'd keep his mouth shut.

"Lots of excitement in town lately, Miranda," Laura agreed pleasantly. "Folks have been waiting for the Wedding Wing's grand opening."

"Will your parents be visiting for any events?"

"No, they won't."

Miranda frowned over her champagne glass. "I'm surprised. I thought they'd want to share in your shining moment."

"They've been sharing all along." Laura gave a light laugh. "You know my parents. Hands-on and behind the scenes. They've been helping me conceptualize the honeymoon suites."

Dale hadn't known this. Not once in the entire time that he'd worked with Laura had she ever mentioned *parents*. He eyed her over the rim of his glass, watched her and Miranda exchange a neutral glance.

Miranda passed off her glass to her husband. "Your mother must have helped arrange for the loan of that gorgeous Mireille Marceaux in your Wedding Wing lobby. I can't imagine how else you got Westfalls's headmistress to pull it out of storage. She wouldn't even acknowledge its existence while we were in school."

"My mom keeps telling me Ms. Cecilia is mellowing out in her old age so I told her to prove it." Laura smiled, and Dale recognized this smile as a real one. "The whole theme of Falling Inn Bed sort of fits with the painting, don't you think?"

Miranda laughed, a sultry sound that was also the closest thing Dale had heard to an unaffected response from the woman since they'd met. "Agreed. It's a lot better on your lobby wall than hidden in a storage room at Westfalls, where the students devote their formative years to speculating on its 'inappropriateness.'"

"Did its 'inappropriateness' live up to your expectations?"

"I must admit it's a bit of a disappointment," Miranda said. "The painting's gorgeous, of course, but I'd imagined something more than a seminude wrapped in mist."

Laura laughed and two things struck Dale in that moment. The first was a sharp memory of making love to Laura wrapped in mist last night. Such a sharp memory, in fact, that he had to shift from foot to foot to ease the sudden pressure of a seam in the wrong place.

The second was that while he'd been working with Laura a long time, he didn't have a clue about her personal life. She'd never once mentioned parents or any family in town, and he'd never once thought to ask.

You're a bad boy. Bad boys drive fast cars and chase faster women.

Touché. He'd been interested in Laura for one reason and one reason only. Looked as though he'd have to correct this oversight if he wanted to be considered a serious contender.

Which came as an unexpected third realization.

He *did* want to be a serious contender.

Obsession or something more? Dale still couldn't say, but all his sleepless surprise last night, all those unanswered questions today, suddenly made sense.

Despite the fact that Laura had convinced herself he couldn't be anything more than a man of her fantasies. Despite the fact that he didn't have a clue how to prove he could be more. Despite the logistic problems of their work situations.

He wanted to be the man of Laura's dreams.

10

"SOUNDS LIKE THERE'S a story here, ladies," Tyler said. "What's the deal with the painting?"

When a waiter walked by, Dale exchanged his empty champagne glass for a full one, knowing he'd never been this thirsty in his life. The cool drink went down hard, and that had nothing to do with the quality of the label and everything to do with Laura, who'd managed to turn his night upside down, hell, his *life*.

And she didn't have a damn clue.

She chatted with her guests, the ultimate professional, expertly sidestepping past history with her old schoolmate and maneuvering the conversation back to her grand opening.

She didn't have a clue that her invitation had thrown his life into upheaval, had made him lose sleep, lose *control*...and had landed him in a situation he had no idea how to handle.

"You've heard of Mireille Marceaux before?" she asked.

Troy nodded. "Miranda has filled me in on all the local legends."

"A French painter from the latter half of the last century," Tyler added. "She's best known for her erotic paintings, although posthumously renowned for her landscapes, too."

"Very good, gentlemen," Laura said. "After her death, she bequeathed her estate to Westfalls Academy."

"They built a house and named it for her," Miranda added. "The dorm Laura and I shared was there."

"As part of her estate, she left a number of paintings. Some were landscapes of our area, which they display in the Marceaux House. Others were erotic, like the *Falling Woman*."

"From what my mother has told me, some term in the will meant the school couldn't sell any of the paintings. Of course that left them with a problem about what to do with them. They could display the landscapes, of course, but the erotic paintings weren't exactly appropriate for the student body. So they were sealed up in storage and left to gather dust."

"And like Miranda said," Troy added, "to inspire class after class to imagine the forbidden images on those canvases."

"Until my mom convinced the headmistress to loan me one to display during the grand opening," Laura said. "I thought it would bring the Wedding Wing luck."

Miranda arched a dark brow. "Which raises the question, Laura—how did you know what the paintings looked like?"

Laura tipped her flute in salute. "It pays to have a family member on staff."

Dale latched on to this detail about Laura's personal life. Miranda was Senator Prescott's granddaughter while Laura's mother had been on the payroll at the exclusive school they attended. Did that explain the undercurrent he felt between these two?

"So what's the tie between Westfalls Academy and Mireille Marceaux?" Tyler asked. "From what I've heard, no one knew anything about her. Her work was hailed among the golden Manhattan set, but she didn't run with the crowd."

"That's the mystery," Laura said. "No one knew anything about her life, let alone of any connection to Westfalls. And believe me, people have spent the past fifty years trying to find one. We've heard everything from trysts with a married lover who lived in the area, to visiting an illegitimate child from said lover."

"Maybe it reminded her of her native France. Who knows?" Miranda said offhand. "After her death though, it was discovered that she owned property on the river. It took years to go through probate, but Laura's parents eventually acquired it to open their artist colony."

Artist colony? Dale glanced down at his date, supposing he should have known that a woman with such unusual views on romance wouldn't be the product of conventional bankers or businesspeople.

"Dale, don't tell me Laura didn't mention her parents' artist colony, either?" Miranda asked.

Had he not been completely distracted with ideas about what the man of Laura's dreams was made of, Dale might not have looked so surprised. He might have rallied a smoother response, too. As it was, he just blinked stupidly, leaving the question hanging in the sudden silence.

Laura stepped into the breach. "Discussions about parents fall in the reality category, Miranda, and what I do around here—" she raised her flute to indicate the ballroom and beyond "—is pure fantasy."

"Are you telling me you don't do reality in your personal relationships, Laura?"

"A bedding consultant can't create wonders like the Wedding Wing and the Naughty Nuptials without inspiration."

Laura lifted her gaze and flashed him a smile that made him feel like she'd never smiled at another man in her life.

Miranda eyed them skeptically. "So you won't be hosting your own wedding in your new addition any time soon?"

Before Laura had a chance to answer, Tyler asked, "Doesn't our bedding consultant believe in marriage?"

Laura laughed, an easy, real laugh, and Dale was getting practiced at telling the difference. "Of course I believe in marriage. But I also believe in romance and in enjoying every second of the way to the altar. Dale calls me a romantic idealist, and I have to admit the description fits."

Just last night Laura had explained her fixed views about the man of her dreams, yet here she contradicted herself by idealizing flings. Why was he getting the sense that she had something to prove to her old classmate?

He turned the thought over in his mind, tested the possibility to see how it fit.

And it fit, damn it.

Laura might not have been able to forget about him after he'd left town, but something had prompted her to write that invitation. As he watched these two old schoolmates subtly interrogate each other, he suspected that reason was more involved than wanting eight orgasms a night.

ABOUT THE LAST THING Laura wanted to do was talk about Miranda, but after two orgasms that left her legs vibrating so she could barely move, how could she deny Dale anything? Especially when he sat behind her, drawing the brush through her hair with such soothing strokes.

She decided one good turn deserved another, and to her surprise, she didn't mind. For once she'd shone instead of looking like a hayseed in front of Miranda. Her welcome reception had gone off better than she'd dared hope. Her guests were content. The press seemed receptive. The Naughty Nuptials was officially underway. So far so good.

Forcing her eyes open, Laura gazed out into the bedroom. Tonight she'd remembered to throw open the doors, and the waterfall splashed steadily, the sound only adding to her drowsy feeling of contentment.

With the starlight bathing Lovers' Lagoon in a wash of silver, her senses lulled into the misty perfection of the suite and of the man who sat silent behind her, his hard body contrasting sharply with the gentle attention he lavished on her with the brush.

"Go ahead, ask your questions, Dale." She would indulge him the way he'd indulged her since crawling between the sheets.

Fair was fair, after all.

"I got the impression tonight that you and Miranda weren't the best of friends," he said.

"We weren't any kind of friends. Just schoolmates in the same year and dorm. A lot of the same classes, too."

"I thought it might be a little more than that."

Laura laughed softly. "A little, maybe."

He didn't reply, and she thought he was waiting for her to elaborate.

"Why so curious?" she asked. "Does my history with Miranda really make any difference?"

"No difference at all." He dragged the brush to a halt in midstroke. "I want to know more about you. We've known each other for two years and you've never mentioned your family."

"You've never mentioned yours, either, Dale," she said. "We generally talk about work. Or flirt."

"*I* flirted. You stopped flirting when I asked you out."

"That's true."

"I want to talk about more than work and sex. I want to know you, Laura. I want to know more than what sort of atmosphere you're creating in the Wedding Wing and where I have to touch you to get you to breathe out those little sighs that make me crazy."

A tingle zipped through her at his admission. She wanted to know why he suddenly wanted to know, but she couldn't go here. Not with Dale. Not when she was so wrapped up in having sex with him that the slightest push would have her thinking romantically idealistic things that were off-limits.

Instead she asked, "Isn't talking about this kind of stuff against the fling rules?"

"Nope. It's like show-and-tell. I'll show you mine if you show me yours."

"How do you know I'm interested?"

"We're naked, Laura." He exhaled a breath that managed to sound thoroughly offended, yet at the same time imply that his reasoning should be obvious. "You just came and so did I—"

"I came twice."

"All the more reason to play the game. It's polite."

That made her laugh. "Okay. I wouldn't want to breach the rules of casual sex."

He ground his softening erection into her backside. "Are you so sure this is casual?"

For him, yes. But for her unfortunately, the answer could all too easily be no. And leave it to a man experienced with women not only to notice, but to call her on it. He was talking about erections and sex, but Laura hadn't ever had casual sex before, only committed sex where her emotions were involved and futures were possible. While she was slinging around her share of bad girl attitude, it wasn't without effort.

She had no future with Dale. That was why she'd nixed a fling with him from the start. He would be leaving town after the grand opening, and she couldn't afford to forget that. She was vulnerable to her emotions and had to reserve her idealistic views about romance for her work at Falling Inn Bed and for relationships that had potential futures.

Romance and sex just seemed a natural fit. It was one of the things she loved best about her work—helping couples explore their relationships. Of course not all of them wound up in commitment, but the ones Laura dealt closely with usually ended in marriage and happily-ever-after.

Dale had been the exception, and one she hoped she didn't live to regret. "I'm at a bit of a disadvantage here, Dale. I'm not all that familiar with casual. I'm trying to stay focused on the here and now so I do this fling right. Sharing our personal lives when we haven't discussed them before seems pointless."

"Sure you just don't want to talk about Miranda?"

Dale was entirely too perceptive for her own good. "Perhaps."

Dropping the brush onto the mattress, he leaned back against the pillows and gathered her against him. "I've got an idea, Laura. Do you agree that I'm familiar enough with flings for the two of us?"

"Absolutely."

"Then why don't you follow my lead on this. I know that you're looking for the man of your dreams and I respect that. Let's just enjoy what we have together and not overanalyze the details. I won't steer you wrong. You have my word."

He pressed his mouth to the top of her head, a casual gesture that felt *right*. She'd known this man for a long time. He might be a bad boy, but he was also a gentleman. If he promised to steer her right then she could trust him to take the lead.

"All right, Dale. Show me yours," she said softly, rewarded when he tightened his arms around her.

"I'm a late-in-life baby with two brothers over a decade older than me. They're both in construction. My parents, too."

"Your mom?"

"Works as the office manager of the family company."

"But you don't work for them?"

Dale shrugged. "I did through high school and college. The family company is based out of San Francisco and does most of its work there. ADF uses them whenever we've got crews in the area. But I wanted to see the world and not be bothered with the hassles of owning a business."

How much more of a reminder did she need about why emotions and sex couldn't mix with this man? He was a jet-setter. She had a life in Niagara Falls. "So what do your parents think about you traveling the world and not working in their business?"

"They'd like me to be a part of it, but they don't need me. My brothers have everything under control. They've already got my nephews and nieces helping out on different jobs and gearing up my dad for retirement."

"Sounds like a nice normal family. Where does your need to see the world fit in?"

He chuckled, a warm sound that filtered through her, feeling slow, warm, *perfect*. "I'm special. The family's been catering to me since the day I was born."

"You were a little brat?"

"A little brat *prince*. There's a difference."

Now it was her turn to laugh. "Well, that explains a lot. You're so used to everyone kissing the ground you walk on. No wonder you couldn't get over the fact that I'd turned you down."

"Do you think that's the only reason I want you?"

She wiggled her bottom, so his fading erection wedged silkily between her cheeks. "Not the *only* reason."

His laughter ruffled across her ear, sending a tingle of memory through her, reminding her of the way his hands felt on her skin when he touched her, the way he felt sinking that rock-hard erection deep inside, the way she recalled all these things just by hearing his laughter.

"I've been around a long time without making love to you, Laura. It's given me a chance to see past your beautiful face and your delicious body. Will you be surprised if I tell you how much I appreciate the way you make everyone around you feel like they're important? How you make your guests feel welcome, like Falling Inn Bed is a home away from home?"

"Yes," the word slipped from her lips on a sigh. And she was surprised. By how this man could talk so openly about the way he felt, how he could make her tingle from head to toe with his whiskey-voiced admissions.

But, perhaps she shouldn't be surprised. She'd been watching him charm everyone around him for the past two years. His easy charm was simply a part of the man he was, part of what had attracted her to him.

"Does it surprise you to know how much I like surprising you?" he asked. "I do, you know."

"Good thing. I'd feel terrible if I bored you after only a few days. We still have *weeks* left."

"You could never bore me, Laura." He breathed the words and she shivered again. "That's why I want to know all about you. So tell me how the daughter of art colony owners grows up to become a bedding consultant of a romance resort?"

"Just lucky, I guess," she said lightly. "Okay, my life in a nutshell…I'm the only daughter of two artists. My dad's a sculptor and my mom's a painter."

"Did she teach art at your school?"

Laura shook her head. "I'm afraid she was a little too avant-garde for Westfalls. It's a very conservative place."

"Which would explain the hidden erotic paintings."

"It does. My mom took a break from her career to work as CFO. One of her perks was my tuition. It's a hideously expensive school, and at the time my parents were funneling most of their earnings from their commissions back into their artist community to keep it running while it developed a name. My mom wouldn't compromise on my education, though." She laughed softly. "And all I wanted to do was go to public school."

"Is this where Miranda comes in?"

"I didn't move in her circles. My parents weren't living hand to mouth, but they were different. Typical artists. Wrapped up in their work and completely oblivious to keeping up with the Joneses and all that."

She paused, considered the best way to explain Miranda's influence in her life, without going into all the gory details that she didn't like to think about herself.

"Miranda is…well, *Miranda*. She's like the town princess. She's got the name, the money and the standing in the community. It used to irritate her whenever people compared us."

"Why did people compare you?"

Laura knew questions would invariably wind up here, a place she'd made peace with only because she'd accepted that she didn't have answers....

A place that made her feel as if she wasn't good enough.

She couldn't share this with Dale. He wanted to know about her, not deal with her emotional baggage. Her past was past. *Over*.

But one of the things Laura had learned through the years was that no matter what people thought of her or her family, only she had the power to feel good or bad about herself. If people chose to judge her, the problem was theirs. Right now she chose to feel good, which meant not dredging up a past no one could change. She might have to deal with Miranda at her grand opening, but she wouldn't invite their past into her present. And especially not into bed with Dale.

"Miranda and I were the same age and in the same year at school," she said simply. "My mom worked there so I naturally drew attention. You've got to understand, Dale. Niagara Falls might look big, but it has a small-town mentality."

He gave a gruff laugh. "So I noticed. The neighboring towns, too."

His dry tone made her smile. "I still don't understand why you're so put out about rave reviews."

Hooking his ankles around hers, he hitched her higher, rested his chin on her shoulder. "I didn't know it would bother me. It does."

"Why?"

He shrugged and she could feel flexing muscles warm and supple along her back. "I'm only concerned with what one woman thinks about me."

It wasn't what she'd expected to hear. He was getting too personal tonight, surprising her with intimacies that she didn't think should be a part of casual sex.

Maybe she was tired from a sleepless night or keyed up from the stress of the events. Either way, all this talk about their lives made it too easy to think of him as something more than a fling. Exactly what she couldn't let happen.

"Why did you let Miranda think we'd been dating for two years?" he asked.

Laura was suddenly glad her hair covered her face so he couldn't see her blush. She'd been asking herself the same question since the words had popped out of her mouth. Worse still, she'd done the exact same thing when Miranda had arrived—pretended to have a date when she'd had no idea whether Dale would show up alone or accept her invitation if he did.

"Old habits die hard, I suppose," she replied honestly. "I couldn't seem to come up with a way to correct her that wouldn't sound like I'd just picked you up for this event."

"You did pick me up for this event. Did inviting me have something to do with keeping up appearances for Miranda's sake?"

Ouch. There was no censure in his voice, just curiosity, but the question came completely out of left field.

"Why would you think that?"

"You had no problem turning me down because you didn't do flings. I wondered why you suddenly changed the rules."

"I told you." She tried not to sound defensive but didn't think she managed it. "I expected to stop thinking about you after you left. I didn't. The grand opening seemed the perfect time to explore our chemistry and get it out of the way."

"And you need to get it out of the way because thinking about me interferes with the search for the man of your dreams?"

Okay, there was subtext in that question, but Laura didn't know what it was. They'd already had this conversation and she wasn't sure what he was looking for.

Twisting in his arms, she tipped her head back to see his face. The star-washed darkness sliced across his features, casting shadows along his stubbled jaw, making his expression harder than their afterglow should allow.

"Did I offend you by leaving our relationship open to interpretation?" she asked. "If I did, I'm sorry. Miranda isn't part of my life anymore and I didn't see the need to get into awkward explanations, especially with Tyler around."

"Our relationship isn't anyone's business."

"Then what's bothering you?"

He lifted his hand to her face, brushed away stray hairs from her cheek, traced the long strands behind her shoulders. Something in the gesture seemed tender, out of sync with the moment when there were questions between them, uncertainty.

"The little brat prince grew up to be a big brat prince." He flashed her a grin that eased the moment, dissolving her insides into jelly in the process. "I realized that I don't want to be your trophy date. I want you to want me for myself."

"I do."

"Then prove it."

He dipped her backward so quickly that she gasped. Her hair swept out behind her and suddenly his mouth was on hers, kissing the sound from her lips, giving her a chance to convince him.

Laura did. In the darkness she proved to Dale that what she felt for him had everything to do with her and nothing to do with a woman who'd always had the ability to make her feel substandard.

But much later, as she lay curled in his arms while he slept, sated and wide-awake long after she should have passed out, Laura stared into the starlit darkness and wondered if her reasons had been as clear-cut as she'd said and if she was being honest with Dale, and herself.

WHEN THE TELEPHONE rang at the crack of dawn, Laura grabbed for it and mumbled a sleepy greeting.

"Laura," Annabelle said. "The throne room. Now."

An invitation to Ms. J.'s office in *that* tone was more than enough to awaken Laura and shoot her adrenaline into the red zone. "On my way."

Slipping the phone back onto the cradle, she glanced over at Dale, who burrowed into the covers and didn't awaken. After pressing a kiss to his shoulder, she slipped out of bed and hurriedly got dressed, refusing to speculate on what had happened to warrant this meeting. She wouldn't borrow trouble, especially when she walked into Ms. J.'s office and knew by her co-workers' expressions that trouble had found her.

"What's wrong?" She braced herself against the doorway.

"We've just had some news," Ms. J. began with a look of such careful neutrality that Laura actually held her breath. "Not necessarily bad news, but a change of plans."

"What plans?"

"Benjamin Harris won't be covering the rest of the grand opening. The assignment of a lifetime is calling him away."

"He's flying out today to cover some Alaskan nudist colony that Tyler hooked him up with." Adam looked so disbelieving that under any other circumstances Laura might have laughed.

But *her* grand opening coverage was no laughing matter. "Who'll be replacing him?"

"Another reporter," Ms. J. said. "Benjamin will brief her on his way to the airport. She'll be here in time for the Bad Bachelorette Party."

"A woman?"

Ms. J. nodded. Annabelle looked stoic. Neither Bruno nor Dougray had anything off-color to say, which was a sure sign of trouble. And Adam...

Laura assumed by his frown that he knew full well what a female reporter meant.

He'd get to play escort.

Sinking back against the doorjamb, Laura rubbed her temples to ease the ache growing there. Who else was there but Adam? Forget Bruno. He had a kitchen to run. And Dougray...as much as she loved him, their new reporter would be treated to comic genius that would make the Naughty Nuptials resemble a Keystone Cop comedy.

Not exactly what she'd had in mind.

Her assistant Frank would present the inn and the events perfectly, but he wasn't a department head. Laura didn't want their new reporter to feel slighted in any way.

"Well, this is a turn." She sounded a lot calmer than she felt. "We were counting on Adam to hold down the fort while we hosted the grand opening events."

"There's an up side," Ms. J said.

"Really? And what would that be?"

"The editor felt bad that Benjamin dropped the assignment before our grand opening even got underway, so he's sending someone with a connection to our featured guests."

A cold chill iced over her spine as Ms. J. said, "Miranda Knight's sister."

The moments that followed were like one of those unearthly silences that blanketed the world after a heavy snowfall. Then an image of a woman bloomed in her mind, a gorgeous woman with bright red hair who'd been a year behind her at Westfalls. Victoria Ford might not be as perfect as her perfect big sister—who could be?—but she was still Miranda's sister.

There was no way on earth Laura could expect fair coverage for her grand opening, let alone the rave reviews needed to launch the Wedding Wing into the big leagues.

She glanced around at her co-workers, all the people who'd placed their faith in her dreams and her abilities. Wonderful insightful Ms. J., who'd hired her recognizing what Laura could bring to the position, trusting her instincts even though Laura had no prior experience.

Dearest Annabelle, who'd not only shown her the ropes of working in an upscale hotel but who'd become so much more than a mentor. She'd become a good friend.

Dougray and Bruno, both were always available when she needed them. How often had Dougray helped out in a crisis or made her laugh after her day had taken a nosedive? And Bruno whipped up special meals for guests at the drop of a hat and fed her whenever she forgot to stop and eat a meal.

And then there were the other department heads who weren't fellow stockholders—housekeeping, reservations, grounds, the shop owners and even Adam. His workaholic ways aside, he'd been a rock in every crisis, coolly handling the kinds of unconventional situations that could arise when a hotel combines romance and guests.

They all believed in her. Not one had ever questioned her ability to pull off the Naughty Nuptials. She knew they wouldn't hold her accountable for this turn of events, but Laura also knew that wouldn't matter—she held herself accountable.

She should have swallowed her pride and aired the personal reasons she hadn't wanted the Knights as the Hottest Honeymoon couple in the first place. If Miranda had never shown up, then the managing editor wouldn't have sent her sister to cover the grand opening.

Did inviting me have something to do with keeping up appearances for Miranda's sake? Dale had asked her, and in the darkness of late night she'd tried to answer that question.

Now the answer seemed obvious.

Her past wasn't as far behind her as she'd thought.

And as she glanced around at her co-workers, all of whom were looking to her for reassurance that there wasn't anything to worry about, Laura didn't know which was worse. Having Dale help her face that she'd been deceiving herself or having Miranda and her sister running loose at her grand opening.

11

DALE'S ROLE AS BED buddy and grand opening arm candy altered dramatically when Laura walked into the Castaway Honeymoon Isle, looking as if she'd been hit by a train.

"What's wrong?" he'd asked, all thoughts of hunting down a manufacturer's phone number forgotten.

She stared at him blankly, as if she hadn't expected to find him here and wasn't sure what to say. He'd still been sleeping when she'd slipped out this morning, and if not for the missing number, he'd be working with a crew on the problem skylight right now.

"Laura, what's wrong?" he asked again.

"Benjamin left. He had an opportunity to break a story on an Alaskan nudist colony. The paper's sending another reporter."

"This is bad?"

"They're sending Miranda's sister. She'll be here in time for the bachelorette party."

While Dale hadn't known that Miranda had a sister who was a reporter, he had suspected there was a lot more to the Laura/Miranda story than Laura had told him. Obviously she'd left out some important details. He hadn't pushed her to share more because he hadn't considered knowing important. What had been important was figur-

ing out how to live up to her views about being the man of
her dreams so he didn't get the boot when this grand opening ended.

He'd decided that he wasn't going to run when love hit
him upside the head, as Clyde had said. He was going to
take a page from the old bartender's book and be smart
enough to know when to stay put.

But seeing Laura so obviously rattled only drove home
how underqualified Dale was for this job. The man of her
dreams would know how to make her feel better. Dale's impulse was to drag her into bed until she couldn't remember a world existed outside the Castaway Honeymoon Isle,
let alone details about changing reporters. Which only
went to prove that he didn't have a clue what he was doing
because there had to be another way besides kissing to
wipe that stricken look off her face.

All right, first things first. Crossing the room, he took
her arm and steered her away from the bedroom and all
thoughts of kissing. He slid a chair out from the dining room
table, and said, "Sit. Now tell me what the problem is."

When she lifted her gaze, the worry in those beautiful
eyes nailed him hard.

She was off guard, uncertain, and he could practically see
the wheels in her head spinning, as if she debated what to
tell him. Here was a perfect chance to figure out how to help.

Dragging a chair around, Dale sat down, sliding his
knees between hers, reaching for the hands she'd folded in
her lap. "What's the problem with Miranda's sister?"

She inhaled a deep, shuddering breath then exploded.

"Victoria Ford is part of Miranda's family and they *always* make sure my family knows we're beneath them.
They *never* miss an opportunity to make sure others know

it, too. How on earth are we supposed to get unbiased press for the Naughty Nuptials with her covering the event? She'll be looking under every quarter round to find dirt because of who I am."

Dale forced himself to look past the way her flushed cheeks made her eyes seem even brighter and said, "You sound like you're talking about the Hatfields and the McCoys."

"I am." She heaved a dramatic sigh. "Not the feud but the mentality. Miranda's family have been looking down on my family my whole life simply because we're Grangers. They carry all the weight around here and we're the nonentities. Life is grand as long as we stay out of their way and don't overstep our boundaries. Most people knows that."

Dale tightened his grip on her hands. "Not Westfall's headmistress. She lent you her painting."

Laura dismissed his words with a frown. "Ms. Cecilia's an anomaly. She was my mom's teacher at Westfalls before she became headmistress. You have no idea how much garbage she got when she hired my mom. To Ms. Cecilia's credit, she wouldn't back down. She maneuvered the trustees into a corner so they couldn't get around the fact that my mom was the most qualified person for the job. Short of refusing her appointment based on their bias, they couldn't prevent her hiring."

Dale's gut told him he was still missing a chunk of the picture here. "So your mom went to Westfalls? What about Miranda's mother?"

"Oh, yeah. This has been going on since long before I was born. Trust me, Victoria's going to waltz in here, looking for any way she can to make me look bad. I'm the *bed-*

ding consultant, Dale. This is the *Naughty Nuptials* campaign. How hard will she have to twist things to make Falling Inn Bed appear like some sordid sex palace? I wouldn't be surprised if the senator starts a crusade to shut us down. We'll all be out of jobs."

He wanted to reassure her but anything he said would be bullshit. He still didn't have all the details of what appeared to be a multigenerational pissing contest. He didn't know this reporter or what she might capable of. Laura could be entirely justified in her worries. And once again he regretted the two years he'd had to find out about Laura, time wasted running from his obsession.

Now he wanted to prove that everything about her did matter. He wanted her to share her secrets and tell him about her family. So he gave her hands a reassuring squeeze and asked the only thing he could think of. "What can we do to keep her focused on the story and not her personal feelings?"

Laura sank into the chair, leaned her head back. "Victoria can be as professional as she wants, but she'll still be expecting trash from me. And I just got done reassuring Ms. J. and everyone that our biggest problem would be Adam escorting her to the events. It was a lie, Dale. I should have told them why we shouldn't have invited Miranda in the first place. If I'd have been up front, none of this would have happened."

Dale thought he understood why she hadn't been up front. Laura took on life full-steam ahead with a very unique outlook that had been hailed as visionary. She wouldn't have asked for concessions based on her past history with Miranda Knight. She would have faced her past head-on. There was no way to have foreseen these consequences.

He didn't think Laura would agree. She pulled away and dropped her face into her outstretched hands, and he stared down at the top of her neatly braided head, feeling uncertain and inadequate. He finally gave in to the urge to kiss her and pressed his mouth to all that shiny blond hair.

"Perhaps you should let Ms. J. and the others know about your concerns now, so they'll have a clue about what to expect."

She exhaled heavily. "You're right. It's the only thing to do otherwise they'll be sandbagged by the crappy reviews. And with Adam escorting Victoria… Oh, this is a nightmare."

"*Not* a nightmare," he said, taking her hands in his and bringing them to his lips. "Just a minor setback. One we can deal with."

She lifted her gaze to his, and he saw relief sparkling in those crystal depths. "You're right."

He was *right*, and that was a start.

If Nick Fairfax, the biggest womanizer on the planet, could prove to Julienne that he was marriage material, then Dale could convince Laura he was at least worth a second look after the Naughty Nuptials ended.

LAURA STARED AT Dale, not quite sure how to respond to his suggestion that they skip out of the sex-toy shower. Standing in the inn's adult shop beneath a half mannequin wearing a neon green chastity belt, he looked wildly bad boy with his hip cocked against a glass display case that housed sexual apparatus from Ben Wa balls to eye-catching dildos in a variety of shapes and sizes. He shot her a smile that suggested sex would cure whatever ailed her.

Laura smiled back, her mood lifting. He'd gone to

some trouble filling his shopping bag so they could pretend they'd participated in the search, which raised the question…

"You bought all the items for the sex-toy scavenger hunt? How did you know what was on the master list? I only passed out the clues to our guests."

"I asked Dougray to let me inside your office while you were having lunch with Jackson and Delia and their parents."

"And he did?"

That roguish smile widened, all the more potent for the shelves of sexy paraphernalia surrounding him. "He likes me."

She wasn't sure whether or not to be irritated. She certainly wasn't surprised. If Dougray made one more crack about Dale being *her* man… "Why did you rifle through my desk and steal the master list?"

"So I could give you a break. Something fun, so you'll feel better." Slipping his hand around her elbow, he steered her toward the archway that connected the toy shop with the lingerie boutique. "Natasha is holding a private viewing studio for us."

That wasn't the explanation she'd expected, but Laura appreciated his efforts. Having a meltdown in front of him this morning had surely broken some fling rules. Since he'd been gentlemanly enough not to call her on it, she supposed the least she could do was go along. "But, Dale, this is Delia and Jackson's bridal shower. We have to participate."

"And how can you do that? You coordinated the event so it's not like you don't know where everything is hidden. We'll just disappear for a little while and head back in time for the unveiling and the buffet. All your guests are out hunting so no one will miss you. We'll be back to give out the prizes." He held up the bag. "And I've picked up every item on the list. No one will ever be the wiser."

He'd thought of everything and her heart was going all soft and squishy around the edges. "Why a private viewing studio? Why not sneak up to our suite?"

He smoothed his hand along her arm, a possessive touch that sent a tingle through her. "Because I want to buy you lingerie, Laura. And I want you to model."

"I appreciate what you're doing, Dale, but you don't have to buy me anything. You're doing so much already. Escorting me to all these functions...not to mention the sex."

"This isn't about paybacks," he said so seriously that she frowned. "I'm distracting you. You haven't smiled once since you told the rest of the staff what was going on with Miranda's sister. You told me everyone understood why you handled things the way you did, but you don't seem to be cutting yourself the same slack. You did what you thought was best, Laura. Forget about it now. You don't have to deal with your new reporter until the bachelorette party, so don't."

"You're being very sweet, you know."

He nodded. "And supportive, too."

"Yes, and supportive."

"Not exactly what you expect from your bad boy, hmm?"

He sounded so impressed with himself that Laura couldn't help but laugh. "As a matter of fact, it isn't."

His stoic edges softened. "Well, it's not entirely selfless. Seeing you naked distracts me, too."

Before she could reply, Natasha, the designer of her own lingerie label and owner of this boutique, stepped out from behind the counter.

"Your private viewing room is ready, kids."

A tall, elegantly dressed woman in her early thirties, Natasha had been a neat fit at Falling Inn Bed ever since she'd proposed opening her own boutique on the promenade. Her lingerie designs were erotic and fashionable and with the growing success of her online affiliate, her association with Falling Inn Bed had provided both her business and the inn with great exposure.

Reaching for a ring looped around her wrist, Natasha withdrew a key and dangled it before them. "Now you go have fun. You deserve to after working so hard to pull off this grand opening. If anyone asks for you, I saw you heading in the direction of the atrium."

"You just keep them walking," Dale said.

Then Laura found herself whisked toward the back of the boutique to the viewing studios where customers enjoyed private modeling sessions.

Natasha unlocked the door and motioned them in. "Have fun." She slipped out and Laura caught sight of Dale's reflection as he locked the door behind her.

Like everything else around the inn, this studio had been designed with vintage in mind. The antique dressing screen, beaded blown glass lamps and boudoir chairs were all a spinoff of the Roaring Twenties' Speakeasy suite in the main hotel. The effect was low-lit and romantic and the sight of the garment rack, where sexy lingerie in all colors and designs hung, escalated Laura's pulse until each beat thudded in her ears.

Dale raked his gaze over her, a look that wasn't so much hungry as warmly promising as he moved to the sidebar where champagne and orange juice had been provided. "I knew you wouldn't drink, but I thought maybe you'd take a few sips if I prettied it up."

She nodded. *Anything* to ease the sudden dryness in her mouth. Dale wasn't acting the way she'd expected him to act after she'd breached the rules of a polite fling earlier. First he'd asked personal questions about her past, and now he was deliberately being supportive and arranging wildly romantic interludes to distract her from her worries.

Laura hadn't realized until that moment how much she'd been relying on Dale to play his part in this whole affair. By behaving like she expected him to, he didn't give her a chance to forget their fling would end after the grand opening.

As she accepted a champagne flute and sipped, Laura realized she couldn't put all the responsibility on him. It wasn't fair.

I won't steer you wrong. You have my word.

She'd given him her word, too. She'd promised she could handle a fling.

Slipping her arm through his, Laura led him toward the garment rack. "Ready for the show?"

His eyes danced over her, a look that reminded her of the way they felt together, skin against skin. "Ready."

Choosing a blue peignoir that was both elegant and completely see-through, he fanned his hand beneath the sheer mesh to reveal just how transparent it was. "Oh, I like this one. I can imagine you wearing this."

Her sense of unreality grew at his words, that turned-on feeling she got whenever he looked at her with that hungry expression, whenever their nearness held the promise of sex.

She accepted the hanger while he turned his attention to the shelf above the rack. He inspected the array of sexy heeled slippers, and something about the sight of this man carefully considering her footwear choices seemed intimate, as if he wanted to share even the most personal tasks with her.

His fingers grazed hers as he handed her a pair of slippers with a whimsical swirl of powder-blue boa, and Laura smiled seductively before retreating behind the screen.

Undressing to the sounds of Dale pouring drinks and settling himself in one of the boudoir chairs blew away any remaining sense of reality. This was a moment of pure fantasy, and shedding her jacket, she peeled off her shell, aware of the cool air on her skin, the shimmer of silk mesh as she slipped on the peignoir. Her sense of anticipation heightened in the quiet, her excitement at imagining Dale's expression when she emerged.

She forced herself to stay focused on the moment, to still her racing thoughts, not to analyze what was happening between them and zero in on the goal of enjoying each other every moment they were together.

Sultry mood music played over a sound system and suddenly it was just Laura, her lover and this wonderfully romantic setting. Who cared what would happen when Victoria Ford arrived? Who cared what would happen when the Naughty Nuptials was over and Dale left town forever?

She'd have to deal with all that reality soon enough. But now…she'd designed the Wedding Wing to indulge in the joy of being a couple, and she and Dale qualified.

Slipping her feet into the slippers, she stepped out of the dressing room for the start of her performance.

A *memorable* performance.

Dale sat in the boudoir chair with his legs spread out before him, looking expectant and indulged and oh-so hand-

some as his gaze devoured her in a hungry sweep. He
didn't say a word, just sipped from his flute and twirled his
finger in the air, motioning for her to spin.

Laura did as requested, turning slowly on her toes in a
move honed by years of dance. Indeed, with the tri-fold
mirror reflecting her from different angles, she felt aware
of her body and the sheer physicality of her movements in
a very familiar way. Or maybe it was just the look on
Dale's face that made her so aware of her every move,
made her feel decadent, *bad*.

He watched her as if she was the most beautiful woman
he'd ever seen, as if he'd never wanted a woman more.

It was a powerful feeling, even more so when he said in
a gravelly voice, "This was such a good idea."

"You have lots of good ideas, Dale." Gazing over her
shoulder, she caught a glimpse of herself in triplicate and
inspiration struck. "So do I."

Rolling her hips, she watched the silk shimmer in reflection with the motion, a fluid, sexy move that obviously
looked as good as it felt given the sharp exhalation of
breath that came from Dale's direction.

That was all the encouragement Laura needed.

She started up a sultry rhythm, moving sinuously as she
rolled her shoulders and arched her back, swaying to the
rhythm of the piped-in music. She could feel the familiar
calm that always happened when she danced, the very reason she'd kept dancing through high school, college and
now as her exercise of choice.

Her moves were simple, but dancing chased away everything except for the sweet release of tension and her
awareness of the man who watched.

She could sense his gaze upon her, feel the heat of her

body's response to her uncustomary boldness. She not only danced for his viewing pleasure, but was reflected in the mirrors, giving him a view from all angles.

The peignoir swayed and shimmered, the silk sheer enough to treat him with glimpses of her swaying backside, the outline of her parted thighs. It was the boldness of the sight that inspired her to add another sexy twist.

Raising her hands, she brushed her palms across her breasts, a barely there touch that evoked an immediate reaction as her nipples drew to tight peaks beneath the silk.

A glance over her shoulder proved she had Dale's undivided attention. He'd leaned back in the chair, legs stretched before him, hands gripping the sides, the champagne flute forgotten on a nearby table. His expression had sharpened, his eyes had grown hooded in a look of profound appreciation and...*restraint*.

He devoured her with his gaze. His fingertips disappeared into the poufy chair arms with his death grip on the chintz. Now wasn't for touching. Now was for pleasure, for proving she could create memories of their time together.

So Laura pivoted slowly as she loosened the ribbon at her throat to let the peignoir fall open. Arching her back, she leaned forward then back again, a liquid movement that made her bare breasts spill from the parted fabric, swaying heavily as she kicked up her tempo.

She raked her gaze over Dale's hungry expression, smiled at his surprise when she caught her nipples and pulled, a slow, thorough move that lifted her breasts and made her gasp at the sheer eroticism of the thrill bolting through her.

Then she spun away and slipped behind the screen.

By the time she'd completed her second costume change, she'd nearly forgotten life existed outside of this viewing studio, that she still had guests on a scavenger hunt. She immersed herself in this unique opportunity to enjoy the romantic atmosphere she had created for couples.

And one glimpse of herself in the stretch lace two-piece that left her midriff and a significant portion of her backside bare awoke something daring inside her. She felt challenged to bring Dale to his knees. She wanted to prove to him, and *herself*, that she could stick to the game plan no matter what, even though her feelings kept sliding from her grasp, and thoughts of romance, of promises and tomorrows and forevers, kept stealing in when her guard slipped.

This time Dale let out a groan when she stepped from behind the screen, and Laura smiled at the need in that sound, the frustration, the *desire*. She treated herself to a glimpse of him, the way he shifted uncomfortably in his chair.

She let him observe her body from all angles, twirling slowly to give him ample opportunity to appreciate just how much this skimpy outfit didn't cover. The heeled slippers—little gold numbers this time—hiked her legs up. She wished she could unbind her hair just because she knew he'd like it, yet her braid showed so much more skin.

Rolling her neck, she sent her braid flying, liking the playful motion. These little short-shorts had a wealth of potential, and with a laugh, Laura started up a new dance, more action this time, lively moves that didn't match the music but mirrored the throbbing thrum of her pulse.

She allowed herself a glimpse of what she looked like in the mirror, and let her gaze sweep over the bold image she presented, all pale skin and bare legs, the flirty little outfit leaving nothing to the imagination. She could see the blush of her nipples through the mesh, the V of hair between her thighs. She liked the way her muscles shifted with the provocative moves, and when she caught sight of his reflection, she knew Dale liked the way she looked, too.

He'd leaned forward on the plush chair and braced his elbows on his knees. His chest rose and fell on sharp breaths, but his look was pure sex. Laura had no doubt that he was feeling the effects of her performance as much as she did.

And she felt them, big-time.

She caught his gaze in the mirror and the moment reminded her of the last time they'd stood in front of a mirror—when he'd first touched her in the Castaway Honeymoon Isle. His gaze had promised her pleasure while his touch had turned fantasy into a reality.

Only then he'd had the control. He'd brought her to orgasm and watched while she went to pieces in his arms.

Now, he was the audience.

Rolling her shoulders, she dipped down, down, *down*…her braid brushing the floor and her muscles stretching as she lifted her backside high. She heard his sharp intake of breath as the mesh stretched tight across her most private places and she knew he was getting a serious glimpse of the goods.

"Laura, I think I've met my match in you."

Somehow she'd never realized how powerful being wanted could be. But Dale's throaty admission inspired her to even greater boldness, and slipping her fingers between her thighs, she let him watch her touching herself.

"Dale, I'm not sure I should take that as a compliment."

"You should, trust me," he ground out, low and raw, and the sound of his hunger combined with the light caresses on her skin made her shiver. "You test my control."

"This is a good thing?" Rocking her bottom from side to side for good measure, she made sure he got a clear shot of her fingers.

His low groan assured her. "It's a very good thing. You challenge me, Laura Granger."

She found it hard to imagine how she could challenge a bad boy with a reputation the size of Dale's, but she didn't question him further. Right now wasn't about explanations or analysis—it was all about pleasure.

And she didn't want distractions. Not when her pleasure was mounting, whether from her intimate touches or from simply knowing that Dale struggled to keep his hands to himself, Laura didn't know. But she knew she'd never felt this way before, and she liked the feeling. *A lot.*

Costume change number three had her wearing a satin babydoll with a padded bodice for some hike 'em up cleavage. The top fastened right below her breasts and then flared open to reveal every inch of skin down to the teeny-weeny matching thong that rode low on her hips.

"Oh, that's sweet," Dale said when she stepped out from behind the screen, and she couldn't resist bending over to readjust a strap on the slipper, treating him to a shot of her backside in triplicate just to refresh his memory. The thong disappeared into the cleft of her bottom, and Laura straightened, twirling in front of the mirrors and surveying herself. "It doesn't show much skin compared to the others. What do you think?"

"I think I want to pull down that thong with my teeth."

"Maybe we don't need to see skin, after all."

But she showed him some anyway.

Raising her arms above her head, she shimmied around in a full circle as the hem rode up to her waist, revealing the thong in all its glory, all the skin it didn't cover.

"You look good enough to eat, Laura."

"I'll have to take you at your word," she said in her silkiest voice when he shoved himself out of the chair and stalked to the sidebar to pour another drink.

"That's a winner, too," he said without looking at her. "Add it to the pile."

He looked delightfully frazzled around the edges, and she savored the feeling of knowing he was coming apart with her every carefully aimed salvo.

"There hasn't been one outfit you don't like. Are you always this agreeable?"

"Can't say."

"Why?"

He gave her an amused grin. "I don't usually shop for women's clothing."

Now that he mentioned it, shopping for clothing seemed like such a *couple* thing to do that she wasn't surprised he hadn't done more before. And along with that feeling came more power, and a sense of purely feminine satisfaction that he'd taken *her* shopping—especially for something so intimate as lingerie.

Sidling close, she cut off his escape to the chair and pressed up against him, whispering, "I'm glad you brought me here."

His arm shot around her waist like a whipcord, anchoring her so close, she could barely breathe. Then his mouth came down on hers, a wild combination of sweet champagne and fierce hunger. A kiss so greedy that her knees turned to jelly and she leaned against him for balance.

"Oh my, my, my, my, Laura." He breathed the words against her mouth. "I'll be dreaming about you for the rest of my life."

Not *fantasizing*, but *dreaming*, and in Laura's mind there was a difference. While she knew Dale didn't make the same distinction, she couldn't help being captured by the deep-throated lust in his voice. She'd accomplished mission objective today. The man of her fantasies had sex on his mind.

So did she. Her sex throbbed in time with her pulse, and when Dale dragged his mouth away, she protested with a groan.

But then he caught the edge of the bodice with his teeth and snapped it away. One breast rolled out of the cup, and exposed her pouting nipple.

Dale caught it, a careful, teasing, tempting bite that made her moan. And when he sucked it inside his mouth with a slow, moist pull, Laura's legs grew boneless beneath her.

"Let's make love." She barely recognized the voice as her own, but with him sucking on her breast and sending shock waves through her, she was lucky to have gotten the words out.

He didn't bother with an answer, just held her tight as he speared his hand between her thighs and brushed aside the thong. He found her moist and ready, and Laura moaned again as he zeroed in on her needy places, could only respond to his lethal touches that brought her to climax as she stood there gasping.

It was over that fast, and when she could think again, she could only press a kiss to the top of his silky head and sigh.

"Do you still think this was such a good idea?" she asked. "I feel great, but you look uncomfortable."

"Uncomfortable is an understatement." He gave a snort of not entirely amused laughter. "Is there anything in this place you didn't design to make couples horny?"

"If there is, I'll fix it."

He gave another gruff laugh but didn't let her go.

"I won't send you back to the scavenger hunt horny, Dale."

Raising his hand to her face, he brushed his fingers against her cheek, a gesture that seemed oddly tender in the heat of the moment. "But I didn't come to make love to you, Laura. I came to admire the view."

"You don't want to make love?"

"I *always* want to make love." A grin played around his mouth. "But I didn't bring you here to do anything but distract you from worrying about tonight, and I did."

He'd surprised her. Dale had remarked before that there was always time to make love if she was already undressed…

"You wanted to make me feel better," she said, understanding dawning. "Dale, that's so…noble of you."

"I told you, being a bad boy doesn't mean I'm degenerate."

"I never said it did."

"It was there."

"No, it wasn't." And it bothered her that he thought it was. "I never meant to imply you were degenerate. I wanted you to know that my eyes were wide open when I sent my invitation, that I wouldn't be under any mistaken impressions about what our relationship could be. I did think hearing about lots of happy women would make you feel good. Obviously, I was mistaken. I don't understand why you're being sensitive about this."

In a sudden move, he dragged her around and sank down into the chair, pulling her into his lap. This new vantage made her feel every inch of her bare skin but not because he was fully clothed. Rather it was his serious expression that declared this moment was about a lot more than sex.

"I'm not sensitive, Laura. It's just…" He exhaled heavily, reaching for her braid which had gotten caught between them. He rearranged it over her shoulder, fingering her hair thoughtfully. "I know my dating history doesn't make me look good. But that's not all I am, and I want you to see that."

This admission was *so* not what Laura had expected. She hadn't had the slightest idea that calling him on his past behavior would make him feel the need to prove himself, which just went to show how far out of her league she was with this man.

"I do see that. And I think you're a very noble man," she said, willing him to hear her words, to accept the truth. "I'd never have sent my invitation if I didn't. I know you think Miranda had something to do with that, and while I honestly didn't realize it at the time, I think you might be right."

Lifting her hand to his face, she caressed his cheek with the same familiarity that he touched her. And here it was…the admission. She wasn't sure if this was breaking a fling rule, but she needed him to understand.

"I thought by letting Miranda and Troy attend the grand opening that I'd prove I'd put the past to bed. But now I see it's not as behind me as I thought. Dealing with Miranda again has only shown me that I *still* don't like feeling second best."

"You're number one with me, Laura."

She thumbed the strong line of his jaw, smiled. "I wouldn't change one second we've spent together."

Her admission sounded so intimate in the hush between them that the vintage studio, the quiet music and all her bare skin faded beneath her need for him to believe her.

And when his fingertips tightened around her jaw, and he tipped her face up to meet his kiss, Laura knew he did.

_12_

VICTORIA FORD, Tori as she'd introduced herself to the management staff upon her arrival, was no less intimidating than her big sister but in a surprisingly different way.

Laura had seen her often in the Westfalls hallways and the common room of their shared dormitory. While they'd both lived in Marceaux House, over a decade had passed since. The woman, as opposed to the young student in Laura's memory, had come as something of a shock.

The physical characteristics weren't so far off from Miranda. Like her big sister, Tori was of average height and delicate build, which managed to make taller Laura feel like a giant. The blue eyes were the same deep shade, but her hair was wavy rather than curly, a lush red instead of black.

Miranda presented herself as the vision of perfection, calm, cool and collected, capable of remaining equally so facing the press or in the path of an oncoming tornado. Tori, on the other hand, _was_ a force of nature. She radiated a presence that no one could miss. She was, quite simply, a woman designed to be noticed.

She'd blown into Ms. J.'s office with no less force than a level three twister and announced her excitement at having the opportunity to step into Benjamin's place. It was fate, she'd declared, because with her connections to the Hottest Honeymoon couple and the bedding consultant, she should have been assigned this grand opening from the start. Not to mention that many reporters would have given their right arms to collaborate with Tyler Tripp on a project.

Laura hadn't known how prestigious it was to work with Tyler, but two things did strike her before the introductions ended. The first was that Dale had been dead right with his advice to explain the situation with the Ford sisters to her co-workers. Had Laura not explained, they'd have all been left openmouthed when Tori had blown through the door with her announcement to capitalize on that situation.

Miranda would *never* have played the personal hand. She would have kept their past history to herself until she'd discovered how much everyone already knew. Miranda operated subtly, controlling the chance of messy repercussions.

Which had led to realization number two: the escort situation for their newly assigned reporter was destined for disaster. Miranda's perfect decorum was more along the lines of what Adam could comfortably handle. Tori's waltz-through-the-door-and-leave-no-one-standing style had the assistant G.M. scowling before he'd gotten into Ms. J.'s office.

She'd shaken Laura's hand and said, "Well, well, well, I get to investigate the Laura Granger up close and personal. This will be interesting."

Emphasis on *investigate*, which added another layer of personal innuendo, and Laura knew right then that Tori would eat Adam as an hors d'oeuvre before gobbling her for the main course.

Then she drew a line in the sand. "Be forewarned, *bed-*

ding consultant, I'm here to get the real scoop on what you're doing around here. I want the down and dirty."

Before Laura could recover from *that*, Tori turned on Adam. "I assume you won't want me attending your events stag. Do you want me to invite a date or will you supply a tour guide? Someone in executive management, perhaps."

Adam looked as though he might burst a blood vessel at just the thought of attending events with *this* woman, but he stepped up to the plate like the professional he was. "I'll be escorting you to our grand opening functions."

"Great. I'll be writing articles daily to report on those functions and keep our readership up to speed. In between events, I'll research the history of the inn and interview staff and guests. I'm going to be pretty demanding, Adam Grant."

"I'll make myself available," he said in a voice Laura recognized as expecting the worst.

And it looked like he'd get it, too, because Tori flashed him a smile that said, "Watch out!"

By the time the interview ended, Laura knew they were all in trouble. Taking a page from Tori's book, she placed her cards on the table after escorting the woman from the office.

"I know you visited us for Miranda's wedding," she said. "But I can arrange a grand tour if you'd like, introduce you to our shop owners and, of course, I'll acquaint you with the Wedding Wing myself."

"I'm counting on it. I was here for my sister's wedding and I have to tell you she was mighty put out you didn't coordinate her event. I think she wanted you to wait on her hand and foot." She gave an offhand shrug. "Personally, I was impressed with how you weaseled out of the deal.

Trust me, it's not every day Miranda gets turned down and let me tell you, there's nothing worse than a bitchy bride."

Laura had no clue how to respond to that admission. Fortunately, she didn't have to because Tori was too busy taking in the main lobby.

"There's a story in this place and I intend to find it," she said. "You've been setting this town on its ear since you started this whole bedding consultant thing, but you've managed to keep it clean enough that none of the movers and shakers around here ever have anything to object to."

Laura could hear the *yet* in there. "It's easy to keep things clean. We *are* clean. We're a romance resort—"

"I know, I know. I read all your spin." Waving a dismissive hand, Tori slowed as they passed the toy shop.

At first glance the display behind the pristine glass appeared to be nothing more than luxury gift baskets filled with personal items decorated in the colors of summer flowers. But Laura knew those baskets were filled with sexual enhancements and stepped up her pace to avoid confronting Joy Jelly, Motion Lotion and Peterbutter two seconds after she'd claimed to run a clean establishment.

No such luck.

"Pleasure and Sizzle, a naughty nipple cream." Tori shot her an amused glance. "Squeaky clean, I see."

"Do I need to be worried?"

"Not if you're telling me the truth and running this place on the up and up," Tori replied. "I want the scoop, and I'll get it. If you're asking me if whether I'll be biased because of our family situation, let's just say that I'm not looking to blast you unless you deserved to be blasted."

"I hear a *but* in there."

Tori laughed. "*But*…I've got a more personal perspective on you than Benjamin did, or Tyler Tripp for that matter. I'm probably looking for different things in my story. You're interesting around here, Laura, and the locals like to read about our families. I intend to do whatever it takes to make my coverage of this place shoot the circulation through the roof. I've got an agenda."

"Proving yourself?"

She nodded and patted the laptop case slung over one shoulder. "That, and furthering my career. Unlike my big sister, who's living the life my family expects her to live, I'm a career girl. You are, too, so I'm sure you understand what that entails."

What Laura understood was that Tori Ford wasn't at all what she'd been expecting, and she still had no idea if that boded well or ill for her inn. But the woman had at least been up front about her intentions—her sister would never have been—and that gave Laura something to work with.

Directing Tori to the Wedding Wing's front desk, she said, "Let's get you checked in."

With a glance, she directed the desk clerk to stand aside and went into the system to upgrade Tori's room assignment from a nice corner room to the Wedding Knight Suite.

In Ms. J.'s office, Tori had mentioned looking forward to working with Tyler. As the bedding consultant, it was Laura's job to facilitate romance in any way she could.

While Tyler was definitely too bohemian for her personal tastes, he was a handsome, ambitious man who'd proven he appreciated romance. Tori was a beautiful woman who shared a common interest in journalism, and if there was any way at all to distract this woman from eating Adam for a snack, Laura was not above matchmaking.

"I have to tell you that I was shocked when you managed to get a Mireille Marceaux erotic on loan from West-falls," Tori said and Laura glanced up from the computer to find her staring at the *Falling Woman* with a frankly disbelieving expression. "Miranda told my mother that you used your personal connections to get the headmistress to approve the loan."

Laura didn't know much about Tori's relationship with Miranda, but if they were communicating through their mother, she suspected they weren't too close. This came as no real surprise when Laura thought about it. If being compared to the perfect Miranda had affected *her* life so dramatically, what would it mean to be the woman's *sister*?

Just the thought diminished some of Laura's animosity toward the new reporter. "Nothing manipulative. I just asked my mom to mention it to Ms. Cecilia, then worked up a proposal."

"You must know how the town's been buzzing ever since word got out."

"I do."

Tori shot her an assessing look. "You wanted the buzz for your grand opening."

"I didn't think it would hurt."

She pulled a thoughtful moue, as if Laura had surprised her, too. "Smooth move."

Laura smiled in acknowledgment of the compliment, produced a card key and said, "Let's get you settled into your suite."

"Suite, hmm? I happen to know that Benjamin stayed in a regular guest room. I know that because I wasn't aware you even had any regular rooms until he told me." She arched a skeptical brow. "Are you sucking up to me, Laura?"

"I didn't think it would hurt."

Tori grinned. "If nothing else, this is going to prove an interesting few weeks, don't you think?"

Laura met her deep blue gaze, a gaze similar to Miranda's, yet strikingly different.

And she felt a flicker of promise inside.

She might not have withstood the test of dealing with Miranda and their history as well as she'd hoped, but here was another chance to handle things better.

Returning Tori's smile, she said, "I do."

DALE SHOULD HAVE known to expect the unexpected from Laura when the men and women split up for the respective bachelor/ette parties. She had Delia's guests currently dining in the spa's garden café, a place where Bruno created health-conscious dishes and fruit shakes laced with proteins and mineral immune-system boosters. From there they'd spend their night mud-bathing and pedicuring and enjoying whatever else women did in a spa.

Laura had refused to tell him what she had in store for the men, but the second Dale stepped into one of the Wedding Wing's ballrooms to find it transformed into a gangster-era gentleman's club, he'd known Jackson's guests had fared much better than the ladies. A stage had been set up as the focal point of the room, complete with rich red velvet curtains, professional lighting and acoustic sound. Wingback chairs surrounded small tables, and an all-male waitstaff refreshed cocktails and food from an impressive buffet.

Scantily clad rockette-style dancers filed onto the stage to applause and catcalls, beginning the first act of sexy skits reminiscent of Gypsy Rose Lee and the Ziegfeld Follies. Dale found the whole show an event to remember and as far as he could tell, he wasn't the only man present to think so. Laura had gone straight to the heart of male fantasies while managing not to piss off the father of the bride.

By the time dim light illuminated the room during the first intermission, Dale was more convinced than ever that he'd do whatever it took not to let Laura get away.

"I don't believe Laura," Tyler said to Dale and Troy, who sat with him at the table. "Where does she come up with this stuff?"

Dale laughed over the rim of his beer glass. "I wish I knew. She's got a gift."

"That's an understatement," Troy said. "Miranda was dying to know what she had planned for a *bad* bachelor party. After that scavenger hunt this afternoon, I think she was worried."

"Speaking of—" Dale turned to Troy. "You made a good showing. Second place was nothing to shake a stick at with those riddles. I couldn't figure out what the hell she was talking about in a couple of them."

"I hear you," Tyler agreed. "I would have been dead last if not for the bride's parents getting sidetracked while I was looking for that minidildo in the main lobby. What was up with that? Laura gave Major General Wallace a different map than the rest of us. He and his wife got lost in the offices looking at vintage photos and reading about the history of this old place."

Dale gave an offhand shrug. "Don't have a clue, Tyler, but it's no wonder you nearly came in last. I hate to break it to you, man, but you weren't looking for a minidildo in the main lobby. It was a butt plug."

Tyler almost choked, but Troy smiled and said, "You give my compliments to Laura. She walked a tough line with her party tonight and made the cut. Doesn't look like there's anyone in this place who's not looking forward to act two."

"You got it."

"There's the major general," Tyler said, shoving his chair back. "I've been trying to catch up with him to arrange a time for an interview." He strode away, leaving Dale alone with Troy.

"So how are you and Miranda enjoying the grand opening?" Dale asked.

"It's a lot different than the first time we were here."

Dale couldn't tell whether this was good or bad. "I'm guessing your wife is glad her sister will be covering it. Where do you stand on the issue?"

"She's my sister-in-law." Troy gave a shrug. "Where do you think I stand?"

"Fair enough. Laura mentioned that she didn't want you two to feel excluded with everything focusing on the bride and groom." Putting a good word in with the reporter's brother-in-law couldn't hurt.

"Tell her not to worry. Miranda and I were long overdue a vacation and there's a certain irony to returning to the scene of the wedding."

Given his unsmiling expression, Troy might have been talking about the scene of the *crime*, but the guy seemed genuine when he said, "You tell Laura that I appreciate how decent she's been. She's gone out of her way to welcome us. I'm sure she won't hear it from Miranda."

"I'll tell her." Dale raised his glass to his lips, drank. He recognized when opportunity knocked and decided to go for it. "So what's up with that? Laura told me that she and your wife weren't friends in school, that people always compared them."

"I suppose it makes sense. Prescott's a big name around here," Troy said, as if that explained everything.

"This whole small-town thing is way over my head. It's like people haven't got anything better to do than nose into other people's business." As he'd learned firsthand. "But tell me something, Troy. I get the part about your wife. She's news. But what's the big deal about Laura—the artist community?"

"I'd guess the family connection."

Family connection? Dale stared stupidly for a moment before comprehension finally dawned. "Are you saying Laura and Miranda are related?"

"They're cousins. You didn't know?"

Dale shook his head. "Distant cousins?"

"*First* cousins as in their mothers are sisters. It's no deep dark secret. Senator Prescott isn't allowed secrets. Neither is his family."

There was subtext in that statement but Dale couldn't dwell on how being related to a senator might affect a family. Not while still absorbing the fact that Laura was also affected and that she hadn't told him something so simple, and important, about herself.

Dale didn't have to wonder why.

He hadn't earned the right to be trusted with her truths. She expected no more than a fling with him and as she'd said last night, she didn't want to break the rules.

"Any idea what's between them?" he asked.

"Not really. Whatever happened took place a *long* time before I came into the picture. Miranda has only said that Laura's mother ran off with someone the senator didn't approve of. Laura's father, I think."

Dale nodded. "Sounds a little extreme but like you said,

this all happened a long time ago. Sure explains why people would compare her to Miranda, though."

Troy frowned. "Yeah, well, all I can tell you is don't be so quick to judge. Laura gets off a lot easier than my wife does. There are a lot of expectations in the family. Laura's exempt by default, and most of the time Victoria refuses to step up to the plate. All the pressure to put on a good show falls on Miranda."

"I don't know enough about the situation to form opinions."

But that would change soon enough. There was a lot more happening with Laura's family than she'd told him and until she decided to share…which wouldn't happen until he proved himself more than a fling.

With that goal in mind, Dale sat through the second act, not enjoying this half of the show, but formulating a plan of action. Discovering this piece of the puzzle helped him fill in the blanks about what Laura had told him last night.

He understood why she would be so inclined to prove herself to Miranda, and to protect her parents from people who viewed them as a cut below Senator Prescott.

The situation was ironic, really. Here he'd been scrambling around for chances to prove he could rise above his press and be more than arm candy for the Naughty Nuptials. But that wasn't the only thing he needed to prove. Dale needed to make Laura understand that he wasn't one of the people she'd grown up with who were fascinated with why Senator Prescott had disowned his eldest daughter and her family.

The only person he was fascinated with was Laura, and she had nothing to prove to him.

Dale was in so far over his head here that he couldn't

help laughing. Peering up at the stage at a group of beauties who would have once enthralled him, he was now so preoccupied with a certain blonde he'd barely noticed them.

Dale thought he understood why so many folks ran when love found them.

But by the time the bachelors finally disbanded, he had the start of a plan, and swinging by the front desk, he penned a note to Annabelle that began:

Hey, gorgeous, I need your help....

"WHAT DO YOU mean you're kidnapping me?" Laura asked. "I can't leave the inn."

Dale had clearly lost his mind or somehow warped ahead a few weeks into the future after the Naughty Nuptials had ended. Yet he stood beside her in this elevator, looking so good in his custom-made suit that hinted at all the sculpted muscle below.

Leave the inn? She wasn't sure she wanted to push her luck that far. She'd survived the bachelorette party and staff interviews with Tori last night and a personal tour of the property this morning.

"Wear the blue dress you wore to dinner the night I came to town," he said. "You promised to wear it so I could slide my hands under all that lace. I'll be able to drive and feel you up as long as you navigate."

"Navigate where?"

"It's a surprise."

"What about the arrangements for the dinner tonight?"

"You've taken care of everything." He scowled. "All the staff has to do is pull the room together, Laura, and I think they can do their jobs without you standing over them. We've got a luncheon engagement. We'll be back in plenty of time for you to check the room setup and get dressed for dinner."

"A luncheon engagement? Where?"

He whipped out an envelope from his jacket pocket. "With some folks I want to meet."

Laura slipped a finger through the seam, recognized stationary from her own private stock—the very same she'd used for his invitation to the Castaway Honeymoon Isle. "Been making yourself at home in my office again, I see."

He nodded, unrepentant as she scanned the invitation.

You are cordially invited to dine at the Niagara River Artist Retreat. Russ and Suzanne Granger, hosts.

"My parents are hosting a luncheon?"

He depressed the emergency button, and Laura grabbed on to him as the elevator jerked to a stop. He only smiled, plucked the invitation from her and slipped it back into his pocket.

Now it was her turn to scowl. "If you keep hitting that emergency button, people will think your company does terrible work. A brand-new elevator shouldn't break down like this."

He looked much more interested in her than his company's reputation. Slipping his hands inside her jacket, he skimmed his palms down her ribs.

"I want to meet your parents," he told her. "And I want to get you away from the inn for a breather before the wedding." He rested his cheek on the top of her head, inhaled deeply.

She couldn't miss what he was trying to do here—make her feel better just like he had during the scavenger hunt. Resting her cheek against his shoulder, she steeled herself against his thoughtfulness, reminded herself not to get all squishy and to simply enjoy the moment.

"So how'd you finagle an invitation?" she asked. "You didn't just call them up and ask them to invite you, did you?"

"Of course not." He sounded offended. "I coerced Annabelle into helping me. She arranged your afternoon off with Ms. J. and introduced me to your folks. A piece of cake after the way she helped you out with my invitation and scared off my date."

She laughed. The way this man manipulated *her* coworkers into working for *him* was nothing short of pushy. "When did this take place?"

"While you were taking your new reporter on a tour of the Wedding Wing this morning. Annabelle got your parents on the phone. I told them I'd been lusting after their daughter for the past two years, I thought it time to introduce myself. They invited us for lunch."

"You're kidding?" She hoped.

"All right, I didn't say anything about lusting after you."

Much to her parents' disappointment, no doubt. Dale couldn't know they'd have loved to hear about a bad boy in her life. They'd never cared much for her dating criteria and had been after her to "let go and live." But Laura knew they were biased, as head over heels now as they'd been upon meeting.

Unfortunately, their sort of love didn't come without a price, and while her parents had willingly paid it, Laura had lived with the consequences, too, which is why she insisted on similar interests, goals and lifestyles. Simple things, but essential...or at least she'd always thought so.

Until meeting Dale Emerson.

Reaching up, she brushed a thatch of silky hair from Dale's brow. "What did you tell them—that you were my *friend*?" Her parents would ascribe their own definition, of course.

"I told them we were dating."

"Dating? I thought we were having a fling."

He rolled his eyes. "I wasn't going to tell your parents that. Besides, flings and dating aren't mutually exclusive."

"Yes, they are. Dating implies a future, and we've only got the Naughty Nuptials. You have no idea what you're getting into here. I don't have normal parents. I thought I told you that."

"I want to see for myself."

"I don't understand why." She couldn't get away from the question. Flings implied temporary. Dating implied romance. Laura couldn't do romance. She couldn't even *think* romance. "This is against the fling rules."

"Shh." Lowering his face, he brushed a kiss across her lips. "I'm the one who knows the rules here, and you promised to trust me about that."

True, but that was before realizing she couldn't trust herself. She couldn't even skirt the topic of romance. Not with Dale's imminent departure looming.

"I did promise to trust you, but I didn't expect you to go behind my back and start colluding with my co-workers to change my schedule."

"You weren't around so I made the arrangements," he said, obviously not getting the point. "I wanted to meet your parents and I wanted to get you away from this place for a while. No work. No worries. No Miranda. No Tori. Lunch with your parents makes sense."

"Are you sure you don't want to sneak upstairs?"

"What is it with you and sex, Laura? Is that all you think about?" He nibbled her top lip, proving that she wasn't the only one who was thinking about it.

"That's all I'm supposed to think about. Especially since

you're one up on the orgasm count after that side trip from the scavenger hunt." *Supposed to* being the point. But Laura didn't think he'd want to hear that she needed sex to distract her from romance every time he did something thoughtful.

So she squirmed against him, instead, savoring the warm rush of awareness that pulsed through her. "When I'm with you, I can't help it. Too much deprivation for too long, I think."

He laughed, a warm sound that burst softly against her lips. "I thought that once, too."

"You've changed your mind?"

He shook his head and looked thoughtful.

"What do you think is happening then?" she asked, suddenly breathless.

"I'm still trying to figure it out. I've got some ideas though. I'll tell you about it sometime."

"Tell me now."

"No. I haven't figured it all out yet. It's hard to think straight with all the romance flying around this place."

She felt suddenly, unaccountably relieved and gave a laugh. "You're supposed to get caught up in the romance around here, Dale. Falling Inn Bed is a romance resort, remember?"

"Trust me. I got that part."

"I do trust you." Nibbling his lower lip, she kissed her way around his mouth, was rewarded when that hardness against her tummy gave a throb. "I trust you to pleasure me."

"If you keep that up, this elevator won't start moving anytime soon." He finally reached for the button.

The elevator lurched into motion, and Dale hurried her into their suite to change. She tossed on her blue dress at his request, and while she dressed, she tried to make sense of his actions. She appreciated that he'd put forth this effort, but wished he hadn't. The more wonderful he was, the more difficult she found it to keep her thoughts on sex where they belonged.

With everything going on with the grand opening, Laura was counting on Dale to keep their fling just a fling, and as they drove out of town toward her family home, she gazed out the window and warned herself not to misinterpret his actions.

He might be a die-hard bad boy, but he was still a very charming and decent man. He'd witnessed her stress over work, shared her revelations about Miranda, helped her cope with Tori's arrival. Of course he'd be thoughtful and caring.

But as she watched him, his profile sharp against the sunlit window, Laura realized what was happening here—Dale was bringing out the best in her. In helping her face her past. In keeping an open mind with Tori.

Between his orgasms and his thoughtfulness, he was tangling up all the romance she created at Falling Inn Bed with all the romance she shouldn't be feeling in her head.

"Why are you staring at me, Laura?" he asked. "You look so serious."

She was serious—*seriously* in trouble—because the man of her fantasies was turning into the man of her dreams.

13

LAURA GAZED AROUND the familiar terrain with a growing sense of determination as Dale wheeled down her parents' drive. He couldn't have known it when planning this trip, but home was exactly where she needed to be right now— the perfect reminder of why she'd always had such decided ideas about the differences between the man of her dreams and the man of her fantasies.

Home was a tribute to soul mates and the power of love and a much-needed reminder of why she wasn't giving in to it until she found the perfect man.

Her parents had renovated the late 1800s farmhouse to include their studios and serve as a retreat for artists who wanted to hide from life on the surrounding acres. They'd originally added a wing to the two-story gabled structure, and through the years had built two more, which lent the place a rather sprawling look.

Footpaths led from the house down to the river and with the outbuildings that served as mixed media studios presenting an assortment of rooftops through the trees, the whole compound had a very rustic, isolated feel.

A place to inspire the muse.

Dale slowed the car and parked beside a wooden sign that read Niagara River Artist Retreat, Circa 1981, that one of their woodworking alumni had created a few years back. He swung his gaze from side to side to take in the bronze sculptures dotting the landscape in grottoes carved from the forest's edge.

His eyes widened. "Your father's the sculptor, right?"

She nodded, not bothering to add that her father had a penchant for the sensual. She thought that much would be obvious from the life-size bronze of a naked woman with her arms raised above her head as she worshipped the sun like a pagan goddess. Appropriately, she'd been named *Sun Goddess*.

Laura hoped to display one of her dad's pieces after returning *Falling Woman* to Westfalls. She'd considered one of his sculptures for the grand opening but had worried about its reception. He was *her* father, after all, and Falling Inn Bed walked such a fine line between sex and romance even when it wasn't intentionally in the spotlight....

But now that she'd set the tone with her loan of the erotic Mireille Marceaux, displaying one of his pieces would be completely appropriate.

"So you come by your appreciation of romance and sex naturally," Dale said.

"My parents are one big love affair. They've been married for thirty years and they're still honeymooners. You'll see."

"So I shouldn't be surprised they raised an idealist?" Something about his expression seemed wistful when he gazed around. "It must have been interesting growing up here."

"Definitely interesting. And frequently embarrassing with my parents running around like two kids in love. But we always had something going on. Not a year passed when they weren't expanding their residency programs or building a new facility. Last year they added a digital imaging studio inside the house. And the year before it was that clay cooperative workshop over there." She pointed to a nearby structure.

Dale followed her gaze, then said, "Let me get your door. I'd really like to see the place. This is my first artists' retreat." After circling the car, he extended his hand to help her out. "Why didn't you become an artist? You must have had plenty of inspiration growing up around all this."

This encompassed everything, including a sculpture of a whimsical and scantily clad fairy beside the porch stairs.

"I found my creative outlet here," she said. "Part of sharing a house with artists means making them feel welcome. I helped out by cooking in our community kitchen and cleaning guest rooms while our residents worked in the studios. Hospitality gives me the best of both worlds."

Dale didn't release her hand. "You do have a gift for making your guests feel welcome, Laura. And you've flexed your creative muscles at Falling Inn Bed. Jackson's bachelor party was brilliant. Troy wanted me to tell you that."

"Thank you—"

"Cherish," her mom's voice called out through the opening front door. "Come on in. We can't wait to meet Dale. Daddy will be out of the studio in a sec."

"Cherish?" Dale arched a dark brow.

"Long story. Not important." She directed him inside.

An eclectic mix of history and art, the Niagara River Artist Retreat was a world unto itself. The only telephone line ran into the office and hurried lifestyles slowed to a crawl when the residents turned onto the dirt path that led to the farmhouse.

For the three weeks to three months of a residency,

every waking hour was spent in artistic expression or communing with other artists. It was a cool place and Laura was glad Dale liked it. Not everyone did, as she'd learned firsthand.

Her mom flung the door wide, showcasing herself, waist-length hair streaming down her back, ankle-length skirt flowing around her slim form. Laura kissed her mom's cheek and introduced Dale.

"Suzanne Granger." Mom extended her hand and smiled. "It's such a pleasure to meet you, Dale. I'm glad you called. Cherish stopped bringing boys home after one of her dates told the class she'd modeled for my husband's *Sun Goddess* out there on the front lawn. We had to adopt some big dogs to keep those curious boys off the property."

Dale laughed, his eyes twinkling with amusement at this unexpected tidbit. "Did she model for it, Mrs. Granger?"

"Suzanne, please. And I'm afraid Cherish has never let her daddy cast her. She has let me paint her, though. My art tends to be more conventional than my husband's."

Dale's gaze trailed back to Laura. "Your art must be very beautiful with your daughter as your subject."

Laura could feel a blush stealing into her cheeks. As always, Dale couldn't help charming everyone he met, and judging by her mom's smile, she wasn't immune.

Then again, Laura couldn't remember ever meeting anyone immune to Dale in all the time she'd known him. Laura herself was no different.

"Where's Daddy?" Laura asked, wanting to get away from this open door where the sunlight showcased her blush.

"He's casting today." Her mom moved behind them to pull the door shut. "Come on, Dale, we'll show you around until my husband surfaces from his work. Messy stuff. It takes a while."

While they meandered through the big house, Laura and her mom took turns explaining the functions of the naturally lit studios and showing him the unoccupied guest rooms, until her dad finally caught up with them inside her mom's studio where they'd been looking at a portrait of Laura as a girl.

Her dad was even taller than Dale, who had to be at least six-two. He strode into the studio, winking at Laura before he scooped her mom into his arms for a kiss. Laura watched as her mom melted against him as if they hadn't seen each other in weeks.

"So how'd you like being the third wheel?" Dale asked.

"I had good days and bad. I've learned to appreciate what they share as I matured."

Her dad was a friendly man, with silver hair cropped close because he couldn't be bothered going into town for regular haircuts. Laura had inherited his fair coloring, and when he finally turned his attention on them, he caught her in a hug.

"Cherish, we haven't seen you in weeks," he admonished with a smile in his deep voice.

"The grand opening, you know, Daddy. It's been crazy."

She'd barely introduced Dale before her mom attempted to whisk her away into the kitchen to leave the men to get acquainted. "Come on and help me get lunch on the table, Cherish. Maybe Daddy would like to show Dale his studio. He's working on a new commission."

Dale didn't need to be asked twice and turned his charm on full-blast as her dad led him from the room. Laura stood there, listening to Dale fire off all the perfect questions to get her dad talking about his work.

For some strange reason she felt silly and nervous and jumped when her mom slipped a hand on her arm.

"So who's Dale?" she asked.

"A friend who's escorting me to the grand opening."

"He told us you were dating."

"Just for the Naughty Nuptials," she explained. "He lives in California and will be heading home as soon as Hottest Honeymoons is over."

"He wanted to meet your daddy and me. That doesn't strike me as the action of a man who has leaving on his mind."

"Trust me on this."

"Do you want him to go?"

Leave it to her mom to zero in right to the heart of matters. "It's not like that with us."

"Whatever you say, Cherish." Turning on her heels, she headed into the kitchen without another word.

The meal turned out to be a comfortable affair around a picnic table on the back porch, where they could all enjoy the sunshine, fresh air and an awe-inspiring view of the river— her mom's favorite thing to do on a sunny summer day.

Dale tossed aside his jacket, loosened his tie and ate heartily as if his burger was fine sirloin rather than all-natural soy protein. He handled the organically grown avocado and bean sprout salad like a champ, too, and even earned praise from her dad for trying a freshly juiced vegetable concoction that was so brutally green she'd seen grown men pale at the sight.

"What's different about this one, Suzanne?" her dad asked, eyeing Dale curiously.

Her mom cocked her head and considered Dale openly. "He's handsome, intelligent and definitely charming, but there's something else...."

Laura bit back a smile as Dale shifted his gaze between her parents. To his credit, he bore up under their scrutiny well.

"Oh, I know what it is, Russ," her mom announced. "Dale's *interesting*. He's not one of those cookie-cutter businessmen Cherish seems so fond of."

"Thank you," Dale said, earning a laugh from her dad.

Been here, done all this before, Laura thought. And if it wasn't bad enough that her parents were critiquing her date, worse still was where this conversation was headed.

"Dale's an architect, Daddy. He designed and built the Wedding Wing."

She needed a distraction, *before* her parents launched into their opinions of her dating preferences. She'd never sold them on the man of her dreams versus the man of her fantasies theory and she never would. Her parents believed in soul mates.

"An architect, Cherish?" her dad asked, surprised. "You're dating an artist? The last I'd heard you'd scratched them off your list at what, sixteen?"

"Fifteen," her mom corrected.

"An architect is different than an artist, Daddy."

"You tell yourself that, Cherish," he said mildly. "I'm curious to know if your architect shares that opinion. How about it, Dale?"

"Actually, I do consider myself an artist during certain parts of the design process. Especially with restoration work. That's my specialty."

"See that?" Her dad nodded approvingly.

Dale shot her a smug look, clearly recognizing when goodwill was on his side. And in true charming Dale fashion, he ran with it. "Excuse me, but I have to ask. Why do you call Laura Cherish? She said it was a long story and not important."

"Not important." Her mom huffed and got up from the bench to collect the plates. "It's only her name."

"Cherish Laura," her dad clarified. "She didn't start going by her middle name until she started school."

"It's a beautiful name." Dale swept a gaze over her that suggested he thought she was as beautiful as her name, and Laura suppressed the tiny tingle of pleasure, knowing the man was just caught up in her parents' madness. "It's an unusual name."

"Not so unusual where Cherish was born," her dad said.

"Where was she born?"

Laura shot Dale her own smug look. He had asked for it and now he was going to get it. Double barrels, if she knew her parents. And she did.

"Cherish, haven't you told the man *anything* about yourself?" her dad asked.

"I was born in a commune," Laura told Dale to get this show on the road. "As in hippies, beads, fringe, free love and all that."

"*Not* free love," her mom announced from the doorway. "Your father and I were married long before you were born, young lady."

Her dad chuckled. "Love wasn't free in the seventies, Dale. It didn't even come cheap. Don't let anyone tell you different."

"I didn't realize they still had communes in the seventies. Wasn't that a sixties thing?"

"Took a while to perfect the community lifestyle. We caught it when it was good."

Laura got to her feet to help her mom clear the table.

"My parents abandoned conventional society to embrace a natural setting more conducive to their art."

"But Cherish changed all that." Handing over his plate, her dad clearly enjoyed a chance to tell his story to a new audience. "She was around five and as smart as a whip. We schooled the kids ourselves in the commune, and one day we were having a discussion about disease and death. It was heavy stuff for the younger ones, but we didn't want to shield our kids from the world and wanted them to understand the facts from us rather than a biased media."

Her mom reappeared and slipped back onto the bench to continue. "One of the children got spooked, and Cherish stood up in the middle of the lesson to reassure him he had nothing to worry about. She told him that we lived in our own world and all the bad stuff that happened out in the 'other' world wouldn't happen to us."

"Out of the mouths of babes..." Her dad picked up the story. "Suzanne and I took a hard look at Cherish, like that 'other' world might see her. She was the prettiest thing, Dale."

"She looked like an urchin." Her mom scowled. "Her hair was tangled halfway down her back and her bare feet were filthy from running around with the boys. We'd been reared in that 'other' world and had chosen our lifestyle, but Cherish hadn't. We decided we should provide her with some balance...."

"And offer her some varied perspectives and different experiences, so she could formulate her own opinions."

"We succeeded, and then some."

Laura couldn't help smiling as Dale's gaze shifted between her parents as though he was watching a table tennis match.

"So how did you handle the transition?" Dale asked, finally turning his gaze to her.

"I endured. And grew up to be a perfectly normal person in spite of my unusual early childhood."

"I don't know about that, *Cherish*." Dale raised his glass of sun-brewed herbal tea in salute. "I've never thought of you as normal. Isn't that the reason Tyler's filming a documentary?"

"What documentary?" her mom asked.

"It's nothing, really," Laura said. "Just an industry documentary about the grand opening."

"It *is* something," Dale corrected. "Laura is being hailed as a visionary in the hospitality industry."

"A visionary?" Her dad blew her a kiss across the table. "You always do me proud."

Her mom didn't look quite of the same mind. "Is that why you invited Cecilia to that party tonight?"

She shrugged. "The opening reception was just a good opportunity to let her slip in to see the Mireille Marceaux she so generously lent me. It has been excellent promotion for the inn."

"She tried to coerce me into going as her date, you know. She hates to attend these sorts of functions alone."

"I told her to bring someone," she said in a would-be-casual voice. She'd never thought for a second her mother would actually consider the invitation. "I want her to enjoy herself. So are you going to come?"

Laura held her breath.

"As of yesterday morning, no. But if this is such a big deal, Cherish, maybe I should go. I know Cecilia would appreciate a chauffeur. She isn't as comfortable on the road as she used to be. She won't even take the car out when there's snow."

"Not necessary, Mom. I'll send someone to pick her up."

While Laura appreciated the support, she knew the last thing her mom wanted was to attend a formal banquet tonight. And the last thing Laura wanted was her mom and Miranda and Tori together in the same ballroom.

Of course, her mom dismissed her. "What do you think, Russ? Should I go?"

"Did I mention that Miranda and her husband are the Hottest Honeymoon Couple?"

"No, you didn't." Her mom's gaze narrowed. "I read it in the paper."

"Oh, well, her sister is reporting on the event."

"I knew that from the paper, too." Her mom's gaze narrowed more, and Laura knew it didn't matter what she said, her mom would stubbornly do what she thought best, even if it meant dragging out one of her beautiful party gowns entombed in the back of her closet.

"Laura gets so busy working these events that I wind up fending for myself a lot, Suzanne," Dale said. "I'd enjoy a chance to hang with you and your friend. We'll enjoy the banquet and take some of the pressure off Laura."

Her mom smiled appreciatively.

Her dad inclined his head in approval.

And Laura…well, she hadn't shared some of the more interesting parts of her family history, so she had no one but herself to blame that Dale didn't have a clue why her mom attending this function would be such a disaster.

Almost as big a disaster as how she melted inside at the way Dale kept stepping in to make things better.

DALE WAITED UNTIL Laura disconnected the call and replaced the cell phone in her purse before asking, "Will there be any problem accommodating your mom at the rehearsal dinner tonight?"

"No."

"Then do you want to tell me why you're so stressed out about her coming?" he asked while driving toward Niagara Falls. "The whole point of getting you away from the inn was to make you feel better. I don't think I accomplished mission objective."

"Oh, Dale. It's not your fault. I appreciate your offer to sit with Mom and Ms. Cecilia. That'll help a lot."

"No problem. But I want to know what's bugging you."

He could only push so far. Laura would either open up or not. He found it hard to believe that Russ Granger and his art could have driven a wedge this size in such a powerful family, but after meeting her parents, he thought he understood why Laura hadn't told him all the details about her relationship with the senator. She tried to protect her parents, which might explain why she'd warned him about how unusual they were.

Dale thought he'd passed that test, and since he'd gotten an unexpected chance to be supportive again, he would have chalked the afternoon up as a success. But one look at Laura and he wasn't so sure.

She sat staring out the window with her mouth tightly set. He wanted her to share her thoughts. Wanted it so much that the want was like an ache. He only had Risqué Receptions and Hottest Honeymoons left to prove he could be more than the bad boy she thought he was. To overcome years of choices and too much gossip that were now biting him in the ass.

Could he prove himself in a the time left?

Damn straight. Just the thought of Laura thanking him for the orgasms and kissing him good-bye after the grand opening ended... One thing Dale knew was women, and this woman wanted him. No question.

He wanted a chance to prove he could be the man of Laura's dreams. He didn't know what that entailed exactly, but he wanted a chance to find out. Toward that end he'd spent a good part of his morning—when he wasn't colluding with Annabelle to arrange this visit—talking with his boss.

In Dale's mind he had to have something to prove he was worth a closer look, and with Nick's help, he thought he'd come up with just the thing. He'd planned to spring this on Laura after meeting her folks, but he'd have to rethink that plan. Now obviously wasn't the time for surprises.

But he couldn't share anything with Laura until she opened up about what was bothering her.

"I liked your folks," he said to get her talking again. "I'll agree that they're not your run of the mill parents, but they weren't all that strange. Romantic. Definitely into natural foods. From what you said, I wasn't sure what to expect. They liked me, too."

"You think so?"

"What's not to like?"

She made a sound that might have been a laugh.

"I think I'll invite myself back again next week. Maybe dinner this time. I'd like to meet some of their art residents. Your parents made them sound like family."

"Why are you doing this?"

"Doing what?"

"You know what. You're so interested in my life outside bed I'm beginning to think you're getting bored with the sex."

"Ouch." Time to put his money where his mouth was. "For the record, I'm interested in *more* than the sex. I want to know what makes you tick. I figured out today where you inherited all that romantic idealism. I don't think I've ever seen a couple more content to be around each other as your parents. Pretty inspiring stuff."

"You know what makes me tick, Dale. We've been working on a project together for two years. I'm not sure about you, though." She eyed him warily. "My parents inspired you? I thought romantic idealism made bad boys run in the opposite direction."

Love slaps you upside the head when you least expect it.

"Sometimes," he admitted, but like Clyde, he was going to do whatever it took to catch his woman. "But are you so sure bad boys have to stay bad boys forever?"

Something about that made her frown harder, because she swiveled around, hiked her knee up on the seat and faced him. "Are you talking about leopards changing their spots? Why would they want to?"

"The right woman can make the difference," he said simply. "I've seen it happen. My boss's wife started out as just one more beautiful date. Now they're the happiest couple I know. Your parents are that same kind of happy."

"No doubt there," she agreed. "My parents are the happiest couple I know."

"Explain something to me then. How can the daughter of the happiest couple you know establish such strict criteria for the man of her dreams? Did your parents have a laundry list of qualities they looked for before they fell in love?"

It was a leading question, and Dale held his breath, hoping she'd open up and elaborate on what was bothering her. Maybe even share a few of her secrets.

She didn't answer for so long that he thought she wasn't

going to. Then she finally said, "No, they didn't, and I'm afraid it created some problems."

"What sort of problems?"

Laura sighed. "Family stuff. My mom came from a wealthy family and they had a lot of expectations for her."

"Miranda and Tori's family."

Laura's eyes widened. "You know?"

He nodded, keeping it casual, not letting her know he was disappointed that she hadn't told him herself. "Troy mentioned it at the bachelor party last night. So what happened?"

"My mom wanted to pursue her art and that wasn't really an option for a Prescott."

"Why?"

Laura shrugged. "The senator, I guess. He had certain expectations of his daughters, one followed them, one didn't."

"That simple?"

"I really don't know. I do know it's all old news. This stuff happened long before I was born, so to me it's just the way things have always been. My mom defied her father by living a life he doesn't approve of. She married a man who didn't meet his criteria so he cut her off and never looked back."

"Sounds harsh."

She shrugged. "Being disinherited has a definite down side but I'm sure my mom would do it all over again in a heartbeat. She's happy in her marriage and in her work and in her life. She values those things more than anything else."

"What about her daughter?"

"I wouldn't change it, either. But living with my parents has given me a profound respect for love. I choose to exercise a little more control before I'm swept away."

And there it was, the reason Dale had been looking for.

Now he had something to work with because he knew what Laura hadn't admitted yet—she'd already been swept away.

14

LAURA RETURNED THE TELEPHONE receiver to the cradle, amazed how one call could shoot her pulse rate into overdrive. She must have looked as shell-shocked as she felt because Dale emerged from the bedroom, where he'd been dressing for the rehearsal dinner, took one look at her and asked, "Who was that?"

"Miranda. She's invited her parents and wants them added to tonight's guest list."

"You're kidding. Why?"

She shrugged, dearly wishing this was some sort of joke. "I was so surprised, I didn't ask. But I should have. What on earth could have possibly prompted Mr. and Mrs. Ford to show up on my doorstep tonight of all nights?"

Dale's frowned. "What did you tell her?"

"That I'd add them. What else can I do? Miranda's my guest. If she wants her mother here… And I don't want to ruffle Tori's feathers, either. Not when she's handling my press."

Smoothing the front of her navy silk gown, Laura was amazed at how wonderful she'd felt just moments ago when dressing. She'd admired the way the silk flowed into the full sweeping skirt, had decided to wear her hair down to complement the simple princess neckline and please Dale.

Now she felt underdressed and unprepared to deal with the night ahead. Her mom would be in that ballroom tonight. Grangers and Fords did not mingle at functions as a rule. "I told them I'd be downstairs to greet them."

"I'll go with you."

Even on the verge of hyperventilation, she couldn't help but notice that Dale hadn't finished dressing. "You're not—"

"Nothing I can't do in the elevator." He tossed his bow tie around his neck, grabbed his jacket from the back of a chair and motioned her toward the door. "Let's see what's going on."

As they headed to the elevator, she willed herself not to panic. Dale was with her, and if nothing else, he distracted her with his hurried efforts to dress between floors.

"Do I look all right?" he asked, making a final adjustment to his bow tie.

She smoothed his ruffled hair. "Dashing. As always."

Then the elevator stopped. The doors opened.

She could see Miranda, her husband and parents standing in front of *Falling Woman*, looking so impeccable in their evening wear they might have stepped off the cover of *Fashion Weekly*.

Though she'd seen Miranda's parents often at school functions, Laura had never said more than the occasional hello when proximity demanded. Speaking with these people hadn't been part of the equation. They moved in separate circles and though everyone in town knew they were all related, they never acknowledged that connection among themselves. They just didn't.

Up close, Carolyn Prescott Ford was a striking woman, as polished and poised as Laura's own mother was natural and energetic. She'd passed along her flaming red hair to Tori, but Laura had never realized how much this woman looked like her own mother until right now when they stood so close.

Dale slipped his hand around her elbow and led her from the elevator. His touch steadied her, made it so much easier to plaster on a gracious smile.

"Good evening, Miranda and Troy," she said in a voice that epitomized hospitality. "Mr. and Mrs. Ford, it's a pleasure. This is the Wedding Wing's architect, Dale Emerson."

The introductions bought her a respite, and Laura had a chance to calm her breathing and decide how best to assume control. From the squared shoulders and forced smiles, she knew everyone had geared up for an awkward situation because no matter how they came at it, this situation was awkward.

But making guests feel welcome happened to be Laura's specialty. If she could sell her guests on romance and make Falling Inn Bed feel like a home away from home, she could get these uptight socialites to blend in. Estranged family or not.

"How wonderful that you were able to join Miranda and Troy tonight," she said. "I see Miranda has been showing you our good luck charm. We were so fortunate to acquire *Falling Woman* for our grand opening. She's been very well received."

"As I mentioned to you, Laura's mother helped arrange the loan from Westfalls," Miranda said to her mother who only inclined her head.

"In fact, my mom and Ms. Cecilia will be at the banquet tonight to enjoy their contribution." There, it was out on the table. Forewarned was forearmed. Laura would never send her guests into a loaded situation intentionally.

"Victoria mentioned that," Mrs. Ford said.

Laura couldn't help but wonder how that information had gotten out when she'd only called to add her mom to the list on the ride back into town.

Had Tori been snooping in places she shouldn't snoop?

Laura couldn't think of any other way she could have known. Even more worrisome was the thought that someone on the inn's staff was responsible for the leak.

Dale glanced down at her and the frown in his eyes made her suspect he was mulling over similar questions.

"We have an exciting night planned," Laura said, slipping her arm through his, a silent gesture to get this group moving toward the ballroom. "This is one of our more conventional functions." She'd hope they didn't look too closely at Bruno's menu. "It'll be a night of dinner and dancing and making friends. I'm sure you'll feel welcome. I just need to make an adjustment to the seating arrangements."

"It's kind of you to take the trouble, young lady." Mr. Ford smiled and seemed to genuinely appreciate the effort.

"No trouble at all." She swept an arm toward the ballroom. "If you'll join me, I'll see you to your table."

And seat these people far across the room from her mom.

There was no small talk as they entered the ballroom, just the sudden silence of people who didn't know what to say to each other. Total strangers would have had an easier time of it than blood relations with so much history between them, which Laura decided simply went to prove that DNA didn't count for much.

But she'd have never felt such a surge of pride walking

into the ballroom with strangers. This feeling came from knowing that her guests peered around the room, taking in every detail and judging her by what they saw.

Laura might have been an excommunicated member of this family but that didn't mean she couldn't host a bash as well as any of them. And tonight, she hosted a fantasy.

The grand ballroom had been arranged to perfection. Colorful summer blooms adorned linen-draped tables. Crystal glassware sparkled beneath the glittering overhead chandeliers, and the band played mood music at the volume perfect to fill the vast room, yet not hinder guests from conversation.

Delia and Jackson had been seated at the head table with both sets of parents and bridesmaids and groomsmen nearby. Other guests meandered in, directed to their seats by uniformed staff.

It was one of these gentlemen she caught as they walked into the room. Quietly issuing her seating changes, she slowed her pace just enough to give the usher a chance to effect those changes before they reached the table.

"Here we are, Mr. and Mrs. Ford," Laura said, both pleased and grateful for her staff's efficiency. "You'll be seated beside Miranda and Troy. Tori's at this table, too, and I imagine she'll show up soon. We're keeping her busy. When we last spoke she was playing nearly a week's worth of catch-up with this assignment."

And Laura hated to think about what else.

When her guests took their seats, she smiled. "Please enjoy yourselves tonight. If you need anything, let me know."

"Thanks, Laura," Troy said.

Dale nodded in greeting and led her away. As soon as they were out of earshot, he leaned close and whispered, "You were brilliant."

"Do you really think so?" She sounded winded, almost as if she'd held her breath during the entire crisis and only now remembered to breathe.

"I do." He peered down at her with such heat in his gaze that Laura felt her tension melt away. "Now tell me how Tori could know your mom was coming tonight."

"She shouldn't know unless she was snooping where she shouldn't have been. But I'm not sure how to ask without putting her on the defensive. I can't sound as if I'm accusing her."

"My lovely *gracious* Laura." He brushed a kiss across her forehead. "I know you'd be more diplomatic."

She wasn't so sure. "I can't deal with this right now. I've got to go catch my mom and give her a heads up before she walks into this ballroom unprepared."

Twining his fingers through hers, he led her toward the entrance. "Can't have that. Although I got the impression your mom was made of tougher stuff."

"She is, but I feel responsible. I'm the only reason she took on Miranda and Tori tonight. But the perfect Ford sisters aren't the same thing as *my mom's* sister. She deserves a chance to prepare herself."

"Agreed."

They caught her mom in the valet line. Laura had seen her formally dressed on so few occasions that seeing her all dolled up still had the ability to make her feel like she was a young girl looking at a fairy-tale princess.

"Oh, Mom, you're gorgeous."

She wore a burgundy silk gown cut so skillfully that it

dripped off her and swirled around her ankles like a cloud. Her eyes twinkled like the uncut gemstones sparkling at her ears and throat, pieces her dad had commissioned an artist in residence to design a few years back.

"Oh, Cherish. I can't look nearly as beautiful as you. She's the belle of the ball tonight, isn't she, Dale?"

"She is indeed, Suzanne, although please keep that to yourself. The bride's a personal friend."

Her mom laughed and introduced her companion. A tall, almost severe woman, Ms. Cecilia, known as the commandant among the Westfalls alumni, looked like she could run a school with a thousand students single-handedly. Age hadn't dulled her tough appearance, and in her typical straightforward fashion, she'd worn black. It lent a rather stylish air to her otherwise austere appearance.

"*Falling Woman* has been such a hit," Laura told her. "I'm sure she's responsible for the grand opening's success."

Ms. Cecilia lowered her cheek for Laura to kiss. "I'm delighted she's bringing you luck, dear girl."

"So far so good. Okay, Mom, I don't want you to freak but I had some unexpected guests show up."

Her mom flipped her hair back off her shoulders, a gesture of utter insouciance. "Hit me."

"Miranda's parents."

She shot a narrowed gaze at Ms. Cecilia. "What are the odds of them showing up the first time I've gone out since you roped me into that stupid fund-raiser?"

"It was for a good cause, Suzanne," Ms. Cecilia said haughtily. "But never you mind about tonight. I'm sure Laura had the sense to seat you at separate tables."

"Across the ballroom," Dale said.

Ms. Cecilia nodded. "Problem's already been solved."

"Well, I was ready for Miranda and Victoria." Her mom waved a dismissive hand. "What's two more?"

"Two happens to be my lucky number tonight, ladies." Dale looped arms with both women. "Shall we? I'm sure Laura will visit whenever time permits."

"I'll be there for dinner." She couldn't help but smile as he escorted them away. He had them both laughing before they'd gotten halfway across the ballroom.

She sighed in relief and thanked her lucky stars he was here to help her with this nightmare. One glance at Miranda's table proved no one had missed her mother's arrival and not one of them looked nearly as reconciled as her mom.

DALE SAT AT the table, making the most of his chance to impress Suzanne and Cecilia, who chatted as if they hadn't seen each other in years. For all he knew they hadn't, and as busy as the conversation kept him, he still found himself watching Laura as she greeted her guests and convened with her staff.

She'd worn her hair down and the crystal-cut chandeliers threw shimmering light over that amazing fall of pale hair as she moved gracefully through the crowd. He'd have never known she was stressed over hosting her mom and Miranda's parents at the same function. Her so-kissable mouth smiled easily and snatches of her silvery laughter managed to catch his attention from all around the room.

She was accomplished at hiding her feelings, and now that he understood the dynamics of her family relationship, he guessed she'd probably honed her skills during her years at Westfalls. Just the thought was enough to kickstart that possessive feeling as he grew more familiar every day with Laura.

He didn't want her hiding her feelings about him—not to him or herself. They deserved a chance to explore how they felt. He would convince her to give them that chance.

Guests still meandered into the ballroom where staff ushered some to their seats while others paused between tables and on the dance floor to greet friends and acquaintances. Peering around the room, he spotted another chance to further his cause.

"If you'll excuse me for a few moments, ladies," he told Suzanne and Cecilia.

"Go have a good time, Dale." Suzanne smiled, darting a quick gaze to where her daughter stood. "You shouldn't have to spend your night baby-sitting two old ladies."

"Old? Speak for yourself." Cecilia stared her down with a look Dale guessed would make more than a few students nervous.

Not Suzanne, though. She simply rolled her eyes and said, "Go chase my daughter, Dale. She needs a *real* man in her life."

"And you're looking at him." He laughed, appreciating the vote of confidence.

But once away from the table, he didn't weave a path through the guests to the lovely Laura. Instead, he headed toward the main entrance where Tori had just arrived with Adam.

"Adam." He greeted the assistant G.M. and took Tori's hand, brought it to his lips. "You look beautiful tonight."

The bronze gown she wore clung to her slim curves like liquid, and Dale couldn't help noticing the striking difference in his reaction to this fiery-haired beauty. Once he'd have enjoyed Tori's appearance and challenged his buddy Nick for her attention, no doubt grateful for a little excitement at an otherwise routine social affair.

But tonight there wasn't a woman in the place who could hold a candle to the lovely blonde with crystal eyes, quick smiles and enough romantic idealism to make a believer out of him. Times had changed.

And so could a man.

Tori shot a sassy gaze at Adam. "Do you hear that, Mr. Grant? You'll need to stick close so I don't get into trouble."

Dale let her hand slip away with a smile. "I've known Adam since the day he stepped foot on this property, and he's never struck me as a fool."

"Good, because I'll need him to keep me on the dance floor so I can overhear all the juicy gossip."

"I promise Ms. Ford will be well attended tonight, Dale." Adam smiled stoically.

"Just to be sure, how about I hold your place while you head over to table twelve and introduce yourself to the woman in black?"

Tori glanced over his shoulder. "The headmistress of Westfalls."

"And the woman responsible for your loan of the illustrious *Falling Woman*. I'm sitting at her table and thought you'd want to know. The woman in red beside her is Laura's mother."

Dale knew that Adam wasn't buying his explanation for a second, but the man took his duties as host seriously. Dale couldn't shake the feeling that Adam wouldn't mind a break from his charge, either.

"I should introduce myself," Adam said. "I'll be back."

"I'll wait breathlessly," Tori shot back. As soon as Adam was out of earshot she whirled on Dale. "So why do you want me alone? I thought you were Laura's date."

"I am Laura's date," he said with a look that left this woman no room to doubt that his interest was strictly business. "But you're right, I did want to get you away from Adam."

"Oooh, confidence. I like that in a man." Looping her arm through his, Tori led him away from the entrance, getting them out of the line of fire of the door. They wound up near video cameras Tyler had set up to catch the night's action.

"So what's up?"

"I wanted you to know that I'll run interference between your parents and Suzanne Granger tonight. Like you, Laura's working and won't be able to stay on top of things. But I'm sure between me and Miranda—"

"You mentioned this to my sister?"

"No. She looks like she has her end under control, but when your mom mentioned you'd told Miranda that Laura had added Suzanne to the guest list, I guessed you were concerned."

"Personally, it didn't bother me in the least, but I knew Miranda would probably have a cow, so when Tyler told me, I warned her. She'll be fine. She called for reinforcements."

Pay dirt. Tori hadn't been the culprit. Tyler had.

"We did exactly the same with Suzanne. So everyone should be all set, then." Glancing down at one of the view screens, Dale watched Laura make her way through the tables toward the stage. "Whatever it takes for everyone to enjoy themselves tonight."

"Agreed. I can't wait to see what's going on around

here…." Tori shot a gaze across the room at where Adam stood engaged in conversation with Suzanne and Cecilia.

Dale smiled at the implication in *that* and silently wished Adam luck. He'd be playing hardball with this one. The evidence was Tori's scowl when Adam moved away from table twelve and toward the stage and Laura rather than back toward them.

"Doesn't that just figure," she said. "That man is already trying to give me the slip. I'm beginning to think he doesn't know how to do anything but work."

"I'd say you have a pretty good read on Adam for only just having met."

"Not much of a brain bender." Her expression softened into a thoughtful moue. "Well, thanks for the heads-up, Dale. I've got to run. That man is my direct line to the scoop around here and he's not getting away."

Without another word, she spun on her high heels and headed purposefully into the crowd. Dale didn't follow, but glanced down at the view screen for another chance to admire Laura up close. The sight of her in a candid moment kickstarted a longing to get back to her side. To touch her.

The feeling was so intense that he broke away from the sight with a laugh, accidentally nudging the second camera. As he repositioned the view screen, he found himself looking at an image of Suzanne Granger. She was a beautiful, more mature version of Laura, and Dale might have smiled at the sight—had it not been for the unexpected expression on her face.

15

BETWEEN GREETING GUESTS, interacting with the staff and recapping the bridal couple's itinerary, Laura had no chance to worry about how her mom, Ms. Cecilia and Miranda's family were faring. When the ballroom had filled, she cued the ushers to close the doors and headed toward the stage to introduce her bridal couple and begin the dancing.

After welcoming her guests, she invited Ms. J. up to speak a few words and, as she did, Laura finally had a moment to catch her breath. Glancing around the ballroom, she noticed Tori directing her photographer closer to the stage, and Tyler checking his video cameras around the room.

But it was Dale who captured her attention, watching her with a dashing smile, the very smile that promised a night of pleasure once they could head back to their suite.

He looked so handsome in his tux, so at ease at this banquet, charming her mother and Ms. Cecilia—funny, she couldn't remember when she'd stopped thinking of it as flirting—and keeping them occupied in spite of all the estranged family in the room.

When Ms. J. returned the microphone, Laura got Delia and Jackson onto the dance floor, and the band began to play. She left the stage and headed toward the table for a break.

Annabelle caught her en route. "We've got a gate-crasher."

"Lobby?"

"I thought you'd want to handle it."

Nodding, Laura slipped out the main entrance, hoping against hope that whoever was trying to crash her gate wasn't any worse than her surprise guests, only to find... "Daddy, what are you doing here?"

He stood beside the ushers, looking larger than life in a tux. He beamed when he saw her, an expression of such pride that Laura grew all soft and stupid inside.

Covering the distance, he took her hands and kissed her brow. "You look so beautiful, Cherish. And your mother..." He let his eyes flutter shut. "That's why I decided to come. Something told me I'd want to be here. Not a problem is it?"

"Of course not, but where did you find those clothes?"

"Rental place. Can you believe they had something in my size?"

Laura thought it likely rental stores carried a gamut of sizes but had probably dusted off this one for him. He looked so handsome with his silver hair and his neat black tux that she could only lean up on tiptoe and kiss his cheek.

"Come on, Daddy. I'm sure mom will be glad to see you. Turns out that the Fords showed up to be with their daughters."

"Now see there, Cherish. You always laugh at me and my gut feelings, but here's a classic example of why I listen to them."

"No argument tonight." But Laura thought his feelings had more to do with him disliking being separated from her mom than any psychic abilities.

She led him into the ballroom, where he surprised her by dancing her onto the floor. "We'll blend in better," he said with a laugh. "Maybe I'll slip by the Fords unnoticed."

Laura thought that unlikely, given that he stood a head taller than most of the crowd.

"Do you remember the last time we danced?"

"How could I forget?" She rested her cheek against his shoulder.

It had been when Ryan Stratton had asked her to be his date for their eighth grade dance at Westfalls. By the day of the dance, he'd taken so much flak from Miranda and company that he'd told her he'd rather skip the dance than show up with her to be tortured all night.

Laura had packed her dress away in the back of her closet and had settled into her room for a night of reading Jane Austen, who never failed to sweep her away into a world where she could forget what happened in this one.

Her dad had shown up and asked her to walk with him. She hadn't had the heart to refuse when she saw that he'd brought her a corsage. They'd walked along the river, Laura wearing her orchid, and her dad reminiscing about when he'd met her mother. He'd told her that all the heartbreaks of the past had disappeared once he'd met his soul mate. They'd danced beneath the stars to the music of the river.

She wondered if Dale believed in soul mates.

The right woman can make the difference.

"I don't think those people have smiled since they let your mother get away," her dad said.

"Who?"

"Your mother's sister and her family. But then it can't be much fun living in that gloomy old mansion with the senator."

"Daddy."

"Well, it's true, Cherish. Trust me on this." He waltzed her around the edge of the dance floor, still working them steadily toward the table where her mom sat. "It's sad, though. They've lost out on so much. Your mother. You."

"You're biased."

"I am."

They enjoyed another dance before Laura took her dad to the table, and unsurprisingly, his arrival had her mom gushing over how her thoughtful husband always managed to show up exactly when she needed him most.

"Honestly. Have you ever seen anything like these two?" Ms. Cecilia asked dryly, but her indulgent smile told Laura that she was just as charmed no matter what she said. "They haven't been away from each other for more than a couple of hours."

Laura laughed, but before she could answer, Dale had hopped up from the table, and asked, "Do you have a minute?"

"Of course," she said. Checking in on Bruno in the kitchen could certainly be bumped down on her to-do list in favor of a few stolen moments with Dale. "What's up?"

"I need to tell you something. Not here." He scanned the ballroom then led her around the dance floor.

When he finally got her to a shadowed alcove between potted palms and the main entrance, he spun her to a stop and said, "Tyler told Tori about your mom being added to the guest list."

"How do you know?"

"I went on a fishing expedition. Paid off."

It took a moment for his words to register. "Okay, I'll buy it. Ms. J. gave Tyler carte blanche around here to pull together his documentary, so he could have been around when Annabelle was making my changes to the guest list, but Dale, what possessed you—" Laura broke off when she saw the smile in his eyes. "You're trying to fix things again, aren't you?"

"Couldn't pass up another golden opportunity. And there's something else I want you to see."

Curiously she watched as he leaned over the two video cameras and tipped up the viewfinders before he scrolled through footage of the rehearsal dinner.

"Are you sure you should be touching those?" she asked.

He dismissed her concerns with wave of his hand. "Already cleared it with Tyler. I just have to make sure I set them back where I stopped them. But it'll take me a minute to find what I'm looking for. Wait until you see this, Laura, it just jumped out at me."

Footage of the event looped through the viewfinders and Laura caught flashes of herself, staff members and guests. Dale kept glancing at his watch, before stopping both cameras.

Directing her attention to one, he began clicking the images forward. "Here we go. Watch this."

Reaching for her hand, he pulled her close so she could see an image of her mom, so exquisite with her sable hair and ivory skin, except for the expression that played across her beautiful face.

"Do you see what I see?" he asked.

Her mom's features reflected her emotions like a mirror in a look that would have been fleeting if Dale hadn't played it out frame by frame, an expression that arced from devastation to longing…to a sorrow so profound that Laura had never seen her mother look quite so sad, so alone…to a resignation that years had honed to knifepoint sharpness.

Dale's hand tightened around hers, and she knew exactly what he saw—the ache in her mom's expression, a look this film had captured and immortalized.

"Do you know what she was looking at when this footage was filmed?" Laura asked, but suspected she already knew.

Dale flipped the viewfinder of the second camera around to reveal an image of Carolyn Ford, and, as she had earlier, Laura could see past her own self-consciousness and resentment to the incredible similarities between the two sisters. Not only in their features, but their expressions. Only this woman's face showed the painful hurt of a sister who'd never learned to deal with her loss.

"Oh, Dale." She exhaled a sigh that made her heart ache, and Dale reached up to stroke her cheek.

"I didn't want you to see this to make you sad. I just thought you might want to work some of that Falling Inn Bed magic on your family."

"What are you talking about? What magic?"

He traced the line of her jaw, stared down at her with such a thoughtful expression that her heart gave another throb. "I think what you do here at Falling Inn Bed is special, Laura. You do love and not just the romance kind. I don't know what caused all the problems with your family, but I do know what I see on these tapes. I think it would be a shame to miss an opportunity when you, Tori and Miranda are together and might be able to make things better somehow."

I don't think those people have smiled since they let your mother get away, her dad had said.

Laura had believed there wasn't much love in the Prescott family. She'd been wrong. This film proved there was more than enmity between sisters. She might not understand everything that had driven the family apart, but they'd all let past hurts and expectations blind them to each other....

When she glanced up at Dale, at the concern on his handsome face, she knew he was right about something else, too.

Falling Inn Bed did specialize in love.

"Dale, I—"

"Ms. Granger," a male voice interrupted and, turning, she found herself face-to-face with Ray Jay, one of the prep cooks. "Bruno asked me to find you. He can't get a hold of you on the radio, and he needs you in the kitchen."

"I'm on my way."

She turned to Dale, who only pressed a kiss to her brow and said, "Go on, we'll talk more later."

After dealing with a crisis involving a raging Bruno and a few quick decisions about the second course, Laura was demoted from problem-solver to distraction and promptly tossed back out of the kitchen.

She returned to the ballroom to find her parents dancing like Cinderella and Prince Charming. Dale had managed to get Ms. Cecilia out onto the dance floor, too, and Laura stood on the sidelines watching these people she cared for have fun.

Most of her guests were having fun, too.

Her bridal couple beamed, clearly enjoying their place in the spotlight. Even Delia's mother waltzed around smiling in her husband's arms, her face wreathed in smiles, another guest obviously caught up in the magic that was Falling Inn Bed.

Remembering Dale's words, Laura glanced over at the table where she'd seated the Knights and the Fords. She watched as Tori got up and took off with her photographer, leaving behind a table full of unsmiling people.

Laura couldn't remember ever seeing Miranda looking so unhappy. She usually managed to keep on a happy face in public…but apparently that wasn't the case when it came to dealing with Tori. And this wasn't the first time tonight Laura had witnessed a look of such loss and longing between sisters.

Dale was right. She needed to give Falling Inn Bed a chance to work its magic because she couldn't close her eyes now, not when she might actually have a chance to make the situation better. She, Miranda and Tori were together for the first time since school. Could she ignore an opportunity to at least try?

No. Not when she suddenly understood why her dad felt sad for his estranged in-laws. And she couldn't help feeling sad, too. Not only for the unhappy family watching Tori walk away without a backward glance, but for herself. She'd wasted so much of her time believing the grass was greener. The perfect Ford family suddenly didn't seem so perfect, after all.

As Laura gazed out at that ballroom, at family members who didn't acknowledge their connection, she realized that she'd been right about one thing—blood and DNA didn't make a family. Love did. Good, bad and unusual, the Grangers loved each other more than anything else. That's why her mom had come to this function tonight. That's why her dad had shown up, too.

There didn't seem to be much love among the Fords. The senator had given away a daughter. Nieces didn't know aunts. Sisters didn't have sisters. Why? Because one man's expectations for his family were more important than the family members.

Laura thought about those expectations, knew in her

heart that although she'd never met the senator face-to-face, she'd allowed herself to be guided by his standards, too. She'd believed she wasn't good enough, had molded her self-image based on his yardstick.

And her expectations for others.

She thought of Tori, who'd been up front with her about the Naughty Nuptials coverage when Laura had expected her to walk in and pan the event. While she *still* might pan the event, she'd promised to at least get the story first before passing judgment. She'd given Laura a chance.

Laura hadn't been nearly so fair. When Carolyn Ford had named Tori as the one to pass along news about the guest list, she'd assumed Tori had snooped where she shouldn't be snooping.

She'd expected Tori to be deceitful because she was Miranda's sister. Laura had been guilty of the same crime as those who'd always judged her as less than Miranda's family because she was a Granger.

And Tori hadn't been the only one she'd judged unfairly.

She glanced at Dale, who looked so utterly handsome with his silky black hair and dashing grin as he charmed Ms. Cecilia. She'd dismissed him from the start as a bad boy and had backed up her judgment with evidence. She hadn't gotten to know him or given him a chance to know her. She hadn't been honest with him or herself about her reasons for wanting a fling.

Yet all along Dale had been honest with her. He'd taken her at her word, trusted her to play by the fling rules and had been equally forthcoming when he'd wanted more.

I want to know more than what sort of atmosphere you're looking to create in the Wedding Wing and where I have to touch you to get you to breathe out those little sighs that make me crazy.

Sure, he was a bad boy, but wasn't she learning firsthand that he was so much more?

Yes.

Since the day he'd returned to town, he'd been changing right before her eyes, and while she'd noticed, she hadn't appreciated what those changes meant.

The right woman can make the difference.

Was Laura willing to let expectations blind her to the perfectly wonderful man who'd smuggled her from the sex-toy shower and kidnapped her away for a worry-free afternoon? The man who'd dressed in an elevator to be by her side when she greeted the Fords? The man who'd gone on a fishing expedition with Tori to prove he could be supportive? A man who so obviously cared?

No. She wouldn't let expectations blind her to this perfectly wonderful man, not when the man of her fantasies had turned into the man of her dreams. She didn't know if Dale would be interested in seeing her after the Naughty Nuptials ended—especially given their long-distance logistics—but she would be honest with him and see if there was any chance to turn their fling into a real relationship.

Her mom had found the courage to follow her dreams and live life by her own expectations. A life filled with love. Yes, she'd had to make sacrifices, but to hear her mom tell it, the rewards had been equally great. Laura would do no less. Not if there was any chance to prove to this bad boy she could be his right woman.

She caught up with him as the band slowed the tempo to a ballad, and he escorted Ms. Cecilia back to their table.

"I'm free," she told him. "Would you like to dance?"

Reaching for her hand, he brought it to his lips and brushed a kiss across her knuckles that made her melt. "The pleasure will be all mine, my lovely Laura."

She sighed a sigh that made him smile and turned around to lead him onto the dance floor…and found herself staring directly into a man's broad chest.

"Oh, excuse me," she said automatically and glanced up to find her dad smiling down at her.

"Go have fun, my lovely daughter."

Laura blushed beneath his knowing gaze, but Dale didn't give her long to dwell on her dad's laughter. He sidestepped them both and led her onto the dance floor and into his arms.

"So you didn't tell me why your dad showed up," he said. "Timing couldn't have been better."

"He felt like he needed to be here. He thought mom might need him."

"I like your parents."

"Even though they reared a romantic idealist like me?"

"The nut doesn't fall far from the tree. And I think there's a lot to be said for romantic idealism."

"A convert?"

He arched a dark brow. "You shouldn't be surprised. Between this place and a fling with the bedding consultant, I didn't stand much of a chance."

She didn't reply, nor did she protest when he tucked her close against him, fitting every inch of his body neatly against hers, making her feel right. Once upon a time, she might have insisted on keeping a reasonable distance for appearances' sake. But tonight she mixed business with pleasure and hosted a celebration for guests, family and friends.

Tonight, she had an example to set. It was her job—and her passion—to sell her guests on the merits of romance.

And now she had to let herself experience it, too.

"I want a chance to prove I can be your right woman, Dale."

He tipped his face back to look at her, his gaze narrowing. "Really?"

She nodded.

He searched her face for a long time, and then his expression softened. He didn't say a word, just held her close while they swayed in time with the music, and she savored the feel of his arms around her, was grateful that she'd finally come to her senses and recognized him for the dream man he was.

"It'll be tough but we can make it work if we want," she said.

"What'll be tough?"

"Having a long-distance relationship."

He just shrugged.

"You're not concerned?" she asked, surprised.

He shook his head. "We won't be having one. I don't want a long-distance relationship."

"Oh, well, I—"

"All that jumping on planes to see each other. All that saying good-bye." He shook his head as if he couldn't think of anything worse.

All she could do was stand there and try to reason through his reaction. Just because he'd been thoughtful and had talked about the *right* woman didn't necessarily mean he'd want to tackle a real relationship that had a serious logistical problem. And just because she'd finally realized he was the man of her dreams didn't mean she'd get her chance to prove she could be his *right* woman.

But even as she tried to understand, something deep inside rejected the reasoning. He couldn't dismiss her out-right. She wouldn't let him. What they had was special, and she simply wouldn't take no for an answer.

"It's not impossible, Dale. In between visits, we can talk on the phone. Or e-mail."

He scowled. "You think phone calls and e-mails will be enough after seeing you every day while I built the Wedding Wing? We've been together even more since I came back for the grand opening. I'm spoiled. I don't want phone calls or e-mails."

"The little brat prince grew up to be a big brat prince?"

"Damned straight."

"Then what do you want?" She tried to sound casual, unaffected. She didn't want to put on any pressure, wanted to leave him an out to take if he chose.

"I told you about my boss, the one who met the right woman, didn't I?"

She nodded.

"It so happens that when I talked to him the other day, he was moaning about something that gave me an idea."

She waited, not sure what was coming but suddenly feeling breathless, her insides winding tight with anticipation.

"As the owner of a large company, Nick has to spend a certain amount of time running his business. But ever since he got married, he'd rather be spending his time in the field with his wife. He was handling both ends until I talked him into branching out into construction with your project. Now he's got so much on the business end that he can't keep up while he's in the field. It's making him nuts."

"And…"

"And…since I created the problem, it seems only fair that I help fix it."

"How?"

Dale smiled, took his sweet time answering her question to give her a chance to appreciate the full effects of his smile. "We'll split ADF into two divisions—preservation, which he'll run, and construction, which I'll run. But Nick only agreed to split up the company if I agreed to become a full partner."

"And?"

"And he'll keep his offices on the West Coast and I'll open new offices."

Her whole body gathered on the edge of a breath, and she could barely gasp out the question. "Where?"

He chose that exact moment to extend her over his arm in a sexy dip that brought their hips together and his thigh wedged cozily between hers. "I was thinking that since we already had a West Coast office, I might open an eastern one. Say in…Niagara Falls."

Laura just stared at him, torn between surprise and the urge to fling her arms around his neck and hug him tight. She stayed put, daunted by the idea of knocking him off balance and landing them both in a heap on the dance floor.

"I thought you didn't want the hassle of running a business."

"I didn't when I was twenty-five, Laura," he scoffed. "Times have changed. *I've* changed."

"But this sounds so…*permanent*. Are you sure this is what you want?"

He brought her upright so fast that she gasped at the collision of their bodies, all hard muscle and male energy against soft curves. He captured her gaze with eyes that left no room for doubts, and she stared back, studying his face feature by handsome feature, unable to deny the truth she saw there.

"I've been gunning to get on the road since I was ten, and never once in all these years have I ever wanted to slow down. Until now. When I'm with you I feel like I've come home."

She sighed, so caught up in the moment that she did loop her arms around his neck. Lifting up on tiptoe, she brushed her mouth against his, and he caught her in a kiss that promised a chance for a future together.

"I like being with you, Laura," he whispered against her lips. "When you're working and when you're upset and especially when you're feeling sexy." Another slow kiss. "Think about all that lingerie we bought. I'm not going anywhere until I see you wear all of it."

She couldn't help but laugh.

"I'll still have to travel, but not all the time. Maybe you'll come with me sometimes, and when you can't, we'll miss each other and give phone sex a try. What do you think?"

"It sounds perfect."

"Are you sure?" He broke away and peered down at her with a skeptical look. "The last I heard you were looking for the man of your dreams to share your goals and bring out the best in you. I was pure fantasy stuff—good for sex but not much else."

And she'd honestly believed that. She'd judged him and had never once taken a closer look, had simply expected him to behave as a bad boy and nothing else.

"You're so much more, Dale," she said softly. "I was too blind to see it. Forgive me."

His arms tightened around her, and she rested her cheek against his shoulder, content to dance in silence, to absorb the possibilities between them, to enjoy being together.

"There's nothing to forgive." His voice grew heavy and

intimate. "You didn't miss a thing. I was everything you said I was. Except degenerate."

"I never said that."

He chuckled, a deep velvet rumble close to her ear. "I've been telling myself I was obsessed with you because we talked so much sex while building this place. But I was wrong. I'm in love with you, and I don't want the boot when the Naughty Nuptials is over. I want a chance to prove I can be the man of your dreams."

His words filtered through her warm and solid, and Laura tipped her head back, needing to see his face, the promise in his eyes. She smiled at what she saw there, let him see everything she felt inside.

"You already are."

Epilogue

JACKSON AND DELIA celebrated an early afternoon wedding in the atrium. Sunlight flooded the forest setting and Dale felt confident that Falling Inn Bed would have no further trouble with the problem skylight. If they did—he glanced over at the woman sitting by his side, crystal gaze misty as she watched the couple exchange vows—she'd let him know. He'd be right on hand to fix it.

This wedding wasn't grabbing him by the throat the way it seemed to be grabbing Laura, but he knew the event was special. The bride wore white, the groom wore tails and they looked happy—all requisites for a decent wedding, according to the bedding consultant. What impressed him more was the contentment he felt sitting beside her in this place they'd created, his design with her vision, tangible proof they were good together.

He thumbed away a tear from Laura's cheek when Jackson kissed his bride and the minister directed the guests to welcome the new husband and wife.

Laura turned her head and pressed a kiss to his hand, and he smiled at the zip of awareness that shot through him.

What was it about this woman?

He'd been asking that question since they'd met, and he finally had his answer…she was the *right* woman.

Taking the container that turned out to be a small plastic replica of a dove with Jackson and Delia's names and wedding date imprinted on the wings, he cupped it in his hands, watched as she unscrewed the head off her own.

"Bubbles." She held up a tiny wand.

"Nice touch."

Puckering her lips, she let loose a stream of miniscule bubbles as the bride and groom walked the aisle to applause. Then she shot him a sidelong glance and hissed, "Blow."

"Be still my heart."

"Don't you ever think about anything but sex?"

"I asked you the very same question and you told me you couldn't help it. Ditto."

She laughed and the silvery sound filtered through him, natural and right. As the bedding consultant's escort, he had a certain standard to maintain, so he got with the program and blew bubbles as Jackson and Delia passed by.

His two favorite interns paused to acknowledge them. Laura and Delia hugged while Jackson extended his hand.

"You two come work for me again," Dale said. "You're welcome on my team anytime."

"You name the time and the place, boss," Jackson said and Delia kissed his cheek. Then the newly joined couple continued through a pathway of floating bubbles.

Dale glanced down at Laura, her cheeks flushed, her misty eyes shining, and knew he'd never seen a more beautiful sight.

"You know," he said. "As long as I'm relocating to Niagara Falls, what do you think about getting married?"

With the wand still poised at her lips, she lifted her gaze. "Is that a proposal?"

"Yes." He blew bubbles her way, a stream that landed on her nose before bursting. "Marry me, Laura."

"Are you caught up in all this wedding madness?"

"No. This is pure selfishness. The thought of driving home after I make love to you is bumming me out. I don't see why I should set up a house I don't want to live in. The only place I want to be is with you." Leveling the wand, he aimed more bubbles her way, laughed when they made her blink. "So, what do you say?"

"The only place I want to be is with you."

"That's exactly what I wanted to hear," he said, placing the wand back into the novelty dove.

Dropping the whole thing into his pocket, he reached out to grab Laura, heedless of the guests that were filing out of the aisles in the wake of the bride and groom. He wanted a kiss to seal the deal, and she proved herself more than willing to give him what he wanted when she wrapped her arms around his waist and melted against him.

Romance was in the air today, as it was most days at Falling Inn Bed, and he was glad.

"Cherish." He gave a soft laugh. "I do, you know."

"What?"

"Cherish you." The words echoed in his mind. "That's a song."

Laura scowled. "Where do you think my parents came up with the name?"

"Where does the Laura come from?"

"My grandmother. She died when my mom was young."

"You've got a lot to share with me about your life. I want to know everything."

"It'll be my pleasure."

His, too. And if anyone had even suggested to Dale that

spending time at Falling Inn Bed would turn him into a man so obsessed with a woman that he'd propose marriage, Dale wouldn't have bid on the Wedding Wing job.

But now...as he held the right woman in his arms, crooning a stanza of an old seventies tune in her ear, he wasn't sorry. Not when Laura laughed that silvery laugh and smiled a smile meant only for him.

"I didn't know you could sing, Dale."

"There are lots of things you don't know about me, and now that we'll be together, think how much fun we're going to have finding out about each other."

She rested her cheek against his shoulder, closed her eyes and exhaled a satisfied sigh. "Can't wait."

"Me, either." And he meant it.

Don't miss a visit to the next sexy suite
at FALLING INN BED. . .
Sneak a peek at Tori and Adam's story
RUN FOR COVERS
coming in November 2004

1

ADAM'S SIMMERING-BENEATH-THE-SURFACE passion had called to Tori and geared her up for an explosion, but his mouth parted over hers almost softly, as if he was poised on the edge of a breath and hadn't quite committed to the course.

Had Tori's hands been free, she would have slipped them around his neck and drawn him into a real kiss, convinced him with her mouth and tongue that he wanted nothing more at this moment than to kiss her.

But her hands weren't free.

They were playing this game by his rules so she could only keep her face tipped toward his as he brushed his mouth across hers again, tempting her with the moist silk of his lips and the taste of his warm breath.

Then he swept his tongue inside.

It was a thorough kiss, one that let her savor the growing heat. His strong hands held her face anchored as he explored her mouth, and a strange feeling of being possessed took hold, an exciting, out-of-control feeling that made her toes curl.

She wanted to wrap her arms around him and press her body close, but she could only return his kiss. She wanted fast and furious, but he championed a slow introduction that tantalized her until her hands instinctively tested the restraints.

Was he teasing her as payback for teasing him?

Tori didn't know, but if that was Adam's game, it was effective. By the time he let his fingers drift down her neck, her tension had mounted so much that she could feel his touch straight through her skin, a liquid heat that sank deep.

With each stroke of his tongue, her whole body felt alive, as if every nerve burst like the fizz in good champagne. He slanted his head to deepen their kiss, and she met him eagerly, tangled her tongue with his, touching him the only way she could right now. She was half-tempted to admit he was driving her wild, but she couldn't talk and kiss at the same time.

And there was no contest between talking and kissing…the longer he kissed her, the more her body responded. Her breasts grew heavy. Her nipples tingled. Every muscle in her body felt aroused with the air circulating between her thighs.

He caressed her throat in a steady motion, and she grew breathless, her chest rising and falling so her nipples almost grazed his shirt. *Almost*.

This was torture.

Which, Tori supposed, was the point of the restraints. She could only focus on how she felt. She was so caught up in their kiss that his hands slipping down her neck didn't register until he rounded her shoulders, zeroed in on her breasts. His fingers cupped her in a smooth move, an erotic touch that made her gasp.

Adam caught the sound with his mouth, a throaty chuckle that became part of their kiss. He toyed with her, *goaded* her. If not for the restraints, she wouldn't have been able to keep her hands off him, and through the daze of arousal, Tori understood his game.

The very same game she'd played with him.

He wanted to tease her and tempt her until she insisted he satisfy this ache inside.

He wanted a reaction.

But Adam hadn't given her what she'd wanted. The man had sat on a massage table butt-naked while she copped feels of his body and *still* resisted her. She'd wanted to shred his composure until he couldn't resist her, and even though he'd finally given in, there was nothing out of control about him now.

If he thought she'd give in after one kiss—even a devastatingly delicious kiss—Adam Grant had another thing coming. He wasn't the only one making up the rules to this game.

Restraints or no restraints.

Tori gave a melting sigh and swirled her tongue over his lips, a promise. While he might have all the control right now, he wouldn't always be the one in charge....

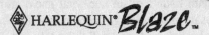

In Harlequin Blaze, it's always

GOOD TO BE BAD

Don't miss

Debbi Rawlins's

latest sexy, red-hot read
available November 2004!

When Laurel and Rob are reunited in
GOOD TO BE BAD, sparks fly. They can't turn back,
nor can they turn away...and when an explosive secret
comes to light at their desert dig site, the temperature
isn't the only thing that's hot, hot, hot!

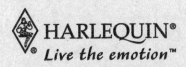

Blaze™

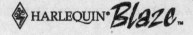

HARLEQUIN® *Blaze*™

Falling Inn Bed...

**One night between the sheets here
changes everything!**

Join author

Jeanie London

as she takes you to the hottest couples'
resort around. In this resort's sexy theme
rooms, anything can happen when
two people hit the sheets.

Read how falling in bed can lead to falling in love with

October 2004 HOT SHEETS #153
November 2004 RUN FOR COVERS #157
December 2004 PILLOW CHASE #161

Don't miss these red-hot stories
from Jeanie London!

Look for these books at your favorite retail outlet.